# 2004: AN OLYMPIC ODYSSEY
Heidi Neale & Nick Manolukas

Sarasota, Florida

# ACKNOWLEDGEMENTS

If George Beres hadn't come to the Peralandra Bookstore in Eugene, Oregon on the evening of April 7, 1998, this book may never have been conceived. We were on our first book tour, and after we took him on a video trip through time into the heart of ancient Greece, he told us about the Sacred Truce and his aspirations for the 2004 Olympic Games in Athens. He planted a seed that night, which over the past five years has grown into the book you're holding in your hands. Thank you, George. We look forward to the day when the Truce is honored once again.

We began writing this story in earnest during the summer of 1999, on the island of St. John in the US Virgin Islands. We were living amidst the tropical beauty of the National Park, just a short distance from Frances Bay. It was a magical and inspiring place, and we're grateful to Helen Michaels for renting her chantier to us.

By August 2002, we were finally ready for some feedback on the manuscript, and fortunately, we had the help of a number of interested and insightful people.

We'd like to start off by acknowledging our editors, John J. Manolukas, for his thoughtful analysis, imaginative ideas and abundant commentary, and Lethea Erz, for her keen eye and remarkable clarity of thought where language and culture are concerned. Our readers, Hal Neale, Ruth Holt Chavez and Beth Brockenshire also gave us their precious time and attention, carefully reviewing the manuscript and providing invaluable feedback. Your comments, ideas, questions and concerns have influenced the story in a multitude of ways, and so, we offer all of you our sincere thanks.

A special ευχαριστώ to our gifted teacher, Maria Pasparáki, for launching us off on the study of the Greek language. Our dear aunt, Katherine M. Kyriakides, and long-time family friend, Lela Haidos, also helped us with Greek pronunciations and sayings. Many thanks.

Again, our gratitude to Bleu Turrell for another beautiful cover illustration. We continue to be astounded by your ability to transform our semi-defined sense of what it *might* look like into a stunning visual piece with deep mythological significance. It nicely sets the tone for the story we want to tell. Thanks again also to Lightbourne for your talented cover design work. And to Ryan Meis, we offer our sincere thanks for your creative interior design and fabulous map of Greece. You're a pleasure to work with, and we wish you much success as you pursue your artistic path. A particular note of gratitude to Kurt Wolf and the Ringling School of Art and Design for their unwavering support. We also greatly appreciated having access to the outstanding collection at the School's Kimbrough Library, and enjoyed working with their excellent staff. Indeed we owe our thanks to the many librarians who've assisted us at public and private libraries throughout the hemisphere. For book production, our thanks to Central Plains Book Manufacturing.

We'd also like to acknowledge Marie Manolukas and the late Nicholas J. Manolukas. The two of you instilled in your children a profound love for the Greek culture, without which we may never have embarked on this odyssey. To the late Peter N. Manolukas, who died of Thalassemia more than a decade ago, we will continue to draw from your courage, strength and sense of humor as we traverse the journeying ways.

A special thanks to Howard Neale who helped tremendously with the dream and vision sequences in the story, and our heartfelt gratitude to those of our family and friends, too numerous to name, who have been so supportive and enthusiastic about this project. All of you have touched our lives in significant and meaningful ways.

Our deepest appreciation once again to Dr. Riane Eisler, author of *The Chalice and the Blade*, *Sacred Pleasure* and many other books and articles, for her revolutionary theory of Cultural Transformation, and for introducing us to the work of the late great archeologist, Dr. Marija Gimbutas, to whom we've dedicated this book.

To the Greens of Florida and beyond, the work we've done together has inspired us, and infused our storytelling with a strong sense of purpose. Your creativity and dedication give us hope that our aspirations for a just, sustainable world will one day manifest themselves in a true participatory democracy.

Finally, we would be remiss if we didn't offer our eternal gratitude to our very own Triumvirate: Sam, Min and the Minoa. Keep us laughing, please.

# AUTHORS' PREFACE

Readers please be advised: the reality depicted in the pages to follow is vastly different from the one most of us are experiencing during these first few years of the "New" Millennium. What started on a hopeful note of worldwide celebration has rapidly disintegrated into a perilous and fearful time. The Doomsday Clock, first introduced at the beginning of the Cold War, is right back where it was initially set, 11:53 p.m., a mere seven minutes to nuclear Armageddon.

To help address this alarming situation, and ensure we stay relatively sane amid the unbelievable insanity surrounding us, we decided to create an alternative reality, one which puts forth another possibility for our human potential. For inspiration, we looked to the ancient poet, Hesiod, who wrote about a "Golden Age" of civilization, existing long before his time of the 8th century b.c.e. According to his account, the people of that distant Age "lived as gods with carefree hearts completely without toil or trouble...[and] in harmony and in peace managed their affairs with many good things."*

We began to wonder what became of those blessed ancestors, and whether there was something of them left in the stories.

With these questions in mind, we proceeded to enter the maze of Classical Mythology in search of answers. We were greeted at the gate by a guard with shield and spear, and throughout the arduous expedition encountered warrior heroes at every turn. They hid in every nook and cranny of the bulwark, and appeared in every conceivable configuration, trying to scare us off with their horrific tales of domination and violence. We laboriously made our way through layers of co-optation and obfuscation, feeling very much like the beleaguered Odysseus, lost on a seemingly endless journey, trying desperately to find our way back home.

Fortunately, throughout the shadowy corridors of this otherwise impenetrable structure, Ariadne's Thread remained, faithfully guiding us back through time toward the older Civilization. In the overwhelming majority of Classical tales these connections are apparent, and each offers clues to the earlier origin of the myths. During our sojourn, we've come to believe that the tales of the Golden Age, or Garden of Eden, have their roots in the actual lives of our Neolithic ancestors.

Mythology shapes a society's worldview, and it seems obvious that a significant factor contributing to our present global predicament has been our long-standing cultural and literary tradition of glorifying, and even *deifying,* the figure of the warrior hero. We believe that if new heroes could be created, who didn't rely on the disastrous might-makes-right philosophy, humanity would once again be much more able to envision a different future for itself, one where the Doomsday Clock is nonexistent and our collective potential is more fully realized.

With this scenario in mind, we've written *2004* and the accompanying *Interpretive Guide*. The idea also inspired our first book, *The Coming of a New Millennium,* where the roots of the current story originate. In *New Millennium*, on the last Winter Solstice of the Second Millennium, Dr. Zoee Nikitas discovered a 3600-year-old Linear A tablet on the island of Kríti in Greece. When she deciphered what came to be known as the Minoan Message, a bifurcation point occurred in humanity's cultural evolution, and the whole of society was thrust in a new, life-affirming direction. A sudden, radical shift of consciousness occurred, and with it, the Great Reawakening began.

The Minoan Message chronicled the cultural transformation which took place in so-called prehistory – how our ancestors, who were peaceful, creative agriculturalists, had lived sustainably and in balance for many thousands of years, until they were overrun by nomadic warrior tribes who worshipped the blade. The last of the Partnership cultures, the Minoans, lived on for many generations, because as an island people they were protected by the natural barrier of the sea. However, when they learned the Thíra Volcano would soon erupt, they realized they were facing the end of their way of life. So they recorded their history on the Tablet, and with great ceremony buried it deep in a cave, where it remained until the late 20th century.

When the Message was deciphered, and the life of the Minoans revealed, other peoples of Planet Earth were drawn to their own prehistories. In the Middle East, as the faithful discovered their common Partnership heritage, they embraced its philosophy, and long-awaited peace finally came. From there it spread around the globe, sparking another cultural transformation which fundamentally changed the course of the future.

*2004* takes place in this alternative reality, where remarkable changes have occurred. The United Nations has reorganized itself into a democratic body and a budding global democracy has emerged. The Security Council has been abolished, and in its place an elected, and truly representative Global Council created. Nations still have a measure of sovereignty, but are no longer given free reign to act solely in their own self-interest. The International Olympic Committee (IOC) has become part of the UN, and the Olympic Charter is again being honored. As a result, the Games have been de-commercialized and sponsorship by privately owned corporations abolished; support and funding are instead coordinated by a nonprofit foundation operated by the IOC.

The globalization movement has also democratized. Autocratic world trade institutions have been dissolved, and corporations, both transnational and local, are now required to operate in the public interest. Governments have adopted a new code of ethics for world commerce, incorporating extensive standards for human rights, fair trade and sustainable practices. Economies have shifted away from militarism and excessive consumption, and are increasingly moving toward locally-based, environmentally responsible industry and agriculture. A global currency, the geo, has been introduced and entirely new exchanges have developed.

As these changes have taken place, peoples' beliefs have also changed, a process which is further accelerating the transformation. Massive reforms have been initiated, and in a few short years, tremendous progress has been made. Access to basic needs, such as food, shelter, medicine and family planning has been greatly improved, and infant mortality rates have begun to fall.

For those living within these pages, a new Golden Age has begun.

For those of us trapped inside the Perpetual War Machine, it's hard to imagine. But try. Imagining a different human potential is the first step to making a new reality possible. For a very long time we've been told, "it's just the way it is." Well, it's not. It's the way we make it. So, please, suspend your disbelief with wild abandon. It may be our only hope.

With Faith in Humankind,
Nick Manolukas & Heidi Neale
Sarasota, Florida
August 26, 2003

*Morford and Lenardon (*See* Bibliography).

BLACK SEA

*Hellespont*

◉Troy

Límnos

Lésvos

Turkey

AEGEAN SEA

*Hermos*

◉Ephesus

*Meander*

Míkonos

*K i k l á d e s*

Náxos

*D o d e k á n i s o s*

Thíra (Santoríni)

Ródhos
(Rhodes)

Kríti

Knossós ◉

∧∧  ∧∧∧∧
Díkti Oros (Mount Díkti)

Invocation

Interpretive Guide

*Ancient Muse!*
*Born of the Cosmic Egg as the Great Radiance unfolded*
*Source of all Inspiration!*
*Infused in the web of Creation, and within Mother Earth Herself*
*With your singing, Life flourished, and over countless eons,*
*we grew to hear and celebrate your song*
*You showed us how to make the harp and play the flute,*
*and with us you danced and danced*
*Until the day you were carried away to Mount Pieria where,*
*seated beneath the majestic willow, you sang on...*
*The people of Mount Helikon claimed you next*
*dividing you in three: Memory, Meditation and Song*
*Then Apollo took you to the Delphic Shrine*
*stripping you of your healing powers and incantations*
*addressing you as the nine of the Ennead*
*Though despite the many changings of your Name*
*You have lived on throughout the ages,*
*in seemingly infinite variation*
*to this modern day*
*Where your voice continues to inspire All who live*
*on this fragile water droplet adrift in Space.*

*With respect, and gratitude in our hearts, we invite you*
*Come to us now if you so desire*
*Grace our prose with your poetic touch*
*Allow our seeds of Love and Peace to nestle into fertile soil,*
*where they will be well received,*
*Someday sprouting into tender shoots*
*and flowering once again.*

# 1

## THE CAVE ON MOUNT DIKTI

$A$ wretched shell of a man sat crumpled, slouched up against the damp, moss covered wall of the cave. Strands of tangled gray hair hung lifelessly over his still, weather-beaten face, merging into his full gray beard. The dim light of a single oil lamp cast a warm glow on his haggard form, gently coaxing him from his slumber, when suddenly, at the mouth of the cave, loud clanging castanets rousted him awake.

"Aauugh," he cried, trying to raise his once thundering voice. "Cease that infernal noise and be gone! Oh, how my head has ached these many a thousand years...."

The music abruptly stopped, and he relaxed a little, slumping back against the rocks. He ripped a tattered piece of cloth from his once fine tunic, and wiped his perspiring brow. Out of the corner of his eye, he saw something move in the depths of the cave. A goat emerged from the darkness, and much to his surprise, addressed him.

"Ala-a-a-s, long suffering Zeus of the Aegis, who once possessed the wide Heavens, do you not recognize those fine musicians?"

Startled by the familiar voice of the handsome goat, he was unable to answer.

"Indeed, you owe your life to them," she went on. "For, do you not remember, that without their music to conceal your crying, your father, Kronos, would have swallowed you up at a sweet, tender young a-a-age."

Zeus stared at her, wide-eyed, and then it dawned on him. "Of course, they are the Kouretes."

"Indeed," affirmed the goat, chomping her cud slyly off to the side of her mouth.

He squinted. "Is it *you*, Amalthea, the blessed one whose milk sustained me as an infant?"

"Yes. It is I."

"Then, this is the place of my birth, on Mount Díkti, in my dear homeland of Kríti."

"You are correct."

He scrambled unsteadily to his feet. "But how did I come to be here? I had been wandering long in a great wilderness, cold, with a limited supply of meat and no sweet wine." He leaned on the cave wall, and shook his head. "I do not know how this has come to pass."

"Rest easy, Zeus, you will find the answers you seek," Amalthea said, as she turned away and disappeared into a dark recess.

"Surely this must be the work of the Gods," Zeus said, now to himself. "But we have been scattered on the wild winds for so long, even I, Greatest of the Immortals, cannot recognize the spinner of this web.

"Could it be that ignoble son of mine? The one who stole my precious thunderbolts and cast me from my rightful throne, winning favor with those wretched, puny mortals. The great Apollo, Lord of Light and Reason, hah. He denies my power and influence, but he is a fool.

"Or perhaps it is Athena. My once favorite and most loyal child, who has long since abandoned me...

"...or Hera, *most* wretched one. Yes, of course, it is you who must be the source of this villainous plot, no doubt in revenge for the many lovers I conquered in my blessed youth. Oh, sweet Memory recall the joyous time, when I could take any woman I desired – whether in my form as a magnificent bull or delicate swan, or as any creature which might have fancied my delight." He closed his eyes and dreamed of his former vigor.

"Zeus, Son of Rhea and Kronos, our parents," a female voice said, interrupting his vision.

"Hera?" he questioned, startled.

"No, dear brother, it is I, Demeter," the elder Goddess answered, stepping out from behind a cluster of stalactites and into the lamplight. "For many ages I have had great concern for you, since Typhon carried you away in that frightful cyclone of wind and rain. Alas, it looks as though you've not fared well in the hinterlands. Poor brother."

"Do not pity *me*, Demeter! Reserve that condemnation for yourself. Demeter of the Bountiful Harvest, yet look at you. You're an old woman, a crone."

"Yes, it is true. I am old, and I have suffered greatly. These last 5,000 years have taken a terrible toll. The Mortals held powerful dominion over me, held me in their clutches until I was close to death. Though, since the time of the Reawakening, I have again tasted the sparkling water from the spring of eternal youth. The lines which crease my weathered face are receding, and daily, more of my strength returns."

Zeus considered her diminished being and softened his manner. "I look with anticipation to the day when your countenance is fully restored, sister."

"And I wonder what the future holds for you, Zeus. You who were once called Lordliest of the Mighty by Mortal and Immortal alike. The world has changed much in the ages since you ruled from snow-capped Olympos, omnipotent and unchallenged. Indeed, the Reawakening has transformed the world of the Mortals, as well as that of the Gods, has it not? Tell me, Zeus, have you yourself partaken of the nectar of transformation?"

Before he could answer, the sound of a thundering chariot drew them to the mouth of the cave, where a set of four black stallions pulled a marvelous golden coach to a stop. Out stepped Zeus' three daughters, Athena, Aphrodite and Artemis, each magnificent in her own right, and together shining with radiance so brilliant it momentarily overwhelmed him.

Confident and strong they entered the cave, and Athena, Goddess of Wisdom, stepped forward and addressed them.

"My sisters and I bring you blessed greetings, dear Aunt," she said, taking Demeter's hands in her own. "Your health is returning swiftly and it pleases me to see it!"

"Thank you, my nieces," she replied, embracing each of them. "You, most lovely of Goddesses, as luminescent as polished gold under a mid-day Sun."

Athena turned to Zeus. "Greetings, father. It has been some time since last we were together. I'm sorry to see that you are not well."

"So, now my neglectful daughter is showing concern for me."

"You attribute to me a quality which should be reserved for yourself, Zeus, but I do not care to discuss that further. Instead, I will question you on a different matter. Was it you who bade Hermes to ask us here, to the glorious island of Kríti?"

He glared at her with contempt. "No. It was not. I have spent many torturous years in the wilderness, and it is only by the sheer greatness of my own will that I have found my way here to this sacred cave. Not one of my ungrateful daughters came to my aid during my terrible desolation. Not one of you championed me, as I had done for you so many times before. And especially you, grey-eyed Athena. For this you shall pay dearly."

"You are in no position to threaten me, Zeus, but you are partially correct. While I have not abandoned you, I have most certainly abandoned your philosophy. I have learned the futility and danger of the way of the warrior hero. In light of recent events, I have found diplomacy and discussion to be far more effective in meeting an opposing view. Domination and violence are merely the crude and ineffective weapons of a less creative mind."

"How *dare* you, insolent child!"

Athena laughed gently. "It has been so many Moons since last we ate the fruit of the Sacred Tree, has it not, my sisters? The Ancient Wisdom has been returned to us, and the world has changed. You have obviously not yet accepted this, gray-haired Zeus."

He grunted in reply, and was about to berate Athena further, when his splendid daughter, Aphrodite, the eternal Goddess of Love, sauntered toward him. Her perfume filled his wide nostrils, sending a spiral of wooziness about his diminished form. She danced in a circle around him, her sheer skirts encasing him in a bubble of resplendent warmth, effervescent like the sea foam from which she had sprung – when suddenly, she thrust her fist before his face. Around her delicate wrist a metal cuff was tightly bound, and at the end of its well-wrought chain an empty shackle dangled.

"You speak of how you *championed* us, dear father, yet so many centuries ago, you cruelly bound me to my loathsome brother Ares, god of war." She shook the chain, then withdrew her arm and continued flowing illustratively around the room.

"Surely you recall how, at the time of our last meeting, you ordered my own husband, Hephaistos of the Magic Forge, to construct these wicked bonds, condemning me for all time to the iron grasp of Ares! For millennia, he dragged me through bordellos and battlefields from here to lands most distant and back again. For what seemed like an eternity, I was subject to his evil will, but as you can see, I have cast him off!" She twirled around.

"The Great Reawakening has brought me some freedom from your maniac son, yet I still wear the demon chains," she shook the manacles again. "Once Mighty Zeus of Olympos, I demand you now remove them."

"I, I will not be spoken to in this manner. I am your Father, and it is *you* who should be obeying me!"

Aphrodite smiled sadly, almost apologetically. "It is beyond your power. Alas, I believed that to be true. No matter, I will rid myself of it with or without your help."

Zeus turned away from Aphrodite and approached his third daughter, Artemis, who appeared in her youthful form as a tall and graceful child of about 13. He placed a gentle hand on her shoulder, and spoke more softly. "My dear Artemis, Goddess of the Wild Earth, why did I not see you in the wilderness?"

"I now live in the land of Gaia, who is grandmother to you, my father. You left that land of harmony and balance long ago and journeyed into another realm, a wilderness where domination, fear and violence are the natural order of things. I admit, I too once dwelt there, with my silver bow and arrows at the ready, but I will venture there no more." She shuddered at the thought of it. "It is a shrinking wilderness, and I pray soon there will be no space left for it at all."

Zeus was taken aback. "Why do you threaten me with your evil charms, my daughter, so young and pleasing to my eye?"

"I speak no evil charm against you, Zeus, I merely speak my truth. You have come partway back from your desolate exile, and I can only hope you will choose to walk further. The opportunity to complete the crossing is upon you."

As he started to respond, a cocoon of golden light suddenly materialized beside them. Inside it, magnificent Hera, luminous Goddess of the Sacred Marriage, coalesced and then emerged in her full grandeur. She courteously greeted each of her family members, but when her eye came upon her husband, her demeanor hardened.

"Well, look at you, Zeus. I see you have retained little of your former splendor."

"Do not be deceived by my appearance, oh despicable Hera. I can call upon my powers at will, and let me assure you, they are still formidable. But I will not be provoked by you, jealous wife, or by my unruly daughters."

"Same old story, tired Zeus," Hera sighed. "Still, you do not understand that the source of my emotion is not jealousy, but rather a painful broken heart. I loved you once, and our marriage held such promise when first we were united. But you honored not our sacred vows, and were unfaithful to me in matters of the heart. You used your mighty power to spread your seed through violence and conquest, while I was ridiculed and blamed as jealous wife. True, in my anger I struck out against those you victimized, but I see now it was a desperate attempt to regain my stature. I was a fool to try to vindicate myself using your brutal means.

"And woe, when I dared question your deplorable actions, you cast your cloak of fear upon my body, and threatened me with bolts of lightning. Those fearsome, painful strikes which severed me from my heritage. But now I have rediscovered that distant ancestor, whose identity you worked so long and hard to conceal."

"Of what nonsense are you trying hopelessly to speak?" Zeus questioned, straining not to show his fatigue.

"Since the Reawakening, I have been reunited with our great, great Grandmother. The one you hid from me. The one you continue to fear. She is the Minoa, and she has told me of my true past, unobscured by your lens of domination. I am far, far older than you, Zeus, both in age and in tradition. I am a daughter of the Early Ways, from which you have severed your own connection. You still fear this tradition, Son-Lover Zeus, I can see it in your weary eyes, but you need not. For, at its root it is not the way of fear, but the path of life's beloved celebration."

Somehow, Zeus mustered a voice which surprised even himself. "Time indeed may have changed some things, but Destiny has not yet sung her final song."

Just then, he noticed a harsh, mechanical sound coming from outside the cave, growing louder and louder, becoming a deafening roar. He felt compelled to go see what it was, and the others followed him outside.

A helicopter circled overhead, and as it landed nearby, Zeus stood defiantly, with arms crossed and head shaking. The hatch clicked open and unfolded into a shining stairway, then out stepped magnificent Apollo, in the prime of his life, in robes of glistening gold.

Zeus immediately stepped forward and accosted him. "Well my far-famed son, do you not look fine, all golden and glowing and brilliant. Apollo, Lord of Light, favored by mortals since ancient times, do not forget this I say to you: you may now feel confident in your royal place, but do not be too arrogant. Be wary of your *own* successor, for his triumph may soon be at hand."

"That's good advice, Zeus. It is a shame you didn't follow it yourself when you ruled the Heavens," Apollo retorted, as he brushed his father aside and approached the others.

"Greetings Goddesses of the Panthaeon! I am pleased to see you, each with your unique and startling splendor. Ahh, and my dear sister, Artemis, allow me to step closer and embrace you, for it has been far too long. How I have ached to see you again."

Artemis opened her arms to Apollo, and the children of Leto and Zeus embraced. When they released each other, it was Artemis who spoke. "I am pleased to hear this, brother. Perhaps now the balance and harmony we once enjoyed can be restored, as I have been restored since the Muses returned to my company."

"And so I have come to understand their proper place is with you," Apollo replied hesitantly, "though I do miss their companionship."

"They are your handmaidens no more, Apollo, but perhaps in time they will visit you again of their own accord."

Suddenly, a galloping bull, fast approaching, drew their attention away. The wondrous beast had fiery eyes and gilded horns, and on his back rode glorious Dionysos, God of Ecstasy, with a crown of ivy and a flowing indigo robe, carrying his staff high overhead. Satyrs and Maenads appeared, sounding castanets, drums and reed pipes as they danced amongst the Immortals. Flowers and ivy sprang up from the Earth, twisting and curling their way around the mouth of the cave. Bunches of grapes burst forth from new vines and a nearby spring transformed into a fountain of ambrosia, shooting up from the ground.

Dionysos dismounted the bull and cast off his robe, revealing his beautiful bronze body, clad only in a small red wrap around his slim waist. "My dear family, so good to see you. It has been so long since we have all come together, and to help us celebrate this momentous occasion, I have taken the liberty of bringing sweet ambrosia in limitless quantities. Please, lovely nymphs, go now amidst my distinguished family and share with them the good things we have brought."

"Dionysos!" Apollo yelled over the cacophony. "You ever self-indulgent, hedonistic fool, we did not come here to inebriate ourselves. We have been brought together by Hermes, the Messenger, yet we know not why. This is the question we must consider."

Swaying her hips to the rhythmic music, Aphrodite danced her way over to Dionysos. "Calm your anxious mind, Apollo. We can discuss the purpose of our gathering *and* sample his ambrosia." She kissed Dionysos on his smooth cheek, then pulled a golden goblet from thin air. He filled her cup with the immortal drink and she sipped the nectar, smiling.

"I agree," Hera said, also moving to the festive music. "We will know soon enough why we've been brought together. Hermes is doubtless on his way, swift-footed one that he is. In the meantime, I am in need of some refreshment."

"Dear Lady of Argos, what a pleasant surprise," Dionysos replied, bowing down low. "Allow me to pour you a generous cup." He did so, then from behind his back pulled a bouquet. "And to add to your pleasure, I present you with these fragrant flowers, fresh cut from the meadows of Díkti."

"Most gracious of you, Dionysos," Hera replied, taking the flowers and sipping the ambrosia. "Mmmmm, truly divine."

"I too would delight in sampling your concoction," Athena said, approaching her brother.

"Goddess Athena, you look most splendid in your fine garments, woven no doubt by your own Immortal hand. It would be my honor to pour it for you."

Dionysos then gestured to the others with wide-open arms. "Come come, Artemis, Auntie Demeter, and Apollo, most level-headed one, are you *certain* we cannot tempt you? Oh, and poor, poor Zeus. You look so exhausted, dear." Dionysos glided over to his woebegone father. "There, there. Please, take just a sip, as it will help to strengthen you. You've been so tormented by the ravages of the wilderness." He filled a goblet and held it out to Zeus.

Zeus snatched it from his hands, swallowed the drink down in one gargantuan gulp, and then hurled the goblet against a jagged rock. With a remarkable blast, it shattered into a thousand shining slivers, then vanished. Though he tried not to show it, Zeus himself was surprised at his power, as was everyone else.

Suddenly, Apollo gestured toward the cave. "Behold those fantastic lights emanating from the Earth! Surely, it must be Hermes at last. Come, let us go in and greet him."

They all followed Apollo into the cavern, and Zeus trailed behind, fuming at having been upstaged once again.

Colored lights shot forth from a point suspended in mid-air, as if split by some unseen prism. As they approached the source and formed a semicircle around it, the light beams suddenly curved and twisted into a whirling vortex, and all at once, Hermes emerged, youthful as ever. When his winged sandal touched the floor of the cave, the portal collapsed into a diamond of light and disappeared. He stood before them and raised his wand. Two living serpents wound their way around it, and his whole marvelous form glowed with awesumnal radiance.

"Greetings most esteemed Goddesses and Gods of the Panthaeon. I am pleased to see us all together once again…"

"Yes, yes," Zeus interrupted. "Why are we here?"

"Greetings to you as well, my impatient father. I have asked you all to return to Kríti, this fair and pleasant isle, as it is the place where the Minoan Message was created. The Minoa herself has beckoned us here because the Transformation is not yet complete. Indeed, it now faces a grave and serious threat. Ares, most detested of the Immortals, is spinning a web of destruction."

"Yes," Athena affirmed, with concern in her voice. "I have sensed it. The peace and prosperity we have enjoyed since the dawn of the New Era is at risk. Our very existence is in jeopardy."

Apollo erupted in fury. "Ares, you bloodthirsty barbarian. In your brashness you would destroy us all! Tell us, Hermes," he went on, trying to regain his composure, "what more do you know?"

"I will give you an honest answer, Phoebos Apollo. I learned of it first from the Minoa herself, when I visited the distant past. She warned me then that a time of great danger would come, and bade me to beware of the god of war, because she knew he would again resurface. I left her world and returned to the present, seeking to track him down. I went to the Great Barren Wilderness, and hidden in my own dimension, I watched him. As had been foreseen, I found him recruiting henchmen. Ares spoke with fire on his breath, whipping up the evil winds of fundamentalism. I heard the admission, from his own wicked mouth, that he is indeed building an army of Mortals."

"That scruffy, flea-bitten band," Zeus interrupted. "I wouldn't call them an army!" He raised his arms in great lamentation. "Oh, the legions I once commanded, I..."

"Yes, Zeus," Hermes continued, "I agree, they are a pitiable hoard, but they're ruthless and their numbers have grown. They are on a quest of retribution and vengeance, determined to restore the old order, and Ares himself is slipping further into insanity."

Aphrodite looked at the metal around her wrist. "So his power has solidified. Perhaps that's the meaning of the persistence of this cuff. Indeed, it has grown tighter since I cast him off."

Apollo stepped forward and addressed his father. "So, Cloud Gathering Zeus, how is it that you know of Ares' band of mortal henchmen?"

Zeus glared at his son, on the one hand wanting to lash out in defense of himself, but on the other, wanting to be more cautious, so he said nothing.

Apollo turned to Hermes. "Tell us, Hermes, during your travels in the wilderness, did you encounter Zeus amongst the conspirators?"

"Yes," Hermes replied, directing his comments to Zeus. "I did see you there, in conversation with your hateful son, but I heard not the words you spoke."

Apollo confronted Zeus more forcefully now. "Perhaps your threat against me is not an idle one after all. Exactly what was it you plotted with the dreaded Ares?"

"I have no need for an army of mortals," Zeus responded coolly.

"Then, what was it you discussed?" Apollo pressed.

"I will not be subjected to your questioning, my brazen son."

"So be it, Zeus, but let me be clear, if you are in league with Ares it will be your undoing." Apollo turned back to Hermes. "Tell us more about this horrific plot. Do you know the time and place of Ares' planned destruction, and the means by which he intends to carry it out?"

"All I know is that it will occur at the Olympic Games, this summer, in our beloved Athens."

"What?" cried Zeus. "That wretched son of Hera is planning to mar my Sacred Games?"

"He *is* my son," Hera retorted, "but *you* are his father, and you have taught him well your ways of violence. And, in regard to the Sacred Games you claim as your own, need I again remind you that I presided over them long before you forced the Mortals to build that ostentatious temple at Olympia."

"This is not the time to set that record straight," Athena intervened. "The Games are in danger, as is the city which bears my name! We must set aside our differences, and unite to prevent this calamity from occurring."

"Woe be unto us," Dionysos exclaimed, "if Ares succeeds in his plan of hideous destruction." He plucked a golden mask of tragedy from the damp air and placed it in front of his eyes. "A return to the days of the warrior kings and their bloody rule, masculinity unfettered, out of sweet agreement with the Sacred Feminine." He cast off the mask and it vanished. "We simply cannot allow that to happen, dears. I'm with you, wise Athena." He summoned a full amphora and poured another cup of ambrosia for Athena and himself, then invited his family to partake. "Who else will join us in opposition to the god of war?"

One by one they refilled their chalices, until Zeus alone was without. Finally, after a long silence, Hera raised her voice and put the question to her husband. "What is your intention, Zeus? Will you join with us to prevent the disaster? Or will you stubbornly cling to your old ways and aid Ares in his destruction?

Zeus of the Aegis hesitated, looking into the eyes of his family. Then, as a distant thunder rumbled, he began taking on a glimmer of his former magnificence, growing somewhat taller and stronger. His robe no longer appeared as a shabby rag and his gray, knotted hair regained some of its silvery luster.

"Hera, Queen of Heaven, fear not my intention, for I too am horrified by the prospect of the destruction of our Games and the city of Athena. It saddens me that you think I'm capable of such abominable acts, but no matter. I declare to you now, and will prove to you in time, that I am allied with you, and with the rest of my family."

He summoned a robust chalice of Dionysos' ambrosia to appear in his waiting hands, and lifting it high in the air, made his pledge. "Now let great Gaia, wide Ouranos and the flowing waters of the Styx bear witness, we will unite to stop the god of war!"

As the Immortals brought their goblets together, a hearty ringing sounded, reverberating throughout the cave.

"So then," Apollo boldly reaffirmed, "we are resolved to combine our talents, to cooperate to foil Ares' loathsome plan – but mind you Zeus, do not attempt to deceive us, for I will be watching. In the meantime, I now propose we leave this womb and travel through our spheres of influence, collecting information as we go. Then let us reconvene at my, I mean *our*, sacred Oracle of Delphi and consult its wisdom."

One by one, each in their own turn consented to the plan. However, before they went their separate ways, Athena, daughter of Metis, stepped forward with one further request. "Please, follow me into the deeper recesses of the cavern, as there is another of whom you must become aware."

She led them down the steep path, their collective brilliance illuminating the passageway. At last, they reached the bottom, and behind a curtain of red and gold stalactites, lay a small pond, framed by a row of spectacular stalagmite columns at the back. A blue sky with white clouds appeared on the surface of the clear sparkling water, and the Goddess spoke.

"There is a Mortal who will become indispensable to our plans, and I shall introduce him to you now." The clouds parted, revealing an image of the handsome Greek hero, fast asleep. "His name is Herakles Speros, son of Maria and Alexander, and a son of Athens, born there 22 years ago. The family moved across the Sea's wide ridges to America, when he was a boy. He has since become a fine young man, a scholar and athlete, and the favored Olympic contender in the decathlon. He is clever and brilliant, indeed godlike in many of his finest qualities, and he is most favored by me, so bid him great glory and do him no harm."

Aphrodite looked upon his beauty and smiled. "I have the perfect mate for him..."

"He *is* a handsome boy," Hera said, admiring him, "with that golden body and those curly brown locks. Though I cannot help but wonder, could this be our long lost Herakles of the Twelve Labors?"

Apollo of the Rational Mind scoffed. "Herakles, *reborn*?"

"Impossible!" Zeus declared. "I myself gave that godlike human the gift of immortality. How could he have been reborn as a mere mortal?"

Hera spoke then to Athena. "You know him best of all. Do you believe it to be true?"

"Surely he is brave and strong, but this Herakles also possesses a vast intellect, and he is diplomatic and gentle in nature."

Dionysos laughed. "Doesn't sound like the hairy brute who bullied his way around the ancient world to me."

"No he does not," Athena concurred, "but perhaps if he were reborn, he would take on more flattering attributes. I know I feel a great love in my heart for this Mortal, and I have not seen the immortal Herakles for some time.

"Here, I give you the opportunity to decide for yourselves. Peer into the Mortal Realm and see young Herakles with your own eyes. Meanwhile, I will go to him and beckon him to join us at Delphi."

# 2

## HERAKLES ALEXANDER SPEROS

$A$s Helios' chariot came up and over the winter horizon, long, low rays of sunshine crept in the window, enveloping Herakles' face in a pool of golden light. He opened his amber brown eyes, then closed them again, not wanting to leave the Realm of Dreams. In his mind's eye, a familiar figure lingered – *the Goddess Athena*. He reached for his journal on the bedside table, trying to hold on to her illusive presence.

*She appears to me as the shining Athena of old*, he wrote, *but gone are the goatskin aegis and spear, and she wears no helmet of bronze. She stands alone, yet behind her in the distance are others, shadows receding into the mist of my subconscious. She has a message for me:* Come to Delphi. *I can hear her saying*, come to Delphi before the Games begin.

He sketched a picture of her beneath his journal entry, feeling her essence in his pencil as each line came forth from the tip, curving around her strong shoulders and trimming the edges of her fine gown. He spent a few minutes completing it, then looked at the image. Her eyes stared back from the page with a seriousness, a sense of gravity he felt in the pit of his stomach. Athena had appeared in his dreams on many occasions, sometimes offering support and encouragement, like before an important meet, and other times, like when Iphe died, to comfort and console him. But this dream was different; she was clearly instructing him to do something. Again, he heard her voice echoing in his mind. *Come to Delphi. Come to Delphi before the Games begin.*

His mother's clock twittered with a sparrow's song, urging him to get out of bed. He went in the bathroom to take a shower, and as the warm water poured over him, he tried to remember more, but Athena's parting message was all he could recall.

He toweled himself off in front of the full-length mirror, and at 6'2" and 190 pounds, he was in the best physical shape of his young life. He gently untangled the thick strands of his dark brown curly hair and combed them neatly back into a short pony-tail, then ran his hand over his chin. At the rate his whiskers grew, he could have a full beard in less than a week. One of these days he might just do it, but it would have to wait until after the Games.

He retrieved his great grandfather's single blade razor from his shaving kit, ran it over the sharpening strap a couple of times and then checked it, *sharp enough.* He held it up to the window and let the sunlight stream through its crystal handle, splitting the beam into a rainbow of colors. Twirling it between his thumb and forefinger, he sent the kaleidoscopic pattern cascading around the room.

Then, looking in the mirror, he smiled and spoke out loud to his reflection. "I know, Iphe, I heard you. We *can't* be late today." He lathered up and carefully drew the blade across his face. When at last he completed the morning ritual, he allowed himself another look in the mirror. *Why would she speak to me of Delphi just before I'm supposed to testify before the Global Council?* No clear connection came to mind, so he shook it off and went back into his room.

He rummaged around his suitcase for his socks and underwear, then went to the armoire to retrieve his new white collarless shirt and black linen suit. After he finished getting dressed, he went out into the living room.

His mother was overseas at another international conference, this one being held at the Hague. Though the apartment seemed empty without her, he could still very much feel her presence there. Mementos and pictures covered the tables and shelves: Mom with her sisters, his dear aunts, and more with uncles and cousins and godparents at various points in their lives.

Then he noticed an unfamiliar bronze piece, an award of some sort, in the shape of the African continent. He carefully lifted it off the shelf to get a better look. It was from the United Nations Commission on Population and Development, and had been given to her in recognition of her many years of service as Director of Family Planning Initiatives. "Maria Anastasía," he said her name out loud. It still seemed strange to think of her that way, but he was glad she'd dropped the name Speros after his father, Alexander, had abandoned them; sometimes he wished he'd dropped it too. Carefully, he returned the statue to the shelf, and then noticed another picture which had gotten shuffled to the back. It showed a young and vibrant Alex at the beach, holding a boy in each arm, before they knew about Iphe's blood disease.

And there was his mother's string of komboloi, Greek worry beads. He picked them up and held them in his hands, remembering those little spheres of aqua glass from as early as he could remember. How mom used to rub her worries into each of them, one at a time, slowly, methodically transferring whatever anxiety she was feeling into the bead, then flicking it out of her palm and down the string. After she sent the last one sailing, she'd swing them all back around with a flick of her wrist and start again. It was unusual for a young woman to have embraced this habit, which was customarily reserved for old men.

He went into the kitchen, got himself some vanilla yogurt from the fridge, and added a sliced banana and some granola to it. Then he poured a glass of orange juice and sat down to read the note his mother had left for him on the table.

On the front of the envelope she'd written, *Honeymou, read just before you leave for the UN.* He opened it, and inside was a picture of himself and his twin brother, Iphe, when they were nine years old. They were at the Tholos Ruins, Athena's mysterious circular temple, at Delphi! Suddenly, the hair stood up on the back of his neck and goose bumps chilled his skin.

*Come to Delphi before the Games begin.*

He vividly recalled that day. They'd spent what seemed like hours crawling around in the tall grass, turning over rocks and looking for snakes. He stared at the image of his brother, who was already much smaller than himself, and so frail. *It's been almost four years since you died. How could that much time have passed?*

Herakles blinked away the tears in his eyes, and then unfolded the note and read it.

*My Dear Kleo,*

*I'm so sorry I can't be at the UN for your presentation, but I'll be watching on TV from the "Nether Lands!" I know you'll do a great job representing the Olympic athletes! Hope you enjoy the good luck picture. I wanted to be sure Iphe would be with you today.*

*All my love, Mom*

*He is with me, Mitéramou. He is.*

Herakles folded the note and placed the picture back in the envelope, which he tucked into his inside pocket. After finishing his breakfast, he cleaned up the dishes, brushed his teeth and got himself out the door.

It was an unusual January day in Manhattan, clear, sunny and close to 60 degrees. The cool air was exhilarating, and as he walked across Central Park, he practiced his speech in his mind, feeling the adrenaline starting to surge. Literally *billions* of people would be watching his testimony, and the thought of it quickened his step.

When he got to Fifth Avenue he looked at his watch, and though he still had 45 minutes, he decided to play it safe and take a cab.

"Taxi," he yelled, stepping out into the street as one was pulling over. "United Nations, please."

"Hey, mon," the old West Indian cabbie replied, eyeing him as he got in, "you dat athlete, Hercules or sohm*ting*?"

"That's close, but it's actually Herakles."

"Herakles. What dat mean any*way*?"

"It's comes from the Greek, and it means Hera's Glory; she was a great Goddess during ancient times. Hercules was the Roman's name for the old hero."

"So, you the new hero?"

Herakles laughed, trying to downplay the remark.

"The TV been sayin' so. What's 'at sport you in again?"

"The decathlon."

"Iré. Dey Olympics, dey comin' on soon. You know Alanta, mon? She from down island way."

"The fastest woman in the world."

"Yah, mon!"

A few minutes later, they pulled up to the crowded plaza entrance and Herakles paid him as he got out.

"Good luck to you, Hera*kles*," the cabbie said, driving off.

For a minute he just stood there, thinking about how the UN complex had changed. They'd transformed the area around the building into a park, with benches under tall trees, bubbling fountains and a boardwalk along the river. Such a different feel now than when he was a kid, being chauffeured with his father in and out of there in those stuffy ambassadorial limousines.

He looked at the row of nation-state flags flapping in the mild winter wind. In their midst, rising above, was the new Planet Earth banner, recently adopted by the UN. It was larger than the others, and round, with a blue and white Earth floating in the starry Cosmos. *One Planet, One People*, he read the motto, feeling joyful deep within his heart.

Inside, the UN lobby had also been remodeled. It was now a tall circular room with angular skylights, and off to one side, a large replica of the Linear A Tablet stood, with translations of the Minoan

Message in numerous languages. Across the room, displayed under protective glass, was the UN's New Millennium Charter. Since the Reawakening, millions of people from all over the world had come to this spot, to see the place where the Message had been delivered, where the spark of global transformation had occurred.

Tourists were crowding around, noisily enjoying the exhibits, and it was only a matter of time before the inevitable happened. A teenager saw him, pointed, and yelled his name at the top of her lungs, magnetizing the room's attention squarely on him. Within moments, he was surrounded by excited young people, touching him and clamoring for his autograph. A part of him remained thoroughly embarrassed to be the center of attention like that, but he also relished their enthusiasm.

One of the boys handed him a map. "Can I have your autograph? Here, write it on this."

He took it and retrieved a pen from his inside pocket.

"Me too, me too!" came the excited shouts.

He autographed a few papers and shook some hands until, much to his relief, an official came to his rescue.

"Excuse me, Mr. Speros," she said in a Russian accent. "I'm Ivanna Jadan, the UN liaison for your group."

Herakles held out his hand. "Ms. Jadan, it's good to finally meet you face to face."

"Nice to meet you too." She shook his hand and then spoke to his fans, smiling. "I'm sorry to pull him away from you, but Mr. Speros is due to testify before the Global Council in just ten minutes, so please excuse us."

"Good luck Herakles!" the young people shouted, as the giggling gaggle parted to let them pass.

They walked through one of the several doors leading off from the lobby. Two UN staff were seated outside yet another door, and upon seeing Ivanna, waved them through.

"The Council is eager to hear your presentation," Ivanna said as they went down the hall, "and I am too."

"It's my honor to be here."

As they approached a set of tall oak doors, Herakles' heart fluttered. He'd been to the new UN several times, but never in the inner chambers, which he'd only seen on television. They passed by an undetectable laser beam, and slowly, majestically, the doors opened into the Hall of the Global Council, alive with a growing hum of excitement.

After the disbanding of the old Security Council, it had been totally revamped. The boxy enclosure that was once the domain of the original nuclear powers had been replaced by a large circular room, with a spectacular glass dome overhead. A crescent moon mahogany table followed the arc of the wall, and twenty-one high-backed chairs were placed along it, one for each of the Councilors. The five major population regions, Asia, Africa, Europe, North America and South/Central America, were each represented by three elected officials. In addition, six at-large Councilors were elected from the remaining regions. Leadership positions rotated every six months.

Ivanna directed him to a smaller table, also shaped like a crescent moon, which was directly across from the Council table. "Please, have a seat. We will begin in just a few minutes. If you'll excuse me, I must attend to several matters."

"Yes, of course," he responded. "Thank you."

"My pleasure."

He sat down and swiveled around. The rest of the athletes were being seated in the large gallery behind him, each taking their designated places. He could spot them a mile away in their dark blue and silver warm-ups. *They looked good. A little bit like the new flag come to think of it.* In the overhead booths to his left, the interpreters checked their equipment, and to his right, the networks were set up and ready to go – with two of the cameras pointed right at him! *Stay calm, relax*, he kept telling himself.

The Councilors were starting to take their seats now: an Indian woman in a traditional gold sari, an aboriginal man, whose clothing was patterned with dots and intricate animal shapes, an Arab woman wearing a colorful headscarf, a tall European man in a starched white shirt and double breasted jacket. Then, a Chinese woman, who was dressed in a red silk pantsuit, took the center chair and waited for the last few Councilors to be seated before making her opening remarks.

"Members of the Alliance of Olympic Athletes," President CeCe Kim began, looking first at the large group seated in the gallery. "On behalf of the United Nations Global Council, it is my great pleasure to welcome you, your representative, Mr. Herakles Speros, and those gathered here in chambers and around the world.

"We've come far in a very short period of time. It's only been four years since Dr. Zoee Nikitas deciphered the Minoan Message, and for the first time in the history of human existence, the people of Planet Earth have united under one democratic world government. In our Declaration of Interdependence and New Millennium Charter, we've set a new course into previously unimagined realms of possibility. Together, we have begun to reverse the long-standing trends of ecological degradation, economic disparity and runaway militarization we inherited from the previous era.

"We have shared our resources, and side by side, nation by nation, we have resolved many of our most pervasive problems and conflicts. Much of the world is at peace, and for that we are grateful and inspired. But we have more to accomplish still. Some in our family of nations have continued to engage in warfare, both across borders and within.

"Fortunately, the Alliance of Olympic Athletes has a proposal to address this grave and troubling situation. We have been looking forward to your testimony, and, as the networks are carrying these proceedings live, the world also awaits. So, Mr. Speros, I now turn the floor over to you."

As Herakles took a breath to begin, surely the Goddess Athena herself must have graced him, for suddenly he took on a glowing radiance, appearing larger than life as he spoke with winged words.

"Good day, Honored President, and Illustrious Members of the Council," he said, looking at each of them. "Thank you for allowing us to present our Resolution to Cease all Hostilities.

"The inspiration for our proposed Resolution comes from the 8th century b.c.e., a time when the people of the Greek city-states lived with perpetual warfare. Yet, in anticipation of the Olympic Games, the warrior kings agreed to the Ekecheiría, or Sacred Truce, which called for the cessation of all hostilities. People could then safely come from far and wide to Olympia to compete in sport. It's hard to imagine, isn't it? That in a world of untold barbarism, the Sacred Truce remained the ideal for over a thousand years.

"Perhaps they were recalling an earlier time, a time the poet Hesiod described as the Golden Age, when our ancestors lived harmoniously and sustainably, in balance with the greater Web of Life. The stories of many cultures reflect a similar Garden of Eden tale, and an emerging body of scholarship now suggests they have their roots in the actual lives of our prehistoric ancestors.

"So powerful was the yearning for those peaceful times, that the Classical Greeks were inspired to lay down their arms, and come together in a spirit of friendly competition. That tradition would ultimately be remembered as a high point of their culture. Unfortunately though, when the modern Games began in 1896, attempts to resurrect this ancient and revered custom were unsuccessful.

"The omission is hardly surprising, given we were about to enter the 20th century, which sadly, turned out to be the most destructive period in all of human history. The rapid growth of our technological sophistication, combined with our philosophy of domination, led us to increasingly more lethal capability, resulting in two world wars, the development, use and massive stockpiling of chemical, biological and atomic weapons, widespread economic inequality, environmental destruction and terrorism.

"We were on the brink of catastrophe, when a mere four years ago, we finally awakened from our enduring fugue. Enough of us finally said *enough*, and cultural transformation swept the globe. We began our great experiment to create a new Golden Age.

"Today, we seek to take the next step toward that new reality. And so, in anticipation of the 2004 Olympic Games, we call on this Global Council to revive the Sacred Truce, and pass the Resolution to Cease all Hostilities. If the last warring nation-states can agree to a cease-fire during the Games, perhaps we'll be able to stop the fighting once and for all. Such an agreement could lead us to the end of institutionalized warfare as we have known it for over five millennia. Ultimately, it could even mean the beginning of an evolutionary leap toward achieving our fullest human potential."

Herakles signaled to the other athletes, who each stood up and held an iridescent card, suddenly transforming the gallery into a glittering golden chalice containing the Olympic Flame.

The Councilors laughed and clapped in delight, and when the applause subsided, the President again spoke. "Wonderful, Mr. Speros, AOA athletes. You speak well and do great honor to your Olympic forebears. I for one am elated to consent to the Resolution, and I urge my colleagues to do the same. Let us now open this hearing and give the Councilors an opportunity to comment and ask questions before we make our decision."

The Native American Councilor, who was from the Iroquois Nation, spoke next. "Our New Millennium Charter requires us to consider how our actions today will affect our descendants seven generations into the future. I believe this Resolution is consistent with our mandate, and will be something our grandchildren will celebrate, for in it rests the ideal of peace between all the people of Mother Earth. This ideal must be realized if our efforts at global democracy are to be fully achieved. I therefore offer my complete support of the Resolution."

"I agree," interjected the Palestinian Councilor. "This is an historic opportunity. If we can stop the fighting during the time of the Olympics, new gates to a longer lasting peace may be opened."

"Right so!" added the British Councilor. "Let me say thank you to the Olympians, and to you Mr. Speros, for taking time away from your training to come here today to present this splendid Resolution. You are the hope of the future!"

One by one the other Councilors spoke, adding their support for the Resolution, until finally, the President tested for consensus.

"Are there any blocking concerns about the passage of this Resolution?" she asked.

The chamber went completely silent for a full ten seconds.

A broad smile spread across the face of President Kim as she announced the result. "People of the World, we have consensus. The Resolution to Cease All Hostilities is hereby adopted.

The Great Hall erupted in applause, the session was adjourned, and Herakles soon found himself surrounded by people shaking his hand and offering congratulations. After a few minutes, Ivanna returned with her staff, and began the process of cajoling the jubilant mass of people toward the reception room.

He knew the scene well, having attended diplomatic functions from an early age. Gliding effortlessly from one admirer to the next, he signed an occasional autograph and graciously received high praises and well wishes. Ivanna introduced him to some of the dignitaries, giving him a chance to use his French and German, and in between conversations, he sipped sparkling cider and had a few hors d'oeuvres.

From an adjoining room, a smooth female voice came over the mic, and like a whisper, snuck its way into his consciousness. She sounded American, but she also had a melodic, Caribbean intonation he found irresistible. He went around the corner to have a closer look, and was surprised to see none other than the fastest woman in the world herself, Alanta January – all 5'11" of her. She and three other athletes, still in their AOA warm-ups, were on a small stage, getting ready to begin. She picked up two cloth-tipped drumsticks and sounded three notes on a steel pan drum, then the others joined in with keyboard and guitars, firing up a calypso beat. Her shoulder-length beaded braids bounced up and around her shining brown face, as her smile and her music filled the room. Herakles stood transfixed.

Unbeknownst to our handsome hero, or anyone else in attendance, the Goddess Aphrodite had arranged for Eros, Cherub of Love, to be at the reception as well that day. High above the impressive room, on the round crystal chandelier, the rosy, winged creature sat, watching Herakles intently. Out of habit he reached for an arrow, but when he found only an empty quiver, he remembered he was supposed to use the Love Dust now instead. It was in a little pouch he'd tied safely and securely around his chubby waist.

He returned his attention to the first of his intended recipients, but upon seeing young Herakles already enraptured, he wondered if the dust was even necessary. However, just to be sure, he decided to bestow it anyway. So he rose up from the light, fluttered over to the defenseless Mortal and sprinkled a hefty pinch upon him. Then, like a hummingbird, he zipped across the room to give Alanta her dose. The love particles rained down around her as he emptied what was left in the pouch, then returned to the chandelier to watch.

All at once, Herakles was overcome. He stared at Alanta, wide-eyed, unable to move, when suddenly her eye caught his, and with a brief flash of light, they were transported elsewhere − onto a ledge at the mouth of a cave, overlooking a deep valley. Together, blissful, they absorbed the energy of the Universe, as a waxing crescent Moon glowed orange on the western horizon, and the Milky Way's clouds of white starlight arched overhead.

Then, just as suddenly, he was back in the reception room clapping with everyone else. Alanta was looking right at him, smiling, as the music ended in exhilarating crescendo. Breaking the trance, she turned away to acknowledge her audience.

*Did she see it too?*

She took a bow with the other musicians, and then obliged the crowd by playing another upbeat island song. He would have stood there, spellbound, for the rest of the day, if Ivanna hadn't approached him with another diplomat in tow.

"Mr. Speros," she said, stepping right in front of him, wrenching his attention away, "I would like to introduce you to Ambassador...."

He followed Ivanna's lead and went through all of the motions by rote, completely distracted by the thought of Alanta. No matter where in the room he went, or with whom he spoke, he felt as though he was suddenly part of her, attached to her, like Theseus at the end of Ariadne's thread. He kept glancing her way, making sure she was still there, and a couple of times he thought she might have been looking at him too. In his heart, he felt an irrepressible longing for her.

When she finished her set, a group of people surrounded her as she left the stage. He'd have to find just the right moment, get away from whoever this was, and approach her.

Ivanna asked if a photographer could take their picture and, in the few seconds the flash lingered in his eyes, Alanta had slipped away. When he looked back toward the stage, she was nowhere to be seen. A terrible sinking feeling came over him. *Where could she have gone? It was just a second ago....* He excused himself to go in search of her, and walked around the perimeter of the room. Nothing. Then he noticed the French doors leading out to the balcony, and thought maybe she'd gone out for some air. He rushed outside and looked around, but again, there was no sign of her. He leaned over the railing and looked down at the park below, then out over the East River. *I need to talk to you.*

At that moment, the doors swung open, and he turned around to see her, walking out onto the terrace toward him.

"Now, don't you be startled," she said, with that irresistible accent. "It's just that, I was hoping to meet you, Hera*kles* Speros. I'm Alanta January."

She held out her hand and he clasped it gently, feeling the magic in her touch.

"I was hoping to meet you too," he replied, grinning. "Your music was fabulous. I loved it. Where did you learn to play like that?"

"In the Virgin Islands, where I was born. You ever been there?"

"No, but I like to travel, so maybe someday I'll go."

"If you like the music, you should go 'round carnival time. Everyone dresses up in wild, colorful costumes and they all parade down the street. The party goes on days!"

"That sounds great, but I'm afraid it'll have to wait until after the Olympics, you know, training and all."

"I hear ya. It kinda takes over your life, doesn't it?"

"It sure does. This hearing's been a nice break in the routine, though. I've really enjoyed it."

"Me too. I only wish it would last a little longer. I've gotta get back to Orleans day after tomorrow, and I haven't even made it to Central Park!"

"Well, you do have tomorrow..."

"I was thinkin' about it, but I really don't know my way around..."

Herakles knew he was supposed to be back in New Haven the next day to resume his training, but right now, Aphrodite was putting words in his mouth and events seemed out of his control. "Well, maybe I can show it to you! Central Park is my back yard."

"You would? I'd love that." She grinned impishly.

"Absolutely. What time are you free?"

"Well, I've got no plans for lunch..."

"Are you staying at the hotel, with the other athletes?"

"Uh-huh."

"There's a great restaurant near there, if you like Thai food."

"Never tried it."

"Do you like spicy?"

"Oh yeah!"

"Then Thai it is. How about if I meet you in the hotel lobby at noon?"

"You got yourself a date, Hera*kles* Speros. "

Just then, the doors flew open and Ivanna came out onto the balcony. "Excuse me, I'm sorry to interrupt the two of you, but we're all being seated for the luncheon. If you'll follow me please?"

Herakles couldn't have cared less about lunch, especially since he knew he would be sitting apart from Alanta. But at least he had a date for the next day. He pulled himself away from her, and they reluctantly followed Ivanna inside. He was seated with a group of Councilors and Olympic representatives, but throughout, his mind remained fixed on Alanta. Alanta.

Alanta.

He could think of nothing else. They spotted each other half-way across the hall, managing to exchange a few long looks, but soon they had to go their separate ways. Herakles had committed to a US Olympic Committee fundraiser that afternoon at the Metropolitan Museum of Art, and had to leave soon after lunch. He hoped he would have a few more minutes with her, but once the media was allowed into the reception, both of them were in-undated. He barely managed to get out in time to make it to his next engagement.

Throughout the fundraiser, he felt invigorated, re-energized. The spark which had ignited in him earlier that day was bursting into flame, and he took on an even brighter radiance as he ad-dressed the crowd. He described the UN proceedings, and when he announced the passage of the Resolution, they gave him a standing ovation. The New Yorkers were proud of their adopted son, who was now poised to become an Olympic champion. They got out their plastic cards and slid them through the machines with glee, enthusiastically showing support for the emerging Olympic ideal.

After a day like that he should have been exhausted, but as he lay there in bed, tossing and turning, he was very much wide awake. All night long he kept going back to that mountain with Alanta, sharing the beauty of an orange crescent Moon suspended over the valley. *It was so real, the place* must *exist. Did she experience it too? What if she didn't? What if she did?*

He tried counting out steps in his mind, running around the track, faster and faster, trying to wear himself out. Around 2:00, he finally fell into a sound sleep, but it only lasted about three hours and then he was wide awake again.

At last, as Dawn emerged from the blackness of Night, he was able to start the day. He put on some heavy sweats and went to Central Park. The sky was clear, the air felt fresh and as the Sun came up, he did his t'ai chi exercises in John Lennon's memorial garden. When he was all warmed up, he started off on a long run through the park, hoping it would help pass the morning.

It did, just a little, but another eternity elapsed before it was time to get ready for his date. He showered and shaved, then spent a long while fussing about what to wear. He finally decided to go casual, so he threw on his favorite Himalayan sweater and jeans and headed out the door.

However, and woe to come for poor Herakles, in the fog of his preoccupation with Alanta, he forgot to call his coach with the news that his plans had changed.

As he approached her hotel, he noticed a little corner newsstand. On the cover of the *Times* was a picture of him at the UN with the headline, *Global Council Adopts Cessation Resolution*. He skimmed the article and thought, overall, it was pretty favorable, especially because it mentioned the fundraiser and called for more contributions. He put it back, gave the vendor some change, and then ducked into the flow of people cruising by on the sidewalk. Though he got a few, "hey, aren't you?" looks, he managed to make it the rest of the way without causing a scene.

A large crowd had gathered outside the hotel, with everyone vying to get a glimpse of the Olympic athletes. His chances of getting past them unnoticed were slim, so he quickly devised a plan to go through the underground parking garage instead. It worked perfectly. The elevator took him right to the lobby and as the door opened, so did the one across from him, and all of a sudden there she was, in an African outfit with wild black and gold geometric designs. He motioned for her to come across the hall, she scooted into his elevator, and they snuck out through the garage together, unnoticed by the fawning throngs.

As they walked along the busy avenue, Herakles pointed out architectural details of various buildings, with special emphasis on the prevalent Greek influences. They made one quick stop at a flower shop, and he bought a bird of paradise from the old Mexican lady. A few minutes later, they reached the little Thai place called Tarn Tip.

This was Herakles' very favorite restaurant, and over the many years he'd eaten there, he had developed a close relationship with the Thai family who owned it. A few months had gone by since he'd been in, and they were glad to see him. The three daughters came over to say hello, then the father came out of the back with a perfect vase for the flower. He arranged it on their table just so, then bowed and smiled and shook Herakles' hand. Next he turned to Alanta and, placing his hands together and bowing, welcomed her to their restaurant. Herakles spoke to him with the few Thai expressions he knew: good day, how are you, thank you, your food is always delicious and so forth, and as usual, the father was thrilled to hear it.

The smells of coconut curry, lemongrass and ginger took Herakles back to his travels there. He told Alanta about the beautiful beaches and turquoise seas in the Gulf of Thailand, and about his trek from Mae Hong Son in the foothills of the Himalayas, where he visited a remote village of the Karin hill tribe. Each story sparked memories of her own travels, and over lunch they went around the globe, getting to know each other a little along the way.

Herakles kept trying, nonchalantly, to direct the conversation toward the vision he'd had, but she wasn't following his lead. Each time he tried to steer them toward that moment during the music, she took off on another tangent: her steel pan orchestra experiences as a child on St. Croix, full Moon drumming at the old sugar plantation ruins, beach parties with calypso and reggae bands. It was all intriguing to him, but he wanted to know about the vision, without inadvertently influencing her perception of it – if she had one. He sensed there was something more behind her enthusiastic words, though she seemed to want to be cautious.

They had a delicious meal, and a complimentary dessert of homemade coconut ice cream and fried bananas with honey. Herakles took the flower up to the counter and placed it off to one side, near the wall, then paid the bill. The Thai mom came out to thank him, and he complimented her meal by saying, "alloy ma kahp." She blushed and went back into the kitchen, and the two of them left in a flurry of waves and smiles and bows.

They hurried across Fifth Avenue, but once they got to Central Park, both of them slowed down to a much more leisurely stride. Because it was such a mild winter day, the park felt alive. Dog walkers, frisbee players, musicians and vendors were all out enjoying the beautiful Saturday afternoon.

"Let's go this way," Herakles said, walking up a little path into a grove of trees.

They followed the trail to a small bench overlooking the reservoir. Across the water, Manhattan skyscrapers rose above the tree line of the green urban oasis.

"It's beautiful...in its city kinda way," Alanta said, putting her sturdy black boot up on the back of the bench, and stretching out her leg. "How long you been here?"

"My family came to New York from Athens when I was 13, so I lived here about five years before moving to New Haven. My mother still lives here most of the time, and since I'm only an hour away by train, I've come back a lot over the years."

"Over the *years*," Alanta laughed. "Listen ta you. You make it soun' like you're a hundred and four! How old are you any*way*?"

Herakles blushed, "22."

"Me too! When's your birthday?"

"December 9th."

"Dohn' tell me! Mine's December 6th! Born under the sign of Sagittarius."

"Gateway to the heart of the Galaxy."

"What do you mean?"

"From our perspective here on Earth, whirling about in an outer arm of our galactic spiral, when we look toward Sagittarius, we're looking at the center of the Milky Way."

"Iré! Where'd you learn that?"

Astronomy was one of my father's interests and he turned me on to it. After the Games, I'm thinking about pursuing it more; I've always wanted a telescope."

"I'd love to look through a telescope."

"When I get one, I'll invite you to a star party."

She smiled. "So we got another date."

"I hope I don't have to wait till then to see you again!"

She switched her legs on the bench. "So anyway, why did your people come here, to the States?"

"Actually, my mom is second-generation Greek-American. She was born and raised in St. Paul, Minnesota, but she moved to Greece in 1980, after meeting and marrying my father there. She was hesitant to live overseas, but she agreed to do so with his promise that they'd someday move back. Fifteen years later, when he was appointed Greek Ambassador to the UN, he was finally able to fulfill that promise. She'd enjoyed living in Greece, and we got to travel all over when I was a kid, but by then she was ready to come home."

"So no wonder you were so *smooooth* yesterday at the hearing. Old stuff to you, huh?"

Herakles shrugged. "Well, thanks but, I never testified before! Just brief appearances at diplomatic affairs, corralled together with the other children."

"Well, you did an excellent job representing all of us."

"Thanks. By the way, I've seen your PSAs on environmental sustainability. They're right on. You're putting out some great ideas."

Now it was her turn to blush. He was surprised he could see it beneath her mocha brown skin, but he could.

"Thank you. Let's keep going, okay? I'm not used to being so still."

"Follow me," Herakles said, continuing along the trail.

"So, do you have any brothers and sisters?" she went on.

The question. Herakles didn't answer right away. He never knew how much to say without being too depressing...

"Hello? You still there?"

They emerged from the trees onto another, wider walkway and then he finally answered. "I did have a twin brother, Iphikles, but he died shortly after the Millennium."

She gently touched his arm, stopping him. "I'm sorry. If you don't wanna talk about it, that's okay."

"No, it's all right," he said, walking again. "We didn't think he'd live as long as he did. He had a genetic blood disorder called Thalassemia, or Cooley's Anemia. It's found mostly in Mediterranean populations. It's like sickle cell anemia, in that the red blood cells are misshapen, which interferes with the body's ability to expel heavy metals like iron; after awhile, that causes organ failure. One of the most promising treatments is a bone marrow transplant. I was a match, but unfortunately, the transplant failed. He died shortly after the operation."

She sighed heavily. "Oh, I'm so sorry."

"I still can't believe he's gone. He was so courageous, and he never let his illness interfere with living his life. I can't tell you how much inspiration I draw from him to this very day." A tear rolled down his cheek and he wiped it away with the back of his hand. "Enough about me. Tell me about your family."

"Alright," she said, patting his back reassuringly. "Where should I start? I'm from St. Croix – okay, quick geography quiz. Tell me where it is."

He smiled, because he knew exactly where it was. "Let's see, I think it's part of the old West Indies, not too far from Puerto Rico."

"Very good! Most Americans have no clue where the Virgin Islands are! Since we gained statehood I think a few more people might know, but I still get a lot of blank stares."

"That must have been a beautiful place to grow up. Are your parents from there too?"

"No. My mom and grandmother are from the island of Dominica, most recently at least, and my dad and his family are from St. John."

"Are they athletes, too?"

She laughed. "No. Momma's a biology teacher and Daddy's an organic farmer."

"Any siblings?"

"Nope. Ahm deh *ohn*ly one."

He loved how she slipped back and forth between her American and Caribbean dialects. "Well, on this beautiful January day, I can't resist asking where your last name came from."

She paused a second, then answered in a more somber tone, staying with her island accent. "Ah mention mah daddy family cohm from Sain*John*."

"Yes?"

"We take dat name from a slave boy named Janu*ary*. He live on deh island in the 1600s."

*Slavery,* Herakles thought. *Jesus.*

"It's incredible," she went on, switching back, with a bit of an edge to her voice. "Slavery had not been seen in any institutionalized form for a thousand years, then those Europeans became addicted to sugar. Where was the old 'war on drugs' then?"

He sensed this was a rhetorical question so he waited, and sure enough, she had more to say on the subject.

"Want a quick history lesson?"

"Okay," he answered tentatively.

"In 1733, the Danes had control of St. John and sugar was their business. At that time, there were over 100 plantations on that tiny island alone, all running on the back of slave labor. The summer brought hurricanes, drought, insect plague and a merciless new slave code. When a new group of captives, who had been tribal royalty in Africa, were brought in, they decided they'd rather die than live in bondage. So, on 'deh night a deh silent drum' they incited the slave revolt. When a dozen of them tricked their way into the garrison, took over the fort and then spread the call for rebellion. The revolt lasted about six months, ending only after the Danes sent in more soldiers to starve the rebels out. By the end, the last of them committed suicide rather than face torture and execution by their masters. My ancestor, a young boy they called January, witnessed the mass suicide, and was forced to testify about the incident in a Danish court. We don't know why they chose that name for him, but it stuck, and it's been passed down now for almost three hundred years."

Herakles didn't know how to respond.

"That's okay," she volunteered, sounding a little more light-hearted again. "You don't have to say anything. Slavery was a terrible thing, but it's a long time over. Hopefully for good."

"Let's hope so," he agreed.

"My turn again," she continued. "I've read you're a Rhodes Scholar. So, when are you going to merry old England?"

"We'll see. They agreed to give me a two-year deferment for

the Olympics, and I still have a year and a half left."

"And what will you be studying?"

"International relations."

"Oh, so you'll be following in your father's footsteps, huh?"

"No. Well, not exactly; we wear *really* different shoes."

"How's that?"

"He had more of the old dominator mentality, you know, he who carries the biggest stick makes all the rules. I'd like to work in the new UN, to help continue the reforms, and be a part of this emerging world democracy."

"So, do you see yourself on the other side of that Global Council room, as an elected *mem*bah?"

He blushed again, putting his head down a little. "Well, maybe.... So, how about you, Alanta? What are you going to do after you win all those record-setting gold medals?"

"Dohn you jinx me now," she replied, tugging on his sleeve. "I'm pretty sure I'll be going to medical school after the Games, but I haven't decided which one yet. I've been accepted to three, one on the East Coast, and two on the West. Right now, I'm leaning toward Stanford. The West Coast seems to offer more in the areas of non-traditional medicine and the spiritual aspects of healing, and that's really going to be the core of my practice. So, I don't know, I guess I'll be making my decision soon after the Olympics, depending on how that all works out."

The two of them went along like this for hours, covering nearly the whole of Central Park and most of each other's young life. Soon the Sun began to set, the sky turned pink, and before long, all the journeying ways would be darkened. However, Herakles didn't want to see the day come to a close, so he tried to extend it. They could drop in at the Museum of Modern Art, for some wine and cheese at the photography show opening, then he'd cook them a nice dinner, or....

But woe, and to his great sadness, she'd promised to meet up with friends for a long-planned dinner and show. So, resolved the day must end, he walked her to the nearest park entrance and started to hail a taxi, when much to his delight, the thoughtful Aphrodite interceded. Suddenly, as if from thin air, the most glorious carriage in all of New York pulled up to the curb beside them.

A magnificent black horse drew the black lacquered coach, and the driver tipped his tall white hat. Herakles and Alanta looked at each other, and with a silent *why not?* they hopped in. The cozy seat brought them closer together, as the horse started off in a trot. They turned back into the Park and onto a road with no cars, and for a few minutes, left the city far behind. Only then did Alanta bring it up.

"So, I'm not sure how to say this without sounding like a crazy woman, but yesterday I had a, vision let's call it, when I was playing at the reception."

*Finally!* Herakles turned a little more toward her, looking intently. "No, it's not crazy. Please, tell me what you saw."

"It was somewhere I'd never been before. A cave on the side of a mountain, with a ledge overlooking a deep valley. An orange crescent Moon hung low on the horizon, and the Milky Way arched overhead."

Herakles' eyes got bigger and bigger as she described the place he'd been.

"You were there, Hera*kles* Speros. I guess I was still playing the whole time, but it felt like I left the reception room with you."

"Maybe we did leave that reception room, because I experienced the exact same thing!"

Her deep black eyes searched his own and she asked him seriously, "you ever seen that place before?"

"No, and I've never had a vision like *that* before, either."

Alanta smiled. "I have."

"You have?! When?"

"One other time, during my coming of age ceremony, when I was turning 13. My Gran'mama Lily had learned the ritual from her grandmother, when she was a girl growing up in Nigeria. We made a bush tea using special herbs, and shared a vision of our home village in West Africa, in the past. An ancestral Spirit spoke with us, and told me to prepare for a great challenge I would one day face. It was an awesome, shared experience, just like with you in the cave. Very real and very powerful."

"Yes, I felt that power too. Incredible. Somehow though, I had the sense that our experience was in the *future*."

"Yeah, it seemed that way to me too."

"I wish we could go off in search of that mountain together, right now," Herakles said as he looked away, suddenly feeling sad.

Alanta touched his chin with her slender fingers and slowly turned his face toward her. "We both know that's not possible, but hey, we saw it ourselves, you and I together again in that amazing place!"

Herakles wanted more than anything to kiss her, when unexpectedly, she leaned over and kissed *him* on the cheek. Just then, a flash of a camera went off, startling them both. They turned to see a sole photographer fleeing across the grass.

"*Great!*" Herakles exclaimed. "What if he's with one of those horrendous tabloids? That is *not* something we need right now."

Alanta leaned up against the side of the carriage and covered her eyes with the palm of her hand. "If that happens, my coach is gonna freak."

That's when Herakles remembered he'd forgotten to call his own coach. "Oh, no! Mine is going to have a fit – for more than one reason."

"What are we gonna do?"

"There isn't anything we *can* do, except maybe hope and pray he was just a tourist."

"No chance," she said, shaking her head. "The way he ran off like that, he's going straight to the press. I'm seriously thinking about running after him."

Herakles laughed. "I have no doubt you could catch him, but then what would you do?"

"I don't know. Maybe if I offer him enough money, he'll wipe the memory."

"And then one of his cronies would get a picture of the exchange. I can see it now."

"You're right. It might only make things worse. We're just gonna have to deal with it."

"I don't think we have a choice," he replied, as the carriage turned onto the busy street toward Alanta's hotel. "When can I see you again?"

"Soon, I hope. My email is Alanta@PlanetEarth.net, so write me and we'll figure it out. Okay?"

"Okay."

"Now, you better get on out of this carriage before we come too close to the hotel, or we're gonna have ourselves more than *one* picture to worry about."

He gently took her hands in his. "All right. I had a *fabulous* time with you today, and I will dream of our next meeting. Until then." He kissed the top of each hand, and then jumped to the ground, running alongside the driver to give him some money. Then he stopped to let the carriage pass. She blew him a kiss, and after lingering a moment more, he disappeared back into the park.

# 3

# THE REMNANTS OF CHAOS

Little did Herakles and Alanta know, but before they went to sleep that night, their picture had been transmitted to the other side of the world, to the Kingdom of Qatar, at the edge of the Arabian Desert. The small country was actually a peninsula, a finger of land jutting into the waters of the Persian Gulf. On its shores, in the capital city of Doha, it was mid-day, and the light of a relentless Sun reflected off the glass and steel buildings of the city center, creating a horrific glare. Above them all, the TExxonMobico Tower rose like a gleaming pillar in the arid blue sky.

High up in the penthouse suite, the holdouts of the once mighty CHAOS organization convened. The four remaining constituents sat grimly at the long mahogany table, amidst scores of empty chairs, waiting for the meeting to begin. On the east wall, their once brilliant Carrera marble plaque, which had been salvaged from their former headquarters, was now yellowed with the tinge of stale smoke. Spelled out across the stone, yet barely readable, was their holy acronym and business philosophy: *Corporations Have Authority Over Society*. Their authority, however, was tenuous at best.

The Millennium Effect had wreaked havoc on their global military-industrial alliance. Their customer base virtually evaporated, government regulation increased, and stockholders and minions deserted their companies in droves. The massive shift in social and economic priorities had left them scrambling to keep their dwindling empire from collapsing all together.

To ride out the cyclone of change, they chose the course of obfuscation and isolation. New corporate entities were formed to further limit their liability and add extra layers of tax protection. Oil acquisitions were accelerated in an attempt to control the sinking market and ensure crude supplies for the duration of the so-called "Reawakening." Because of its remote location and near total dependence on oil, Qatar was chosen as the best place from which to orchestrate a suitable response to the temporarily changed circumstances. They convinced their long-time business associate, the King, that if he stayed the course with Big Oil, he would be well taken care of. So, as the other oil rich nations opted to diversify their economies and develop alternative energy sources like solar and wind, His Majesty broke ranks and went with CHAOS.

The Chairman of the Chairmen, Mr. WestLockMartBoMc-Douglas, *et al*, was still alive, but he was not well. The former king of the corporate realm sat noticeably diminished in his overstuffed black leather chair. He'd lost some weight in the last few years, and his diamond rings slid on his fingers as he impatiently tapped the tabletop. When last we saw our corporate nemesis, he was in his prime. Arms sales were up and he sat fat and happy, manipulating the course of world events with merely the bark of an order. When the Millennium Effect occurred, he believed it to be just another bothersome public relations issue which could be controlled through CHAOS' vast media monopoly. However, he had underestimated Ben Gerrard's Earth News Network and the power of the Minoan Message. In the aftermath, as the ideals of sustainability and corporate responsibility began to flourish, CHAOS lay close to ruin.

In the past four years, the cartel had seen the withdrawal and transformation of several of its key conglomerates. The Chairman of DizzeyUniversal went the way of the ratings and began taking responsibility for the content of his entertainment. He led the industry in setting new programming standards and revolutionary anti-violence protocols, which acknowledged the media's link to violence. He started GNN, the Good News Network, and it was wildly successful. All of a sudden, there was a blossoming of entertainment which put forth positive messages, and his philosophical shift had helped make it possible.

The Chairman of ExxoToyMitsu finally acknowledged that petroleum-based technology was a dead-end road, so he sold off his oil production interests to his former associates and bailed. He formed a new company, SolarUNlimited (SUN), by consolidating and redirecting his remaining assets toward the development of solar-powered industries. He retrieved a few of the old patents from the Vault of Buried Technologies, and by 2002, the company had launched a new line of solar cars, which quickly became the hottest personal transport vehicles on the market. His success had contributed to technological breakthroughs, which extended into other sectors. Soon, most of the fossil fuel-burning energy plants had been converted; and huge monorail projects were initiated, which were destined to replace city busses and cars in municipalities around the globe.

As a result of the public's boycott of genetically modified and pesticide dependent agriculture, the Chairman of food production giant DAM/Nabco split from DowPont PetroBioseuticals® and changed their name to Organico. He shunned the norms of agribusiness and embraced sustainable, organic farming, embarking on an impressive program of topsoil decontamination and reclamation. Warehouse after warehouse of toxic chemicals were removed from the market, and pesticide production plants were converted to recycling facilities. He too dipped into the Vault and retrieved previously unreleased research, which detailed the unpredictability and potential hazards of genetically modified food and medicine. His efforts ultimately led to an international moratorium on dangerous biotechnologies.

So, after the big defection, CHAOS membership was reduced to the Chairman, his nephew Arthur Hayes, media baron Ruther Burdock Unlimited, former tobacco tycoon Morris Reynolds and dear friend of the Chairman's, Mr. PetroBioseuticals® himself, DowPont – affectionately known as DP.

The Chairman still controlled the weapons manufacturing wing, and now, most of the world's remaining oil production interests as well, but business was declining and the financial stability of the entire operation was at risk. The momentous market shift away from a military economy had forced him to diversify. When his nephew stepped forward, looking for a chance to prove himself, he gave it to him. Arthur had proposed converting 30% of the Chairman's vast production capability toward the peaceful use of military technology. Begrudgingly, and in deference to his obligation to protect The Margin, the Chairman left Arthur in New York to develop the whole new division.

Arthur shined in his new role. Under his leadership, war technology was suddenly being used for altruistic purposes: enhancing medical technologies, restoring and protecting the environment, and pursuing the scientific exploration of Earth and Space, just to name a few. He was responsible for billions of geos coming in, and although the Chairman wasn't about to admit it, Arthur's success was financing much of the rest of the CHAOS machine.

DP had remained completely loyal to the Chairman, swearing an oath to the bitter end. As did Ruther, although now his media holdings had been reduced to a single, but still influential network, CHAOS ONE. Finally, there was poor, pathetic Morris Reynolds. His health had deteriorated so significantly in these last few years that he now needed a respirator and several personal assistants to attend to him. He too remained completely loyal to the Chairman, confident that somehow, someway, they could all regain their former glory.

"Let's get this God damn show on the road," the Chairman demanded, as he fumbled with the chair's built-in remote control pad. When it was working, he could summon gigiquads of information from their vast computer network, or interface with the CHAOS Satellite Comnet. When it wasn't working, as was often the case these days, it only raised his blood pressure. He pounded the remote with his fist, and their very large video screen came to life with an image of the blond-haired, blue-eyed Arthur Hayes.

"It's about time, Goddammit," the Chairman continued. "Can we finally get started?"

Ruther, Morris and DP all nodded, chortling.

"The latest threat to our global empire of free trade and profit comes once again from that God Damn United Nations. They just passed a resolution that, if signed by our remaining clients, would cease all hostilities during the Olympics. This would result in a significant loss of revenue during the next quarter. And, even more alarming is their ultimate goal: completing their insane mission of global disarmament! The way things have been going lately, we can't afford another damn moratorium. We have got to do something to spark our sales and return this division to a state of health. I'm not just gonna roll over and die dammit! Now, what are we going to do about this?"

"Give it up, Uncle!" the televised Arthur responded. "Don't you see, the future isn't in arms sales, it's in the *peaceful* use of our military technology. I say we focus our efforts on that. Look at these figures." A pop-up window appeared beneath him on the screen. "We've got a phenomenal growth curve going here and there's no reason we can't sustain it. In fact, if you'd invest a little more in my division, I think we could see even greater profits."

"No, Goddammit!" the Chairman declared. "I'm not going to stand by and watch all our hard work converted into these sissy ass uses. This dip in arms sales won't be permanent, history proves that. We simply have to act to hasten the natural order of things."

Morris Reynolds removed the respirator mask from his face

to light up another cigarette. He pounded weakly on the table in front of him, and spoke with as much force as he could muster. "Peace is not addictive, I say, it's *not* addictive."

"I agree," added Ruther. "Aggression and warfare are simply inherent in human nature. This *peace* is only a passing fad."

"Passing fad or not," DP retorted with a venomous barring of teeth, "it has negatively affected The Margin. Weapon sales are plummeting and that's pulling down the whole sonofabitchin' thing; if we can't get 'em back up, we're all going to be shit out of luck."

"Well," Ruther interjected, "it seems we have a choice to make. Are we going to divert our remaining assets toward the peaceful use of our military technologies; or are we going to hasten conflict in the world to boost sales? It's that simple."

"Our infrastructure is in place to generate massive amounts of weapons," the Chairman replied flatly. "It would take forever to duplicate our present capabilities for *peaceful* purposes. Shit, we'd be looking at less than 40% profits for *years*, and it would all be in those God damn geos. I say we go for the big money again, the big dollars. We break the peace and we rake it in. If we play our cards right, we can take back our other markets in the process."

"Do you have something in mind?" DP asked with one of his glacial sidelong looks.

"As a matter of fact, I do," the Chairman replied slyly. "Let me tell you about a few new friends of mine. They call themselves One God One Way, or OGOW for short. Basically, they're the last of the militant monotheistic fundamentalists – a loosely allied network of thugs with operations around the globe. They're very much opposed to any form of world government, and I think we could collaborate with them, work to achieve all of our goals. We were thinking that just a few well placed strategic interferences would deter those nations from signing on to that God damn resolution."

Arthur stood up and leaned over his desk, filling their room from the screen. "What? My God, Uncle, have you no limits? I will not be part of *any* alliance with a terrorist organization. You've gone too far this time."

"Sit down and shut up," the Chairman bellowed. "I appointed you and I can dismiss you – and I will with another outburst like that."

"You're wrong, Uncle. You've grown disconnected from your once vast empire and the realities of your underlings. My colleagues will remain loyal to me because they believe in what they're doing. Yours, the few who are left, no longer do. They've been deserting you in droves, and you still act as though you're in control, when in reality, you're not. The world has changed and is continuing to change faster than you can comprehend. Your once great power is now largely within your imagination. But at some level, you must know that – to stoop to an alliance with funda-mentalists, you'd have to be desperate. Well, let me be clear with each and every one of you. I will *not* be a part of it." He terminated his transmission and the screen went black.

The Chairman raised an eyebrow. "I didn't think he had it in him. But God damn him anyway, we don't need Arthur Hayes. If my plan is successful, business'll be booming, and he'll be beggin' me for his old job back."

"So what kind of 'strategic interferences' do you have in mind?" asked an intrigued DP.

"Bombings, of course – but not too much collateral damage; just enough to get people's attention."

"What exactly do these potential associates expect from us?" Ruther wanted to know.

"That's the beauty of it. We simply supply them with the bombs, and they'll do the rest. Hell, they don't even need the new stuff, so we can kill two birds and dump off some of the old sur-plus."

"Good," replied DP. "I wouldn't want to spend too much on this enterprise. Those terrorists are such low-lifes, but I think a temporary alliance with them will work nicely, so I'm willing to go along."

Morris nodded his assent, his weak wrists trying to support two thumbs up.

"Ruther," the Chairman questioned pointedly, "are you with us, or against us?"

He hesitated, but then agreed. "Count me in."

"All right then, we've got a deal," affirmed the Chairman. He pushed a button on his keypad and the larger-than-life picture of Alanta kissing Herakles in the carriage appeared on the monitor. "Moving on to some related business, one of our minions managed to get this picture of that cocky little Greek boy who had the gall to get up there and demand an end to all hostilities. I think we should use it to undermine that son-of-a-bitch and his God damn resolution. A nice sex scandal always works to discredit people and this one is interracial to boot. What do you say, Ruther?"

"Oh, I like it. I like it! It'll weaken support for the resolution *and* divert attention away from our campaign, should people begin asking too many questions. I'll run it immediately. By the way, when will we see the first explosion?"

"Three, maybe four days."

"I'll have cameras standing by. Tell me, where will they strike first?"

And so, from their far-off desert oasis, blinded by the glare of avarice, the Chairmen of CHAOS conspired, intent on setting in motion their plan to sabotage global disarmament and recover their lost riches.

# 4

# ON THE SHORES OF NEW HAVEN

Herakles had never been in Grand Central Station at this early an hour on a Sunday morning. It seemed unusually, almost unnervingly quiet as he crossed the cavernous room. Overhead, the fabulous constellation mural adorned the ceiling, somehow more vivid in the solitude, more expansive without the surging masses. He lingered beneath it a moment, listening, letting the stillness in.

As he approached the ticket counter, an old man was leaning in toward the window, carefully counting out his money to the agent. The gentleman got his ticket and put his billfold away, then looked at Herakles and smiled. *There was something familiar about him*, Herakles thought, nodding pleasantly. The man winked and tipped his hat, then shuffled off toward his train. Herakles turned to the agent and slipped some money under the window. When he looked back, the old man was gone. He looked at his watch, 5:14. *Better hurry up.*

The doors were closing as he jumped aboard, and the train left right on time. He put his bag in the overhead rack and took a seat near the window. As they started their slow, rumbling trek out of the dark labyrinthine tunnels, he leaned against the side of the car and closed his eyes. Images of Alanta flowed through his mind: in the cave with the waxing crescent Moon over the mountains, playing the steel pan at the UN reception, eating Thai food at Tarn Tip, blowing him a kiss from the carriage. He felt so dreamy and wonderful thinking about her, so free from all concern. However, at the periphery of his bubble of euphoria, annoying sounds clamored to be heard. Loud, mean sounds, trying to punch their way through and wrestle his attention away from her. He tried to will them to cease, knowing he'd have to experience them live and in person soon enough, and at that thought, the bubble burst.

*No relationships, no television, no phone calls, no Internet*, he could hear his coach saying in that thick East German accent. *I want your total focus to be on your training. 110%. Do you understand me? 110%.* The coach who didn't even want Herakles to testify at the UN, let alone take an extra day to *goof off.* Carl Richter, the celebrated Olympic decathlon champion of the 1960 Games, the legendary coach who'd brought many aspiring athletes to greatness, and Herakles' unrelenting taskmaster for the last 18 months. He was stubborn and set in his ways, demanding yet stingy with praise, and definitely a control freak. In the beginning, Herakles felt honored that Carl had agreed to train him, but now he was starting to wonder if he would be better off with a younger coach who believed a little more in positive motivation. *Too late, I have to make the most of it. But what about Alanta? How would Coach deal with that?* He didn't want to keep her a secret, but he also didn't want to hear Carl say no.

The train came above ground, yet it was still so dark he could barely tell. Only the raindrops pelting against the window gave it away for sure. They sped along through the urban sprawl of White Plains...Greenwich...New London...Fairfield...and finally, as the first light of day was trying to worm its way through the overcast sky, they arrived at New Haven station.

Herakles grabbed his stuff, and turning up his collar, stepped onto the platform and into the damp cold. He hurried down the stairs, and fortunately, a taxi was there waiting. It was 6:45, which meant that he still had a good hour before he had to see Carl; plenty of time to psyche himself up for the confrontation.

However, try as he might to reframe the situation, anxiety and gloom seeped into his bones with the chill. Fog enshrouded the landmarks of New Haven Green, Harkness Tower and the turrets of Old Campus, which now looked more like a scene from medieval London, complete with an oppressive sense of foreboding. By the time they got to the field house, it was drizzling an icy rain, and he was thoroughly dreading what lay ahead. He paid for the cab, ran up to the tall door and heaved it open.

"Where the *hell* have you been?" Carl barked, scaring him half to death.

"Uh, I apologize Coach, but, didn't you get my call?" He started for the locker room. "I left a message on your answering machine last night."

"Yes," Carl replied, following him through the doorway. "I heard your message and I repeat, where the *hell* have you been? You were supposed to meet me here *yesterday* morning."

Herakles got all the way to the lockers before turning to face him. "As I said in my message, I had to stay in New York for another day. I'm sorry I didn't call you earlier; I should have, but it slipped my mind." He opened the locker door and Carl slammed it back shut with a thwap of his palm.

"Slipped your mind, did it? Damn. Well, tell me, what was so pressing, so important that you let it completely disrupt your training schedule?"

"Oh, come on Coach, it was only one day."

"Don't give me that bullshit. We only have a handful of 'one-days' left. So, what's your explanation?" Then, without waiting for an answer, Carl whipped a copy of the *Daily Post* at him. "Does Alanta January have anything to do with it?"

Herakles picked up the paper and there it was, his worst nightmare. The picture of Alanta kissing him in the carriage, with an oversized headline trumpeting, "Olympians Unite!"

"What were you thinking?" Carl went on, pursing his lips and parking both hands on his hips, looking madder than ever.

"It was an accident. Look, I'm really very sorry about this. I promise, I won't let it happen again."

"You're damn right you won't let it happen again or you'll be looking for a new coach."

"We'll be more discreet in the future, I promise."

"Your future is the decathlon, and I'll warn you to remember that. The Games are now only six months away. Six months! You simply can *not* let a woman distract you now. Not at this critical time."

"She's not a *distraction*, Coach, she's an enhancement to my life."

"You're not to see her until after the Games, do you understand me?"

"You're being totally unreasonable, Carl."

"Kleo," he thrust his forefinger in Herakles' face. "I told you from the beginning. No relationships. Now you decide, either her or me."

Herakles flung Carl's arm away and looked him straight in the eye. "I knew you wouldn't understand. You're just like my father, it's your way or no way. Damn your stubbornness."

"What'll it be then? It's your choice."

"I'll do what you ask of me, but I think you're absolutely wrong."

"Let me hear it. You *won't* see her until after the Games."

Herakles looked away, trying to keep his own anger in check. "I won't see her."

"Good. Now dress and get your tardy ass out there. I guarantee that by the end of the day you won't be giving Alanta January another thought."

How wrong Coach was, because from that moment on, Herakles would never let her out of his thoughts again. He knew how he felt, and he knew she would only make him stronger, faster and more able to endure the grueling punishment Coach was trying to inflict – tripling the number of sprints, doubling his 5k run, then adding extra reps and extra sets in the weight room. He reached deep inside himself to rise to the occasion, to the point where even Carl seemed surprised. It wasn't until well after the Sun had set, with Herakles still going strong, that Coach called it a day.

Finally, he'd get something to eat. As is customary for serious athletes, Coach determined his dietary requirements and planned the meals, but Carl took it further, obsessing about what Herakles ate, asking detailed questions, trying to catch him sneaking something that wasn't in the regimen. He'd gotten grilled over what he had in New York, and of course, he couldn't even hint that he'd eaten a vegetarian Thai lunch.

Usually, when he wasn't in detention, he got three solid, if somewhat carnivorous, meals each day. Carl had signed him up on a school meal plan, so breakfast was at home, but every afternoon and evening the two of them would take the shuttle bus to the grad school cafeteria on York Street. Tonight, because it was so late, the dining room was deserted. They sat across from one another, but Herakles didn't look up and Carl didn't speak. With each echoing sound of their silverware, the silence between them seemed amplified.

He got back to his apartment around nine. After he kicked his shoes off on the mat and set his bag down in the hall, he went into the living room. He'd moved in during his fourth year at Yale, and had never really found the time to furnish or decorate the place, but it was still pretty comfortable. Aside from his bedroom furniture, he only had a futon, and a second-hand coffee table and chair, though he did have an awesome sound system, with CDs spilling out of the racks. Next to them sat the acoustic guitar he had always hoped to learn how to play. On the wall were two prints, Monet's *Water Lilies* and a Newport Jazz Festival poster. Filling the remaining space were a variety of plants. In one corner, he'd hung an old hammock, and ivy and philodendron had not only taken it over, but were growing around the room, creating a virtual arboretum.

He went over to the sliding glass door and looked out. The view was usually pretty good from his 16th-floor apartment, but tonight, through the cold winter rain, he couldn't see much at all. One of the tall, Neo-Gothic stone towers of Old Campus became partially visible for a minute, and then it slipped back into the mist. The light of the streetlamps managed to filter through the dense, moist air, but he couldn't make out the harbor at all. As he was just about to go back inside, a sparkling diamond of light appeared in a small break in the clouds. *Sirius. It must be.* The brightest star in the Heavens, peeking through to give him a glimmer of hope.

He went back in and closed the door. *Coach can forbid me from seeing Alanta, but he can't stop me from contacting her, and I'm going to do it right now.* He changed into his heavy cotton sleeping shirt and turned down the comforter, piling the pillows into a nice backrest against the headboard, then he retrieved his laptop from the desk, climbed into bed and thought about what he wanted to say. He wasn't accustomed to his new voice-activated computer, so it still felt a little strange telling it to "log on," but he did, and it did, and as soon as the connection was confirmed, he began their electronic relationship.

Subject: Waxing Crescent Moon
From: Herakles@Gaia.net
Date: January 7, 2004
To: Alanta@PlanetEarth.net

Hello Alanta, I hope you made it safely back to New Orleans. I've been thinking about you and our wonderful meeting all day. I can't get the vision of the waxing crescent out of my mind – nor do I wish to.

Did you see today's *Daily Post*? I can't believe people still buy such trash. Thank the Immortals that most of the tabloids went out of business after the Millennium. Can you imagine what it would be like if this happened in the old days?! My coach, recovering cold warrior that he is, actually *threw* the paper at me. He was thoroughly enraged by the whole thing, and he forbade me to see you until after the Olympics. I'm so sorry. I hope you understand. He was literally ready to walk out on me if I didn't agree – but he won't keep me from thinking about you all of the time and writing as much as possible.

What Carl just doesn't understand is that the positive feelings I have for you will only *help* me prepare for the Games. Thanks for coming into my life!

Subject: Waxing Crescent Moon
From: Alanta@PlanetEarth.net
Date: January 8, 2004
To: Herakles@Gaia.net

To me, the waxing crescent signifies a new beginning. Each day it'll grow larger and brighter until it reaches fullness, and this is what I hope for our relationship!

Even though I would've loved to see you again too, I don't know how we could have pulled it off anyway. So, dohn worry mon. We'll be together in our thoughts and dreams. And *visions.*

Well it may be the new days, but people still like to gossip and CHAOS ONE is feeding right into it. I watched that crummy channel for two hours last night and not one mention of the Resolution – just idle chatter and incessant speculation about us. They even interviewed people who said they knew me, but I had no idea who they were!

Jimmy and I sat down and had a heart-to-heart. He was totally cool with our getting together, though he thinks we should be as private as possible because of the "race" thing. He worries that we'll get distracted from our athletic goals because of the way others might react. I assured him we'd lay low till after the Games, which, given the situation with CHAOS ONE, is probably not a bad idea anyhow.

His biggest concern however, was with me getting too involved with the political stuff. I got to hear the story all over again about how Tommy Smith and John Carlos got their careers ruined in Mexico City in 1968 – all for wearing a black glove to show solidarity with the Civil Rights movement. It was Jimmy's first Olympics and he wore the glove too, but he was up in the stands and lucky for him, didn't get his picture taken. I have to admit, I can see what he means. Ours was a completely *personal* thing, and now it's completely out of our hands. Kinda scary, but I don't really think they can wreck our careers over it. Still, since the Resolution has been adopted by the Global Council, I think I'm gonna back off the activism for awhile. I hope you understand.

Well, gotta go. More soon.

Subject: coaches
From: Herakles@Gaia.net
Date: January 8, 2004
To: Alanta@PlanetEarth.net

You're so lucky to have an understanding coach. Part of me wanted to walk out on Carl, but I knew the bargain when he agreed to train me – though I never really believed all the stories I'd heard about him, till now! He's working me harder than ever, but thinking about you gives me the strength of a thousand!

From the moment Eos shows her rosy fingers at Dawn until Helios disappears into Night, I do think of you, Alanta January, and the magical day we had together.

Subject: Magical Day
From: Alanta@PlanetEarth.net
Date: January 10, 2004
To: Herakles@Gaia.net

When I'm working out, I play the whole day over in my head, like a movie. It's funny, isn't it, how in retrospect events can seem larger than life?? Yet, this really *does* feel larger than life, somehow. Doesn't it?

Subject: LIFE
From: Herakles@Gaia.net
Date: January 11, 2004
To: Alanta@PlanetEarth.net

I know what you mean. Yet, I don't know what it all means. Know what I mean?

Subject: meaning
From: Alanta@PlanetEarth.net
Date: January 12, 2004
To: Herakles@Gaia.net

Yes. And no. The most fundamental of all questions: What does it all mean? I say nothing, noh-*ting*, unless you have someone to share it with.

Subject: it
From: Herakles@Gaia.net
Date: January 13, 2004
To: Alanta@PlanetEarth.net
   I'd like to share it with you.

Subject: it
From: Alanta@PlanetEarth.net
Date: January 13, 2004
To: Herakles@Gaia.net
   Me too. :)

Subject: it
From: Herakles@Gaia.net
Date: January 14, 2004
To: Alanta@PlanetEarth.net
   Knowing that will sustain me, at least until after the Games.

Subject: school bus bombing in Kashmir
From: Alanta@PlanetEarth.net
Date: January 18, 2004
To: Herakles@Gaia.net
   I just heard about the terrorist bombing. I can't believe people can be so cruel. My heart goes out to those families. I hope this doesn't lead to retaliation and keep them from signing the Resolution – and they were so close to signing. :(

Subject: Kashmir
From: Herakles@Gaia.net
Date: January 19, 2004
To: Alanta@PlanetEarth.net
   It's all so horrible, and so predictable. The last vestiges of the dominator regression asserting themselves. However, I believe we

have the collective ability to overcome it, and I'm glad to see the UN is trying to bring both sides back to the table.

-Kleo.  PS Are you sure you want to be talking about this?

Subject: jerks
From: Alanta@PlanetEarth.net
Date: January 20, 2004
To: Herakles@Gaia.net

Sorry I haven't written in a couple of days, I've been a little preoccupied by the jerks from CHAOS ONE. They've been phoning the field house and snooping around my neighborhood. Why can't they just disappear? Have you seen what they're saying about us? It's disgusting! They even released some pictures of me which most definitely do not depict reality – they must be digitally creating them! And yet, they still have the *nerve* to call themselves "fair and balanced." *#@*!!, it makes me so pissed off mon!!! xo

Subject: jerks
From: Herakles@Gaia.net
Date: January 21, 2004
To: Alanta@PlanetEarth.net

Try not to think about them, Alanta. Keep focusing on your training, and remember, the rest of the world doesn't see you that way. Those "reporters" are pestering me too, rooting around looking for something to sensationalize, but Carl will only stand for so much. Yesterday, he threatened to call security. Hopefully they'll be on to something else soon.

It *is* disgusting, especially how they're focusing on the racial "problem." What's the problem? Thinking it's a problem is the problem. (Jimmy sure made that call!) I miss you.

PS What is "xo?"

Subject: xo
From: Alanta@PlanetEarth.net
Date: January 21, 2004
To: Herakles@Gaia.net
   You've been here how long and never seen that? x = kiss and
o = hug. It's a kind of short hand. I miss you too.

Subject: Myanmar
From: Herakles@Gaia.net
Date: January 25, 2004
To: Alanta@PlanetEarth.net
   Another bombing, this time in a market place in Yangon,
hundreds of people killed – it's total madness. I can't believe the
government would do it. With their recent concessions and peaceful overtures, they've given every indication they're getting ready
to renounce the dictatorship and recognize the pro-democracy
movement. This doesn't make any sense.

Subject: Myanmar
From: Alanta@PlanetEarth.net
Date: January 25, 2004
To: Herakles@Gaia.net
   ENN just reported that the Myanmar government is denying
any responsibility. If they didn't do it, then who did?

Subject: Myanmar
From: Herakles@Gaia.net
Date: January 26, 2004
To: Alanta@PlanetEarth.net
   I wish I knew. I'm starting to get really nervous about the
Resolution. These bombings are jeopardizing all of the negotia-
tions.

Subject: The Resolution
From: Alanta@PlanetEarth.net
Date: January 27, 2004
To: Herakles@Gaia.net
I'm prayin' for the best.

Subject: the pattern emerges
From: Herakles@Gaia.net
Date: February 2, 2004
To: Alanta@PlanetEarth.net
First Kashmir, then Yangon and now the Government House in Kinshasa...three bomb attacks in three weeks, progressively worse each time. And no one has claimed responsibility for any of them. Whoever is behind it is obviously trying to undermine the Resolution, and unfortunately, they're succeeding. I'm afraid Bogotá will be next. I hope not, though. Somehow, the UN has *got* to pull everyone together.

It's so hard to concentrate. My running times are slipping and my jumps are the worst in years. I know I should tune out recent events, but I'm finding I just can't. And here I am, going off about it to you, who shouldn't be dwelling on it either.

Maybe the bitter cold has something to do with freezing my optimism into a solid block. Two degrees below zero right now. Have you ever felt a cold like that?

My American calendar says today is Groundhog Day, halfway between the Winter Solstice and the Vernal Equinox. I can never remember how it goes: the shadow means spring is, or is not, six weeks away. Either way it's too long. In my mind I escape by returning to the wildflower fields of my homeland, where I can smell the scent of the blossoms. I pick one and send it to you. xxxooo, h

PS In western Kríti, where my great grandparents are from, there's a big festival every February 2nd. It's held in honor of the Panayía Arkoudiótissa, the Mother of God of the Bear. It's a name the locals give to the Virgin Mary, which remembers Artemis, the Goddess of Wild Creatures.

Subject: 2 below
From: Alanta@PlanetEarth.net
Date: February 10, 2004
To: Herakles@Gaia.net

Thank you for the flower from Greece! I'll take it as a good luck charm for both of us to ace the qualifiers, so we can be there, together, in just a few short months! And that Resolution is going to be signed, so thaw out your block of pessimism and believe it.

And no, I have never felt 2 below. Not even close. Coldest it gets here in Orleans is about 30, maybe high 20s and that's rare, and plenty cold enough. This island girl has never even seen snow. Ooooooo – chills my bones just thinkin' about it.

You remembered the xxxs and ooos! Go ahead and take some back for yourself! Alanta

Subject: Athens
From: Herakles@Gaia.net
Date: February 11, 2004
To: Alanta@PlanetEarth.net

You're right. The news isn't so bad this week, nothing else terrible has happened and the UN is persisting. To Athens! Kleo

As he said, "send," the brief pulse of digitally-coded electricity zipped off into space, destined for the screen of the beautiful Alanta. Truly, the realm of wing-footed Hermes in a modern incarnation! The Messenger, swifter now than ever before, faithfully conducting Herakles' most intimate thoughts and feelings through a vast electronic web.

"Home page."

The Eagle Nebula appeared, with its mighty green and orange column of star stuff spanning light years across the Heavens. At the very tip of the massive cloud of gas and dust, a new star was incubating, waiting to burst forth. Would it develop a planetary disk at some point in the distant future, eventually evolving into a world capable of life? Perhaps intelligence? He loved contemplating the possibilities.

"Search for Alanta January."

A long list of web sites appeared and he scrolled down until one caught his eye: *Alanta's Journey, March 2004 issue African Roots magazine*. He opened it and suddenly, the face of the woman who'd charmed his heart was smiling back at him from the monitor. She was on a beach somewhere, probably in the Caribbean, with palm trees and blue sky, an image so vivid he could almost smell the fragrant breezes. He looked at the picture for a long time, imagining himself with her on that perfect beach, longing to be with her right now.

Finally, he went to the article.

### ALANTA'S JOURNEY
### By Gloria Taylor

Alanta January. Most of us know her as the fastest woman in the world, and that is a title she rightly deserves. At the age of 22, she has already set the world record for the women's 100-meter sprint three times, most recently at the Track and Field World Championships in Paris last year. However, there is much more to this young woman than her impressive running abilities. Her story, and the story of her family, is a remarkable history of the African diaspora and a testament to a way of life rooted in Mother Africa Herself.

For Alanta, her tale begins with her grandmother, Gran'mama Lily. Lily Khana was born in Nigeria in 1942, near the delta of the great Niger River – the largest flood plain and wetland in the whole of the African continent, where each day millions of gallons of water pass from the mountains to the sea.

Gran'mama Lily grew up in a rural setting, where her mother's people, the Ogoni, farmed the rich, fertile land. They shared the fruits of their labor and labored for the betterment of the village, each contributing what they could, depending upon their particular talents. The women of Lily's family had the gift of knowing plants, and for countless generations they had been among the healers of the Ogoni community. By the time she was a young woman, Lily had learned the secrets of the ancient craft from her mother. Just how far back their healing wisdom goes, nobody knows, but she claims the tradition stretches into the *hundreds* of generations.

Ms. Lily's father was from the Yoruba tribe, one of the largest and most powerful in all of Nigeria. He was an educated man who came to Ogoniland after his appointment as local magistrate. He did not share the patronizing attitude of some of his fellow Yoruba when it came to the Ogoni. Rather, he served with an open mind and soon learned to appreciate the way of life they had kept alive.

Nigeria was a British colony at that time, and with his position, he could have afforded to live extravagantly compared to most of the Ogoni. But he didn't, choosing instead to live simply, like the rest of the villagers. Though not everyone accepted him, he was generally well-liked and respected, and Ms. Lily's mama took a special liking to him. The two of them bridged their cultures and forged a loving and strong relationship.

When Ms. Lily turned 17, she married a local man named Nelson Eleme, who was three years older than she. Tragically, just as their young lives were beginning together, Big Oil was beginning its operations in the heart of Ogoniland. It was a development that would ultimately sweep Lily and Nelson into a cataclysmic chain of events.

When Nigeria gained its independence in 1960, more big multinationals came in, acquired vast tracts of land and littered the once pristine countryside with oil rigs, refineries and miles and miles of pipeline. It signaled the beginning of the end of the Ogoni way of life. Homes were seized and people displaced, while a handful of corporations raped the land and reaped the profits.

Ms. Lily's father spoke out against the injustice of it all, but the oil interests already had the government in its back pocket, and they were not about to put up with his protestations. He was pressured into keeping quiet, and when he continually refused, they removed him from his position. Still, he persisted in trying to stand up for the Ogoni, and in 1961, when a pipeline explosion took his life and the life of Lily's mother, Lily and Nelson were convinced it had been intentional.

Though they were grief-stricken and frightened, they pulled together all of their courage and organized with other villagers to try to stop what was happening. Sadly, their resistance was quickly stifled by the merciless crackdown which followed. Within a few months, Nelson and six others were arrested on bogus charges, tried by a military tribunal, and then publicly executed by the government officials who'd been bought and paid for by Big Oil.

Oh, how she cried when her beloved husband was hung before her eyes, and though she was nearly beside herself with grief, she could not afford to fall apart. She had her young daughter, Grace, to take care of. When the government seized her property, she fled with her baby, a bag of clothes and a few personal items, and the "talking drum" Nelson had given her as a wedding gift. She changed her name back to Khana, her mother's family name, then went far away to the sprawling capital city of Lagos. She used what little money she had to rent an alley-front store around the corner from the central market, and for almost three years, eked out a living by selling herbal remedies and potions – all the while hiding from the police and trying to cope with the horror of what had happened.

She would sit with Grace on their porch off the back room of the shop, singing and playing her drum, keeping Nelson alive and with them in spirit. One day in 1963, a musician named Azikiwe, who was new to the city, came to her to be treated for a sore throat. He'd strained his voice, so she created a special herbal blend and sent him along his way with strict instructions to drink the tea three times a day, and give his voice a rest. Two weeks later, he came back to the shop, feeling wonderful and well. He sang her a song in gratitude in his strong, smooth voice, and she picked up her drum and played along. It was a beautiful start to a friendship and collaboration which would go on to span the next four decades.

In 1967, Azikiwe formed his own band, the African Rhythms, and asked her to play percussion. Juju music was bursting forth as a new musical sensation, fusing the age-old drumbeats with jazz, blues and rock and roll. Within a few years, it had won over the

Nigerian music scene, and they were at the leading edge of the phenomenon. By 1973, they were touring internationally.

Ms. Lily and Grace traveled with the band throughout Africa, Europe, Japan, America and the Caribbean, and in 1975, she built a little house in the town of Calibishie on the island of Dominica. Grace turned 15 that year, and Ms. Lily had thought it best for her to stay in one place to finish high school. Back in Nigeria, a military coup had just taken place, so returning there was out of the question. Lily had tasted real freedom and opportunity and she wanted to make sure Grace was able to "walk that same path."

For the next twenty years, Ms. Lily spent a lot of time on the road with the Rhythms, though she always returned to her adopted island paradise to reconnect with her community, work in her garden and as she puts it, "refill the well."

In 1993, when she retired from the band, she again felt the desire to return to her homeland, to work for the sovereignty of her mother's people. She joined OPM, the Ogoni People's Movement, a nonviolent protest group led by the celebrated writer, Ken Balewa. The organization's mission was to restore the Niger Delta by reversing the environmental and cultural devastation wrought by decades of oil extraction. When Balewa and eight other OPM activists were publicly executed by hanging in 1995, she stepped forward to take a leadership role. According to Ms. Lily, "the murder of Ken brought back all the pain I'd held inside since Nelson was killed in 1961, and I felt compelled to get more involved."

With her help, OPM reached an agreement with a reformed wing of Big Oil, requiring them to dismantle their operations in the Delta and restore Africa's largest natural wetlands. Reparations amounting to over 30 billion geos were paid out to the Ogoni people, who were then granted limited self rule from the government of Nigeria and a voice in the new UN. Lily was asked to run for the presidency of the new Ogoni Republic, but she declined, expressing her desire to live on Dominica and let the younger generation of leaders and activists shape their own future. She has since remained in semi-retirement, though on special occasions, she'll still take her talking drum and go back on the road.

Now, Ms. Lily's daughter Grace, Alanta's mother, enjoyed the life of a traveling musician, but she was much more of a home-body at heart. In Dominica, she settled right in to her new routine of going to school, tending the gardens and experimenting with herbal concoctions. In 1977, Grace began work on her biology degree at the University of the Virgin Islands on St. Thomas. She did well in her studies and enjoyed the student lifestyle. During her fourth year, she took a trip to St. John, a tiny island across the channel, in search of a manchineel tree – an extremely toxic and dangerous plant whose chemistry she wanted to study. She had no way of knowing that the one-day excursion would end up changing her life forever.

She rented an old jeep in the small port town of Cruz Bay and headed out to the East End. Up and down the bumpy, steep road she went, passing beach after white sand beach along the seven miles of winding North Shore Road. Out beyond Frances Bay, nestled in a tropical hammock near the Annaberg sugar plantation ruins, she found her tree and carefully took a specimen. Before heading back to town, she decided to try to make it all the way to the end of the island. She drove through the tiny village of Coral Bay, and the road quickly narrowed to a dirt two-track. Then, as she came around a corner, she encountered a small herd of bray-ing donkeys, completely blocking the way. She looked out the window to her left, and noticed a little stand. Tacked up on its roof were two signs: one that said "Vi's Snack Shack," and the other, "Conch Fritters." Since she couldn't go any further, she parked the jeep out front and had a seat at the sole picnic table, in the shade of a big tamarind tree. A young man was helping Vi move some furniture, and according to Grace, it was love at first sight.

Christian January V was handsome, earthy and smart, and he had a vivaciousness in his personality which immediately appealed to her. He joined her at the table, and they had lunch and talked the afternoon away. He and his family had been on the island since the 17th century, when they were brought there from Africa to work on the sugar plantations. He could trace his family name back to 1675, when his ancestor, then just a boy, witnessed the mass suicide of slaves who had revolted, and for a short time, seized control of the island. The slave boy testified to the Danish overlords that he too had been encouraged to kill himself rather than surrender. But he wanted to live, so he fled, hiding in the rainforest until he was discovered.

The boy January's descendants continued to work the plantations even after their emancipation in 1848, some 15 years before the Emancipation Proclamation was decreed in the United States. The era of the big plantation finally waned, and by the turn of the 20th century, it was practically over. So, St. Johnians began working the land for themselves, eventually building a strong community which carried them through the next fifty years. Then, in the 1950s, billionaire Lawrence Rockefeller discovered the island. He bought up half of it and created a national park, overnight transforming St. John into a tourist mecca. It was the beginning of the end of their agricultural way of life – the way of life Christian wanted to hold on to, even though it was becoming more and more difficult to make a living.

When Grace got a job teaching high school biology on the neighboring island of St. Croix, they decided to marry and relocate there. They bought some land for Christian to farm, built their own house and made a go of it. By the end of the next year, Alanta Grace January would take her first breath of frangipani-scented air.

Alanta remembers her childhood as a happy one, closely connected to the land and sea. She spent hours in the family garden, learning the science and herbal lore from her mother, and cultivating prize orchids and planting fruit trees with her father. She loved working the land, feeling the soil, and watching the miraculous cycles of nature in their endless and elegant dance. She also loved the ocean, and would often go fishing down at Mango Bay, right near her house. Usually though, unless she got lucky in the first twenty minutes or so, she'd get hot and bored and end up underwater herself, investigating large stands of elk horn coral surrounded by schools of tropical fish. Alanta also had her grandmother's love of music. From the age of five, when she performed in her first carnival parade, she's played the steel pan drum.

Alanta says that she and her Gran'mama Lily were always like two peas in a pod. An older and younger version of the same adventurous spirit. One was short and spry with salt and pepper hair, and the other tall and lanky, with a full head of beaded black braids, but kindred souls nonetheless. From Ms. Lily, she learned to dream the big dream, and to believe that anything is possible.

Her Gran'mama also helped her learn to manage her asthma, which ironically, led to her track and field career in the first place. She was 14 when she had her first really serious attack. She'd been helping the people at church clear out an old attic, which had been gathering dust for decades. After a few whiffs of the moldy clouds, she found herself struggling to breathe, and ultimately ended up in the emergency room. The doctors diagnosed allergy-induced asthma and set her up with the latest pharmaceuticals to control the symptoms.

At first, Alanta withdrew, afraid she might have another attack. She stayed away from the garden and avoided the trail down to the beach. Instead of roaming the countryside with her friends, more and more she was staying inside by herself. When she started drawing inward emotionally, her parents got very concerned. The girl they sometimes called "Sparks" was losing her vibrant glow. But thankfully, Gran'mama Lily had a plan. The school year was almost over, and Alanta would spend a good part of the summer on Dominica with her.

During the following two months, Alanta transitioned back into her old self. With Gran'mama Lily's help, she learned how to maintain a self-healing mental state through the use of herbal remedies and meditation techniques. They spent hours drumming and singing, hiking up to the falls, kayaking on the ocean and generally embracing life together. Alanta had no asthma to speak of, and when she returned to St. Croix, she felt strong and renewed.

One day, when she was playing basketball with some friends at school, the track coach came by. After a few minutes watching her zip from one end of the court to the other, he invited her to try out for the team. He needed a sprinter and Alanta agreed to give it a go. Once she started running, she couldn't stop, and the faster and stronger she became, the fewer asthma attacks she'd have. With her coach's guidance, she began setting records, and by her third year, she outran all the boys on the team. As her fourth year approached, she was being recruited by a number of major universities.

When she found out the legendary Jimmy Johnson was interested in coaching her, that decided it, and the rest is Tulane history. She set school records during her first two years, and most likely would have qualified for the 2000 Olympics in Sydney, if she hadn't had an asthma attack because of a freak drop in barometric pressure on the day of the trials. She recovered quickly though, winning the World Championships the next three years in a row and setting a world record for the fastest women's 100 meter run each time. Can she better it at the Olympic Games in Athens? She thinks she can.

Alanta believes her adventure has just begun. She says, "the Great Reawakening has taught me that we're all spiritual beings who are interconnected in time and space in ways we are only now beginning to understand. I look forward to the journey, along the way remembering to embrace the divinity within myself, and doing my best to manifest it out there in the world." Perhaps this is the key to her remarkable career.

Alanta January will be representing the United States in Athens, Greece for the 2004 Summer Olympic Games. She will compete in the 100, 200 and 400 meters, as well as the 4x100 and 4x400 relays.

*Gloria Taylor is a doctoral student at the University of the Virgin Islands. Her first novel, Jumbie Bay, was awarded the Turnbull Literary Achievement Award in 2003. She lives on the island of St. Thomas in the US Virgin Islands.*

As Herakles said "page one," Alanta's picture again filled the screen, with her impish smile and big, dark eyes looking back at him. He stared at her face for the longest time, trying to digest what he'd just read. Now that he knew some of her family's remarkable story and their connection to history, he started to sense the incredible depth of her being. Eventually, he pulled himself away, shut down his computer and went to sleep, wishing they could be together that minute.

Time apart from her seemed to pass ever so slowly, but pass it did, and the Great Wheel turned, leaving winter behind for another year. The crocuses, daffodils and tulips finally emerged from their hibernation, each bloom trumpeting the annual reunion of the Goddesses Demeter and Persephone. Their long winter of separation had at last ended, and as mother and daughter were reunited in their endless cycle of seasons, so too were the northern climes spared an endless cold.

As springtime swept across the land, Herakles rejoiced in its returning. Spring fever had long beset him, and being outside cured his claustrophobia and rejuvenated him. Corresponding with Alanta had helped ease his longing during their own separation, but it had been a difficult time. They'd shared their training successes, and their deep concerns over the latest terrorist attacks, as well as their frustration about the "scandal," which had remained very much in the news. CHAOS ONE continued to criticize their interracial relationship, but fortunately, most people either shrugged it off or got caught up in the romance. Would the "Olympic lovers" both win the gold? And would their relationship survive the Games?

The bets were on, but one thing was certain. Herakles was head over heels in love with her, and he was hoping that beneath her Xs and Os she felt the same way about him.

# 5

# CRESCENT CITY

Alanta crouched low to the ground, head down, in her starting position, carefully placing her fingertips as close to the line as possible. With a mighty exhale she closed her eyes and focused on Ashé, the power to make things happen, just as Gran'mama Lily had taught her. In her mind's eye she saw the cheetah, running swiftly, effortlessly, across the African savannah, gliding over the brush with paws barely touching the ground, the scent of grass and freedom filling her nostrils.

The gun sounded and she became that cheetah, with long, brown muscular legs propelling her forward and powerful arms slicing the air, chasing her dreams down the unbroken stretch of track.

"Excellent," Jimmy called out, jogging over to her. "That's more like it. How did it feel to ya?"

"Better. I think I'm finally gettin' back in sync."

"'Bout time! We've been through a lot this week." He smiled with his toothy grin and showed her the stopwatch. "You keep it up and you might just set another record. I'd sure like to see that!"

"Me too, Jimmy."

"All right, it's a good time to call it quits. You did great today, Ajay. You really turned the corner. To celebrate, I think you should take tomorrow off. Take some time for yourself. We'll pick up Monday morning, 'kay?"

"'Kay," she replied, smiling too.

She bee-lined to the sauna, and as she sat back against the cedar wall, she felt the heat envelop her, infuse her, and finally, enable her to release the last lingering remnants of physical and emotional strain she'd been holding in. It had been a trying week, but thankfully, it was ending on a good note.

She couldn't figure out how it happened. She and Jimmy had always been able to work so well together, with virtually no conflict at all. But then, in the four months since New York, things had begun to change. It wasn't too noticeable though, until just these last two weeks, when Alanta's performance began to slip. That's when she realized they were much less able to address it in their usual positive manner. They were both edgy and agitated with each other, and it got worse and worse until Jimmy finally came out with it. Then it all made sense.

He actually believed they'd made an *agreement* that she would keep her mind totally out of the political realm, when she had remembered their conversations completely differently. Yeah, on occasion they'd talked about Alanta not being "too political," but she never promised not to read a newspaper or watch tv.

He passionately reiterated the Mexico City incident, and how racial issues and politics can mess with your entire career, but she just didn't believe it. True, you can't control what someone might send out over the e-waves, as she recently found out herself, but Kleezy's politics have only made him more adored by the whole world. Besides, Tommy Smith and John Carlos have become important historical figures who will be long-remembered for their acts of courage. Bless his heart, but Jimmy was stuck in the old days, when race discrimination was the norm. Old fears sure do have their ways of persisting, even in a changed world.

Then, after the argument, once she worked through her own defensiveness, she started feeling guilty for keeping it from him. She thought he might have suspected she was paying attention to certain things, like the progress of the Resolution, and when he said as much, she felt like she'd really let him down. He looked so hurt that she would keep him in the dark like that, and she felt terrible.

Then it was downhill from there, starting with the worst asthma attack she'd had in years. It got so bad at one point she almost called an ambulance, but then that second cup of black coffee clicked in and, thank the powers that be, it finally broke. She awoke that next morning with every muscle in her neck and back aching from the struggle to breathe. She called Jimmy and they apologized to each other and made up. He was especially sorry when he found out about the attack, and told her to stay in bed. He came over right away, made her breakfast and brought enough food for lunch and dinner.

The rest of the week, her performance stunk. Her timing was off, her strength had been sapped and she really started to worry. The US Olympic Trials were less than six weeks away, and she was nowhere near where she wanted to be.

She promised Jimmy she'd stop pressing Kleezy for information, cut out the Internet news, and mentally distance herself from politics. He was glad to hear it, and so to put it behind them, he took her out to her favorite pizza place in the French Quarter. Their reconciliation helped turn her attitude around, but it wasn't until this morning that she finally felt like she was really on the mend.

After a cool rinse in the shower, she went back into the sauna for a few more minutes. She breathed in the warm, dry air and exhaled slowly, feeling it soothe her recovering lungs. As the sweat emerged from her pores, she imagined it cleansing her from the inside out, flushing away all the yuck, all the insecurity and all the impediments to her resolve. There was no way she was going to let another asthma attack keep her from competing in *this* Olympics.

That thought propelled her up and into the shower for the final cool rinse.

She hopped on her bike and from the stadium rode the short five blocks to her house in the University District. She lived in the cottage of an old cotton broker's home, part of a large estate which had been built in 1853. She came up to the tall wrought-iron gate, and swung it open just hard enough to zip her bike inside, before it sprung back to a close with a loud ker-*chink*. As she walked up the long entrance and around the bubbling fountain in the courtyard, she analyzed the architecture of the old place, suddenly realizing that the tall pillars along the broad front porch were Greek in de-sign. She always knew that, she supposed, though she hadn't ever really connected it before. The new awareness made her feel closer to Kleezy and to Greece, and for the first time all week, she sensed the butterflies of anticipation and excitement fluttering in her stomach.

She went behind the big house to her apartment and heard Ruger's familiar welcoming howl, as he and his mother, Patches, came bounding off the back porch to greet her. As she parked her bike, the two beagles eagerly vied for her attention. She tried to indulge them, but by no means were they satisfied when, after a few minutes, she shooed them off and went inside.

The small one-bedroom cottage had wood floors and shut-tered windows, and an eclectic array of decorations: her painted wooden cheetah sat crouched, ready to pounce from one corner, and in another, her steel pan drum waited to be played. A large colorful batik covered one wall, and across from it hung a vibrant Haitian painting depicting a group of dancing women. Next to it, she'd placed a series of three African masks, one above the other. Her cozy bedroom was right off the living area, with long strings of glass beads hanging in the doorway.

She dropped off her gear at the front door and went straight to the fridge, pulling out the pot of spicy lentil soup she'd made earlier in the week. *Tonight's gonna be an early one*, she thought as she put it on the stove. After dinner, she was going to make a cup of chamomile tea with honey and lemon, and then crawl into bed for a long, restful sleep. And that's exactly what she did.

She awoke early the next morning and decided to go straight outside and start the day in her garden. That always put her in the right frame of mind, and besides, it was overdue.

The air was fresh, the soil damp, and the tangle of weeds came right out. As she started turning over the dirt with her trowel, and crumbling the clumps with her hands, a rich, earthy scent rose up, permeating her being. She loved the cool feeling of it between her fingers, and was always amazed by the living creatures who would suddenly be revealed. It was the beginning of the cycle, when all things were renewed, and anything was possible.

Makin' a proper bed, her daddy used to say, was the most important part of the process. She smiled at all the memories of the three of them, her parents and her, in their garden. Things grew all year long on St. Croix, so the changing of the seasons wasn't quite as noticeable, but Grace and Christian always made a big deal of the spring planting. Treated it differently than the rest of the year-round work.

She sprinkled in the organic fertilizer, turning and mixing and sifting until she was satisfied it was evenly distributed, then she planned out where everything was going to go. This year, she decided on herbs, peppers, tomatoes, cucumbers and zucchini. She surveyed her newly prepared garden, thinking about the transformation it would be undergoing over the next few months. As it began its phase of new life, so too would she begin anew. The conflict with Jimmy had put a lot of things in perspective for her, and she believed that, with it behind them, she was ready to move into her own transformative period – from Olympic hopeful to Olympic champion.

There was just one last thing she had to do today to make it all happen: plant some seeds so they could start taking hold. She thought about it for a few minutes, and then it came to her. *The habenero peppers from last year. Perfect!* She got them from her cupboard inside, then placed three of them in the ground in a triangle, about six inches apart. With a little water, she wished them good luck and then moved on to the rest of her day.

She washed up and poured herself a large glass of mango juice, deciding on a bagel, and some yogurt and fruit for breakfast. Then, she packed her bike bag with some trail mix and two energy bars, filled her water jug, tucked her beaded braids into her bicycle helmet and took to the streets.

Past the homes of her neighborhood and the University buildings she rode, all the way to the tracks, where she had to stop for the old Charles Street trolley. Some teenaged boys leaned out of the window as the car rolled past, waving and calling out, "hey, it's Alanta January! A-jay! A-jay!"

She waved back enthusiastically, then crossed the tracks and turned onto the wide-open bike trail which wound its way through majestic Audubon Park. It led her under the branches of the gracious old oaks, and around the picturesque pond, where two herons stood still and silent in the shallow water.

She came out of the park at the red brick church and stopped her bike again. The bells were ringing and the people were filing in, with the men in suits and ties and the women wearing fancy hats, and children running around the yard, trying with futility to delay the inevitable. The scene brought back a flood of memories of growing up on St. Croix, where she'd been baptized in a red brick church a lot like this one.

Her daddy was raised in the Moravian Christian tradition, and had felt very strongly about continuing it after he and momma were married. Grace knew the scene going in, and even though she thought it was a bit too rigid, she went along with it because it offered the stable community she'd been hoping to find.

Alanta went with them to Sunday services every week, and had enjoyed it well enough, especially the church picnics. However, from a very early age, she was also getting a radically different religious perspective from Gran'mama Lily, whose spiritual practices were much more diverse. Originally rooted in the traditions of her native Nigeria, they'd been modified and expanded to include elements of many different cultures Lily had experienced during her 25 years on the road. From her, Alanta learned about the study of comparative mythology, as well as how to reach spiritual states through drumming and dancing. This blending of traditions created in Alanta an appreciation for the many ways of seeking to know the Mysteries of the Universe.

She left her neighborhood and headed east, soon linking up with the path along the Mississippi River. As she rode, a steamboat blew its horn and the tourists waved from the shore.

On she went to Jackson Square, and as she passed by Saint Louis Cathedral, an old Black man wailed soulful notes on his tenor sax, as a handful of street vendors set up their booths for the day. She continued on the cobblestone streets through the French Quarter, where people were just waking up from the usual rowdy Saturday night before. A few shopkeepers were sweeping their porches and others were just opening for business. Past the rows of colorful shotgun shacks she went, admiring the flowers in their brightly painted window boxes.

She decided to take the back streets all the way to City Park, and then spent a while on the trails there, weaving through the antebellum oak trees, which were virtually dripping with Spanish moss. Then she really pushed it the last couple of miles to Lake Pontchartrain, where she stopped and took off her helmet for a few minutes, letting the breeze cool her down. As she walked her bike along the shore, she remembered the book she'd read about the African rituals which had taken place in the 19th century. The legendary Voodoo Queen, Marie Laveau, conducted mysterious ceremonies, *right here*, invoking ancient spirits and practicing "black magic."

Suddenly, the wind picked up and white caps started breaking across the expansive lake, which now looked turbulent, unsettled, even under the clear blue sky. The timing of the gust and her thoughts amused her, but it also gave her the creeps, so she decided to turn around.

She headed back to town via the Esplanade, the shady, tree-lined street where a number of the big cotton brokers' homes were located, some of them beautifully restored. At Rampart Street, she hung a right, and when she came upon Louis Armstrong Park, she thought of the perfect place to take another break – Congo Square.

She followed the path to the central courtyard, which was paved with concentric circles of red bricks and surrounded by trees. She had a seat on a shaded bench, and thought about the history of the place.

It had long been a gathering spot of the Oumas, the original indigenous residents of the area, who, for countless generations, had celebrated their seasonal corn festival there. As the slave trade grew in the 18th and 19th centuries, so did the sympathy of these Native Americans, who knew well what to expect from European treachery. Though they hadn't been officially stripped of their sovereign rights, yet, they were being systematically driven off of their land. They formed alliances with the Africans and, in time, joined their families together as well. On weekends, when the slaves were allowed, they met here to barter and socialize.

Local tradition evolved into a mixture of different African customs, Native American practices and the Christianity which was forced upon them. Their music formed the basis of what was to become the uniquely American sounds of the Black spiritual, blues, jazz, rock'n roll, and ultimately her favorite, funk.

She sat there with eyes closed, imagining herself traveling backward in time, decade after decade, trying to get a sense of what Congo Square might have been like. From the hip-hop and punk of the 90s and 80s, to the afros and funk of the 70s, the psychedelic 60s, and the 50s with bobby socks and pleated skirts, post-war 40s, depressing 30s, and before the Crash, in the "roaring 20s," it must have been a sight. She tried to imagine flappers and zoot suits and Scott Joplin music....

Then as she approached the turn of the century, she found it harder to imagine. What would Reconstruction have looked like, or before that, before Emancipation, when the African slaves met here with the Oumas? It must have been just a dusty circle, with a few wooden benches and crates set up for people to sit on.

In her mind's eye, she tried to imagine the scene – women dancing, men playing drums, children running around – then suddenly, she felt warm and a little dizzy. The light around her started to dim and a figure appeared. It was Gran'mama Lily, sitting in the center of the square, absorbed in the playing of her talking drum. Entranced, Alanta listened to the beat, growing louder and louder, until all at once it stopped. Lily's image receded and in her place a young woman appeared, dressed in a long, beige gunny-sack skirt, and tattered white blouse and head wrap. The figure then started walking toward Alanta, slowly, measuredly, moving as if she were almost floating above the ground.

"Who are you?" Alanta asked tentatively.

"You ain't afraid?" the Spirit replied, now right in front of her.

"Not really," Alanta answered, gazing into her ethereal eyes.

"Good." She sat down on the bench.

"Who *are* you?"

"You know."

Alanta stared at the Spirit, seeing in her face an image of her own. "You're my ancestress. The one who was brought from St. John, almost ten generations ago."

"Yes."

"You must have come through New Orleans."

"On my way to Atlanta."

"I'm your namesake, in a manner of speaking."

"You sure are."

"What's your real name?"

For what seemed like forever the Spirit just looked at her. Finally, she answered. "I had no name, but I did have a dream. Over and over again I'd see myself runnin' away, with the wind carryin' me to freedom."

"Did you ever try to escape?"

The Spirit looked away, staring straight ahead. "No. I was too scared of the whippin' I'd get if I was caught. But don't you be afraid, Alanta January."

"Afraid of *what?*"

The Spirit didn't answer.

"Afraid of what?" Alanta pressed.

The Spirit rose and again faced her. "You'll have to run, like you never run before. For the both of us, run, with a good strong wind at your back."

With that, the Spirit faded away and Alanta opened her eyes. The birds were chirping in the trees overhead and bright sunshine streamed through the branches. She stretched out her legs and for a long time remained there, staring into the center of the court-yard, thinking about what had just happened.

Later that night, she decided to give Gran'mama Lily a call and tell her about the daydream.

"The ancestors are with you and all around you, and so am I," Lily responded.

"Thanks, Gran'mama, that's reassuring. I've been so upset."

"The whole world has been upset by the resurgence of violence, Lanna, and I'm sure you're feeling some of that. Try to focus on the hopeful signs. All the factions in the Congolese conflict have finally agreed to the UN Resolution, and I've got to believe the others will come around too."

"I hope you're right Gran'mama."

"I trust that I am," Lily replied matter-of-factly. "Now tell me more about that Herakles Speros."

"We've been emailing a lot and talking on the phone. I like him, Gran'mama, he's gentle and sweet, funny, kind, and really smart – and he's an incredible athlete too. I think he's got an excellent chance to win a gold medal in Athens."

"That's wonderful, Lanna. Will you be seeing him again anytime soon?"

"Well, the Olympic Trials are in six weeks, but I don't know how much time we'll be able to spend together there. Both of our coaches think it would be best if we saved that for after the Games. I can't wait. I think there's really something between us."

"Good for you both! I look forward to meeting him in Athens."

"You're coming to Greece?!"

"As long as you qualify. I talked with your parents last night, and we're making our plans."

"Oh, Gran'mama! I'm so *psyched*. I want you to know I'm gonna give it my absolute best, for you, and for all of my ancestors."

"I know you will. Love you."

"Love you too."

She hung up the phone, thrilled that her Gran'mama was coming to Athens. It reaffirmed her determination that nothing was going to stand in her way this time, not asthma, or politics or manufactured scandals. She stretched out on the couch, now feeling confident that she'd be able to handle whatever obstacles she would have to face. Not only was she going to compete in the 2004 Olympics, but she was going to win five gold medals, a feat no track and field athlete had ever accomplished. *I'm gonna do it*, she kept telling herself, *I'm gonna do it.*

# 6

## HOMEWARD BOUND

Earth continued her year-long journey around the Sun, and by mid June, as Helios' golden chariot approached its most northern point, Alanta and Herakles were briefly reunited in the city of Sacramento. For it was there, in the sprawling Metropolis in the heart of the Great Valley, that the US Olympic Track and Field Trials took place.

The weather was hot and the track fast, conditions which worked to the benefit of them both. Alanta qualified in all three of her solo events, coming in first in the 100 and 200, and a close second in the 400. Her performance also guaranteed her a spot on the 4x100 and 4x400 relay teams, so her dream of winning five gold medals was now a distinct possibility. Herakles relied on Carl's strategy of winning the running events, and it came through for him, just as it had at the World Championships. He easily took first in all four races, and more than held his own in the jumping competitions, placing second in both the high jump and long jump, and third in the pole vault. He wasn't all that pleased with his performance in the throwing contests, but he still won the decathlon by 41 points, a comfortable margin over the other contenders.

Because of the persistence of the CHAOS press, and Carl's clear instructions, he and Alanta had agreed ahead of time to play it very cool at the Trials. They'd been able to catch glimpses of each other, but only from a distance and sporadically at that. The cameras were everywhere. However, after it was over they planned a secret sunrise rendezvous. Before dawn on the day of their departure, they snuck out of their rooms and met in the dugout at the baseball field adjacent to their dorms.

They were together only fifteen minutes, yet in that short time the potency of Eros' Love Dust surged. The long embrace, the connecting eyes full of wonder, and their passionate goodbye kiss charged them with excitement and anticipation about what was yet to come.

That was well over a month ago already, and Alanta had been on his mind all of the days in between. She sustained him in a way that was entirely new and wonderful, infusing him with strength and inspiration.

Everything else seemed to be on track as well. He was right where he needed to be with his conditioning, and he was getting along much better with Carl. Even the Resolution was beginning to look like more of a reality. The bombings had stopped and only two nations, India and Pakistan, had yet to sign on. All troops had been withdrawn from the borders and both sides were negotiating through the UN. As optimism was growing in the world community, so too was he feeling more confident of its ultimate success.

Training-wise, since the running and jumping events were coming along nicely, Carl now wanted him to concentrate on the javelin, shot put and discus. Of the three, his favorite was the discus, though he still had a way to go before he could out throw the reigning Olympic champion, the self-described Awesome Aussie, Maximilian Leach. Max had previously won the decathlon by dominating all three throwing events and placing in some of the running and jumping events. This strategy had worked for six years straight, and so when Herakles surprised everyone with his impressive victory at the Worlds in Paris last year, Max became overtly abusive, verbally assaulting him afterward in the locker room. The experience convinced him that Max was the most vulgar, ungracious individual Herakles had ever encountered. Consequently, he was determined to do everything humanly possible to ensure the honor of winning the gold did not go to that ingrate again. Every point he could pick up in his least best events could be the one to help him surpass Max, so he turned to the discus with heightened motivation.

As he picked up the smooth, heavy discus, he thought about his ancestors at Olympia, readying themselves for the competition, just as he himself would be doing in a few days. He extended his arm, gently swinging the disc, imagining it flowing out of his hand on the crest of every ounce of momentum he could summon through his fingertips. He took position, and when every fiber of his being was in accord, he flawlessly performed the wind-up, spin and release. Upward toward the stratosphere the discus flew, momentarily disappearing in the blazing sunlight, then falling back to Earth. *Not too bad.*

He got another disc, and Alanta suddenly flashed through his mind — specifically the kiss in the dugout — then he imagined a totally new scenario. They'd meet in New York and spend the next two days together, then he'd be off to Olympia…but it was just a fantasy and he knew it. He'd have to wait until the Games. He took position, smiling to himself as he thought about their real reunion, now less than three weeks away. Again, with flawless precision, he let the discus fly.

"Excellent, Kleo," Carl said with enthusiasm. "Excellent!"

Kleo nodded back, trying to conceal a smirk. *If you only knew what I was thinking, Coach. If you only knew….*

That evening, as he sat by himself on his balcony watching the Sun finally set, he decided to call her. He just needed to hear her voice. They'd only talked once since the Trials, so when the urge overtook him he couldn't resist. He got the phone and placed the call, then laid down on his bed.

"Hello?" she said, evoking a wavy, dreamy feeling in him.

"Hi Alanta, it's me, Kleo."

"Kleezy! Oh sweetness to my ears! Howdja know I was juss thinkin' 'bout you?"

"You were?"

"Yeah," she giggled. "So, you okay?"

"Other than the longing in my heart to see you, I feel great. And I'm totally psyched to go to Greece!"

"It's just three days away now, huh?"

"Yup, I leave on Thursday."

"Heyyyy, howdja work that out any*way?* Everyone else I know isn't going till the end of the month, when the Olympic Village opens."

"When I thought of the idea two years ago, I wrote to the director of the archeological site at Olympia. She got everything approved in advance, and when I qualified, we set the final steps in motion. I'd have gone sooner, but I could only persuade Carl to let me go for two weeks."

"I'm surprised he's letting you go at all, given the trouble you've had with him."

"Well, he was never pleased about the arrangement, but he knew from the beginning it was part of my dream. From the moment I realized that I wanted to compete in the Games, I've felt compelled to go there to complete my training. I suppose, as you might say, I was 'called by my ancestors.'"

"Dey a powerful voice. Bess listen to 'em and do what dey say."

Herakles laughed. "Yes, ma'am."

She laughed too. "Those ancestors of yours sure started somethin' big with the Olympics. Hey, I was thinking, afterward, let's spend a few days together in Greece. Some nice, outta-the-way place. You can show me around again."

"That's a fabulous idea. Is there anywhere in particular you'd like to go?"

"You decide and surprise me. Just make sure it's outta the spotlight, Kleezy, okay?"

"No problem, I know a thousand places where no one would find us."

"I can't wait."

"Me either."

There was a long silence, as neither of them wanted to hang up.

Finally, Herakles went through with it. "Well, I guess I should be going. I have an early day tomorrow, and I'm sure you do too. I'll send you an email when I get to Greece."

"All right, *oh*-kay," she replied, as if she were singing a lullaby. "Good night then. Sweet dreams and safe travels to *you*."

"Good night," he whispered, clicking the phone off. He turned out the light and rolled over on his pillow, savoring the sound of her voice, letting it merge with his consciousness. So rhythmic...so soothing.... He took a slow deep breath and as he exhaled, he closed his eyes and passed into the Land of Dreams.

Next thing he knew, he was standing on a rocky shoreline at the edge of the Sea. He recognized the huge, protruding East Rock, so he knew he was at New Haven harbor, but no boats or buildings were there, just wooded hills. A gust blew through his curly brown hair and fluttered his course-hewn tunic. He breathed in the moist, salty air and cast his gaze across the glistening water. Out in the distance, a white sail rose up over the horizon, coming closer...closer...closer. It was a ship, with at least fifty oarsmen, and at the prow of the craft stood a tall statue of a Nereid, carved out of oak and painted with realistic features. The *Argo!*

Suddenly, without warning, the vessel was upon him, and the wooden figure came to life and addressed him. "Herakles, son of Maria and Alexander," she said with a Siren's voice. "The Goddess Athena bids you step aboard."

Then, as she turned back into a statue again, a glowing, radiant Athena appeared at the railing, with arms open. A long plank extended to the shore and Herakles slowly ascended, cautiously approaching her. He looked into her endless grey eyes, and when he placed his hands in hers, she spoke.

"Herakles, it is time. Come with me now across the Sea's wide ridges, and we will travel back to the land of your birth. I shall guide you safely first to Olympia, and you will make your final preparations for the Games, then we'll continue on to Delphi where you will learn of your destiny. You *must* make this journey. It is of vital importance."

The Goddess called upon Zephyros, the West Wind, to fill their sail and soon they were underway. The deep ocean waves lapped up against the side of the ship, as they sliced through the cool, wine colored water.

"Goddess Athena," Herakles said in Greek, marveling at her glorious presence, "I have many questions for you."

"In their time they will be answered, but now, you must rest. Though the *Argo* is a swift ship, it is still a long voyage. I have woven a special pillow for you to lay upon and dream."

He reclined on the large, comfortable cushion and she covered him in a warm blanket of slumber, the gentle rocking of the ship hushing him into stillness...ushering him into Oneness.

In the timelessness of this sleep he met another, the Minoa, with her long, dark curls cascading snakelike around her shoulders and breasts. Two winged griffins, six feet tall, attended her on either side, and a large golden chalice stood before her, holding the Sacred Flame. In each hand she held a serpent high overhead.

"Herakles, my distant descendent," she whispered. "You and your beloved shall weave our golden thread far into your own distant future."

Startled, he awoke to the sound of the oarsmen, singing an unfamiliar song as they steadily, rhythmically, rowed on.

*I'm still asleep.* He got up and looked for Athena, but she was nowhere to be seen.

*The Minoa. She spoke to me....*

He leaned over the railing and looked out past the Nereid, still staring, rigid at the bow. They were approaching Gibraltar, and the narrow strait which separates the great continents of Africa and Europe. As they passed by the mighty rocks, he laughed to himself, remembering a story he was told as a child, about the Pillars of Hercules. *Hah, as if any mere mortal could move mountains to make this path to the Sea!*

Just then, a fierce gale blew up and the terrifying Charybdis appeared, spinning the *Argo* about like a matchstick on its raging whirlpool. He hung on to the railing tightly, and the men scrambled to keep to their oars.

"Do not doubt yourself, Herakles," a low, androgynous voice said to him over the fearsome wind, "or surely you will perish."

As it uttered those words, an enormous wave rushed up and spilled over them, throwing the ship sideways and knocking him down. He slid across the deck and almost off the vessel, clutching the railing at the last second and hanging on for dear life, as the vortex tried to suck him into the abyss – then suddenly, the Sea calmed and the ship again righted itself. A dense gray fog enveloped them in misty rain, and the oarsmen resumed their rowing.

They began a new song, and by the time they finished their tale of the Golden Fleece, the rain had cleared off. The Sun again shone brightly, and as the clouds turned puffy and white, Herakles laid his eyes on the western shores of Greece. A pod of dolphins greeted the ship and led them to a narrow inlet.

They rowed up the quiet river Alphiós, as birds sang and trees dropped fragrant purple flowers along the banks in welcome. When they came upon the dock, the men withdrew their oars and threw the lines ashore. Herakles disembarked and splendid Athena again appeared to him.

"Welcome to Olympia, my dearest Herakles, it is good to see you here. Only the most courageous have dared a crossing such as the one you have now made. I am pleased to see that you have stilled the waters of self-doubt, for you must indeed believe you can move mountains." She took note of his disheveled appearance, and then with a wave of her palm, transformed his soggy tunic into a robe of deep crimson, and neatly arranged his curly locks.

"Now I bid you, please, come with me," she said graciously, taking his hand in hers.

They approached the Sacred Grove of Altis, and much to his delight and wonder, the ancient site of Olympia had been returned to its former magnificence. Gone were the fallen temple pillars and the blocks of marble strewn about the weeds and red poppies. In their place stood tall, gleaming structures, with pediments and friezes painted in vivid colors. The gymnasium, baths, workshops and galleries were intact, all standing majestically amongst cypress and oak. Huge bronze and marble statues of ancient Olympians lined the tiled walkway, and they passed several alters ablaze with silver, gold and burning candles. At last they came upon the temple of the Goddess Hera, fully restored, shimmering with a golden light. Athena led him between the pillars and into the inner sanctuary, where the Queen of Heaven herself was waiting.

The combined radiance of the two Goddesses was more than his mortal eyes could absorb. He shielded them for a moment, but then as they adjusted, Hera's glorious form became apparent – her jet black hair against fair, milky skin, and dark eyes fixed on eternity. She stood before her simple stone altar, which was adorned with candles, flowers and an attentive coiled serpent. Slowly, she extended her slender arms outward in greeting, and spoke to him in winged words.

"Beautiful boy who carries my name, welcome to our beloved Olympia. You are to become one of our greatest champions, young Herakles, but you will face serious and dire obstacles in fulfilling your destiny. You must draw strength from us, for you will need it to overcome the perils awaiting you. The first of many choices will confront you upon your awakening. Take care to choose wisely and remember to be true to your heart."

Athena moved to stand beside her, and when Hera concluded, the two Goddesses merged together in likeness before vanishing in a swirling vapor.

Herakles awoke with a start, this time in his own bed. He sat up and ran his hands through his hair, realizing he was perspiring in great abundance. He went into the bathroom and splashed some cold water on his face, then looked at himself in the mirror. *What was that all about?* He returned to his room and recorded the dream in his journal before he tried to analyze it further. He'd learned to interpret his dreams and trust in the metaphors they contained, but sometimes their full meaning wasn't immediately clear. As Athena had said, the questions will be answered in time. Still, he couldn't help but wonder what important decision he'd soon have to make. Fortunately, he didn't have to wait too long because later that day, after an exceptional high jump, the first part of the riddle was answered.

"Very good, Kleo," Carl affirmed, patting him on the back. "I've never seen you jump so well, and at such an important time in your training. What are you doing differently?"

"Nothing, really. I'm just getting excited to go to Olympia, and I guess the thought is lifting me higher, giving me wings you might say."

"Careful with those wings, we don't want you flying too close to the Sun!"

"Do not worry fearful Daidalos," Herakles laughed. "I shall take great care."

During the last few months, they'd been able to put the New York episode behind them, and return to such light-hearted banter. But alas, it wasn't to last.

"About Olympia," Coach said more seriously. "There's something we have to talk about, and I know you are not going to like what I have to say."

Herakles' good spirits then took flight, replaced by a heavy blanket of doom. "What is it?"

"I don't think we should go."

"What?!" He suddenly felt flush.

"It will only disrupt your training. Don't you see? The Greek government is just using you for publicity – you will have endless distractions. You can only optimize your performance if you minimize your training irregularities. You should remain here until the facilities are open in Athens. That's only two weeks from now."

"Changing the plan will be the disruption, not fulfilling my dream of training at Olympia! Damn it, Coach. We're supposed to leave day after tomorrow, and you agreed from the very beginning. You know how important it is to me."

"Yes, but I have to listen to what my instincts are telling me, and they're telling me it's a mistake. I had hoped you would come to realize this yourself."

"It's *not* a mistake! My performance will prove it to you."

"I don't think we should take that risk."

"Risk? The risk is *not* going." Herakles looked at him hard. "I won't stay here, Coach. I'm going to Olympia with or without you. That's *your* choice."

"Don't threaten me, boy. I know what is best for you. If you want the gold, you will listen to me."

Herakles stared at him a moment, trying to find the words to convince him, but he could tell that Carl had made up his mind, and nothing he could say or do would change it. So he turned and stormed off toward the locker room. He was going to Olympia and he didn't care what Carl said, or how loudly he yelled, there was a greater chance of hell freezing over than of any change in the agreed-upon training plan. Carl would have to come around or he'd go to Olympia without him.

Herakles didn't even bother to take a shower, he just changed his clothes and left in a huff. He headed toward home, trying to figure out his next move, but the anger kept rising, blocking his judgment. When he got to his building, he wasn't ready to go up yet, so he kept walking, hoping that somehow this emerging reality would radically shift. He went through the Old Campus and past the courtyards of Berkeley and Calhoun, then all the way to Woolsey Hall and Silliman. Ever more confused and frustrated, he trudged up Hillhouse Avenue to a small park near the Divinity School, and climbed into the branches of his favorite oak tree. Off in the distance, he could again see East Rock, the huge promontory jutting out into the Long Island Sound, bordering New Haven Harbor.

Just last night, from that very spot, he'd happily sailed away on the *Argo*, bound for his home country. He felt like screaming, and if he were out there with no one around, he would have – from the very depths of his being he would have. He fixated on that distant rock, swinging his legs back and forth under the craggy limb, spinning the dilemma every way he could think of, but it was no use. The dilemma remained and he suddenly felt completely alone. In his solitude, he relived his dream from the night before, and Hera's voice echoed in his mind.

*The first of many choices will confront you upon your awakening. Take care to choose wisely and remember to be true to your heart.*

The chapel bells sounded, affirming her words and crystallizing the conundrum.

He wished he could be with Alanta right now, but that would only be selfish; she still had her training schedule, and the last thing he wanted to do was upset her. Only one other person in the world could possibly understand his situation – his mother. He jumped down off the tree, and broke into a run for his apartment.

He placed the call the minute he got home, and much to his relief, she was in.

"Mitéramou," he said in Greek, feeling on the verge of tears.

"Honeymou, what's the matter?"

"Carl went back on his promise to go to Olympia. He wants me to wait until the end of July and go straight to Athens with the rest of the athletes."

"Oh no! I'm so sorry. What are you going to do?"

"I think I'm going without him."

"Is that wise?"

"When I ask myself that question, I hear the voice of Athena from my dream last night. She said that I *must* make the journey to Olympia, and that it was of vital importance. I believe that deep within myself I have a need to go there, to place my feet on that soil and connect with my ancestors before I compete in the Games. Somehow, psychologically and spiritually I feel that if I don't go, all the physical preparation in the world will be of no consequence."

"Kleo, you've thought this through and your inner voice is telling you directly. Listen to it."

"Thank you for telling me what I want to hear, but do you *really* think I should do it?"

"Yes, I do, and besides, Carl will come around. In the meantime, why don't you visit me? We can spend a little more time together before you go."

"I was hoping you'd say that." He looked at his watch. "If

I hurry, I can catch the six o'clock and be at your place before eight."

"Wonderful! We'll have a nice dinner together. Now remember, bring everything you need for your trip. I don't want to have to overnight a shot put."

He laughed. "I will. I love you."

"I love you too, honeymou."

Fortunately, he was well organized for the trip. Most of his equipment had been shipped ahead of time, except for his discus/shotput/javelin set, contained in its own custom made case. He opened it to make sure everything was in there, then closed it back up and set it near the door. He packed both of his bags full of athletic clothes and shoes, and then realized he would need other things to wear, so he made room for a few shirts and a couple pair of nice pants. He took a quick shower and assembled the rest of his everyday stuff, and then after a final check, headed for New Haven station.

His mind was restless as the train rattled its way down the track to Manhattan, but once he got to his mom's apartment, he was finally able to relax a little bit. Maria made a hearty meal, and then they watched an old black and white movie on tv until he fell asleep. The next day around noon, after a strenuous workout at the local gym, he checked his messages for the first time since the fallout. When he did, Carl's angry voice came booming through the speaker, demanding to know why he hadn't shown up for training, and insisting he wouldn't stand for it. Carl left another, even angrier message that afternoon, and by the following day, just as Herakles was leaving for the airport, the final ultimatum was delivered: either he comes to the field house immediately or their relationship was over.

And so it was. With little hesitation, Herakles hung up the phone, kissed his mother goodbye and hailed a cab for JFK.

# 7

# AN UNHOLY ALLIANCE

The Men of CHAOS convened once again in their penthouse boardroom, high up in the TExxonMobico Tower in Doha, Qatar. The Chairman sat haughtily at the head of their long mahogany table, ordering the minions about with his customary insolence. The underlings scurried around the room, pouring glasses of water and tumblers of Chivas before retreating through tall bronze doors. When the room was secured, the Chairman called the meeting to order. He turned on the very large screen at the other end of the table and it showed a huge graph, loudly proclaiming the overwhelming failure of their bombing campaign. Weapon sales were near rock bottom and the collateral damage was higher than anticipated.

At the sight of the image, Ruther Burdock jumped out of his chair. "My God! I didn't think it would be this bad! We've totally miscalculated the effects of our operation. As reluctant as I am to admit it, Arthur might have been right."

"Don't be an alarmist, Ruther," the Chairman admonished, "and don't mention that traitor's name to me. Things haven't gone exactly how we planned, but that doesn't mean we should give up the fight."

Ruther paced nervously back and forth. "This has all gotten so ugly. So messy. And I don't like the company we're keeping."

"They are a ragged bunch aren't they?" the Chairman agreed, laughing. "I don't like 'em either, but we're going to have to stick with 'em just a little bit longer. We've been thinking too small, that's all. Local bombings just aren't as effective as they used to be. However, we've taken care of that problem, so don't worry about it. One more is all it's gonna take." The Chairman cast a conspiratorial glance toward DP, who nodded back, with the thin mean line of his smile stretching out to both sides of his sallow face.

Ruther noticed their smirks. "What the hell is that supposed to mean?"

The Chairman shifted uncomfortably in his big puffy chair. He hadn't kept too much from Ruther over the years, but with his old friend's support luke-warm and diminishing daily, the Chairman and DP thought it best to set their new plan in motion without troubling him with it. "We're just upping the ante a little."

Ruther looked absolutely horrified. "Upping the ante? Hundreds of people have already died because of this ungodly alliance with OGOW, and you're planning to *up the ante?* What are you going to do next, unleash a plague? Really, we have got to set some limits here. This is getting totally out of hand."

"Don't get squeamish on us now, Ruther, you knew this was going to get ugly. I promise you, just one more bomb will do the trick. We'll be turning those trends around overnight."

"But the bombings haven't worked. We can't continue to kill people over this."

"Quit moralizing, Goddammit. The bombings haven't worked because we haven't been using the *right* bombs." The Chairman looked hard at Ruther, communicating without words the magnitude of the decision he'd made.

"You intend to use a *nuke?*" Ruther waited for a response, his jaw slackening.

"Just one," the Chairman replied offhandedly. "We pulled it out of the warehouse. I mean, they're all just sitting there collecting dust anyway, so we decided to use one of 'em."

"For God's Sake! Now we're the four horsemen of the son-of-a-bitchin' Apocalypse?!"

"We're going to do it in Athens," DP replied, ignoring Ruther's over-dramatization. "At the Olympics."

"I am *appalled*. Have you people gone mad?"

"The way we figure it," the Chairman explained, "it can't fail. The public will be so scared, they'll feel like they have to act to protect themselves. That means security, that means defense, that means a reversal of fortunes. They'll want to invest in technology which makes them feel safe from terrorist attacks. Hell, we're the only ones who can provide that. It's perfectly logical."

Morris got a hold of the laser pointer and the red beam of light started ricocheting around the room.

"Knock that off, will ya?" the Chairman barked. "For cryin' out loud."

Morris nodded from behind his plastic mask and set it down.

"How far along is this hideous plan?" Ruther cried.

"They've got the device in place," replied the Chairman calmly. "We're ready to go."

"Don't tell me you've given control of a nuclear bomb to those fanatics in OGOW? Are you completely out of your minds?"

"They'll do whatever I want them to, whenever I tell them to do it," said the Chairman confidently.

"Then tell them not to detonate that thing! We have to find another way."

"Objection noted, Ruther, but we're going forward with it. After the bombing, we'll dissolve the alliance with OGOW, I promise. Just this once and then we'll go back to the way things use to be. You know, media manipulation and so forth, not such a messy business."

"I will not condone this. I will *not*." Ruther held his ground.

"Don't give me that crap. We're all in this together, and I suggest you accept reality. Sometimes you have to play hardball to stay on top. It's just the way it is."

"That's a hell of a lot of lives." Ruther retorted.

"Since when did you care so much about the loss of lives?"

"This is different. My commercial enterprises never hurt anyone, at least not directly."

"Right, Ruther," DP interjected condescendingly. "There's no link between entertainment violence and real violence."

Attempting to make his own jab, Morris moved his respirator mask aside, but all that came out was a protracted maniacal wheeze.

"Shut up, will you!" Ruther screamed. "I'm talking about the power of the atom. Once unleashed, it has the potential to destroy all life on the planet – including our *own!*"

"That's precisely why it will have the desired effect," the Chairman countered. "People will be so frightened, they'll invest their money, their new *geos*, in all of our latest security gadgets. We're talking a whole new generation of defense weaponry, which can find all those pesky nukes that escaped the disarmament craze."

Ruther started getting frantic, gesticulating madly as he spoke. "How could I have allowed myself to get into this predicament? I never should've gone along with the bombings in the first place. It went against my instincts, but I didn't say anything. Didn't want to be *disloyal* to CHAOS. God*dammit*. Should have gone with Arthur, I knew he was right. Now it's gotten completely out of control and there's nothing I can do to stop it. Damn you, all three of you, and damn myself to. We've become monsters. *Monsters*, I tell you!"

"It's a monstrous world out there, old boy," DP said, as the familiar mean line returned to his ashen face.

# 8

# OLYMPIA

Subject: I MADE IT!
From: Herakles@Gaia.net
Date: July 19, 2004
To: Alanta@PlanetEarth.net

Dear Alanta,

I'm really here, in my beautiful homeland of Greece! The wildflowers are still in bloom, and the red poppies are ablaze with the fire in my soul. I pick one and send it to you.

The trip went smoothly. It was crystal clear as we flew into Athens, and when I saw the Parthenon and all of the Acropolis below me gleaming in the sunlight, my heart started racing. I boarded the first bus to Olympia town, and as we were about to leave the Greek mainland and cross onto the Pelepónnisos, a four-masted sailing ship, called the *Wind Spirit*, glided past us through the famous canal, on its way out to the Gulf of Kórinthos.

We stopped for refreshments in a seaside village and I wandered into a bakery to get a little something. The moment I saw the old Greek yia ya (grandmother) behind the counter, I remembered an occasion with my family that I haven't thought about for years. We'd stopped at that very same bakery on a family holiday when I was a kid – and she was a yia ya then! I know it was her because she was missing her left pinkie. "Got it caught in the oven door," she had told us back then, when we were fascinated by such things. Her almond cookies (kouriambiethes) had set the standard of excellence for all of these years. Nowhere had I encountered a better one, and I assure you, I have sampled them many hundreds of times. So, you can imagine my astonishment when today she presented me with a morsel so splendid, so delicate it simply evaporated into my taste buds. She has somehow exceeded her former accomplishment and perfected the recipe, sending these humble sweets into the realm of the sublime.

I remember that holiday like it was yesterday. My brother and I were six, and he and my parents and I spent most of the summer driving around Greece visiting relatives, eating food and exploring ruins. It's one of the best memories I have of my childhood.

Right now, it's about 9pm and I'm at the "cyberkafenéo," a coffee shop/taverna/ouzeria/computer place around the corner from Katina's (she's the yia ya who's renting me a room). Yia yas are everywhere here, believe me. And, like every other older Greek woman I have ever known here or anywhere else in the world, Katina follows strict protocol where food is concerned. Rule number one: you must have a blinding assortment of pastries on hand at all times, all the while claiming you're running low on your supply and pretending to rummage through the cupboards, searching hopefully for some small tidbit you can spare. Katina retrieved half a dozen containers of my old favorites from her refrigerator and credenza and I sampled them unrestrained. After all, I didn't want to disappoint her.

Honestly, these tavernas never change either – lots of old men, sitting around small wooden tables drinking Turkish coffee and ouzo, playing távli (backgammon), and most importantly, feigning disinterest in everyone and everything around them, when in fact, they're absorbing the whole melodrama like sponges soak up the sea, filtering every edible bit of plankton out of the swirls of ambient conversation to feed their unending appetite for gossip. They seem like character actors in a living theater drama, playing out their parts with the precision that comes with centuries of tradition.

The big news: Carl didn't come with me. The morning after you and I talked on the phone (and a day and a half before we were to leave) he quashed Olympia! He unilaterally changed the plans, declaring that it would be too disruptive to my training. I couldn't convince him that it would be far more disruptive to cancel. No matter what I said, he insisted I would be making a horrific mistake. It was so strange, because just the night before, I had the most vivid dream I can ever recall. I sailed here to Olympia on the great mythical ship *Argo*. We crossed the Sea's wide ridges, barely escaped the terrifying Charybdis and ultimately visited Olympia, fully restored to its former magnificence. During the incredible journey, I encountered the Goddesses Athena and Hera who "told" me that it was *imperative* I make my journey as planned, and further, that an important choice would confront me in my very near future. The next day Coach came out with it.

I decided to heed your advice and listen to my ancestors. Even if this is all in my head, something is trying to tell me something and I want to hear it. So, here I am, coachless, two weeks before the Games begin – but I'm following my dream!

And tonight I dream of seeing you again,

only two more phases of the Moon must pass...

Love, Herakles

He re-read the message and sent it, then straightened the mouse and pad and got up from the low oblong table. As he pushed the chair back in and turned to leave, he nodded to the troupe of players sitting around a large backgammon board over at the next table. They tried to pretend they didn't notice Herakles, but he knew they'd been watching him, subtly, sideways through the thick, course hairs of their gnarly gray eyebrows.

He left the kafenéo, walked a few steps down the street, and then turned around to peek back in the window. Sure enough, the old men were now huddled around the computer screen talking briskly. They probably had a huge network of family and friends on line, who were just *waiting* for some tasty morsel of gossip – the old grapevine updated for a new era. Technology may change, but some things remain a cosmological constant.

He continued on, walking casually through the vibrant little town. Streetlights illuminated the bustling walkways, and the tourists darted about, seeking bargains on the splendid souvenirs. Marble busts of Hera, Zeus and Apollo, replicas of Byzantine icons, and porcelain plates of every size, proclaiming "Athens 2004" were among the most popular. The outdoor tavernas and restaurants were overflowing with people eating, drinking and happily chatting in many different languages. Bouzouki music charged the air, and the smells of grilled fish and souvlaki drifted out into the streets, enticing hungry passers by.

All of a sudden, a teenaged boy shouted his name, and the next thing he knew, he was surrounded by excited fans.

"We'll be with you at the Games!" an American called out. "Great job with the Resolution, Kleo!" yelled another. A small Greek boy wished him "kalí epitehía," good luck, and more people surged toward him with paper and pen. He stayed on for a little while, chatting, shaking hands and signing autographs. When he felt he could make a graceful exit, he withdrew from the crowd and took the back streets to Katina's.

He came to the front door and found the languid Boubalina, Katina's 17-pound calico cat, laying across the threshold. She pretended to be asleep for a moment, then reluctantly opened one heavily drooping eyelid and regarded Herakles carefully. She opened the other eye and leaned back in a luxurious, stretched-out pose, looking at him as if expecting to be picked up.

"Don't even think about it, Boubalina," Herakles said, laughing, as he stepped over her and went inside. He walked up the wooden staircase, carefully trying to avoid the creaking stairs, but to no avail. The oak steps had a personality of their own, worn well by the feet of countless travelers before him.

His room was at the top of the stairs. It had one window, a slanted ceiling and a door which opened onto a small balcony overlooking the quiet street. He went outside and leaned on the railing. *I'm really here. I'm really in Olympia.* He stood there for some time, enjoying the tranquility, before going back inside for a marginally warm shower and bed.

Just before dawn, a renegade rooster came charging through the neighborhood, announcing the break of day. Herakles woke up, thrust the covers aside and jumped out of bed, ready for his "first" day of training. He went over to the basin, splashed some cool water on his face, and then ran his damp fingers through the mop of disheveled curls on his head. He pulled them back into a pony tail and found a towel to dry his face, then poured himself a tall glass of water from a brightly painted ceramic pitcher. Feeling refreshed, he rummaged around his suitcase for a tank top and shorts and got dressed.

As he went down to breakfast, the staircase creaked at a slightly lower pitch, having rested its tired old planks in the stillness of the night. He walked through a narrow hallway, and on the wall, there were numerous family photographs surrounding a large icon of the Virgin Mary, who seemed to be watching over them all.

An open door led out to the little patio, where a trellis crowned with grape vines arched overhead and ripening fruit hung between the white wooden slats. A wrought-iron table and two chairs were set up in the middle of a brightly tiled floor, and on a white lace tablecloth she probably made herself, Katina had laid out her breakfast spread. A nice loaf of warm, crusty bread wrapped in a red checkered cloth sat waiting in a little basket, and she had platefuls of kasseri, romano and feta cheeses, Kalamata olives, hard boiled eggs and pastries, all beautifully arranged next to a tall pitcher of orange juice. Katina herself, however, was nowhere to be found.

He sat down and, though his appetite was prodding him to hurry up and dispense with the formalities, he took a moment to give thanks. He looked at each of the familiar foods, wondering if his Olympic forebears had eaten similar things as they prepared for competition. He closed his eyes, took a deep breath, and an overwhelming feeling of gratefulness welled up, sprouting like a flower within his truest heart.

As he ate breakfast, he looked across Katina's back yard. Behind the fig tree and nondescript buildings, a dark indigo Night was transforming into the pink and orange fingers of Dawn.

When he was almost finished, Katina came out, so he stood up to say good morning. It felt good to be speaking Greek again.

"Kalimeára sas, Kyría Katina."

"Katse, katse. Sit down, my boy."

"Thank you for the delicious breakfast, but you don't have to go to all this trouble every morning."

"What, you don't like it?" She looked at him, worried.

"No no, as I said, it's delicious..."

"Típota! Besides, I don't mind. It gives me something to do. I don't sleep well, just worry all the time. Worry, worry, worry. My children are so far away and my knees are terrible, so I would just as soon get up and make it nice for you. I'll cook your breakfast every day, and your dinner too, just as we agreed."

Herakles knew better than to try to argue food with a yia ya. "Thank you. I appreciate it."

"Of course you do. Now tell me, what about your coach? What happened? Why isn't he here?"

"Yes, well, I'm really very sorry about the other room being vacant. I'll be glad to pay you for it."

"Never mind that. Where is he?"

"Well," Herakles struggled, "he refused to honor our agreement to come to Olympia, and so, we parted company."

Upon hearing the juicy bit of gossip, her eyes lit up. "Too bad for him." She stacked the empty dishes onto her little tray. "You want more breakfast, a few more eggs?"

"No, really, but I promise to make up for it later." That answer seemed to satisfy her for the moment, so he got up from the table. "I have to be going now. I'm meeting the director of the Olympia site shortly. Thank you again, Kyría Katina."

"Parakaló, Kleo, it's my pleasure."

She reached up for his face, and he obligingly leaned forward so she could more easily give him the customary pinch on the cheek. Much to his relief, she turned out to be a gentle pincher, and not one of those mega-twisters who left a big red mark for the rest of the day.

He went back up to his room, brushed his teeth, then grabbed his equipment kit and daypack and headed out. There was no sign of Boubalina lolling about the front entrance, and a cursory look behind the large flower pots revealed no cat. *Oh well.* He continued down the street, and a few people were out and about, but otherwise all was very still and quiet.

He walked to the bus terminal taxi stand, where a middle-aged cabbie was leaning up against the ticket window flirting with the agent. When Herakles approached, the man turned toward him.

"Well, well, well, if it isn't Herakles Speros. We heard you were in town. On behalf of all the people of Greece, let me say that we're delighted you have returned to your native soil to train for the Olympics. Welcome."

"Thank you. It's my great honor and joy to be here."

"It's a pity though that you'll be representing the United States, and not Greece. However, we still wish you good luck. Now, allow me to take you to the site."

"Yes, thank you." Herakles laughed at the cabbie's obligatory laying of guilt. Predictably, the cabbie laughed too, as he took the bags and put them in the trunk. Herakles hopped into the back seat and rolled down his window. It was a short, ten-minute drive down a long, straight tourist road, with rolling hills, olive groves and pasturelands off in the distance. He could barely contain his excitement. This was it. Olympia – where it all began, nearly three millennia ago.

He tried to orient himself to the surrounding geography. The ruins lay in a flood plain at a bend in the mighty Alphiós River, near the point where the smaller Kladeos River flows into it. Both rivers have their source high up in the Arkadian mountains to the east and south. He leaned out the window and looked back up over his shoulder to see if they were still snow capped. It was rare in the summer, but sometimes.... *Nope, not today.* Through the front windshield, he could see a forested mound coming into view. It was Mount Kronos, named after the formidable father of Zeus and commander of the earlier generation of Gods and Goddesses known as the Titans.

He loved thinking about those old myths. From an early age,

his mother had been telling him the stories of the ancient Greeks. They would come to life as she performed little dramas about Gaia and Ouranos, or Hera and Zeus, when he and his brother were ready for bed. She had helped them to understand the larger meaning of those stories, and what they tell us about ourselves, our history, and potentially, our future.

They pulled up to the entrance and Herakles reached into his pocket for a few geos, but the cabbie cut him off. "No. You keep it. It was my pleasure to drive you here." He popped the trunk.

"Thank you," Herakles replied, smiling, as he got out of the cab and retrieved his bags.

The cabbie stuck his head out the window. "Shall I pick you up at the end of the day?"

"I appreciate your offer, but now that my equipment is here, I'll be jogging back and forth. I need the exercise, you know. See you around."

"Very well," the cabbie replied, and with a nonchalant wave, drove off.

A shuffling sound drew Herakles' attention to a short, white-haired man wearing black horn-rimmed glasses, who was coming toward him across the parking lot. A large gold ring with what looked to be a hundred keys dangled from his belt loop, jingling with each left footstep. He called out to Herakles loudly in Greek. "Give an old man a hand, ehh?"

Herakles hurried his stuff over to the entrance, then ran back and offered the man his arm. The elder slipped his hand through and locked elbows securely, in preparation for stepping onto the high curb. As they went up, the old man grunted with determination, and they made it without incident. "There, thank you." He let go.

"You're very welcome, sir."

They both continued to the ticket booth door, and the old man looked him over while he thumbed through his keys. "If you're here to see the ruins, you're early. The gates don't open for another hour."

"Well, actually I'm here to see Dr. Margolis. My name is Herakles Speros."

The man squinted through his thick lenses. "Oh, *you're* Herakles Speros; she said you'd be coming. You'll be signing autographs or something."

Herakles laughed. "I expect to sign a few, yes, but I'm also going to be training here, in preparation for the Olympics."

"Yes, yes, for the Games. Good. Good. I'm happy to meet you." He found the key he was looking for and went inside his booth. The door to the right of the main gate buzzed. "Go on," he said, waving from behind the glass. "Her office is in the museum, second floor. She'll be expecting you."

Herakles acknowledged him and went through. A stone walkway crossed over the River Kladeos, which was now more of a narrow stream in a shallow, rocky gully. He leaned over the railing and tried to imagine how this trickle of water could swell into the torrent that had once overrun the entire area, submerging the temples and monuments, then leaving them broken and buried in mud.

Continuing on, he soon came to a large grove of trees which shaded the bright white marble facade of the modern museum. *I just have to get a glimpse of the ruins before I go in.* He set down his bags and walked a little further until the concrete vanished, giving way to a dirt path. The coarse gravel crunched beneath his sneakers, and when a dove cooed from some unseen perch, he stopped.

The jumble of toppled pillars, partial foundations and scattered marble slabs appeared silver in the shadow of Mount Kronos. Red poppies grew out of cracks in the stones and carpeted the grounds in thick patches. A single ray of sunlight suddenly came streaming over the mountain, illuminating the three remaining marble columns of Hera's ancient temple. He knelt to the ground, gently placing his palms flat against the Earth. Then he closed his eyes and whispered to the wind, "thank you for making this possible."

He took a long, deep breath and exhaled slowly, pushing his palms into the dry ground, feeling the pebbles and dirt with his fingertips. The energy of the sacred place pulsated through him and he felt wonderfully alive. This was where he was supposed to be and he knew it, without reservation. After a few moments, he stood up, brushed off his hands and went inside the museum.

The lights were on but not a soul was in sight, and a glacial silence emanated from the tall ceilings and skylights overhead. Past the empty reception counter, he could see into the large gallery, where the triangular pediments from Zeus' temple were mounted. On one side of the room was the tragic wedding feast battle between the Lapiths and the Centaurs. A glorious Apollo stood above the two enemies, as though he were reminding them of the importance of keeping the Sacred Truce.

On the other side, redoubtable Zeus oversaw the rigged chariot race held for the hand of Hippodameia. And on the far wall, were the twelve square metopes, the stone carvings of the mythical Herakles completing his Twelve Labors. From the old hero's slaying of the Hydra, to his theft of the golden Apples of the Hesperides, they were all there, preserved for posterity.

"Kalimeára sas, Mr. Speros," Agapi Margolis said excitedly, as she appeared on the stairway across from the ticket counter. She was dressed in a cream-colored linen pantsuit, and seemed to be about his mother's age, early fifties or so. Her black wavy hair was carefully pulled back into a short ponytail, looking remarkably like his, and she exuded an air of professionalism. "Thank heavens you made it, with all of the rumors circling about, I didn't know what to think." She held out her hand. "Welcome to Olympia. We're delighted to have you here."

He clasped it. "Thank you for making my dream a reality, and please, call me Kleo."

"You're most welcome, Kleo. Now, I've made all of the arrangements you requested and everything should be in order. Your equipment arrived last week and has been set up or locked in storage. So, if you'd like, we can go out to the field and I'll show you around."

"Absolutely!"

She led him back outside and down the old gravel path into the Sanctuary. They passed the remnants of the archaic gymnasium with its many slim, elegant pillars, shaded by trees with purple flowers. As they came upon the temple ruins, she remarked that the one dedicated to Hera had been built in the 8th century b.c.e., well before the one constructed for Zeus.

"Do you know what was here before that?" Herakles asked.

"Not specifically, but there is persuasive evidence to suggest that it had been a sacred place for a very long time. It was most likely one of the numerous Goddess worshipping sites which thrived during the Neolithic period, approximately 7000 to 2500 b.c.e. And I believe it dates back to the Paleolithic."

"The Old Stone Age..." Herakles echoed.

"Yes."

They continued past the vestiges of the treasuries, where in the Classical times of the 5th century b.c.e., men of the rival city states such as Athens, Sparta and Korinth had given their tributes to Zeus, each trying to out do the other with more splendid displays of gold and statuary. Eventually, they approached the stadium, where the ancient Games had actually taken place. A high stone archway framed the long passage leading out onto the field.

"After you," Dr. Margolis said, gesturing with her hand.

He took a deep breath and started through the portal, his connection to the ancient Olympians intensifying with every step. When he emerged onto the green grass of the field, euphoria embraced him. He set down his equipment and impulsively broke into a run. His enthusiasm was so contagious, that by the time he came back around, Dr. Margolis was grinning with vicarious joy.

"I'm sorry," he said. "I couldn't resist. It's just that I'm so excited to finally be here."

"I completely understand. Now, let me show you what I've arranged. Over there," she pointed to the far end, "is where you will be training. We've cordoned off that half of the field, and marked it as you requested; and as you can see, the jumping areas have also been set up according to your specifications. This side of the rope will be the viewing area. I must remind you, we average 5,000 visitors a day, and I suspect many of them are going to want to watch you train."

"That's okay. As long as they stay behind the rope, I don't mind."

She walked them over to a large sign which clearly outlined the rules in Greek, English, French, German, Spanish and several Asian languages. "One hopes the tourists will read the sign and use a little common courtesy."

"That'll be fine."

"Very well. Now, the tent you see adjacent to the field is for the press. We have issued a number of passes, and I expect reporters will begin arriving later this morning."

"Excellent, thank you."

"Over here," she pointed to a shed under some trees, "is where you'll find the water cooler and equipment storage. There's plenty of room for the items you've brought today." She reached into her jacket pocket. "Here's your key. Spiro, our resident sports enthusiast, will keep an eye on the tourists and the press, and make sure you have everything you need. The autograph stand will be open once a day, in the viewing area. What time do you prefer?"

"Um, how about after lunch?"

"Very well, let's say 1:00 then. Your fans will appreciate it, and I think it will enable us to keep disruptions to a minimum."

"Sounds good. It looks as though you've thought of everything."

"Well, there is one more item."

"What's that?"

"My phone has been ringing off the hook this morning. Reporters. They're asking me to verify rumors that you have come to Olympia without your coach."

"You can tell them I'll be holding a press conference this afternoon and will address their questions at that time."

"As you wish. Spiro will be here shortly, so if you need anything at all, just let him know."

"I can't thank you enough."

"The pleasure is ours. Well then, I can see you're anxious to start, so I'll leave you to it. Good luck, Kleo." She started to walk away, but then called back over her shoulder, "oh, and the ladies in the museum cafeteria are expecting you for lunch. Please don't disappoint them. You may use the private dining room if you'd like." She smiled with the familiar look of one who had also encountered many an exacting yia ya.

Herakles laughed, waving her off as she disappeared through the portal. He slowly turned back around, absorbing the panorama of the monument ruins amidst the old cypress trees, with Mount Kronos and the Olympic training grounds before him. Then he ran across the field, to a shady old oak, to do his morning stretches.

He found a nice grassy patch, and standing with his legs slightly apart, closed his eyes. He took three long breaths, and on the fourth, he raised both arms overhead, then brought them gently down to the front as he exhaled. This was his favorite part of the routine. Carl called it muscle conditioning, but for him, it was so much more. It was a time to loosen his muscles, yes, but also to merge mind, body and spirit.

The tree beside him became his elegant template. His chest the thick, sturdy trunk. Arms, hands and fingers the free-flowing leaves at the end of strong, flexible branches. High into the sky he stretched, beyond the stratosphere, beyond the Solar System to the outer edges of Cosmos itself...then, carried on the swift solar wind, he returned to the leaves, traveling through the veins of the tree and back down the mighty trunk, on through his powerful legs, down, down through the mantel and into the magma, the liquid rock bubbling with creation in the very heart of Earth. His breath slowed as he came into balance, becoming a humble conduit for the energy of the Great Mystery.

His motions were slow and graceful as he grounded himself in space and time, breathing calmly and regularly, stretching each muscle, carefully indulging its desire to reach beyond the confines of his skin. He'd developed his own routine, a mix of yoga, calisthenics and t'ai chi, which varied slightly every morning depending upon how he felt. Today, he noticed a strain which began at the base of his skull and continued right on down his back. All the traveling in those tiny compartments, not to mention the tension between he and Carl, had created a nasty little knot in his neck. He pushed two fingers into the muscle and rolled it slowly in a circular fashion, first counter-clockwise, then clockwise, in synch with his slow, deep breaths. After a few minutes, it started to release, and as chi flowed through the block, his circuit of continuous life energy was restored.

He slid down into a hurdler's stretch, and then slowly bent forward until his forehead touched the ground at his knee. He held it there for a long time, breathing and relaxing, breathing and relaxing, then switched legs. Soon, he felt completely loose and ready to go.

He took another run, circling the field three times, and as he came back to his starting point, a husky middle-aged man dressed in a light shirt and khaki pants came running through the portal toward him. The man picked up speed as he crossed the field, then he hurdled over the viewing area rope, before coming to a gravelly halt a few feet away.

"Herakles Speros!" he exclaimed, bestowing a gregarious hug as though he were a long lost relative. "I am Spiro Vlahandreas, and it is my pleasure to be at your service." He bowed.

"The pleasure is mine," Herakles replied.

"Tell me," Spiro asked in earnest, "what did you think of my hurdle?"

"Excellent! I hope you're not competing in Athens!"

Spiro laughed heartily. "I haven't decided yet, but we shall see, Herakles Speros, we shall see. I can hardly believe my eyes. You are right here, in Olympia! I tell you, I've been here 26 years and never before has an Olympic athlete trained here. This is an historic moment."

"I don't know about that, but I do appreciate your assistance in making it possible."

"Delighted. If you need anything at all, let me know and I'll take care of it. I mean it now, anything at all."

"Well, all right, how do you feel about working a stopwatch while I do my morning sprints?"

"I would be honored."

"I don't want to interfere with your other responsibilities."

"Dr. Margolis has made it perfectly clear. You are my primary responsibility for the next two weeks, and right now, that means working the stopwatch. Where is the device? I would like to practice a few times."

Herakles retrieved it from his equipment bag under the tree, then showed Spiro how it worked. "We'll start with 30-meter dashes, and move up from there. I noticed the lines have already been etched on the field. Do I have you to thank for that?"

Spiro shrugged. "It was nothing."

"Okay," Herakles said, as he double-checked the blocks. "Give me a few seconds to settle into position, and I'll start when you say go."

He slid into them, and moments later Spiro called out, "on your mark…get set…go!"

With a mighty surge, Herakles set his energy in motion. He ran with lightning speed, traversing the short distance in only a few seconds. At the end of each sprint, he'd wait a minute, then get himself in position to start again. And again and again and again until his pulse rate nearly doubled. He loved the feeling of adrenaline rushing through his body and neuropeptides tingling in his head. It was ecstasy!

By the time he completed his sprints, the first of the tourists started arriving, and Spiro immediately approached them to establish observation protocol. Meanwhile, Herakles took several relaxed laps around the field, then stopped for a drink of water. He savored the cool, hydrating liquid, picturing the molecules as they replenished the cells of his body, becoming the fuel which would propel him up, up, and over the high bar.

Spiro had done a nice job of setting up the high jump apparatus and the thick blue landing cushion. He put the bar at 6' – a couple of easy ones first, to work on form. He measured out his steps on the grass, and then with three great strides, launched himself up and over with plenty of room to spare. He scrambled off the cushion and back to his starting spot. Another easy one, smooth and graceful, before he decided to raise the bar to a more challenging level of 6'6". His approach was strong, and his form flawless. He raised the bar an inch or two after each jump, until he reached 7'2", his personal best, and then he added an inch to see if he could top it. He knew he had it from the moment his feet left the ground, and his face was beaming as he rolled off the mat.

But there was no one there to share it with; no Carl to pat him on the back and congratulate him for the accomplishment. *Maybe it was a mistake coming without him — no, I can't think that way. The right decision's been made and that jump confirms it.* He looked across the field for approval from the fans, whose numbers were now growing in the viewing area, and they responded, waving and calling his name. He waved back, realizing he'd have to rely on them for support. Over in the press area, he noticed several camera crews had arrived and were setting up their equipment. Thank goodness Spiro was here to keep an eye on things.

Instead of raising the bar again, he decided it was time for a few long jumps. He took another lap around the field, and his fans cheered as he passed by. He acknowledged them, but kept on going to the starting line, where he stopped to do some preparatory leg stretches. In his mind's eye, he visualized his approach, launch and landing, and the way he felt today, he thought he might just be able to jump a personal best in this event as well. *That's it. Think positive. I can do it.*

When his legs were good and loose, he readied himself for the approach. Starting from the upright position, he took a deep breath and then burst into a sprint, quickly building speed. When his left foot grazed the starting line, he launched himself forward, his powerful limbs lifting him up. He pulled at the air as if grasping at invisible rings, and for a moment felt like he was fooling gravity. At last he touched down in the sand pit, and his momentum carried him forward onto his knees. *Not bad for a first jump, not bad at all.* He got up and came around to check the tape: 26'8" — two inches short of his best jump.

It took four more tries before he bettered his mark, and again, he knew it the moment he launched. After a smooth landing, he checked the tape to be sure, and *yes! 27'*. It had been months since his last best jump, so he was elated, but once again there was nobody there to share it with. Spiro was off keeping the tourists at bay, and Carl? He had to admit, the whole thing bothered him, but there was nothing that could be done. *Right Iphe?*

He walked over to the water cooler and sucked down three more cups. The Sun was getting higher in the sky and the field was starting to heat up. He grabbed a towel out of the ice bucket and buried his face in it, then wrapped it around his neck. Beads of cold water dripped down onto his chest, glistening in the summer light, and he thought he better get the distance running out of the way before it got too much hotter.

He retrieved another stopwatch from the bag, strapped it to his wrist and just before he crossed over the starting line, clicked it on. Within a few seconds he was cruising down the length of the field, and then spontaneously, he leapt up over the berm, dodged a few trees at the perimeter, and emerged onto wide-open pastureland. His long, tanned, muscular legs carried him forth with the grace of a gazelle, and his breathing quickened as his heart pumped faster and faster. Distance running gave him a different kind of a rush, more blissful, heavenly, other-worldly. In this state, he could allow his mind to wander without disrupting his rhythm, and it wandered directly to Alanta January. He relived their meetings in New York and Sacramento, and envisioned their approaching reunion in Athens, as he glided over the ground, adroitly navigating the uneven terrain.

Twenty minutes into it, he circled back, making for a forty-minute run. When he returned to the old Olympic field, he slowed to a walk until his breath returned to normal, and then cooled down again by the ice bucket.

It was 11:45, a good time to stop for lunch. So when he felt somewhat refreshed, he set off across the field toward the excited on-lookers. He waved as he walked past the people in the viewing area, and the reporters began shouting questions from the press tent. "Where is your coach? What happened between you and Coach Richter? Is it true that you're here alone?"

Herakles stopped for a moment to address the journalists. "I'll answer your questions after lunch, say 12:45, right here? I've worked up a bit of an appetite." He flashed one of his irresistible smiles and walked measuredly through the stone portal, where

Spiro waited to escort him to lunch.

"The ladies asked me to bring you into the kitchen," Spiro said, slightly apologetically. "I hope you don't mind, they're very anxious to meet you."

"I've been looking forward to it, but first, I'd like to wash up."

As they walked through the swinging doors into the cafeteria kitchen, a cacophony of clattering plates and chattering people burst forth. Succulent aromas swirled in potent vortices about the room, calling to him, enticing and enchanting him.

When the ladies spotted him, an abrupt and conclusive silence fell upon them – a quiet so striking, so complete, you'd have thought Jesus Christ himself had entered the kitchen bearing wine and bread – but it only took a moment for them to catch their breath and resume their conversation. They fluttered toward him en masse, a flock of doting hens five feet tall, converging on him with out-stretched arms, intent on touching for themselves the living legend standing in their midst. All at once they grabbed at him, pinching folds of fabric on his jersey and twisting folds of skin on his blushing cheeks. They hugged him and patted him, praising everything about him, and there wasn't much he could do but go along with it. He didn't really mind though; he'd been pinched and prodded and poked and jabbed in every possible way, and he knew it was the sincerest form of affection they could muster.

The cafeteria line had started backing up, but only when the tourists began calling loudly for service did the ladies finally let him be. They dispersed back into their familiar domain of boiling pots and cooking trays and simmering saucepans brimming over with the sustenance of Life.

Predictably, the volume and intensity of the discussion began to build as several of the women started putting his lunch together. They argued over every detail, from which plate to use to how many spoonfuls of green bean almandine to give him, but eventually consensus emerged from the chaos and Herakles was presented with a mountain of food. He lavished his thanks and compliments upon them, and then went into the small private dining room to sit down. Before he even took a bite, three of them came bursting through the door with paper napkins and pens in hand, seeking his autograph. Every few minutes thereafter, one or more of the women would enter, apologize profusely, place another napkin on the table and tell him what to write.

Ordinarily, he'd be talking over the morning workout with Carl, who would never have allowed these interruptions. However, since Carl wasn't there, he indulged their demands, enjoying their company. When he did have a moment, he tried to evaluate himself, to objectively analyze the morning's highs and lows, but he couldn't help but wonder if he was missing something. Carl was often able to notice things he had overlooked, and then use them as teaching points to improve his performance. He was a good coach, Herakles had to admit, despite the annoying similarities to his father. One thing was certain, Carl would never have approved of this lunch.

Herakles didn't worry too much about that though, because he knew the food had been prepared with love, and as the women would no doubt profess, with the finest ingredients found anywhere in the world. He enjoyed it all, but the dolmades, the grape leaves stuffed with rice, nuts and raisins, were simply outstanding. Almost as good as his mother's.

When he finished, he slipped out the emergency exit to avoid a lengthy farewell, and fortunately, no alarm sounded. He made his way back over to the field, and as he emerged from the portal, the media and his fans went into a frenzy. He shook a few hands and assured the cheering multitudes he'd sign autographs after he spoke with the press. Spiro struggled to keep order among the excited crowd, who at this point were pressing against the ropes and jumping up and down. As soon as he was in earshot, the gaggle of reporters began shouting questions, thrusting their wireless mics at the air in his direction. When he reached the press tent he had to raise his arms to quiet them down.

"I'll answer questions in a moment, but first I'd like to make a brief statement if I may. I appreciate your cooperation. Thank you. As you know, I have decided to train here in Olympia for the next two weeks in preparation for the upcoming Olympic Games in Athens. I'm delighted to be back in the land of my birth, the land of my ancestors. It's a dream come true for me to be practicing here, at the ancient site of the original Olympic Games, and I am most appreciative of the Greek government and the facility staff for allowing me this opportunity.

"As you must know by now, I have come here alone, without my former coach, Carl Richter. We had a difference of opinion about my decision to train here, and that difference led to the end of our professional relationship. However, I have no animosity toward Coach Richter, and I continue to hold him in the highest regard. He's been an excellent coach who's played an enormous role in preparing me for the Games. In fact, I would like to take a moment to thank him publicly." Herakles reached deeply within his heart and looked squarely into the ENN camera, out into the wider world. "Thank you Carl, for everything you've done for me."

As soon as the reporters realized that Herakles had finished his statement, they began hurling questions, simultaneously and in competition with one another.

"Will you be naming a new coach?"

"No."

"Do you think you can do it alone, without a coach?"

"Yes, I do."

"Did you hear the reigning Olympic decathlon champion, Maximilian Leach, boasted yesterday that he'll be *easily* winning the gold again?"

"We'll see about that!"

"Is it true that you also had a falling out with Ms. January?"

"No."

"Is it true your argument with Richter ended in a fist fight?"

"Most certainly *not*." The reporters who'd asked the last two questions were with CHAOS ONE, big surprise.

"Look, I'm willing to spend a few minutes with you every day if you wish to follow my progress, but please, try to respect my privacy will you? I need you to focus on my training. That's what I'm here for. I face the most important challenge of my life in less than a month and I *must* have your cooperation to make it work. Please, ask me no more questions about Coach Richter or my relationship with Alanta January, all right?"

"Do you still think you can win the gold?"

He smiled radiantly and with confidence. "I will give it my best. Now, if you'll excuse me, I'd like to spend a few minutes with the nice people who have come to watch me train."

He went back over to the growing crowd, and when they saw him coming they erupted in a flurry of paper waving and cheers, each of them vying for his attention. He shook more hands and signed more autographs, and after about twenty minutes pulled himself away, thanking them all for their encouragement. As he headed back over to the field, he replayed the press conference in his mind. Not too bad really, though the two from CHAOS put him ill at ease. Who knew how far they were capable of going?

He broke into a jog and shifted his focus to the afternoon workout, where he'd be practicing his throwing events. The javelin was first, so he started his shoulder exercises, gently rolling one arm, then the other, over his head as he ran. He did a lap, and then stopped under the shade of the knobby old tree to finish warming up his upper body and leg muscles. Afterward, he retrieved his equipment kit from the storage shed, opened it up, and carefully removed and connected each length of the javelin.

The javelin throwing area was along one side of the field, beginning close to the observers' section and extending all the way to the record markers Spiro had set. Without a doubt, this was his best throwing event. A perfectly timed approach, combined with an aerodynamically precise release and full follow-through, compensated for the greater size and strength of competitors like Max. As he neared the starting point, his fans again went wild, waving and calling to him. He took his place in front of them and waited, with eyes closed, until they settled down.

When it was relatively quiet, he slid his fingers into the grip and lifted the slim shaft over his shoulder. The air was mostly steady, though he detected a slight intermittent breeze, so he observed the treetops to see which direction they were blowing. When he had his trajectory calculated and felt ready to go, he started down the runway in a steady, straightforward jog. At mid-point, he extended his arm back so that the tip of the javelin was coming just off his chin, and then, with speed building, he turned into three mighty side steps, completed his cadence and catapulted it over his head in a great outpouring of energy.

It rose up high, and then gracefully arched over and down into the ground about ten feet this side of Max's world record. He jogged over to the landing site and marked it, then plucked the javelin from the dirt and returned to his starting place. He threw it four more times, with each one outdistancing the last, and ended up within six feet of the record and close to his personal best.

Next he took up the shot put, a 16-pound cast-iron ball intended to be hurled through the air in flagrant disregard of gravity's demands. He felt its solid bulk weighing heavily downward in his hand, drawn to its natural resting place on terra firma. This was a strangely contemplative event for Herakles. To a great degree, the sport had traditionally focused on the exercise of raw, naked power, but because of his relative size and weight, Kleo took a different approach, relying instead on eastern philosophies of meditation and chi energy movement. His goal was to tap into the unseen powers of the Universe to the maximum extent possible, and transfer them into the momentum of the shot. To do so, everything needed to be in perfect alignment, perfect harmony.

He attuned himself to the sphere by gently moving it around his body, using its mass to warm up his shoulder, back and neck muscles. When he felt ready, he stepped into the ring and took his stance, cradling the smooth curve of the shot in the nape of his neck. He closed his eyes and visualized his glide, release and follow-through, and then carried them out with a great exhale, propelling the pellet outward. He went through the ritual four more times, each time coming in around 60'. *Pretty solid.*

He saved his favorite, the discus, for last. He felt a special af-
finity with this event because it was the discus which had led him
to the world of track and field in the first place. He was 16 when
he made the decision. He'd been playing football for three years
as a quarterback, when he was chopped down at the knees by an
over-sized linebacker who was bent on hurting him. He tore several ligaments, and though they quickly healed, the incident was
serious enough for him to question why he was involved in the
sport at all.

He really didn't like the game even though he was good at it.
Growing up in Greece, he'd always played soccer, however, when
his family moved to New York, his father had insisted he try out.
At the time, football was wildly popular and Herakles suspected
that his father had pushed him into it in order to impress American colleagues at the UN. And impress he did, because Herakles
had a knack for anything athletic. From a very early age, he could
excel in any sport in the time it took most people to learn the
rudimentaries.

As a first-year high school student he was selected as one of
the best in the state of New York, and at the time of his injury, he
was being considered for all-American as well. His performance
had already gotten the attention of college recruiters. If he'd continued to stay healthy and perform at that level, he was looking
at a multimillion dollar contract to play professional football as
soon as he finished college, or sooner if he desired – but he didn't.
It was too aggressive, too dominating. Players and coaches alike
talked about winning at all costs, and serious injuries were all too
common. Worse, artificial stimulants and steroids were widely
used, which he didn't approve of at all, and he couldn't understand
the vehemence of the fans and the slick commercialization of the
industry. It all seemed so out of proportion to what was really important. Players earning millions of dollars, yet greedily striking for
more. Team owners holding municipalities hostage by demanding
new facilities, tax breaks and environmental exemptions. In his
mind it was tantamount to the barbarism of the Roman gladiators,
beamed into millions of households three, sometimes four days a

week. Fortunately, everything changed after the Millennium Effect, as balance began to be restored to society. The popularity of the game greatly diminished as fans turned to other outlets for entertainment. Caps were placed on salaries and self-regulation by owners was abolished. But that all came long after he'd bowed out.

Because of his injury, he was unable to practice with his team for several weeks, so one day after school, he decided to go to the Metropolitan Museum of Art. They had a wonderful collection of Greek artifacts from Minoan times on down through the ages, and being there always made him feel as though he were back home in Greece, where antiquity and the present intermingle as part of daily life.

As he was exploring the galleries, he chanced upon Myron's famous statue of the discus thrower from the 4th century b.c.e. Though it was an image frozen in stone, the sculptor had somehow captured a subtle grace and movement in the smooth white marble, preserving the illusion of timeless motion. As the athlete wound up his circular spin, Herakles could almost see the disc fly from his outstretched hand, and suddenly, Destiny revealed herself, right there at the Met.

For a brief moment, Herakles saw himself in the future, competing at the Olympics in Greece. The International Olympic Committee had just selected Athens to host the 2004 summer Games, and at that moment, Herakles knew he was going to be there. He began practicing as soon as he fully recovered. That was six years ago already. *Hard to believe....*

He went over to the chalk-drawn ring, where Spiro had kindly put his discus, but before he picked it up he did a few more warm ups, especially focusing on his obliques. Then he took the 4-1/2 pound flying saucer in his hand, and threw it up and down a half-dozen times to get the feel of it. He lightly curled his fingertips around its smooth edge, and precisely placed his thumb to minimize the wobble. After a few swing-backs to orient himself to the turning motion, he stepped into the ring. Before he took his stance, he surveyed the panorama to get his wind-up spot, and a cypress tree stood right at ten o'clock – *perfect*.

As he got into position he visualized the throw, seeing himself as a human spring, with his powerful hips and legs propelling his broad upper body around, creating the force of a spinning vortex, which he would channel through to the disc. He took three deep breaths, then in one accelerating motion, wound up and released the discus, fully extending himself into the throw.

It climbed toward its apex with startling speed and then fell back to the ground with a thud. *Good.* Maybe just a little early on the release, but nice trajectory and distance, and when he checked, it was 223' and just short of his best.

Five throws later, he heard Spiro's booming voice in the distance, herding the tourists and the press corps off the field. Herakles gave them all one last wave for the day, and then headed back over to the running area. He set up the hurdles and waited until Spiro was finished.

"Excuse me, Spiro," he called out. "I could use a hand again, if you don't mind."

"No problem, what can I do for you?"

He picked up his stopwatch and tossed it to him. "I need a timekeeper again."

"I was hoping you would," Spiro replied, catching the watch. "Now let me see, I should stand over there."

"Perfect," Herakles said, walking up to the starting line and crouching into position.

Spiro gave him the "on your mark...get set...go!" and he sprung out of the blocks and raced toward the hurdles, effortlessly gliding over all ten bars.

"Bravo!" Spiro exclaimed. "Bravo, 14.95 seconds."

Herakles circled back around then got down for another run, and another, before finally calling it quits after his fifth rep.

It had been a great first day – everything went as well as he could have hoped, as if it were all an affirmation of his most important decisions in life. How good it felt, like anything was possible, and that's how he wanted to feel during the Games. So he took a moment to ground himself. *Don't get cocky now, and don't peak out too early. Save the best for Athens. Save the best for Athens.*

Spiro helped him put his equipment away and offered him a ride home, but he was intent on running to Katina's. The sinking midsummer Sun was partially hidden behind a cloud, and opaque streams of golden light poured down as if from the breast of Heaven. He admired it for a moment, and then walked off the 3,000-year-old track and field, and through the stone portal. He continued past the ruins, toward Hera's temple. Three rotund pillars stood at the entrance of the large rectangular site, but the rest of it had been tumbled and tossed throughout the millennia by the rumblings of Earth-shaking Poseidon. Filtered sunlight fell gracefully over the pillars and bits of clover grew from the cracks along the length of what remained of the temple foundation. Herakles touched a sturdy column, placing his palm flat against it, concentrating on the memories contained within the stone. As the song of the nearby stream ebbed and flowed, his perceptions shifted ever so subtly, and he found himself inside his recent dream.

The Temple of Hera stood before him, restored in all its former glory. The chipped and yellowed marble now shone forth with smooth and radiant luster, brilliant as the planet Venus on a clear and moonless night. He entered the site and slowly, with reverence, approached the inner sanctum. As if from somewhere else in the Realm of Dreams, he heard the flutter of wings, an echo from the depths of his consciousness. He looked up to see a peacock feather floating gently downward to the marble floor. *The Goddess.* He knelt down to pick it up and as he touched it, the reconstruction vanished. The feather stared at him with its colorful, iridescent eye, and Herakles addressed his benefactor.

"Thank you, Hera, Queen of Heaven, for giving me this glimpse into your ancient world. It is with great honor and humility I come here seeking a connection with my ancestors, the athletes who have walked upon these sacred grounds and touched your enduring spirit. I appreciate being able to complete my final preparation here, and trust that I'll find the strength I need to excel at the Games." He twirled the feather between his thumb and forefinger, and marveled at its luminescent beauty even in the fading sunlight.

Then he tried to figure out where it came from. He looked

up, but saw only clouds above. *Surely I imagined the flutter of wings and the restored ruin.* He looked around, past the toppled temple walls. *Were there any peacocks on the grounds?* He saw only the peaceful quiet of the deserted site. *Could a tourist have left the feather somewhere, only to be carried overhead by some unseen wind? Maybe it's fatigue – it has been an eventful day.* He placed the feather gently on a pillar fragment, and then left the sacred grove with his long shadow trailing behind.

He crossed over the River Kladeos again, and the gatekeeper buzzed him through the main gate with a nod and a wave. He waved back to the old man, then took off down the road with long, easy strides, leisurely traversing the few kilometers to Katina's.

Boubalina strategically blocked the front door to the house, staring at him intently. She was clearly resolved not to let him pass until he demonstrated his devotion to her, so he knelt down and scratched behind her ears. She pressed against him and purred with approval. After a few minutes of feline indulgence, he went inside. He took the stairs three at a time up to his little room, stripped off his sweaty clothes and jumped in the shower.

Feeling clean and refreshed, he slipped into a pair of his favorite jeans and put on a purple cotton shirt and sandals, then went down to the patio for dinner. The aroma of Katina's cooking permeated the house, and Herakles suddenly realized he was famished. He took his place at the little table, just as Helios' golden chariot disappeared in a pink and lavender dusk. The air was cooling now, and it felt wonderful after a day in the heat of the summer Sun.

Katina had selected an assortment of flowers from her garden and made a delightful centerpiece for the table. A basket of warm rosemary walnut bread sat before him, next to a saucer of velvety olive oil, seasoned with herbs and garlic bits. As he was reaching for a slice to dip in the marvelous mixture, Katina came roaring out of the kitchen carrying a serving tray.

"How are you my boy?" she asked excitedly, placing a large bowl of egg lemon soup in front of him. "I hope you are hungry."

"Yeia sas, Kyría Katina. I'm fine, thank you. This smells wonderful."

She nodded with satisfaction, sitting down next to him. "So, eat!"

He dipped his spoon into the thick, creamy soup and sampled it, suddenly realizing that, somehow, his favorite foods tasted even better here in Greece.

Katina placed her elbows on the table with her chin in her palms, watching him. Testing him. "It's too salty."

"No, no. It's delicious, the best I've ever had."

"Good. How was your day? Did your training go well?"

"Very. I think this is going to work out just fine."

"Good.... Do you have a girl friend?"

Herakles held back his laughter, and his soup, but just barely. Greeks were so nosy, and of course she must have some relative she wanted to match him up with.

"Well, sort of."

"I hope it's not that Atlanta February. That's what everyone is saying. I don't believe it. You would never marry a Black girl would you?"

Katina's statement saddened Herakles, but it didn't catch him completely by surprise. He was well aware of the older generation's taboo against interracial marriage, which persisted somewhat even after the Millennium.

"As a matter of fact, I *was* referring to Alanta *January*, and frankly, if I love someone I don't care what color her skin is."

Katina looked shocked. She shook her head and got up from the table, muttering as she went back into the house. "I don't understand you young people these days. You should be marrying a nice Greek girl."

She soon returned, carrying a magnificent platter of food.

"I know it's hard for you to accept," Herakles went on, "but I was taught to treat everyone with the same respect, regardless of their color or creed. And that's what the Millennium was all about, removing the barriers which have kept us divided for all of these centuries. We have to learn to overcome our prejudices, don't you think?"

Ignoring him, Katina removed his soup bowl and set a full plate down in its place. A slight fragrance of nutmeg rose up from the large rectangular piece of macaroni casserole, topped with a creamy white sauce and baked golden brown. Next to it was an overstuffed eggplant with melted feta cheese. A cucumber and tomato salad with olives, peppers and more feta cheese filled the remaining space. "Ehh, I still think you should marry a nice Greek girl," she finally said. "There are many beautiful young women right here in our village. I could introduce you to them."

Herakles knew she meant well, so he set aside his frustration and tried to placate her. "We'll see. For now, I need to concentrate on my training, but after the Olympics, who knows?"

Katina lit up at the prospect. "I understand. First, you will win all of the gold medals, and then you can have your pick of the girls. I'm sorry, I didn't mean to upset you. Can I get you some more pastítso?"

"Thank you. I'd love another piece. It's all delicious."

And so Herakles ate, and ate – though he made sure to save a little room for the pastry Katina had prepared for dessert. She served it hot, right out of the oven, with phyllo crisped to such perfection, and a custard so light and creamy, it came close to touching the divine. There was only one thing left to do after a meal like that: go back into his room, meditate over the day and wait until sweet slumber overcame him. And that's exactly what he did.

He was only beginning to connect with this ancient and mystical place, but it was enough to reassure him that he'd made the right decision. As he lay falling asleep that night, the Spirit of Olympia danced at the foot of his bed, while the voices of his predecessors echoed deep within the recesses of his memory.

Subject: Olympia
From: Alanta@PlanetEarth.net
Date: July 23, 2004
To: Herakles@Gaia.net

Hey. Thanks for your email. You make Greece sound so mysterious, so exciting. I can't wait to get there! Sorry it's taken me so long to write back – things have been just crazy around here. Now, that CHAOS bunch is accusing me of using steroids and they're calling for my disqualification from the Games! They have nothing to base their allegations on except a supposed informant whose name they won't disclose. So, I had to pee on demand to prove my innocence, once again. I can't tell you how sick and tired I am of people always assuming that I couldn't have achieved what I have without using drugs. I know I'm clean, but I don't trust those tests 100%. It freaks me out to think they might actually be able to ruin my dream. (And Jimmy's this close to sayin' I told you so.)

Had a rotten training week – just can't seem to concentrate. I keep telling myself not to let it distract me, but it is. Bigtime.

Tell me more about Olympia and how you're getting along without Carl. I'm so proud of you for standing up for yourself and doing what you believe in. I'm with you in spirit, and in eight days, I'll be with you for *real.* Can't wait.

Missing you, Ajay

PS Is your Delphi trip still on?

Subject: Olympia
From: Herakles@Gaia.net
Date: July 24, 2004
To: Alanta@PlanetEarth.net

I suppose it wouldn't be right to cast the evil eye at CHAOS, but I admit, I am tempted. I'm so sorry they're stressing you out at this important time. Try not to worry though. Their credibility is virtually nil, and these days most people pay no attention to their brand of journalism. Their bogus allegations don't make you guilty, and everyone who matters knows that.

We all have frustrating periods during training, so try not to let this situation bother you too much. You need to put that energy into your practice, and focus on the positives – but you know all of that, and I know in the depths of my soul that you will win the gold.

Olympia has been fabulous and my training is going well, although I could use Carl to help contain the crowds. I've become somewhat of a local curiosity, and every day more people come to watch me practice. The staff has been extremely helpful and they're doing their best to keep the tourists from interfering, but it's becoming more difficult.

I've also got some CHAOS thugs of my own to contend with. They follow me everywhere, appearing from behind trashcans in dark alleys, that sort of pathetic behavior. One even hid in the restroom at the gym where I've been working out! They have no boundaries, no shame. Consequently, when I'm done with my day, I go directly to Katina's. Between CHAOS and the crowds, it's just too disruptive to spend much time in public.

I'm with you in spirit too, and counting the days.

XOXOXOX, h

PS Yes, the trip to Delphi is on. I'm going to consult the Oracle for a glimpse into our future....

# 9

## KRONOS' THUNDER

As Herakles was settling down into the starting blocks, he thought he saw a figure, a man, standing near the stone portal on the other side of the field. Before he could give it any more thought, Spiro yelled "go!" and he was off like sparks from a fire, sprinting full-out toward the hurdles. He easily cleared the first one, and the second and third, but then without warning, the very tip of his shoe clipped the fourth one, and with arms and legs flailing, he came crashing to the ground. He took the brunt of the fall with the palms of his hands, but he had so much momentum, he couldn't keep his chin from driving hard into the gravel. *Shit.*

He got up with that dreadful question, *how bad is it?* hanging in his mind like a cloud ready to burst. He touched his chin with the back of his hand, and crimson blood smeared across his knuckles. Bits of gravel lay imbedded in his scratched and bleeding hands, stinging fiercely. He checked his arms and legs which, other than a couple scrapes, seemed all right.

Spiro ran over to him, shocked by the ungraceful collapse. "Are you injured? Here, let me see."

"I'm fine."

"You need ice for your chin. Let me get some for you."

Herakles walked back to the starting line, shuddering at the thought of his worst nightmare: falling flat on his face just like that at the Games, for the whole world to see. Thank the Immortals that the fans and press had already left for the day – how he abhorred screwing up in front of them.

He played the humiliating moment over in his mind. *What went wrong? Why the concentration lapse?* As he questioned himself in search of a cause, he again noticed the man, and a cramp suddenly gripped him in the pit of his stomach. He couldn't discern the stranger's features at that distance, but instinctively, he knew it was Carl. He wasn't ready for this.

Spiro returned with some ice wrapped in a towel. "Here now, put this on the wound," he instructed, analyzing it. "Don't worry, it's not so bad."

Herakles pressed it against his chin, averting his eyes. "Thank you."

Spiro then noticed the man. "I don't know how he could have gotten in here. Excuse me while I go escort him to the exit."

"No, wait. I know who it is, and I'll talk with him myself."

"Very well."

He held the towel firmly, trying to stem the flow of blood, and once it seemed to be under control he started walking across the field.

*What should I say to him? Do I want him back?*

He was just getting used to training alone, but he had to admit that part of him would welcome Carl's return. As he approached the figure, he initially saw what his expectation told him to see: his old coach, standing there waiting for him. But then, in a few more steps, when he saw the man's mustache, he realized it wasn't Carl at all. It was his father, Alexander Speros!

Herakles froze in his tracks, the sight of him nearly taking his breath away. It had been four years since Alexander had disappeared. No calls, no messages, no visits, nothing. And now there he stood, like an apparition rising from heavy gray mist.

All Herakles knew was that after the Millennium, his father had been forced to resign as the Greek Ambassador to the UN because of his refusal to embrace the ideals of the New Era. Like the others who stubbornly clung to the old dominator ways when transformation swept the planet, Alexander vanished from the public sphere. Then, he deserted his family. Where he'd gone and what he'd done for all this time was a mystery to Herakles, who quite frankly, didn't give a damn. This man had caused his family too much pain, and as far as Herakles was concerned, his father's sudden return could only mean one thing: trouble.

He debated whether to turn around and walk away, as Alexander himself had done, or whether to approach and address him directly. Perhaps give him a few things to think about. He took note of his father's attire, and predictably, Alexander was still very much the old world diplomat, in his dark tailored suit, red striped tie and high-gloss wingtip shoes. He'd grayed over the years though, looking much older than Herakles had remembered.

As his eyes met his father's in stony silence, Apollo and Zeus looked on from beyond, judging the impending contest against their own.

Summoning his courage, Herakles again began walking toward him, closer and closer, until they stood at arm's length.

"Hello, son," Alexander said tentatively in Greek. "It has been far too long."

"That's a matter of opinion," Herakles shot back. "After what you did to us, I can assure you I have *not* been counting the days until your return."

"I can understand that. You have a right to be angry."

"You're damn right I do. And I am. What the *hell* are you doing here? And at a time like this. How typically egocentric and selfish."

"I've come to apologize, and to ask for your forgiveness."

"Cut the bullshit. What do you really want? Are you getting back into politics – looking for a photo opportunity perhaps? Where the hell have you been these past four years anyway? No, don't tell me. I don't care."

"I should have called or written, I know that now. But please try to understand, when the Great Phenomenon occurred, the world changed too quickly for me. I wasn't prepared, and I didn't know how to cope with it. That was difficult enough, but when your brother was dying, something inside me just snapped, and I completely withdrew."

"And now you've clawed your way back to reality and want forgiveness? I don't buy it, father. Why now? Just before the Olympics? No, you're scheming something else. I know you." He blotted another trickle of blood from his chin, trying to be nonchalant about the fresh wound.

"I tell you, son, I am not scheming. I come now because I have finally learned how to trust in my heart, and the time has come for me to follow it. I have searched long and hard and, though you may not feel compassion for me, I have endured much these past four years. I have been alone, as if lost in a vast, barren desert, trapped by an old way of thinking, and unsure of my place in the new society. However, through the experience, I have finally discovered my place, by rediscovering myself. I know now what is truly important. You are my flesh and blood, Herakles. I care about you, and about what you think of me. With humility, I ask for your forgiveness."

Herakles saw the tears in his father's eyes, but he didn't believe they were genuine. And he certainly wasn't ready to accept that Alexander had transformed. "Redemption is earned, father, not granted," he finally said. "You say you've changed, yet you come marching in here with your tragic tale just as I'm preparing for the most important test of my life. Did you give any thought to how your sudden confession would affect *me?* Or my training? I would wager not, and that seems very much like the old Alexander Speros to me."

"Very well, I can see that I have upset you. I assure you that was not my intention. It was a mistake for me to come here, and I will not bother you with my presence again. Good luck in the Olympics, son. I will be proud of you regardless of the outcome." Alexander turned to walk away, but then looked back. "And Herakles, my dear child, whether you believe it or not, I have always loved you and I always will."

Now great tears of lamentation came to the eyes of the son. A part of him wanted to believe his father, to run to him, embrace him and never let go again, but his loyalty to his mother and his unresolved anger held him back. He blinked through the teardrops, willing them away, and stood up straight and tall. "Goodbye, father," he called out after him, "and please, do not return." With head down, the older man walked slowly through the portal, disappearing once again.

Herakles felt his stomach muscles tightening and his jaws clenching, as rage suddenly surged through him with powerful waves, erupting from depths previously unknown. He tried to focus on his breathing, and to begin to reshape the jumbled mess of feelings running wild within him, but before he realized it, his feet had taken him off in a run, jumping him over the berm and past the ruins, then out into the open field. He circled around the back side of Mount Kronos, and for the first time noticed a narrow dirt trail leading up the hill. It was steep, and the dusty gravel gave way a few times under his feet, but he kept on, pushing faster and harder up the rugged slope, until he finally reached the summit, exhausted. When he saw the magnificent panorama, his anger suddenly transmuted to sadness. A profound, silent sadness, which stretched out to the stormy horizon.

Silver mist lightly covered the pasturelands and olive groves off in the distance. The sacred glade of Olympia lay below him, cradled between the two rivers as they meandered through the plain, flowing inexorably toward each other, to their confluence. There they joined together and continued on as one, far out to the sea.... So distant, the sea, and elusive – like his father.

All Herakles had ever wanted from him was his love, but that was the one thing Alexander had never expressed. And now, after all that had happened, he unexpectedly appears and says the words Herakles had longed his whole life to hear.

Suddenly, a tear welled up and rolled out of his somber brown eye. He quickly wiped it away, but it proved only to be the first of many more to come. He tried to resist them, but couldn't. They had been trapped so deep for so long, that when they finally found their way to the surface, he was overwhelmed. One after another, they spilled out in abundance, leaving two broad, salty trails down his rosy cheeks. He cried and cried, from the depths of his being he cried, the tears cascading down to the Earth, seeping into the sacred mountain named for the father of Zeus. A gentle rain began to fall, patting the ground, carefully collecting his bitter tears in a melancholy stream...carrying them on to the river...merging them back with the sea.

Herakles remained atop Mount Kronos until the muted Sun set on all of his childhood disappointments. By the time he came down in the gray dusk of early night, he allowed himself the possibility that perhaps his father could change. It would be taking a grave risk to find out, and if it were once again a deception, his devastation would be complete.... No. He was not yet ready to take that chance.

Sleep did not come easily to Herakles that night. He tossed and turned into the early hours, and when he finally did find slumber, it was anything but sweet. The moment he fell into its grip, he found himself standing alone, naked, in the center of a splendid coliseum. The Goddesses and Gods were all in attendance, watching at a distance from their golden thrones, and an unruly mob filled the stadium seats to capacity. On the field with him were two referees: Alexander and Carl, his father and his coach, standing stiffly on either side of him, each holding a spear in one hand and a shield in the other. Suddenly, a howl went up from the crowd as the heavy iron gate was opened and a tremendous beast came roaring into the stadium. Half lion, half human, it came charging on its two legs directly toward poor Kleo. When the creature was nearly upon him, it cast off its lionskin robe to reveal its true form: a huge, muscular man – the mythic warrior hero, Hercules!

As the demigod lunged, Kleo nimbly sidestepped him and the crowd cheered and whistled. The brute turned around, now furious, and came at him a second time. Like a matador, Kleo once again effortlessly stepped aside, letting Hercules charge past in a cloud of dust. However, as he was not armed with any blade of steel, he'd have to change his tactics with this bull. The dance would not work again. Hercules approached, this time more cautiously, holding his bulky arms outstretched as he looked for a way to grab hold of him. Kleo darted back and forth, keeping Hercules off guard, and the lumbering giant became frustrated and more angry. He came at Kleo and they went head to head, four strong arms grappling, a few steps to the left, and a few back to the right, each seeking to find an advantage, a weakness.

Kleo let up on his resistance, just enough to cause Hercules to overextend, then he jerked his arms downward, releasing the lock. As Hercules stumbled forward, off balance, Kleo took a pivot step to his right and, redirecting all of his energy, thrust his entire body into the brute's knees, tripping the mighty fighter to the ground. He quickly pounced on the broad, sturdy back of the old hero, firmly gripping him in a headlock. It took every ounce of Kleo's strength to subdue him, as he writhed and flailed, with club-like arms pounding the dusty ground and roars of anger and humiliation exploding from his powerful lungs. Kleo struggled on, repositioning himself with each mighty thrust, trying to maintain control. When the behemoth finally showed signs of fatigue, the fans jumped up on their stone benches and yelled, "kill him! kill him! kill him!" Without emotion, the Immortals looked on, and the referees stood silent.

Kleo could have easily finished him off with a mighty twist of the neck, but he didn't. Instead, he released his grip, stood up and walked away from the defeated hero. The onlookers threw stones and half-eaten thigh bones down from the stands, hissing and boo-ing, but then suddenly, their displeasure reverted to excitement. Kleo turned around just as the beast rammed into him, knocking him hard to the ground. As he hit the floor of the coliseum, he awoke with a start.

He sat straight up in bed, eyes wide, breathing heavily. Rivu-lets of sweat poured down from his temples and chilled his back. He clutched at the bedsheets, for a moment seeing the gruesome spectacle again, there in the room in front of him. Flinging the covers aside, he got up and poured a tall glass of water. He drank it down, feeling somewhat revived, then sat on the side of the bed and recorded the dream in his journal, carefully sketching Hercules' fantastic lionskin robe. He checked the time, 5:50. The Sun would start rising shortly, so he completed his account of the bizarre episode and readied himself for another day of training.

He went through the motions of breakfast and the morning workout, preoccupied and irritated, barely aware of the present. Despite the cheery demeanor he manufactured for his daily press conference, it was a fiasco. They wouldn't drop it about the scraped chin, and his fans were sympathetic, but disappointed that their hero had fallen. He cut the autograph signing short and threw himself into the afternoon workout. His concentration was off, and as the day dragged on, it only got worse. Still, he knew he couldn't stop until he faced the hurdles, even though he was dreading it.

It was a solid start, and with strong, deliberate steps, he easily cleared each of the ten hurdles and crossed the line with a decent finish time. Not his best run by any measure, but after yesterday, all he wanted was a good clean one, and that's what he got. He circled back around for another rep, then suddenly stopped dead in his tracks, in utter disbelief. Just inside the portal, a tall figure stood staring at him with powerful intent.

"Spiro!" he called loudly, trying desperately to keep his anger in check. "Would you please escort my father out of here and inform him he will no longer be allowed in to see me?"

"Yes, of course. I will speak with Costa at the front gate as well."

Herakles thanked him, and then trotted over to the water cooler to have a drink. He surreptitiously watched Spiro's exchange, but instead of having the pleasure of watching his father be escorted out, Spiro started running back over to him. The sinking feeling returned to his stomach.

"Kleo," Spiro said, trying to catch his breath, "that man is not your father. It's your former coach, Carl Richter!"

"It is? You're sure?"

"Yes, of course I'm sure. Do you want to speak with him?"

"Uhh...yes...okay. I'll talk to him."

"Very well."

Herakles walked across the field, this time keeping his skeptical eye squarely on the man. No more optical illusions. He wanted to be absolutely sure before he got too close. When he could clearly see Carl's Germanic features, a sense of relief overtook him, and he broke into a jog toward him.

"Hello, Carl. What a surprise," Herakles began, reaching out his hand.

Carl stepped forward, and with his familiar wooden demeanor, gave him the old trademark vicegrip. Though when he noticed the cut on Herakles' chin, his chiseled face softened a little. "Well, I'll get right to the point." He released his hand. "I've come to apologize to you, Kleo. My anger was misplaced. I was furious with you for pursuing this Olympia training – what I believed to be a folly with no place in a serious regimen. First, it pissed me off that I had originally agreed with this ludicrous idea. Of course, I also had the expectation that you would let go of it when the time came. Then, when you insisted on pursuing it, the questions began to gnaw at me. What if it jeopardized your success? What if the Games came and you were not ready? It would certainly be my fault as your coach. I would have failed you.

"That was bad enough, but then, what angered me to the point of irrationality, was that I couldn't see how 'following your dream' as you put it, could be an asset to your performance. And this led me right to my own narrow-mindedness. I have, how do you say, *meditated*, about this, and it occurs to me that I have been trying to deny the importance of your spiritual development. I have trivialized your intangible needs. Your need, like everyone else's, to connect to that which is larger than ourselves, that which nurtures and sustains us beyond our physical existence.

"I have always been more comfortable thinking about technique – counting repetitions, dissecting the discreet elements of a perfect discus throw, analyzing your carbohydrate conversion rates. You have helped me see that a meal is more than a calorie count. That the love and familiar ingredients which go into its preparation are just as important. That the perfect discus throw requires more than the sum of its elements perfectly executed.

"And while I've always known this to some degree, I've recently realized that for most of my life, from my early days in communist

East Germany until now, I have approached athletics as something to be 'mastered.' The exercise of dominion over one's body and one's emotions, in the futile attempt to control them. From you, I have learned that a more effective approach is to find the harmony amongst the different facets of our selves – the biological, emotional and spiritual – and then mix them together in a great hearty brew and drink them down. I know I can be stubborn, but I believe that's a trait we share. If you'll take me back, I'd like to be your coach again."

"Here in Olympia?"

"Yes. I want you to win the gold and I think you need me to do it."

Herakles was astonished. Carl was finally coming around, finally beginning to understand him. He suddenly realized how unfair it had been to link Carl so closely with Alexander. Sure, there were similarities of attitude and habit, but Carl had engendered trust between them. He honored his word and had always been straight with him. Carl was not a conniver and manipulator like his father, and he was sincerely attempting to bridge their differences, where his father's attempt had seemed hollow.

"I appreciate your candor, Carl, and as I feel grateful for all of the good advice you've given me, I'm glad to have given you some insight in return. I'm sorry we had such a strong disagreement, but I have always respected you as a coach. I know I'd never have made it this far without you."

Carl smiled. "Yes, I saw your message to me on tv. Thank you."

Herakles nodded. "I would like very much for you to be my coach again, but there's just one other thing we need to agree on."

"An amendment?"

"Yes. I've made plans to go to Delphi the day before the facilities open in Athens."

"For what purpose?"

"Ordinarily, I never would have told you directly, but since you seem to have had a change of heart, I will. I had two very vivid, very specific dreams, one on the night before I testified at the UN, and the other on the night before our falling out. The Goddess Athena appeared and told me that I *must* make the journey to Delphi before I go to Athens. She, or my subconscious, or whatever you want to call it, told me it was imperative. I feel compelled to go."

"More links to the ancestors, no doubt."

"Yes, Carl," Kleo answered, laughing. "Something like that."

"Is that it? Any other side trips or vision quests you need to accomplish before you compete?"

"That's it. I promise."

"All right," Carl agreed, grasping Herakles' hand in another mighty shake. "Now tell me, what in the world happened to your chin?"

And so Herakles and Carl were reunited. The tension between them was now gone and each man respected the other for what he had done. Many would have gone their separate ways and never spoken another word, but these two had moved through their anger and frustration to a place of empathy and understanding, thereby strengthening their bond from that time hence.

Herakles had hoped it would be enough to help him quell the raging torrent of emotion he was feeling toward his father. But that was not to be, and the next week turned out to be nothing short of a training disaster. Alexander's appearance had opened a wound deeper than he realized, and deeper than he was able to cope with. His attempts at meditation were superficial at best, and the willpower which had always been effective at pushing Alexander to the recesses of his mind simply did not seem strong enough. Like a spirit suspended between worlds, his father's essence hung about him heavier than a wet wool coat, appearing in his dreams, and occasionally even revealing itself in broad daylight. The harder he tried to push it away, the more persistent it became, taunting him with doubt. *You shouldn't have come to Olympia*, it would say to him, *perhaps I wouldn't have found you. What a pity, and you were doing so well....* Yes, he had been doing well, until the unwelcome visit, when everything started falling apart. His timing and balance were off, and his mind unfocused. He'd become increasingly frustrated with each passing day, and though he tried hard to regain his composure, he knew his father was getting the best of him.

He stood at the far end of the runway, holding the long, flexible pole at his side. Like all decathlon events, the pole vault required complete concentration. Unlike the others, however, this event catapulted the vaulter upside-down 19+ feet in the air. He looked up at the crossbar slicing through the overcast sky, and for a moment he doubted his ability to clear it. He shook off the feeling and tried to imagine himself in perfect form – takeoff, tuck, rockback, extension – up and over the bar.

He nodded to Carl, who nodded back, and then he started his approach. His form and timing seemed aligned, but when he planted the pole in the box, somehow he overstepped his mark, completely throwing off his angle – and there wasn't a thing he could do about it. He was committed. Off-balance, he ricocheted up into the air, his feet barely missing the bar, and as he tried to get himself over, his chin smashed into it, ripping off the scab from his previous wound. He landed flat on his back in the pit, and the bar came crashing down on top of him.

The crowd groaned.

Blood streamed down his chin as he laid there, eyes clamped shut, wanting to cry. *Why is this happening? Why now?*

"Kleo! Kleo, are you okay?" Carl called, running over.

Herakles rolled off the mat and sat down in the dirt behind the giant cushion, out of sight from the press tent.

"You need some ice," Carl said. "Hold on. I'll get it." He came back and handed it to him. "Don't worry, everything will be okay."

"I wish I could believe that."

Carl sat beside him. "Look, Kleo, I've noticed the trouble all week. At first, I thought it was just the temporary lack of discipline you experienced with my absence, but now I can see it runs much deeper. Something profound is bothering you. So much so that you're completely out of balance. Your...dimensions are not in alignment," he nudged him, trying to lighten things up.

But the poor dejected soul couldn't even manage to fake a smile. "No. Definitely not in alignment."

"What is it?"

"I don't know."

"I think you do know. Please, tell me. Maybe I can help you."

"I don't want to talk about it."

"Kleo, this is not easy for me to say, because it is so important to reaffirm your confidence at this crucial time, but I believe that if you do not resolve the matter, you could be jeopardizing your chances at the Games."

Just then, out of the corner of his eye, Herakles noticed a camera peeking around the corner of the thick mat. "Will you please do something about them, Coach?" he yelled loudly. "They're driving me nuts!"

Carl scrambled to his feet, calling to Spiro, and the two men converged on the CHAOS reporter. Carl walked him off the field while Spiro informed the crowd and the rest of the press that they would be leaving for the day. When everyone had gone, Carl returned and again sat down beside Herakles, who was now under the sturdy old oak, still holding the ice pack to his chin.

It took Herakles a few minutes before he was finally ready to break the silence. "It's my father, Alexander Speros. He came here the day before you arrived and ruined everything. Coach, I wish you could have seen me before he turned up. I was performing better than ever, and now, I can't...I just can't get him out of my mind. He's everywhere. Even when I sleep, he stalks me, hunts me down in my dreams."

"I see."

"I thought I'd come to terms with those feelings, but after seeing him, I realize I haven't. I've just pushed them aside all these years."

"That's the first step in dealing with those strong emotions, Kleo. Looking at them square on; asking yourself how long you want to hold onto your anger toward him."

"As if it's my choice, Coach."

"Oh, but it is, Herakles. Tell me, do you see yourself feeling this way for, say, five years? Twenty-five? Fifty? Hmm?"

"I don't know."

"But you can agree that, hopefully, a time will come when you will not feel such rage, yes?"

"Yes."

"So begin looking for that place now. Perhaps a resolution with your father will come, perhaps it won't, but how will tormenting yourself achieve anything? Your father will be who he is no matter how you feel about him. Let the anger go."

Herakles lifted the icepack from his chin. "How bad is it?"

"Someone must be looking out for you. It's superficial; it will heal in no time."

"Damn it. Why did he have to come *now*? Why?"

"You know I can't answer that question, but perhaps one day you will be able to ask him yourself. In the meantime, I can only advise you to look into your heart, and try to find compassion for him. Perhaps he too has suffered in ways you do not know."

"*His* suffering?"

"Yes, Kleo. Your father has lived on this Earth for over sixty years. He has undoubtedly experienced many things."

Herakles fell silent. In a little while, he could again hear the birdsong of the forest and the breeze in the treetops, and he brightened ever so slightly. "Well, what now, Coach?" he asked, setting the ice pack down.

"I think it's time to conclude the Olympia chapter of your saga — we were only going to practice half a day anyway. You can get some extra rest this afternoon, and tonight, you'll be on your way to Delphi."

"I don't want to leave on such a sour note."

"Look at it this way, you've started down the path of resolution. It is a new beginning. The first few steps are always difficult, but they will get easier."

Carl stood up and reached out his hand. Herakles grasped it, looking into the deep blue eyes he'd once thought so rigid and stern, but which now seemed gentle and kind. "We'll get through this together, Kleo, I promise." Carl put his arm around Herakles' shoulder and the two men walked off the field.

And so they gathered up their belongings, gave final instructions to Spiro and left the Sacred Grove of Altis for the last time. No crown of laurel, no victory goblet, just a humbled athlete traversing the depths of his soul, comforted by his loyal coach. As they entered the portal leading off the field, Herakles turned around for one more look. Spiro and some of the groundskeeping staff were already starting to tear down the equipment, and the clouds were ready to burst. They turned to leave just as heavy raindrops began to fall, purposefully, methodically from the infinite sky above, anointing Herakles for the initiation yet to come.

After a luke-warm shower and lunch at Katina's, he excused himself to his room. He sat down on the middle of the bed, with his legs loosely crossed and open palms resting gently on his knees. A muted light beam came in through the window, creating a large rectangle on the wooden floor. He concentrated on it, breathing in deeply through his nose, and out through his mouth, trying to relax. A few minutes passed, and as the shape slowly, imperceptibly elongated into a parallelogram, his eyelids grew tired and heavy. Then suddenly, like thick, red velvet curtains falling down upon a theater stage, they shut out the room around him.

In the blackness of his mind's eye, a spiral staircase suddenly appeared, with its pearly white marble glowing in a golden light, beckoning him to descend. He gently placed his hand on the banister, feeling the cool, smooth surface with his fingertips. He started down the stairs, taking a slow, measured step with each breath. One by one, releasing the tension, letting go of his anxiety, moving through his boundaries of reason and rationality, as he searched for his inner self…his deep self.

At the bottom of the stairs, the air grew cold and snowflakes began to fall. He felt alone, afraid, almost panicked, but then a figure emerged from the storm. As it took shape, he realized it was his brother. *Iphe! Is it really you?*

*No, it's really you. We're one and the same, remember?*

*I miss you.*

*I'm always with you in your heart, dear brother, you know that.*

*I need your help.*

*I know. It's about father.*

*He's come back, claiming he's changed, but I don't trust him.*

*Come with me.*

As Iphe turned and walked away, a cruel wind rose up, whipping the flakes into a raging blizzard. Herakles hurried after him, trying to keep him in sight. They went a great distance, trudging through drifts of accumulating snow, until eventually, they came to a tall metal door.

Standing outside were their parents, arguing with each other.

"This could be it, Alex. You have to go to him."

"I can't," Alexander snapped back. "And I won't. I want nothing more to do with him, or with any of you. I'm leaving and I'm not coming back." With that, their father vanished in the tempest.

Herakles looked at his brother, who pointed at the door, urging him to go through. He grasped its thick, brass handle, thrust it open, and suddenly he was at the foot of the bed in the hospital room where Iphe died, four years earlier. Iphe was there, hooked up to IVs and monitors, struggling to breathe, and their mother was at his side, gently stroking his head.

*He never came to see you, did he? Not once.*

Iphe sat up and took the respirator mask off of his face. *No he didn't, Kleo.*

*He didn't even come to your funeral.*

*Boy, are you angry.*

*Your damn right I'm angry — the way he's treated us, and especially the way he treated you. I'm angry that he was never there when we needed*

*him. And about his drinking and volatile, unpredictable temper.*
*What's underneath the anger?*
*I don't know what you mean.*
*What are your deeper feelings?*
*Abandonment. Disappointment. And I'm not sure he ever loved me.*
*Difficult emotions, aren't they?*
*Yes! I need guidance. I need your help.*
*I can't help you. I'm dead. Only you can help yourself.*
Herakles looked at his mother. *What should I do?*

She opened her mouth to answer, but then the hospital room disappeared and he found himself standing in the snowstorm once again. He reached into the whiteness, groping for the staircase railing, and much to his relief he found it. He tried pulling himself onto the first step, but a fierce gale blew him down and backward, nearly knocking him over. He grasped the banister with both hands, and against the great weight of the wind and snow, arduously dragged himself up the steps. At last he could see the top. The snowfall lightened, then stopped, and he started feeling warmer. As he neared the last step, he felt himself coming awake, returning to the awareness of his room.

When he finally opened his eyes, he noticed that the gray sunlight had disappeared. He remained calm and still, allowing the impressions of his experience to settle in. After a few minutes, he laid back on the bed, cradling his head in the pillows and stretching out his long legs. He thought about the vision, and about his brother and mother, then fell into a shallow, restless sleep.

Three hours later, he awoke to the sound of the Olympic anthem coming from his cell phone, somewhere inside his half-packed suitcase. He searched through the clothes and stuff, finally locating it. "Embrós? Hello?"

"Honeymou, how are you? I've been thinking so strongly of you, I just had to call."

"Mom! I'm so glad to hear your voice!"

"What is it? What's wrong?"

"It's father. He came to see me." His voice trailed off.

"Oh, no! What happened?"

"Everything was going exactly as I had hoped, until he arrived. My practices were better than ever, I was feeling the connection to Olympia, drawing strength and confidence from the sheer magic of the place – and then without warning, he just appeared at the field six days ago, full of apology and woe. Three weeks before the most important event of my life! And I knew something was wrong when I set out for those hurdles, then I wiped out, slashing my chin. I had to confront him with blood running down my face. I told him to go away, and he did, but ever since I saw him, I can't get him out of my mind. He haunts me in every thought and I just *can't* concentrate."

"Why didn't you call me?"

"I didn't want to worry you. You have enough to contend with where he's concerned."

"Thank you for trying to protect me, Herakles, but I'm strong. I have room enough for your problems too. Tell me, then what happened?"

"Then, thank the Immortals, Carl came back, and he's been wonderful. It's almost as though he's undergone a transformation. He's being much more understanding, and I think we've worked through our differences. I'm so grateful he returned, but I still can't get you-know-who out of my mind and there's nothing Carl can do about that."

"It's true. Only you can find your peace within."

"Easy to say, but how? I'm furious with him, and I can't seem to tune out the anger anymore."

"Then you must work through it, turn it into something positive. You have a lot of energy invested in your anger, son, so much so that it's consuming you. But if you can turn those feelings of hostility and bitterness into compassion and forgiveness, I believe you will regain your confidence."

"Compassion! Forgiveness! How can I forgive him after what he did to us? Have you forgiven him?"

"I'm trying, though I confess, it has not been easy. However, I also realize that unless we forgive him and transform our pain, he can continue to hurt us."

"I will *not* forgive him. Tell me, why does he deserve it?"

"It's not about what he deserves, it's about the continuation of *your* suffering. You certainly don't deserve this."

"So, you think I should invite him back into my life?"

"That's up to you."

"Would you see him again?"

"For the time being, no, though he's made no effort to contact me either. If he called, I would decide then."

"So how am I supposed to forgive him?"

"He is not evil to the core, Kleo. Try focusing on his good qualities, the ones I fell in love with; the ones which are also present in you."

"Like what?"

"He's adventurous, artistic, witty, and he can be very charming. And you have to admit, he is brilliant."

"Those things are so buried under what he's become."

"This may be true, but you have to understand, Herakles, we're all products of the culture that raised us. Sometimes we reflect the best parts of that culture, and sometimes the worst. As a young child, your father survived the second world war, with the Nazi occupation of Greece. Then he endured the five years of civil war that followed. You and I can't begin to imagine it."

"It doesn't give him the right to desert his family when we needed him most."

"No, it doesn't, but please try to see that many factors have shaped his life. The more you understand him, the easier it will be for you to forgive him."

"I'm too angry to forgive him."

"Please, Kleomou, don't let that anger harden you. You have a heart of gold, and beautiful dreams for yourself and the world – and just look at the world we live in now! Whole nations have learned to transform their age-old hatreds, to forgive their most bitter enemies. You too can transform your feelings, and when you do, it will be as though a great weight has been lifted. Promise me you'll try, for your own sake."

"I'll think about what you've said."

"I'm here whenever you need to talk about it."

"Thanks, mitéramou, I don't know what I'd do without you."

"That goes both ways. You are the light of my life, and I'm so excited to see you!"

"I should be at Thea Vasso's tomorrow evening as planned."

"I'll look forward to it. And I'll look forward to seeing you win that gold. You can do it, Kleo, I know you can."

"I appreciate your faith in me."

"Tell me now, how is Alanta?"

"As you might have heard, she's been facing false accusations of steroid use, and that's been difficult. She's resilient though, she'll overcome it."

"I can't wait to meet her."

"You'll get along beautifully."

"I'm sure of it. Now, you be careful in Delphi, promise?

"Promise."

"And I'll see you in Athens tomorrow night. Call anytime you need to talk, I'll keep my phone on. I love you."

"I love you too."

He hung up and checked his watch. Still over an hour before he had to catch the bus. He turned on the light and surveyed the room, planning his departure. Just a few more things to pack. Thankfully, Carl helped him out with the equipment and his stuff, so all he had to carry was a light backpack with some food and water, and Katina had already seen to that. He collected some of the remaining clothes, and as he passed by the mirror, his reflection caught his eye.

He looked hard at the features of his own face, trying to identify those he shared with his father: high cheekbones, intense brown eyes, full lips, olive skin. For a moment, the face looking back in the mirror became his father's. He blinked the illusion away, but couldn't deny it, he looked more like Alexander than he had ever admitted to himself. So did that mean he had a self-destructive side too? Lurking deep within him somewhere, ready to explode without warning in a fit of rage, or manifesting itself in the overindulgence for which his father was renowned? Herakles had always felt so in control, but now he feared that side of himself which might be there, buried underneath, ticking like a bomb that could go off at any time. *Focus on his good qualities*, his mother had said.

Herakles turned away from his reflection and tried to do as he'd promised. As he threw the last of his belongings together, he searched the realm of his memory, thinking, *good memories, good memories.* Yes, there were the sailing trips around the Greek Isles when he was a child. His father loved being out on the sea, and was usually in good spirits then. They'd sail from one port to the next, eating lots of seafood and meeting up with friends and relatives along the way. And then there were the parties. Alexander would often take center stage to sing songs or tell stories, mesmerizing the crowd with his intellect and humor. For every good memory, a dozen bad ones surfaced, but at least it was a start.

He took a final look around the room and under the bed, then closed up his bags and left. Carl was waiting for him downstairs with Katina, who was drying a fresh round of tears over his departure. He thanked her profusely for her hospitality and excellent cooking, and she shoved two more packages of food in his backpack, making him promise to eat it all. He assured her he would, then said his goodbyes and headed toward the door. The splendid Boubalina even made a surprise appearance, as if to say farewell. She stretched out across the threshold, eyeing him with her languid lids, and purring for further affection. It worked, for a moment, and Herakles knelt down to scratch her behind the ears one last time, before stepping out into the rain.

As he made his way through the cobblestone streets and into the heart of old Olympia town, he had to dodge dripping awnings and jump over fresh puddles to avoid getting his sneakers completely soaked. It wasn't raining too hard at the moment, since the cloudburst two blocks from Katina's, and he thought it might even be letting up a bit. Then he passed by an alley, where the rainwater was gushing out of large orange clay pipes, forming six discreet waterfalls, all flowing together into a formidable stream and collecting in a pond around the drainage grate. *Maybe not.*

A fine mist was rising overhead, encircling the streetlights, creating starbursts against the darkening sky. As he approached the bus terminal, the mist thickened into a steely gray fog, sending a chill down his spine. He found a table under the old wooden awning and pulled a sweatshirt from his pack. He put it on, sat down on a little green chair, and waited for the bus to arrive.

# 10

# THE ORACLE AT DELPHI

Out of the vapor it emerged, like a medieval dragon, with yellow eyes shooting long beams, and metal body groaning to a halt in front of him. Its marquis confirmed his destination: Δελφι. The doors opened with a great ratcheting sound, and he hesitantly stepped aboard.

The old driver peered out from under his black sailor's cap, and something about him seemed vaguely familiar. Not giving it another thought, Herakles handed over the fare and took a seat toward the back of the empty bus. The driver threw it into gear, stepped on the gas and they continued down the journeying ways. Herakles tried in vain to get comfortable in the cramped, hard seat, eventually deciding to use his backpack as a pillow. He leaned up against it and stared idly out the window at the merciless, pelting rain. Surely not the way he had hoped to leave Olympia – depressed, confused and waterlogged. *Trust the path,* he tried to remind himself. *Trust the path I've chosen. When Zeus opens the Heavens to unleash a fierce and unyielding storm, there's nothing to be done but wait. The rain and this long night will eventually pass.*

However, at the moment, that still seemed a great distance away to poor Herakles.

The bus bounced and splashed its way out of town, and soon they were alone on the sparsely lit road. As he stared out into the void, vivid deathbed images of his brother cycled through his mind. Images he'd been able to keep at bay, which, like his feelings for his father, were now for some reason thrust into his present awareness. *Why now?* He kept asking himself, *why couldn't it wait until after the Games?*

Kilometer after kilometer, there was nothing but empty road, until they encountered the lights of Pírgos. As they passed through the small town, thick fog obscured the streetlights and storefronts, and not a single soul was visible. They continued on up the highway, soon coming to a "y" in the road, but instead of going north as they should have, they started heading west into the darkness. *Damn, the old man has lost his way.* It was an easy enough mistake to make in this weather, but still, it was extremely irritating. He sighed with exasperation and went up to the front of the bus.

"Excuse me sir, but aren't we supposed to be driving north by now, toward Pátrai?"

The old man cracked a smile but stared straight ahead, saying nothing.

"Can you hear me?" Herakles said a little louder, "I said I think you missed the turn."

"I am not deaf, young man." He turned and winked. "I can hear you quite well."

"Sir, I apologize for raising my voice, but I'm concerned that we're traveling on the wrong road."

"You are going to Delphi, aren't you?"

"Yes I am, and I know the right road is back there."

"It's not the only way. Sit back and relax, young man, relax."

Herakles still wasn't convinced. He kept silent for another few minutes, but as they headed further off track, he could bite his tongue no longer. "Sir, I'm sorry to interrupt you again, but surely by now you recognize that we took a wrong turn."

"Hang on!" The driver made a hard left onto a bumpy gravel road. "We're almost there."

Herakles grabbed onto the bar to steady himself. "What?

We've just started! There are many more hours to drive."

"You are mistaken," the driver replied, bringing the bus to a stop. "We won't be driving to Delphi at all. We're going to sail there." He opened the doors, took the keys and walked off into the foggy night.

"You must be out of your mind. Come back here! Wonderful. This is just what I need right now." Herakles ran to the back to retrieve his pack, then hurried off the bus. The fog was so thick he could barely see three feet in front of him. "Driver! Where are you? This is not amusing." He listened for a response, but heard only the sea lapping up against the nearby shore. Then a bell rang, and he followed the sound slowly, carefully, down a dirt path to a dock. "Driver? Driver, are you there? Answer me." A lantern appeared in the fog and Herakles could just make out the contours of what looked to be a 30-foot sloop. Finally, he heard the driver's voice.

"I will answer you, Herakles Speros. What is it you wish to know?"

Herakles approached the boat, and could finally see the old man, sitting next to a massive wooden steering wheel under the hanging lamp. "Who are you? And just what do you think you're doing?

The driver laughed. "I am called Mentes, and I am here to escort you to Delphi."

"*Mentes*," Herakles repeated, now laughing too. "Oh, I *see*. An incarnation of the Goddess Athena herself, no doubt, coming here to carry me off on my journey to find my father – just as you guided the young Telemachos to far away places, in search of his father, Odysseus. I get it. Very clever. Okay, who put you up to it? Alexander?"

"This is no deception, Herakles," Mentes replied, now more assertively. "Please, step aboard and prepare to set sail."

"But the port of Itéa is almost two hundred kilometers from here!"

"I assure you, we will be there by sunrise tomorrow."

"In this fog? Are you crazy? The air is barely moving."

"Look," the old man said, waving his hand toward the sky, "the fog is beginning to lift." Sure enough, one by one, the stars became visible. "And Notos is coming with a strong and steady wind." A breeze ruffled the slackened sail.

Herakles was suddenly taken off guard, and he didn't know what to say.

"Don't say anything," Mentes instructed. "Please. Let loose the moorings and come aboard."

Herakles had to admit that the timing of those coincidences spooked him...and just now, it seemed as though Mentes knew what was on his mind and answered him before he had a chance to speak.... Still, the old man appeared harmless enough, and sailing to Delphi was certainly tempting, but the whole idea was preposterous.

Yet, there was also a mystery here he didn't want to try to explain. Looking out over the wine-dark Sea, he felt a stirring deep within, urging him to take the chance. Relying on that instinct, he untied the line and boarded the boat. "Okay, *Mentes*, I just hope you can sail."

"For thousands of years I've sailed."

"Yes of course, what was I thinking? The magnificent bright-eyed Athena can do many splendid things."

"You've sailed too, haven't you, son?"

"Yes, as you must know, when I was a boy."

"Very well then. Raise the main and make fast the headstay!"

Herakles stowed his shoes and pack below, then took hold of the halyard and raised the large white sail up the sturdy wooden mast. He secured the jib sail at the bow and then returned to the cockpit.

"Now pull in the sheet and off we go to Delphi."

Herakles did so, and the smaller forward sail came to life.

Mentes checked the wind. "Trim it in, just a little."

Herakles gave the sheet a tug and tied it off in two figure eights around the brass cleat. A southerly wind filled the sails and the boat responded, momentarily lifting out of the water. Herakles felt his heart flutter, and as they started picking up speed, a sense of exhilaration overcame him – the salty breeze blowing through his loose, curly hair, and the sound of the wooden hull moving through the water. *How strange, I was just thinking about sailing earlier today....*

Mentes put out the lantern, and everything suddenly went black. As Herakles' eyes began to adjust, and he became oriented to their direction, the Universe unfolded before him. Hera's milk sprayed across the moonless sky, creating the arc of our Milky Way Galaxy. Cygnus the Swan and Aquila the Eagle soared through the starry expanse, while gas giant Jupiter passed close to hot, blue Vega, and Venus and Mars set together along the western horizon.

Mentes had been watching him as he surveyed the sky. "To which famous land does the Great Bear lead?"

Herakles smiled knowingly. "If we follow the nose of Kallisto, she will take us to a most well-known land indeed. To an island not 70 kilometers from here, lying low and broad on the waters of this temperate Ionian Sea. Its expansive plain faces east, toward Helios' eternal rising, resting beneath the shadow of leaf-trembling Mount Neritos. It is a rugged place, and to this day, most certainly a fine nurse of women and men. Why, it is none other than sunny Itháki – home of the great Odysseus, the hero most favored by Pallas Athena."

Mentes smiled as if pleased with his answer. "Yes, in days long ago, Odysseus was most favored by me, but now I have found a new hero to nurture."

Herakles snickered. "And that would be me."

"Yes, my young friend. Glory awaits you, but there are great dangers ahead, and you must be at peace to face them."

Herakles didn't like the sound of that. "What do you mean, dangers?"

"They will be revealed to you when you are ready to hear them. However, I will tell you this: you were correct to compare yourself to bold-hearted Telemachos, the dear son of godlike Odysseus. For like him, you are also on a journey to find your father."

"I don't know if I want to find him or not."

"And unlike Telemachos, who held his father in the highest esteem and risked great personal harm to find him, you yourself can find no love for Alexander."

"He doesn't deserve my love."

"Perhaps. In any event, you must heal your wounded heart, for your own sake."

Herakles fell silent as Mentes' words echoed in his mind. He stared out over the water, now with more questions to contemplate than ever. It wasn't enough to be faced with the pain his father had rekindled. No. Now he was on this precarious, wayward journey in the middle of the ocean, and with whom, he knew not.

*Who was behind this inventive charade? And where did they find this Mentes?*

It seemed so much like a dream, yet it was much more coherent than when last he sailed with Athena, to Olympia, from the Long Island Sound – when he woke up safe and secure in his bed. This experience was somehow different. More like those moments in the Sacred Grove, when he found the peacock feather, and with Alanta when they shared the orange crescent Moon from the precipice – when the veil between worlds seemed translucent. After a long while, he looked at Mentes, who again spoke as if in response.

"Trust the path you have chosen, Herakles, for like the meandering way of the labyrinth, your path *will* lead you to center, though it may be a long and circuitous route. And through it all, no matter how far away your destination may seem, you must continue to believe in yourself – lest the Sea send a wave a second time to douse those burning embers of doubt." He winked again.

Herakles stared at him, mystified at how Mentes could know about that, when he was certain he'd only told Alanta. "How do you know of my dream, Mentes? Please, tell me."

"You know the answer to that question. You need only admit it to yourself."

"That beneath the old seafarer seated before me, you're really the Goddess Athena, who herself accompanied me on that voyage. Mentes, I just can't accept that in a literal sense. No offense, but you Immortals are metaphors, projections of the human psyche. You have a great deal to teach us, but you do not manifest yourselves in corporeal form."

Mentes laughed heartily. "My dear Herakles, you must try to understand. You are entering the Mythic Realm, where your reality and what you call metaphor intersect...where the veil between worlds is translucent...." Mentes eyed him closely, seeming to gauge his disbelief. "I have been with you a good many of your years, young Herakles, though you have not noticed me until recently."

Just then, a pod of dolphins appeared, streaming through the water alongside the boat. They temporarily distracted Herakles from his metaphysical conundrum, and he went to the railing, reaching out to them over the side. He could hear their breath on the waves; the brisk spout of the exhale, and the short sucking sound of the inhale.

They had been his guiding spirits since childhood, when he first encountered them while sailing the Aegean with his family. He'd imagined himself as one of them, swimming across the ocean, seeking adventure and companionship, thoroughly enjoying the moment. He always interpreted their appearance as an affirmation, or good omen, which was particularly welcome at present.

Then, as quickly as they came, they left again, disappearing into the depths. He turned to Mentes. "I was half expecting your brother, Apollo Delphinios, to assume the form of one of those fair and pleasant creatures, leap aboard our vessel and try to enlist me to serve at his temple at Delphi."

Mentes smiled. "Indeed, bright Herakles, but I believe Apollo is otherwise occupied at present. You will meet him soon enough."

"Yes, of course I will..."

"Look, there in the distance, to port off the bow. The lighthouse at Mesolóngion. We are approaching the channel which leads to the Gulf of Kórinthos."

"Already? I'll say it's a favorable wind!"

"I have often encountered rough seas at the inlet, and surely, the waters are beginning to rise. You would do well to hold fast."

Herakles returned to the cockpit and braced himself, as the swells rose higher and higher, growing into dark mountains of water all around them. Their craft was tossed about, and waves came crashing onto the deck, sending a chill through him. He tightened his grip, for even if this was a dream, he had no desire to be swept away. Up and over the billowing waves they went, rocking side to side to side.

"Ready about!" Mentes called out, as he released the jib sheet from port and pulled it in to starboard. "Tacking!"

Herakles ducked to avoid the boom as it swung fiercely to the other side, where the mighty wind again caught the jib and filled the main. They continued on through treacherous waters, tacking again and again to maintain their course and speed. Finally, after what seemed like forever, they came to the narrowest part of the strait and the waters began to quiet. Jagged rock formations jutted out from either shore, their sinister forms like shadow phantoms piercing the starry sky. *Surely, Prometheus himself must for eternity be lashed to these monstrous crags….*

The waterway widened as they entered the Gulf, and the ominous cliffs receded into the distance, putting Herakles more at ease. Mentes then called upon Zephyros, who sent an agreeable wind to carry them east toward the port of Itéa. If it held, they should arrive by sunrise, just as he was promised.

He went onto the deck and sat down, resting his back against the mast. For a long time he remained there, staring into the Heavens, feeling peaceful and relaxed, and concerning himself no more with the perplexing questions of his present situation.

Cygnus and Aquila flew with Night toward the west, and soon the Gemini Twins rose in the east, bringing with them the first light of morning. As the early glow brightened, the twin peaks of Parnassós emerged, bold and mighty against the sky. On its lower slopes, under the shadow of tall cliffs, where the great springs tumble out from the Earth, lay the Sanctuary at Delphi.

Mentes brought the boat into the bay and the mountain loomed before them, now embraced by the arms of Eos, in a pink and lavender dawn. As they approached the shore, it suddenly occurred to Herakles that they were completely alone. No other sailboats or ships were anywhere to be seen. As the port came into view he could see the town, which looked much smaller than he'd remembered. And there was no marina, or any boat slips, just a simple wooden dock. Mentes dropped the jib and released the main, expertly guiding the sloop right up next to it.

"I told you I'd have you here by the first light of day."

"Yes you did, dear Mentes, and I kindly thank you. It has been a remarkable journey."

"You are most welcome, bold Herakles." Mentes tipped his cap. "Now collect your things and step ashore. You have an eventful day ahead of you."

Herakles retrieved his belongings and disembarked. "Will I see you again?"

Mentes responded with his now familiar wink. "Push me off, will you? I've got to be getting on." Herakles did as he was asked, and waved goodbye as Mentes glided away.

He put on his sneakers, slung his pack over his shoulder and walked off the dock. As he reached the shore, he turned around for one last look at the boat – but it had vanished. In a strange way he expected that, as he now expected to awaken from this dream and board the real bus to Delphi.

But he didn't.

For life is like a dream as the old ditty goes, and at times we just find ourselves out there, floating on some uncharted stream, not quite sure how we got there or why. When it happens, the only thing to do is continue to row, and so Herakles did just that.

He climbed on top of a large limestone boulder at the shoreline and looked out over the Gulf, wondering what in the world was going on, when suddenly, he heard a fearsome rumble, tumbling down the mountain behind him. Seismic waves knocked the boulder loose, and it shifted beneath his feet in a great lurch forward and then back, very nearly dashing him to the rocks. Luckily, he reacted quickly, and with a mighty leap vaulted away from it, rolling onto the ground.

Poseidon the Earthshaker had turned over in his sleep.

It had been so long, almost two millennia, since the Greeks, Romans, Ethiopians or anyone at all had offered hecatombs worthy of the mighty Sea God. Consequently, somewhere in the hazy, lost fog of time, he laid his immortal body down in his watery realm and sunk into the deepest slumber. To this day he remains there, forgotten jetsam resting on the bottom of an ancient ocean, somewhere in the unexplored recesses of Psyche. Every so often he'll briefly stir, still able, albeit unwittingly, to remind us of his presence.

When the tremors stilled, Herakles stood up and pulled himself together, relieved he hadn't broken anything. He turned around and faced the mountain. Its two peaks, the mighty Horns of the Phaedriádes, towered over him against a brightening blue sky. Then with brilliance, and most excellent timing, Helios appeared, hurling a golden ray of sunlight between the rocky horns and onto the glorious Temple of Apollo, *fully restored*, resting high up on the cliffs.

For a long time, Herakles stared at the temple in wonder, awed by its radiance and beauty. Eventually, as the left hemisphere of his brain began to ask the questions how and why, the right recalled what Mentes had said: he was entering the Mythic Realm, where metaphor and reality intersect.... *What is this "Mythic Realm?" A different dimension of time and space...a delusion existing only inside my head...? Must I give myself over to it to learn its secrets? And if I find the courage to do so, will I risk losing my sanity?*

A few meters away he saw a stone staircase leading up the grassy embankment. He adjusted his backpack and headed up the steps, following the cobblestone walkway to a group of small wooden buildings, shops and tavernas, built along a waterfront boardwalk. A few tables and chairs had been put out in front of one restaurant, but no one was there. He peeked in the window, and it looked normal enough, but again, no one. No activity at all....

He stepped in between two trees, planted in impressive red and black amphorae, and approached the store next door. It was a standard souvenir shop: Athens 2004 Olympic tee shirts hanging in the window, Temple of Apollo pendulum clocks on the wall, a nice array of 12th century Byzantine icon replicas, and the familiar bronze and marble statuettes of Zeus and Athena, all crammed in a tiny display case. Nothing too out of the ordinary.

Suddenly, in the window's reflection, he noticed a lady with blonde hair and a red shirt, standing behind him. *Finally, someone...* but when he turned around, she was nowhere to be seen. Only a whiff of floral perfume remained in the calm air.

Over near one of the restaurant tables, an invisible glass fell to the tiled patio and broke loudly, shattering into a thousand pieces. Around the corner, the sound of laughter echoed off a brick wall. He bolted toward it, but by the time he got there, he found only a deserted alley. It was as though people were there, all around him, but at the same time, they weren't. *What is happening to me?*

All of a sudden he felt the need to flee, and he took off through the alleyway as if the Harpies themselves were flying after him in hot pursuit. He ran through a maze of narrow streets, and then found himself on an old dirt road, leaving the town of Itéa. Within a quarter of a mile it turned into a footpath, which he guessed would eventually go up the gorge. So he kept following it, running faster, faster, all the while thinking to himself, *I can shake this illusion...come back to reality. I'm not losing it....*

The trail soon came to the broad Pleistos River, then turned to follow it north, into the mountains. Still running, he tried to focus on the river, which had for eons been patiently, steadily working its way through the limestone in one long continuous pilgrimage to the sea. *Flush my mind with the clear cool water, flowing steadily over smooth, polished rocks....* Across the grassy meadow, with a panoply of tiny wildflowers calling to him in a chorus of blooming color. *Fresh scent of the blossoms awaken a memory in my soul....* Through an old olive grove which had sustained the people for generations before him. *Sacred fruit which nourishes, sacred fuel which keeps the fire burning....* Entering the forest, winding through the shade of cypress and spruce. *Thank you trees for sheltering me in this rising summer heat....*

Abruptly, the trail came to a fork: straight, continuing along the river, and left, up the valley wall toward the Sanctuary. He veered off, and within a kilometer, started climbing, one switchback after another, after another. Though it was getting steeper and steeper, he kept pushing harder... *I'm not waking up*. And harder...*try to wake up*...and harder...higher he climbed, switching back...and back...and back. 500 meters. Higher. 600...*dizzy...not crazy...not crazy!*

The path was dissipating, turning into a spider web of lightly trodden trails. He pressed on, clutching at the loose, rocky hillside, trying to find his footing, and as he came on all fours, huffing and puffing up and over the precipice, he saw the Tholos, the mysterious circular temple of the Goddess Athena. Its ring of tall marble columns touched the clear blue sky, and from within, a golden light shone forth.

"Do not be afraid, brave Herakles," proclaimed an ethereal voice. "Please, enter."

He got up and brushed himself off, trying to look a little more presentable, and then slowly approached the marvelous structure. He could see a nondescript form inside the glowing light, but nothing else.

"Come," the voice reverberated around him, beckoning.

He slipped between two of the columns, and the light dimmed to a subtle glow. As his eyes adjusted, her exquisite form came into focus. There the radiant Goddess stood, embodied before him. She of the beautiful hair, like a waterfall of chestnut brown curls cascading over her shoulders. She of the splendid robe, woven by the dreams and visions of countless poets throughout the ages.

"Please," she said invitingly, "come closer. I am pleased you fared well on your journey."

"Mentes is an excellent sailor," he replied tentatively. As he drew nearer to her, he could see her unmistakable grey eyes. "Though, if I may say so, you look far more magnificent in this form."

She smiled, nodding serenely.

"So how shall I honor you, Goddess Athena? Do I kneel before you as in days gone past?"

"No, my friend. We are of different realms but we are one. You honor me with your presence, as I honor you with mine."

Herakles nodded graciously in reply.

"I know you have many questions about many things, young Herakles, and they will be answered in due time. However, there is a dire controversy raging deep within your soul, and you must resolve it before you can gain any further understanding."

"My father."

"Yes. When you have made your peace with Alexander, you will be able to continue on your journey. Only then will you be ready to hear the words of the Oracle."

"On the boat, when we were talking, Mentes suggested that perhaps Alexander deserves my love."

"Perhaps he does."

"Will you share your wisdom with me, Athena Parthená?"

She turned and swept her arm toward a circular marble pool, on a raised platform in the center of the Tholos. Trees, flowers and nymphs were delicately carved on its outer shell, and it was filled with clear still water. Four live serpents surrounded it, as if to protect it solely for those whom the Goddess had welcomed. "Come, look into the sacred pool. Learn the nature of your father's past, which has long since been hidden within you."

Herakles carefully approached the basin, as two of the snakes eyed him closely. Athena's breathless whisper rolled across the water and when it stilled, Alexander's face appeared. First, as Herakles had seen it just days ago – a man in his early sixties. Then the image grew younger, and younger still, until he became a boy about the age of six, when he lived in a remote village in the mountains of Greece.

Scenes of the second world war, the German occupation of Greece and then the Greek civil war, with their horrifying images of destruction, violence and bloodshed, flowed through the water...then it stilled again, this time focusing on the young Alexander. He was in a run-down hospital, shut in a small, glass-enclosed room by himself. Quarantined.

"Let me out of here," the boy cried, tears running down his

pale cheeks. "Please! Please let me go!" he screamed. "I hate you. I hate you all."

A nurse wearing gloves and a mask went inside to tend to him. She unwrapped the blood-soaked bandages, and tried to calm him while she changed his dressings. Herakles, shocked, could see the festering, open wounds on his little arms and legs. She carefully cleaned and bandaged them again, then came out to talk with the doctor. The boy sat on the edge of the bed, sobbing heavily.

"He just came in today," the nurse said sadly. "Some neighbors found him hiding under a wool blanket in the crawl space of his family's home. They said he might have been there for some time. His parents, communist sympathizers, were found dead, killed two weeks ago by the nationalists."

"Lord help him, the poor boy. What is his condition?"

"He has a fever of 102, and there are several sites of injury on his arms and legs. All are highly inflamed, swollen and tender, and there are clear signs of infection, possibly emanating from the bone."

"Sounds like osteomyelitis – and we have no antibiotics. Damn it all! The children are the ones who suffer most in war. We'll have to remove the infected tissue and keep him in quarantine for the time being. Does he have any other relatives?"

"No. They've all been killed."

The doctor shook his head. "If he survives, we'll have to send him to the orphanage in Athens."

The medical people disappeared and Herakles again saw the boy close up, as he deteriorated into a frail and listless little figure, near death from pain and loneliness.

The water rippled and the ghastly image disappeared, replaced by Herakles' own reflection in the pool. He looked at Athena with tears filling his swelling red eyes. "His parents, my grandparents, *murdered*. I was always told that they died of natural causes."

"In his own way, perhaps he was trying to spare you the pain you are now feeling."

"I never realized the extent of his suffering."

"Now that you do realize it, what is your intention?"

"My mother tells me I must forgive him."

"Will you find forgiveness for your father?"

"Perhaps now, I can. Never before had I thought of him as that sick, frightened child. Brutalized. Isolated. He never talked about the wars, and I suppose I thought he was too young to have experienced them. Now I see their terrible consequences." He felt heartsick and weary, and remained silent for some time, but then a revelation came upon him, and he brightened. "Then perhaps he never *meant* to hurt us. Maybe he was so damaged himself as a child, that he never developed the capacity to form close, loving relationships, even with his wife and children."

"Let your anger go, Herakles. Forgiving does not mean condoning his hurtful treatment; it only means you are no longer controlled by it. It is within you to release the anger. Come with me." She led him out of the temple and to the edge of the ravine. In her outstretched hand, a chunk of red variegated limestone appeared. "Take this stone." He did so. "Feel its texture, its crevices and cracks. It holds the memory of Earth Herself, and it can absorb your pain and sorrow, returning them to the vast expanse, where they will trouble you no longer."

He looked at the rock, aware of its course texture pressing into his skin, sensing the residual feelings of anger and disappointment flowing out through his fingertips, draining into the lumpen receptacle, freeing his heart of the debilitating weight he'd carried for so long.

"Now, cast it off!" she pronounced, sweeping her arm across the chasm.

With certitude, he hurled it over the mountain, proclaiming at the top of his lungs, "I forgive you, father. I forgive you!"

As the falling stone cascaded down the edge of the mighty gorge, he could hear Echo, resolutely affirming his conviction. The pain which had for so long ripped through the essence of his being, relentlessly tearing at his fiber, flesh and bone, was now gone, replaced by a tender feeling for the suffering little boy trapped inside his father. A wave of great relief swept over him. *Perhaps he is capable of change.* He looked to the Goddess with the gratitude of a shipwrecked seafarer, just plucked from the frigid waters of ever-lasting grief. "Thank you, Shining Athena. I'm most appreciative."

She nodded, smiling. "We must now prepare ourselves for the gift of prophecy. Come. To the Kastalía Spring...." She pointed up the mountain a short distance, to a cleft gushing forth with crystal-line water, and with her other arm, reached out to him. "Take my hand."

As he gently grasped her luminous limb, they were instantly transported to the pool beneath the spring, whisked there by the grace of the Goddess in merely the blink of her eye. The Tholos now lay below them on its plateau, overlooking the steady river Pleistos and the broad, blue-green precipices of Mount Cirphis across the valley.

Herakles stood before the basin, appreciating its simple, natural beauty. Ivy and saxifrage adorned the moist, dripping rockface, speckled with red-orange lichen, and purple morning glories pushed through the cracks, trumpeting Athena's arrival. Songbirds appeared, dipping into the water and darting into the branches of a large fig tree, laden with fruit.

As Athena removed her splendid robe, a twittering mass of swallows rose up from the brush and relieved her of the garment, fluttering with it into the branches. They hung it with great care and then disappeared on the wind. Herakles gazed upon her per-fect nakedness, transfixed, unable to move or speak.

"Come, Herakles of the Golden Heart, renew yourself in the eternal waters of Parnassós." She entered the pool, watching him.

He shyly took off his clothing, and then carefully stepped on the damp moss-covered stones at the edge. As he lowered himself into the cool, clear water, it wholly enveloped him in the magic of its primal essence – surrounding him, protecting him, incubating him. For what seemed like a very long while, he remained sub-merged in the stillness.

Then suddenly, he burst through the surface, gulping great draughts of air. He opened his eyes and a sense of rapture engulfed him, pulling him into seamless union with all Creation. Time stopped, and across the great river valley below, eternity unfolded before him, connecting the past, the present, the future, and every discreet thread of the limitless Web of Existence.

High above him, an eagle called...

...then Herakles became the eagle, gliding through the atmosphere. Far below, he could see the Tholos, the Kastalía Spring and Temple of Apollo, all perched on the edge of the jagged cliffs. Then higher still he flew, above the two horns of the mountain, where the whole of the Greek landscape came into view – the long, narrow Gulf of Kórinthos leading westward to the Ionian Sea, to the east, the deep blue Aegean glimmering in mid-morning sunlight, and in the north, snow capped Mount Olympos, standing alone, bold against a hyperborean sky. He circled three times, absorbing the expanse, then glided back down to the pool, and back into himself again.

Athena was waiting for him nearby, radiant in her shining gown once more. She beckoned him out and with the wave of her arm, dried his golden body and neatly arranged his curly hair. She cloaked him in a short white garment, spun and woven by her own immortal hand, delicate as her ephemeral breath.

"My handsome Herakles, you are now ready to receive the Oracle. However, before we begin our procession, there is something else you must know." He looked at her expectantly. "Prepare yourself to meet the Immortals. The Panthaeon awaits at the Temple of Apollo."

"Athena, this experience grows more extraordinary with every passing moment, but I cannot deny the fear rising within me."

"I know. You're anxious about what is yet to come."

"Yes."

"There's nothing to be afraid of."

He nodded trustingly, resolved to continue onward. Athena started up the Sacred Way, gracefully moving as if carried by a gentle murmur, seeming more to float above the Earth than to move her legs in walking. He could very much feel the solid ground beneath his feet – the well-worn stones laid in the walkway, a pebble through the soles of his sandals – then a faint breeze rose up from the valley, ruffling his robe against his thighs, the cloth so fine, so elegant, it was at the same time there and not there at all. It seemed as though two different realities had somehow become intertwined, and that he was caught between the weft and the weave of a complex and mysterious fabric.

As they approached the monuments and treasuries, Herakles' attention began to drift, to wander back to an earlier trip he'd made to Delphi. In his mind's eye, he saw not the brightly painted statues and pediments of the ancient world restored, but rather the Sanctuary in ruin, as it existed in his own time. Suddenly, he collided with a solid form, brushing by unseen.

"Herakles!" Athena called to him, sounding faint and somewhat distant. "Herakles, you must listen to me!" As his attention focused back in on her, her voice reclaimed its power. "You must keep your mind and spirit present, here with me, or you may slip away before it's time."

"What *was* that, Athena? That invisible force I just encountered?"

"I will share with you what I know to be the truth. Our two realms – yours, the corporeal, and mine, the mythical – coexist, side by side in the same space. When you are in between worlds, as was the case a moment ago, elements of both realities exist. When you fully cross into one, the other recedes into the mist of your imagination. Trust me, Herakles, you have only to decide to return to your world, and you will."

"But on my way up here, I was desperately trying to get back and couldn't."

"These things are governed by your truest desires."

"I see."

"Please, Herakles, it's imperative you remain here until the Oracle has been received."

"I will not disappoint you, Athena."

"Then let us continue."

And so they went up the hill, past the extravagant marble treasuries, each of which vied for favor with the ancient Oracle, their skillfully carved pediments calling loudly with bold color and provocative scenes. However, these were not the familiar images of a distant heroic age – the military conflicts and ravishments, petty kings and monster slayings – upon which Old Society was built. Rather, they reflected the values of the New Society, depicting scenes like the Birth of Cosmos from the Celestial Egg, the Sacred Marriage of Gaia and Ouranos, and the joyful Reunion of Demeter and Persephone.

At the Siphnian Treasury, Herakles stopped to look at the pediment, and was surprised to find that it no longer showed the demigod Hercules fighting with Apollo over the Delphic Tripod. Instead, he saw *himself* receiving it from the God as a gift! He looked at Athena, who only smiled and gestured for them to keep going.

As they rounded the last switchback, they encountered the winged Sphinx of Náxos, rising high above them, resting serenely on her tall Ionian column, welcoming those who came seeking knowledge.

Beyond the Sphinx, the resplendent Temple of Apollo gleamed robustly in the sunlight. Forty marble columns marked the outer rectangular boundary, and at its apex, a magnificent pediment depicted Medusa, with a lioness on each side of her. Behind the temple, the massive Horns of the Phaedriádes thrust upward into the sky.

"Brother Apollo," she announced in her most assertive voice, "it is I, Athena, who seeks to enter, and with me I bring the Mortal, Herakles Speros. Welcome us with arms open." She led Herakles up the marble steps, and for a moment, he was blinded by a glorious light emanating from behind the columns. They stepped inside and gradually, as the evanescent shapes resolved themselves into cohesive form, he realized he was seeing the Classical Panthaeon incarnate: Hera, Dionysos, Aphrodite, Apollo, Artemis, Demeter, Hermes and Zeus all stood before him, wearing robes of the finest fabric, shimmering in the surreal light. Around the chamber hung tapestries of crimson, silver and gold, and flaming torches encircled the immortal assemblage.

"It's about time you got here," Zeus boomed, throwing his arms skyward. "We've been waiting for eons!"

"Greetings to you as well, my father," Athena replied. "I see you have not used this time to acquaint yourself with the finer points of civil discourse."

"Touché," Dionysos snickered, as he took a sip from his ambrosia-filled chalice. "Let the spectacle begin!"

"Dionysos," Apollo sternly rebuked, "can you not refrain from your incessant ingurgitating even for a moment? We face a matter most grave, and still you persist in your merrymaking, unable to appreciate the magnitude of our situation. But alas," he turned to Athena, "let me not forget my own civility and fail to greet my dear sister in a manner befitting her glory. Welcome, radiant Athena. It has been far too long since Parnassós has been graced with your magnificence." He took her hand and bowed. "And this must be young Herakles, of whom you have spoken so highly."

"Yes. It is with great joy I present this most blessed of Mortals, Herakles of the Golden Heart."

"Welcome to our heavenly realm. Well-nigh, you shine with the brilliance of an Immortal."

Herakles could feel the gaze of the extraordinary beings around him, scrutinizing him in close detail. "Thank you, Phoebos Apollo. I am fortunate to be in your company, and will endeavor to do honor to you all."

"Undoubtedly the son of a diplomat. However, you needn't perform any sacrifices today, Herakles, as we no longer require such veneration."

"Speak for yourself, Apollo," Zeus bellowed. "I for one wouldn't mind a few hecatombs for old time's sake."

"Oh please," Dionysos laughed, "*do* slaughter a few oxen for the old boy. It would do wonders for his disposition."

"Forget the silly offerings," Aphrodite purred. "Your mere presence honors us, handsome Herakles, so exquisite to my eternal eye. Tell me, what do you think of my precious gift, the love of the beautiful and swift Alanta?"

"Resplendent Aphrodite, a finer gift could not possibly be conceived, and so I am forever grateful to you. The mere saying of her name evokes in my heart a longing to see her once again."

"And so you shall…"

"No time for that," Zeus interrupted. "Danger is afoot, and there's work to be done."

"Please," Herakles addressed the gathering. "Tell me, why have I been brought into your illustrious realm?"

"Because," Apollo answered, "our wayward brother, Ares, infamous god of war, is plotting to bring an end to this era of peace we have all enjoyed. Athena believes you will ultimately be the one to stop his frightful destruction."

"Me? But you're the omnipotent ones. How am *I* to stop a God?"

"Worry not," Athena reassured him. "When the time comes, we will help you, but first, we must determine what has been learned since last we met on the island of Kríti."

"Fair sister, Athena," Hermes began, "keen-minded and wise. Although you have cast off your armor, I see you still revel in the art of strategy. Therefore, let me be the first to report. As you know, I returned to the desolate wilderness to resume my surveillance, but shortly after my arrival, Ares became aware of my presence and I was forced to flee. How he was able to perceive me, I do not know for certain," he looked hard at Zeus, "though I have my suspicions."

"Do not implicate me in Ares' treachery, brazen son of mine," Zeus retorted. "I have pledged my allegiance to my family and I am a God of my Word."

Hera responded with a hearty harumph, and the others rolled their eyes, except for the budding Artemis, who stepped forward to defend her father. "Let us not be divided by innuendo and suspicion," she said in her lithe and charming voice. "Our ability to stop Ares depends upon our unity. I too had my doubts about Zeus' sincerity, so since last we met, I have spent much of my time with him." She looked at Herakles. "What I have learned is that I hold a heavy anger in my heart for my father, Zeus, as I believe we all do. For, during the years he ruled the wide Heavens, we were all victims of his wrath and domination. Yet, it has been a long time indeed since he reigned supreme, and his own journey has not been easy. He has traversed the barren wilderness, and I believe he has come far along the path of transformation. With our help, his rebirth can be complete. However, now is a critical time, and we must show him our support."

"Thank you, beloved child," Zeus replied, eyeing the others with self-satisfaction.

Dionysos started clapping loudly. "Bravo, bravo! What a remarkable performance. I don't know about the rest of you, but I'm close to tears. Yes. Yes, we should all have pity for once ruthless Zeus."

"That's *enough*," Apollo warned. "It is plain to see that my dear sister Artemis speaks from her heart, and what she says does have merit. I acknowledge that I too harbor anger and resentment toward him; the rest of you do not?"

Each of them readily acknowledged they did, and a bit of a fracas suddenly arose. Athena intervened by offering a suggestion. "Perhaps we could learn to trust you, father, but you must persuade us you are worthy of that trust."

Zeus stood defiantly. "How *dare* you. I am of the greatest generation of Immortals that has ever existed. I fought and won the Great War against the Titans, brought order to Chaos, established stability. Under my rule, the arts and sciences flourished and mortals prospered. Have you no respect for these notable deeds?"

"Oh yes, the *great* war," Dionysos chided. "You always have to bring that up. Well, that happened ages ago and it's time to move on. Besides, no war is great, dear misguided father, and until you realize that, you have no hope for transformation."

"Please," Athena pleaded, trying to diffuse the mounting tension. "These are old arguments, reflective of old patterns which clearly have lost their legitimacy over time. Father Zeus, surely you see how the world has changed, and surely you have changed to some extent along with it. In your time, you were revered for your sole authority and might, but the nature of power is different today. We no longer exercise it for the purpose of manipulation and control, but rather to accomplish worthy goals, such as stopping Ares' violence. Do you not agree?"

"I was not the only one to wield my power over others as it fancied my shifting whims. We all believed in that doctrine of dominance, didn't we? Well, didn't we? I will not bear the brunt of this indictment alone. I will not be demonized in this fashion. If the rest of you will acknowledge your complicity, then I will acknowledge my role and take my responsibility."

Pallas Athena was first to admit her own reliance upon violence and vengeance in the past, showing particular remorse for her jealousy and inexcusable treatment of poor Arachne. Artemis of the Golden Arrows and Far Shooting Apollo denounced and lamented the killing of Niobe's 13 children, which they committed as revenge for the slander of their mother's name. Much to Herakles' surprise, each and every one of the other Immortals followed, confessing their past abuses of power and affirming their allegiance to a more cooperative, egalitarian ordering of relations.

When each had spoken their peace, Zeus delivered his repentance. "I admit. I once relished in the hurling of my thunderbolts and the terror and awe which ensued, but that no longer gives me joy. As my dear daughter Artemis said, I have come far down this path of transformation and I am committed to seeing it through."

Hermes remained skeptical. "That is all well and good, but how then did the brutal Ares know I was there?"

"Yes," Apollo focused his luminous gaze on Zeus, "how do you explain *that?*"

"I do not know, but I will say this: treacherous and insane though he is, Ares is not a fool. He is skilled in the tactics of war, and is therefore wise to the ways of spies. Perhaps your powers of concealment have slipped, swift-footed Hermes, but nevermind. I can also prove my trustworthiness, as I too have valuable information. After reconciling with Artemis, I embarked on a mission of my own.

"I too went back to the wilderness, and when I arrived, the intractable Ares once again attempted to recruit me into his wretched little battalion. I went along with it to see what I could learn about his evil plot, but alas, he subsequently cast me out, for he too did not trust my intent. However, I did manage to see his mortal henchmen, the thoughtless fools, and a more sinister band I have never seen. They agree on very little if the truth be known, but they are united against what they believe to be a grand conspiracy to wrestle power away from their God – some *all knowing, all seeing* monotheistic incarnation who goes by several different names. Ares, the ever so devious one, appears to each of the various sects not as himself, but as their *own* God, then instructs them to join forces with their former enemies. They have sworn by blood oath to champion him.

"The vagabonds have left their wilderness exile and now roam freely over the civilized world, set on horrific destruction. They're responsible for the recent calamities, and they show no remorse over the death of innocent mortals. Finally, their murderous plans do indeed focus on the Olympic Games, for Ares himself acknowledged this to me. Now, skeptical ones, would I have divulged this information if I were in league with my wayward son?"

"It is a good beginning," Athena affirmed.

"The Olympics!" Herakles exclaimed. "What are they going to do?"

"Perfectly diabolical deeds, no doubt," Dionysos remarked offhandedly.

"Have you nothing of value to offer, self-indulgent brother of mine?" Apollo retorted. "Or have you simply continued your reckless carousing as though you have not a worry in the world?"

"Testy testy, Rational One. I'll have you know, since last we met, I have poured many a splendid libation in the hopes of tricking those nasty Mortals into disclosing their secret plans. But woe, I'm sorry to say that most of them refused to touch it and I was unsuccessful in acquiring any useful information – though I did have a devilishly good time." He raised his cup and took a godlike swig. "And you, brother, what have you learned? Do tell."

Apollo's self-confidence abruptly drained away, as all eyes turned toward him. He stood there, motionless, saying nothing, until Dionysos prodded him and he finally replied. "A most dangerous weapon has been taken from my arsenal. I fear.... I fear that Ares may now possess the power of the stars themselves." He suddenly grew agitated, gesticulating as he paced back and forth. "The atom is no longer restrained by reason…"

"You have fooled yourself, nephew," Demeter interjected with great concern, "if you think it ever was. There can be no *reason* in the creation of weapons of mass destruction. I myself tried to warn you of this many years ago, but in your brashness you would not listen."

"Like Zeus before you," Hera added caustically, "you have been misguided by your desire to dominate and control, and now, what we have all feared most has come to fruition."

"I was blinded by the magnitude of my own power, by which I sought to master the Cosmos," Apollo admitted. "It was a fool-hardy belief. I understand that now."

Zeus grunted with satisfaction at his favorite son's confession.

"How could this have happened?" Herakles cried in horror.

"I thought I was entrusting these weapons to *rational* Mortals, but I have underestimated their depravity."

"Fool!" Zeus exclaimed. "Mortals cannot be trusted. Did you not learn the lessons of history? From the beginning, they have honored the deceitful ways of their benefactor, the traitor Prometheus, who stole our sacred fire and gave it to humankind."

"Oh!" Dionysos chimed in. "Do we not remember what happened after *that* infamous misadventure? As punishment, you forced Pandora to let loose the evils upon the whole world from that miserable little jar of yours. Don't remind us. We've been living with the consequences of your tantrum ever since."

"Until now," Aphrodite pointed out. "For remember, Hope too has finally escaped from that jar, and surely the evils are vanishing from the Earth."

"Except of course for Ares and his henchmen," Athena reminded them.

"Yes," Aphrodite repeated, lifting her tightly cuffed wrist. "Except for Ares and his henchmen."

"What say you, Mortal Herakles?" Hermes asked with the weight of human history rolling off the tip of his tongue. "*Can* those of your kind be trusted?"

For a moment Herakles stood shocked, in arrant disbelief that a handful of fundamentalists were placing all of humanity on the edge of a precipice, poised to hurl everyone headlong into the abyss. The peace so painfully recovered after these long millennia was suddenly at risk, and now, before the Immortals of Olympos, he was being asked to justify their faith in the whole human race.

He stood tall and replied with winged words. "I cannot presume to speak for all of humanity, but I can and will speak for myself. I have returned to my homeland of Greece not to seek personal glory and fame, but rather to challenge myself to realize my fullest potential. Along the way, I've made mistakes and harbored ill feelings, especially toward my own father, but with the help of wise Athena, I have been able to forgive Alexander and let go of my animosity. The Millennium affirmed my belief in the values of compassion and love, and those are the emotions now filling my heart. And so I say to you, Blessed Immortals, that I can be trusted to do everything in my power to help you stop Ares and protect the city of my birth."

"Beautiful," Hera said proudly. "You glorify us all with your eloquent words, spoken passionately and with resolve."

And so the Immortals smiled with approval and Herakles took his place amongst them.

"Perhaps now," Athena suggested, "we should consult the Oracle and determine what path to take."

"Yes," Apollo agreed. "Let us proceed into the inner chamber." He parted the tapestry and led them inside, where they formed a circle around the Golden Tripod, which stood over a narrow orifice in the ground. "Dear family," he continued, "after the passing of these many generations, I have come to realize my error in claiming this sacred spot solely as my own. Surely, no one being can rightfully claim to have the exclusive possession of the Oracle.

"So please, join with me in calling forth ancient Wisdom. Focus on the question which must be answered: How are we to stop Ares from carrying out his despicable plan?"

A great silence overtook the gathering.

Herakles stood between Athena and Apollo, feeling their pul-

sating energy as it surged through him and around the circle, co-
alescing with the energy of the others. As the individual identities
blended together, Herakles sensed a new consciousness emerging,
but it was still vague, still distant. As Hermes and the Goddesses
gave themselves over to the merging, so did Herakles follow, letting himself be totally absorbed into the Oneness. When at last,
Dionysos, Apollo, and finally, Zeus, surrendered, a remarkable
thing occurred.

As the circle of energy became complete, a white-hot flame
erupted from the fissure in the Earth, streaming through the
Golden Tripod in a mighty spinning vortex, writhing and shifting
with blinding light. Then, before Herakles' eyes, it coalesced into
the Snake Goddess, with her long, curly black hair flowing down
and around her open bodice. Her long skirt shimmered in fractal
patterns, radiating all of the colors of the spectrum, and in each
hand she held a black snake. Her golden eyes sparkled, the snakes
hissed and then she spoke, her voice deep with the resonance of
the ages.

*My children, grandchildren and infinite great grandchild, at last you
have come together as one. See then with your common vision from whence
you came, for I am the spirit of your ancestors, born in the caves of blessed
Kríti, and I am a descendent of the Earliest One. I am the flame rising
within you, when you allow peace to enter your hearts. I am harmony and
balance and love, the hope for the future.*

*You have come to me seeking Wisdom; you have become one to mani-
fest the answer. Herakles of the Golden Heart, you must find the weapon
which springs forth from the head of Apollo. Trust in your path, for it connects with those of the Mortals upon whom Ares relies. And on the third
day of the Games, you will be the one who prevents the evil destruction
they have planned, thereby protecting the future of all humanity. Then and
only then, shall we gather at the summit of Olympos, where I will lift the
veil which has clouded the vision of Mortals and Immortals alike. So says
the Oracle you have sought.*

Earth took a mighty inhalation, and in a tremendous whirling,
roaring funnel, the Snake Goddess was sucked back into the fissure
and the flame extinguished.

It was at that precise moment, from their high perch atop the tall temple columns, that the Gremlins of Ares sprinkled their Dust of Deception, chanting quietly to themselves.

*Just as the Mortals will be deceived,*
  *so too shall you Immortals.*
*Just as the Mortals will be deceived,*
  *so too shall you Immortals...*

Slowly, Herakles became conscious of himself, and of the Panthaeon resolving again into their individual forms. He caught a glimpse of Demeter, youthful, vibrant, reborn. And the lovely Aphrodite, in pain, doubling over as Ares' cuff gripped her even tighter. With these first thoughts, all of it vanished and everything went dark.

Suddenly, the smell of dust was overwhelming. He felt someone's hand on his shoulder, trying to get his attention, and when he opened his eyes, he saw a black leather boot kicking up more dirt in front of his face. He started coughing and sat up with a start.

"Are you all right, son?" the older man asked, as he tried to get his footing on the slope. "What are you doing way up here?"

Herakles looked at the man's clothing – a modern security guard uniform. *Where am I?* He looked around. *On the side of a hill.* Down below lay Delphi's ancient track and field, with its crumbling limestone bleachers embedded in the mountain.

"Young man?"

"Uh, oh yes, thank you, I'm all right...I was just resting."

"Well you sure went out of your way, I almost didn't notice you. We're getting ready to close, so please start making your way to the exit."

"Okay. Just give me a minute to wake up and I'll be going."

The man eyed him closely. "Aren't you Herakles Speros, that famous athlete?"

Suddenly feeling embarrassed, Herakles stood up and brushed himself off. "Yes, sir."

"Well, good luck in the Olympics, and take care of yourself," the man said as he started down the hill, stirring up yet more dust in the loose gravel.

First thing on his mind, water. He grabbed his pack and retrieved the full bottle, then took a long drink. He wiped his face with his sweatshirt and took a minute to try to shake off his disorientation. Then, slinging his backpack over his shoulder, he went down onto the old stadium field, briefly stopping to observe the surrounds. The Horns of the Phaedriádes still towered behind him, and across the valley, the mountains turned purple in the afternoon light. Far in the distance, he could see the port of Itéa and the waters of the Gulf of Kórinthos. He looked down at the smattering of ruins below him. The Temple of Apollo and Athena's Tholos were again reduced to rubble, surrounded only by the remnants of the once splendid Sanctuary. *I am in the Mythic Realm no more. Yet, I feel Athena and the Panthaeon are a part of me as never before.*

*Have I somehow been given a glimpse of the future…? The destruction of the Games…and the Snake Goddess, who said I have to prevent it…but how am I to stop* Ares?

He started down the Sacred Way, hurrying past the remnants of Dionysos' theatre, where the last of the tourists were snapping their final photos of the day. He continued on by the toppled treasuries, remembering them intact so clearly in his mind. When he turned around for one last look at the ruins, for an instant, he thought he could see that mysterious place he'd spent the day.

Within minutes of getting to the bus stop he was recognized, so he had to set aside his heavy contemplation and turn to more familiar habits. He signed the autographs and engaged in well-meaning banter with his fans until the bus arrived, and then he took a seat in the back, alone, trying to communicate to the talkative crowd that he didn't want to socialize during the trip.

The bus turned around and headed down the mountain, and Herakles saw himself as he was earlier, scrambling up on all fours, hot, sweating, afraid he was losing his mind. *Was it all in my head?*

*If not, then I spent the whole day at a crowded site with no recollection of it. Did all those tourists see me? And how did I get there?*

Once they rounded the last switchback and started heading out of the valley, his stomach called out to him in a clear, resounding voice. He looked in his backpack, and much to his relief, found the food that Katina had prepared. After a while, it seemed to revive him and he started thinking somewhat more clearly.

He contemplated the day's bizarre events and found himself questioning the very nature of reality – had he somehow entered a physical dimension of the dream world and been able to glimpse the future? Or had he slipped into what some would call a psychotic episode?

All he knew for sure was that the experiences had seemed acutely real, and that his gut was telling him he must act on the knowledge he now possessed. But how? He shifted uncomfortably in his seat.

Out the window, the Plains of Attica rolled by, as the bus swiftly carried him to his beloved home.

# 11

## CITY OF ATHENA

As the bus approached the outskirts of Athens, the landmark for which the city is renowned came prominently into view. High atop the Acropolis the Parthenon stood, with its marble columns reflecting the last rays of a golden Sun. Herakles stared out the window at his city in twilight, as it settled into evening under a fuchsia and orange sherbet sky.

Athens, his birthplace and forever his home. He loved how the ancient ruins blended with the modern architecture; the way you can turn a corner, and take a trip through time – just there, the Temple of Zeus, with its immense pillars casting their long, late shadows over the bustling 21st century streets. Roman arches, Byzantine churches, and there's the Cycladic Museum, with its fabulous collection of white folded-arm figures, those serene, feminine marble sculptures dating back to at least 3000 b.c.e. Turn another corner, and behold again the Parthenon, pinnacle of the Acropolis, still holding all of Attica under its hypnotic spell.

*This could all be at risk*, his inner voice said loudly and shockingly to himself. He pushed it aside, shifting in the cramped seat, trying to return his attention to the life outside the window.

Streetside tavernas were overflowing with people, eating, drinking and laughing, and there were a lot more trees than he remembered. As they passed Syntagma Square, he noticed moving sidewalks carrying people around it, from bakery to bookstore to kafenéo and back.

*It could all be gone in two weeks if I fail. No!* He stopped himself. *I won't be able to function if I let myself think that way. Somehow I have to concentrate, and figure out what I'm supposed to do.*

They pulled into the old downtown station, and as he got off the bus, a few more of the riders wished him good luck and asked him for one last autograph. With all of his mental energy, he tried to focus on each and every detail of the interactions, and hold on to the present moment. Anything to distract him from the terrible knowledge that perhaps he alone possessed.

The station offered a variety of interesting diversions as well. It had been completely renovated, and the new motif successfully integrated pre-Classical to post-modern designs. Along one wall, a large exhibit highlighted 4,000 years of ground transportation. Vehicles of the Ages: Minoan pedal cars to chariots, to trains, streetcars and monorails.

A long stairway led up to the platform, where the new monorail could in minutes whisk him to within a block of his great aunt's apartment. However, after spending nearly two hours crunched in that tiny bus seat, he really felt he needed to walk.

As he emerged from the station, he immediately noticed the lack of car traffic. Busses, taxis and bicycles freely used the streets, which had once been jammed only with cars, and much to his surprise, the air was relatively clear, with no throat-burning haze of the infamous Athens smog.

He came to a stoplight, and above the cross-street in front of him, the monorail silently glided by; it was painted with huge, colorful Olympic rings and the words "Athens 2004!" His gut wrenched at the sight of it.

He dashed across the street, and next thing he knew he was all out running, faster and faster, darting around the people on the crowded sidewalk, his urgency growing as he traversed each block. His single thought: his mother. The steadfast and brilliant Maria, his anchor. She'd help him figure out what to do next.

As he approached Vasso's neighborhood, the Plaka, he had to

slow down. This was a popular restaurant area, and tables and chairs filled with happy tourists spilled out onto the sidewalk, creating a vibrant, festive ambiance. He made his way through, for once unnoticed, and turned up the narrow cobblestone street leading to his great aunt's apartment. It had been several years since he'd been there, but he recognized the building immediately.

It was nicely landscaped out front, with fire red geraniums overflowing large pots, and dark green shrubbery growing low around the grounds of the small courtyard. The sturdy stone entranceway was carved with decorative meanders, and it supported a wrought-iron gate with a griffin soldered in the center of the bars.

He found the name on the directory and pressed the button. A moment later the door buzzed and he took the elevator to the 12th floor. His mother greeted him as he got off, and just seeing her shining face helped put his mind at ease. Since their last visit, she'd cut her curly black hair above her shoulders, making her look much younger than her 52 years, and as usual, she was healthy and fit. She was dressed casually this evening, in shorts and a sleeveless blue shirt.

Thea Vasso, who was never too casual, was there as well, appearing in her characteristic stately manner. She was a first cousin of Maria's mother, and now, even in her mid-seventies, she had clearly managed to hold on to her youthful spirit. Her hair was still dyed strawberry-blonde and her forthright demeanor assured him that she was still sharp as a tack.

They welcomed him with love in their hearts and plenty of food on the table. The three of them sat on Vasso's terrace, beneath her vine covered trellis, overlooking a violet-crowned city. They chatted about the Olympics, gossiped about the recent weddings and funerals and told favorite family stories, complete with new embellishments improvised just for the evening. He told them about his trip to Olympia, and Thea Vasso pointed out all of the relatives and friends he should have contacted along the way. She pronounced his hair too long, and gently hounded him for information about Alanta. On into the late hours they drank their tea, ate numerous desserts and caught up on all the news – well, almost all of it.

He couldn't wait for Vasso to call it a night. Finally, at 11:30, she announced she was headed for bed. They helped her take the dishes inside and clean up, then the two of them went back out to the terrace. Herakles hugged his mother with desperation and relief. They pulled their chairs in close, and with hair standing up on the back of his neck, he told her about his odyssey through the Mythic Realm.

She took it all in with her customary patience, remaining calm and nonjudgmental, patting his hand reassuringly, and listening intently until he'd finished his tale. She was pleased to hear that he'd forgiven his father, but when Herakles got to the part about the Oracle and the destruction, she became visibly upset. Never before had his dreams taken on such a foreboding quality, and never before had he seemingly blacked out; she admitted it worried her greatly. They discussed his experience and the metaphorical nature of dreams, but also considered the possibility it was somehow a premonition, a rare glimpse into the future. There was too much at risk to take any chances, she said, urging him to explain it to Carl and approach Olympic Security.

By the time they were through, Herakles was mentally and emotionally worn out. He kissed his mother good night and collapsed on the couch, falling into a dreamless sleep.

The next morning, he called Carl, and over breakfast in the hotel room, again relayed his account, albeit in a somewhat modified version. Herakles feared that if he told Coach the whole story, it would still be too much for him to handle, despite his recent progress. So he characterized the events as having unfolded through his regular meditations.

There he was at Delphi, soaking in the inexorable beauty of the place, musing about the old myths and stories, and when he reached a deep meditative state, he experienced the drama of the Oracle in his imagination. However, because it was so real, so specific and horrifying, he had to take it as some kind of precognition.

Coach heard him out, listening carefully and neutrally. He

affirmed that coming to terms with his father would no doubt improve performance, but he was reluctant to take the "vision" too literally, and was not at all thrilled with the prospect of reporting it to the authorities.

Herakles agreed that from a rational point of view it sounded a little crazy, but urged Carl to look at it as a gut feeling, a concept he knew Carl accepted. He told him what Maria had said: the stakes were just too high to ignore it. "Besides," he said in conclusion, "what harm could it do to notify Security?"

"They'll think you are stark raving mad," Carl replied in a low, even monotone.

"It's a risk I'm willing to take."

"I can see you've made up your mind."

"Will you come with me?"

Carl hesitated for a moment, but then gave in. "You're going to drag me down with you, hmm? All right, if you insist."

And so they arranged a meeting with Ivanna Jadan, their Olympic Committee liaison, for 1:00 pm, giving them ample time to make their way to Olympic Village, check in and get acquainted with the area.

A monorail took them northward through the neighborhoods of Athens, and on to the Olympic complex, which was nestled in a sylvan grove at the foot of Mount Parnitha. At the transfer station, they switched cars for Olympic Village.

The Village had been designed as a modern re-creation of a Minoan town, modeled after the culture which had flourished in the islands four thousand years ago. As the train entered a densely wooded area, the sunlight suddenly became muted; they were approaching the main entrance. The track curved left and right in a gentle s, and they came to a stop in front of the Kríti building. It was a multi-leveled structure, which at its highest point stood five stories tall. Each of the floors had external walkways, lined with red and black pillars, and a bulls' horn frieze adorned the roof.

Baggage assistants retrieved their luggage and placed it on waiting carts, and they stepped out onto a greenstone walkway. When the monorail continued on, they could see the splendid fountain at the center of the large plaza. Blue dolphins jumped through each of the five Olympic rings, as water spouts shot up around them. Flagpoles encircled the fountain, and as each team arrived, their country's flag would be raised. Among the dozen or so already there, Herakles could make out those of Greece, Sweden and Germany, ruffling slightly in the temperate breeze.

Just outside the building entrance, two large black pillars supported an ivy-covered archway, and a sizeable bronze griffin sat on either side of the tall glass doors, which slid open when they approached.

The lobby was in the front of an atrium, which had plants and trees growing on every floor, some in huge amphorae. In the center, the Goddess Aphrodite bathed in the foam of a seashell fountain. Behind her, the four-story wall had windows from floor to ceiling, showcasing the magnificent panorama of the mountains, and the large, green area of the Central Courtyard.

On one side of the window, a huge replica of the famous fresco, *The Bull Vaulters*, had been painted; on the other, a copy of *The Women from Pseira*, with the three stylized Minoan ladies and their long, curly locks. A jazz ensemble played upbeat music over near another waterfall sculpture, and official greeters roamed the lobby, welcoming newcomers – the first of nearly twenty thousand athletes who would be arriving over the next three days. Just now, two different Spanish speaking teams were filtering out of the lobby and over to the monorail, which would zip them around to their respective buildings.

One of the greeters spotted him and made a beeline over. He was very excited to see Herakles in person, and welcomed them both profusely before directing them to registration. They picked up their passes and room keys, and as their building, Santoríni, was right next door, they decided to walk.

They got a luggage cart and went up the ramp to one of the glass-enclosed walkways, and halfway across, stopped to look out over the Courtyard. It was magnificent. For a brief moment, the anxiety evaporated and he felt the thrill of being there.

The Village complex was a circle of eleven interconnected buildings of varying heights and shapes, all arranged around the Courtyard, and each of which had been named after a different island, city or region in Greece. Many had terraces similar to Vasso's, with potted trees, red geraniums and grape vines growing on trellises. The grounds were lush with flower gardens, small ponds with lily pads, and greenery thriving around the stand of old oaks a local farmer had managed to preserve. In the center of the grove, hidden from their view, lay a 60-foot labyrinth mosaic.

"I've heard there's a Cretan labyrinth tucked away in that stand of trees," Herakles said, pointing it out to Carl.

"Why would they put a maze in there?"

"Not a maze, a labyrinth!" Herakles explained. "A maze is a trap, with false choices and dead ends, while a labyrinth is a walking meditation, a spiritual tool of transformation linked with the ancient Minoans, and many other cultures. The participant is invited to walk the winding, curving path to the center, a metaphor for the journey to the center of one's spiritual self. The lesson being, that if you trust in your path, you will find the answers you seek." Herakles was glad to know it was there, because it was a reminder of a message he knew he needed now. He decided he would walk it as soon as he had the chance.

They continued on the ramp, a few moments later emerging into the lobby of the Santoríni building. Decorating the walls were images of swallows and blue monkeys, and larger-than-life replicas of the Minoan frescoes found on the island, including *The Boy with the Fish* and *Room of the Lilies*. They had a large display telling the history of Santoríni, complete with a model of the island volcano before its massive eruption in 1628 b.c.e., when it completely buried a Minoan village in ash. For 3,600 years the town had remained hidden beneath a nondescript hillside, until it was discovered in 1967. Pictures of the archeological dig, at what is now called Akrotíri, showed some of the streets and homes of the lost city. Nearby, a sign announced its recent designation as a World

Heritage Site, and the ambitious plan to fully excavate the area by 2015.

Greenery and potted flowers added touches of nature to the interior space, and he noticed an especially gorgeous living bouquet in a huge gold chalice over by the sitting area. They stepped into the glass elevator and rode it to their respective floors, agreeing to meet downstairs at 12:55.

Herakles was on the seventh floor, at the opposite end of the hall from the showers. It was a simple room, with a desk, a chair and a bed, but it had a spectacular view of the Courtyard and the mountains beyond. He only had about 40 minutes, so he decided to spend the time trying to collect his thoughts for the meeting.

They met as planned and then made their way back to the Kríti building and up to the administrative offices on the fifth floor. Inside, they found Ivanna Jadan waiting for them in the reception area. Herakles had remembered her from New York, and felt somewhat relieved to see a familiar face. He introduced her to Carl, and then, without saying anything about what to expect, she escorted them into one of the interior offices, where two men were seated at a round table. She introduced them to Marco Ramirez, a Peruvian man in his mid-fifties, who was the Executive Director of Olympic Village, and Randall Harris, the burley, red-headed Chief of Olympic Security.

Ramirez stood to shake their hands. "Mr. Speros, Mr. Richter, good afternoon. Please, be seated. Ms. Jadan has informed us that you have information vital to the security of the Olympics." He sat back down. "You may proceed."

"Thank you, Mr. Ramirez," Herakles began. "I have reason to believe the Games are in grave danger. Prior to my arrival in Athens, I visited Delphi, and while I was practicing my daily meditation exercises, I experienced an unusually powerful series of images – a premonition of a great catastrophe..."

"A dream?" Harris asked mockingly. "This is a waste of time."

"Let him continue," Ramirez said, raising his hand in rebuke. "After all, Mr. Speros' ancestors routinely relied on the Delphic Oracle in matters of life and death."

"I know how it sounds," Herakles admitted, attempting to deflect their skepticism, "but I assure you I am not given to hysterical delusions. I have had several premonitions at other times in my life, which indeed came to pass just as I had seen them."

Carl piped up in support. "Many people, including myself," he glared at Harris, "have experienced this phenomenon."

"Or claim to," Harris retorted, glaring back.

"Please, Mr. Speros, continue," Ramirez said neutrally. "Exactly what was this premonition of yours?"

"A fundamentalist group is committed to wreaking havoc with the New Millennium peace. They're responsible for the recent bombings, which are part of an organized effort to sabotage the cessation of hostilities and re-ignite the fires of hatred and fear. All of that senseless violence was only a prelude, however, to their grand finale: a nuclear device they plan to detonate here, in Athens! The most terrible fire of all, born from the head of Apollo him..."

"Hogwash!" Harris blurted out, abruptly standing up, sending his chair sailing across the tiled floor. "I don't have time for these fantasies and hallucinations, when I have real security issues to worry about. Sounds to me like you're on drugs or something, Speros. I'll keep this quiet for now, but I warn you, don't waste any more of my time."

"*Mis*-ter Harris," Ramirez admonished. "That is quite enough. There's no reason to threaten him. I'm sorry Mr. Speros, Harris just takes his job very seriously. I assure you, there will be no repercussions from our meeting today. However, I'm sorry to say that, barring some more objective evidence or at least corroboration, there's not a great deal more we can do about your concerns. Do you have anything else?"

"No, but you've got to believe me!"

"We'll keep our eyes and ears open, and if you discover any evidence of this conspiracy, rest assured, you will have my full attention once again." He got up and held out his hand, and the meeting was suddenly over. Ramirez deferred to Harris and that was that. They left the office in somewhat of an awkward daze, not sure of how to respond to the rebuff.

They found a bench under a dark, shady tree in the Courtyard, and debriefed what had just transpired. Carl kept trying to emphasize how neutral and open-minded Ramirez had been.

"He really was listening to you, Kleo, I believe that. Look, these people are trained to assess security risks, and they've probably had to sift through hundreds of potential threats during their careers."

Kleo wasn't satisfied. "But why did Harris react that way?"

"He's an ass."

Herakles shook his head. "They didn't believe me, and they're not going to do a damn thing about it, are they Coach?"

"No, they didn't believe you, but they will still do their job. You did what you could, and now you have to focus on the Games. It's time, Kleo," Carl implored, taking him by the shoulders. "Success is almost within our grasp. You *must* focus your mind and attention on what you've been working toward all these years."

Suddenly, Herakles felt an overwhelming responsibility not to let Carl down. He stared into those sparkling blue eyes, and for the first time, felt a deep love for this person, this good and loyal man who had stayed by his side. With a lump in his throat he declared his intent: "I will focus, Coach. I promise."

Carl nodded and folded his arms, which was often the prelude to a bit of advice. "Now, as your coach, I strongly recommend you have some fun tonight."

Kleo couldn't help but smile at the unexpected suggestion.

"If I recall," Carl continued, "the rest of the American team is arriving later today. I would hope you'll be meeting Alanta."

"You've really come around."

Carl winked and patted his shoulder, then left to go rest up for the reunion he'd planned with some of his colleagues.

Herakles needed diversion, so he went in search of some company. He wandered back into the lobby, where he found the greeters in the process of welcoming the South African team, 40 or so athletes decked out in their turquoise and yellow warm-ups. He decided to hang around for a while, and before he knew it, he was talking with athletes from all over the world, distracting himself for the time being in everyone else's excitement.

He looked at his watch and his heart skipped a beat. If all went as scheduled, she'd be there in less than half an hour. He decided to find one of those comfortable divans and sit quietly for a few minutes before her arrival, so he slipped out of the Taiwanese assemblage and went into one of the anterooms.

He sat back, closing his eyes and stretching his long legs out in front of him. As his new dilemma came sharply into focus, a heavy sigh welled up and came forth. What would he say to Alanta? How could he "drop the bomb" on her like it had been dropped on him? With all she's worked for, and her competitions right around the corner.... No, he just couldn't disrupt her life like that.

He'd have to keep it from her, hide it beneath a calm, collected demeanor he would somehow have to manufacture, but he knew he had to be careful. Alanta January was extremely perceptive. He'd have to make it *really* good. Suddenly, he felt flush, light-headed, almost ecstatic – *she was going to be here any second.*

He got up to find a water fountain and as he was taking in the cool, refreshing liquid, he heard the musicians strike up their jazzy version of the *Star Spangled Banner.* The American team had arrived and she was now close by! He hurried back into the atrium lobby to find the place filling up with athletes, all dressed in red, white and blue – a sea of grinning faces streaming through the doors, gaping at the splendid surrounds.

He scanned the crowd, from the scallop-shell fountain of the Goddess Aphrodite, past the ensemble and the registration desk, over toward the sliding glass doors – and all at once, she was there in flesh and blood! At that moment of recognition, she caught his eye and her radiant smile lit up the room, fanning into flames the embers burning in his soul.

They hurried across the lobby, trying politely to get through the Yugoslavian basketball team and the Bulgarian weight lifters who kept obscuring their view of one another, until finally, they came face to face. Without hesitation they flew into each other's arms, twirling around, holding on as though they'd never let go.

Then they looked each other in the eyes, silently expressing what words could only lessen. How happy they were. How right this feeling. How promising the future if only they could spend it together.

"Alanta, you're more beautiful than Memory allowed me to recall."

"You're so sweet, Kleezy. I've missed you too. But here we are, together in Greece, can you believe it?" She reeled him in and gave him a kiss on the lips. "I've been looking forward to that."

"Feel free to do it any time you wish."

"Great! I will. So tell me, how 'you been? How was your trip to Delphi?"

"Good, but I'd rather talk about you. How was your trip?"

"Excellent. I just love flying above those clouds. 'Freaks me out a little, bein' so high above the ocean, but it is exhilara*ting*. And look at this place," she gestured around the room, "it's amazing. I am *so* excited to be here."

"It is exciting isn't it?" he said, glazed over with her presence. "Tell me we're still on for dinner tonight."

"How 'bout Thai food? I've been craving it ever since New York."

"I checked, and they have it."

"Great. Let's meet at the food court entrance in an hour and a half; that'll give me a chance to check in and take a shower. Thanks for coming to meet me, Kleezy." She looked him over again and shook her head, smiling, "you sure are fine."

He blushed, and was sure everyone knew it. "I'll see you soon," he said sheepishly, watching her walk away, finally having to wrest his attention from her splendid form.

It was clear that a number of people had seen the exchange, so he decided to duck out of the crowd, and go back to his room for a shower himself.

Rows of cypress trees lined the tiled walkway from the residential complex to the food court, called Pangaia, a huge enclosed area with restaurants offering cuisine from around the world. At the main entrance, a broad marble staircase stood, with two benches on either side. He was a few minutes early so he sat down to wait, but then he was up again, far too excited to sit still. He tried to occupy himself with a large framed map which listed all of the restaurants, and he noticed some unusual ones – Ethiopian, Jordanian, Slovenian – then he heard her voice behind him.

"Kleezy!"

He turned around and there she was, looking more fantastic than ever in an orange and yellow Caribbean print outfit. She threw her arms around him once again, and they hugged each other tightly.

They went up the steps, past a row of red and black Minoan columns, and then through the glass doors into the interior. The complex opened up into an enormous indoor space with restaurants, cafés and bistros on multiple, staggered floors – everywhere, people and activity and food of every kind imaginable. An Italian place with its own piazza, decorated in the style of Pompeii. A German delicatessen with Bavarian décor. A British pub behind the facade of an 18th century schooner. And right next to them, a Greek taverna with live bouzouki music, where a man was just delivering a tray of flaming kasseri cheese to a group sitting at a large round table.

"Lemme see," Alanta said, beaming, "oh-pah! Isn't that what you Greeks would say?"

Just then, the server cut loose with an overly gregarious "oooohh-pahhhh!" and they both cracked up.

"Let's eat there for dinner tomorrow, okay Kleezy?" She placed her hand on his arm. "I want to spend all my free time with you."

He put his hand gently on top of hers, grinning. "Me too."

They continued past the European and Middle Eastern restaurants until they reached the Asian section. A narrow wooden footbridge arched over a pond with goldfish and white water lilies, and as they crossed it, they traveled into the land of Siam.

A young Thai woman, wearing a red and gold sarong, approached them. With palms together, she greeted them with a bow. Herakles and Alanta returned the gesture, and followed her in. She seated them at a low wooden table with colorful woven cushions, amidst potted palms and flowering hibiscus. A little shrine to Buddha had been set up nearby, with burning incense and food offerings in three delicate porcelain dishes.

They looked the menu over and decided on fresh spring rolls, an order of shrimp no-name, mixed vegetables in oyster sauce and a spicy whole fish with red curry. Kleo placed the order, using his limited Thai vocabulary, much to the delight of the staff.

"Now tell me," Alanta demanded, "what's the matter?"

Herakles took a sip of his jasmine tea and tried to appear nonchalant. "What do you mean? Nothing's the matter. We're here, together, at the Games. Everything is just fine."

He set the cup down and she adroitly reached over the table, for a moment taking his smooth chin in her firm but gentle palm. "You got sohm-*ting* on your mind, I can tell. What is it?"

The server brought the appetizers.

"It's my father," he answered vaguely, picking up the large serving spoon. "Here, try some of these spring rolls...and the shrimp. I can't believe they have no-name! That's the actual name of this dish in Koh Phangnga, that little island I told you about last time."

"You were just going to tell me about your dad," she said, popping one of the delicately spiced shrimp puffs into her mouth.

"I was able to work through a lot of my old issues, and I've forgiven him, but I still haven't reconciled with him personally, so I guess I have some anxiety about our inevitable meeting."

She eyed him closely. "That's understandable, but I'm glad to hear you're on your way to closure. You were so upset the last time we talked on the phone.... And what about Carl," she tested, "how's it been since the reunion?"

"Better than ever. He's been wonderful."

"That's so good!" She took her teacup in both hands, holding it up to catch the aroma, then taking a sip. She held it to her lips, and tentatively looked at him over the rim. "And the Oracle? Did you see our future?"

The color suddenly drained from his face.

"What *is* it, Kleezy?" she pressed. "Something happened at Delphi, didn't it?"

"No, it was nothing."

She placed the cup back on the table, then sat back and folded her arms resolutely. "Kleo, you're trying in vain to keep this from me."

"I can't talk about it, Alanta."

"Well, now that you've *admitted* there's something, you *have* to talk about it." She scrutinized him. "Lemme guess, you really wanna talk about it, but you're worried about how it'll affect me. Isn't that right?"

"Yes."

"Hera*kles* Speros! I knew it. Now, don't you know it's honesty and openness that makes us so right? You take that away and what do we got? Nothing. Noh-*ting*."

He looked desperately into her eyes. "I don't want to burden you Alanta, with the Games just two weeks away."

"It'll be more of a burden if you don't tell me." She reached over again, this time taking his hands in hers. "Together we're stronger Kleezy. Believe it. Let me in. Tell me what happened at Delphi."

He squeezed her hands, as tears welled up in his eyes. "It's so horrible...." He took a deep breath, choking back the emotion, trying to get a grip, as she patiently waited. *Where to begin?*

And so he told her the bizarre tale of how he had entered the "Mythic Realm," sailing to Delphi with Mentes, meeting Athena at the Tholos, addressing the Immortals at the Temple of Apollo and learning about Ares' monstrous plan.

As he recited the prophecy, Alanta gasped in horror. "What are we going to do?"

"So you believe me? You don't think I've gone insane?"

"Of course not. You know how I feel about this stuff, Kleo."

"Well, Olympic Security thinks I'm nuts. Carl and I had a

meeting with them earlier today, and they looked at me as though I'd completely lost my mind. The security chief, some thick-necked hulk named Harris, even accused me of being on drugs."

"So what are they gonna do about it?"

"Nothing. Noh-*ting*."

"Oh, Kleezy...I can see why you didn't wanna tell me."

"Alanta, what should I do? I feel I need to act, but I'm at a loss."

Just then, the rest of the meal arrived and the two of them stared at it for a long, long time. Finally, Alanta broke the silence.

"The prophecy said we had till the third day of the Games, right?"

"Right."

"So I think we have time to eat."

He lightened up a little. "You think so?"

She helped herself to the rice. "We gonna need to build our strength if we have to go savin' the world." She placed a couple of good-sized scoops on his plate. "You mind carvin' up that fish? I'll handle the veggies."

They ate their dinner mostly in silence, with the weight of the terrible knowledge hanging heavily over them both. Every few bites, their eyes would lock together for a brief eternity, exchanging all at once the extreme continuum of emotions they were feeling.

"The Cloud o' Dread be circlin' round this place," she finally said.

"I'm so sorry I dragged you into this, Alanta."

"Nonsense, Kleezy. I never end up where I don't wanna go. We're in this together so don't worry, we'll figure out what to do. As Gran'mama Lily says, 'trust your own feet, and they'll take you up the right road.' But we gotta lose that Cloud along the way."

"This is a nuclear attack we're talking about! How do you just set it aside and go on like nothing's the matter?"

"You just do. And in the process, you stay alert, pay attention to the circumstances and the goin's on around you, and when the time comes, the right road will make itself known."

"What if I miss my chance..."

"No. Uh-uh. I don't believe that we've been brought together only to be gettin' blown up into smithereens. You hear what I'm sayin'? We *will* see each other through this, Herakles. As Bob Marley says, 'every little thing, is gonna be all right.'" She squeezed his hand again.

"I hope you're right."

"I am. Now, *oh*-kay, I wanna talk about somethin' else."

"What's that?"

"It's about our plans *after* the Games. We talked about spending a couple of days together, but I'd like to know if you might be interested in maybe makin' that a little more open-ended?"

"How can I think about after the Games, with the threat of..."

"Kleo, you have got to see a future for yourself, or it's sure you won't have one. That goes for anybody, anytime. Now, I give it to ya, we are under some extraordi*nary* circumstances here, but the principle is the same. You got to see it to rea*lize* it. So, about changin' those plans?"

Herakles cracked a smile, and looked into her ebony eyes. "I'd like to see where this relationship can go."

Alanta broke loose with an ear-to-ear grin. "Me too."

And so they made their plans – hiking up Mount Olympos, touring some of the Greek Isles, then sailing over to Monemvasía and crossing the Pelopónnisos to Olympia. Throughout the conversation, they tried to evoke a positive future, intentionally denying the scenario of unfathomable destruction, willing away the frightful specter of nuclear annihilation.

After dinner, they meandered around the Village Courtyard until they found a nice bench near the little pond. There they spent the rest of the evening, sitting closely together with arms interlocked, looking up at the summer stars, not saying too much...bracing for the danger they knew they must face.

Finally, as it neared midnight, he walked her to her building, Náxos, which was right next door to Santoríni. They arranged to meet the next day, and kissed each other goodnight.

# 12

## THE BURDEN OF ATLAS

With his thoughts and emotions bound up in a muddled mess, Herakles stared out the window of his small seventh floor room. Mount Parnitha rose up to meet the Heavens, its summit still caressing Night in this first light of morning. It was a sacred place, where Earth and Sky intersect, and where for countless generations, people have gone seeking the good graces of the Immortals. He hoped they would see fit to bestow upon him some insight, and prayed for the strength to set aside his apprehension, and focus on the Games.

A half-hour later he met Carl, and over breakfast they went through his training schedule. Refusing to allow the possibility of a stray and unproductive thought, Coach laid out the plan for the following two weeks, structuring most of Kleo's time in an effort to keep them both as engaged as possible. Despite what had transpired over the last couple of days, Carl seemed more determined than ever to succeed. Wasting no time, they finished their meal and headed out.

A monorail took them the short distance to the stadium, and they got off at the athlete's entrance. They walked past a huge set of neon Olympic rings and down a long ramp into the locker room, where Herakles changed into his training sweats.

Much to his chagrin, the moment he stepped through the

sliding glass doors of the weight room, he saw the last person in the world he ever wanted to see: Maximilian Leach, the "Awesome Aussie" and reigning Olympic decathlon champion. There he was, doing his "light" workout — bench-pressing about 350 pounds, Herakles' upper limit — rep after rep, making it look so easy, and without even a spotter to help him guide the barbell back into the stand.

Herakles again recalled their last meeting at the World Championships, and again heard Max's parting threat, *I'll see you in Athens, Speros, and I'm gonna kick your ass.* Now here they were, and Max was getting up from the bench, just about to look right at him.

"Speros!" he bellowed with his Australian accent, "I told you I'd be here. I hope you know I'm gonna kick your ass this time 'round, you rookie!"

"Hello, Max," Herakles replied, walking over to the brute and extending his hand. "Good luck to you."

"Ha!" Max exclaimed, grabbing it with a painful grip. "You're the one who'll be needing the good luck, *mate*. The Olympics are *my* domain. I hope you like silver or bronze 'cause I'm takin' home the gold to Goondiwindi once again."

"Don't count on it, Max," Herakles said, jerking his hand free and walking away from the obnoxious creature. However, Max wouldn't let up. He followed him over to the mats, unleashing a barrage of vulgarities and insults. For the most part, Herakles ignored him and proceeded through his normal warm-up routine, knowing from experience that Max was not likely to stop. He knew the Maxes of the sports world all too well, and could expect teasing, intimidation and numerous attempts to break his concentration and confidence. Unfortunately, even after the Millennium, a few competitors still clung to those base tactics. Win at all costs, without giving a damn about integrity, sports ethics and the transcendent ideals of the Olympic Games. For them, it was all about ego and personal glory, and multimillion dollar contracts to hawk one thing or another. It made him sick to his stomach.

Then, Max started in on Alanta, at first taunting him with juvenile, sexist comments about her. When Herakles refused to take the bait, Max continued escalating his crude remarks until he found the last straw: referring to the love of Herakles' life as "dark meat." Well, it was all our noble young hero could do to restrain himself. He jumped to his feet, on the verge of silencing the bully with his fist. Fortunately, at that moment, Carl came in and intervened.

"That's *enough*," he said, stepping between the two athletes.

Herakles stormed out, and Carl followed him back into the locker room. "You can't let Max bother you like that."

"I know, Coach." Kleo replied, trying to get a hold of himself. "I know."

"You have the strength to ignore him." Coach patted him on the back. "Now, let's go see this new track. I hear it's running very fast and that will give you a big advantage over him. Remember, if you can win all of the running events again, you won't even have to place in the throwing events."

"Okay, Coach," Herakles responded, trying to sound confident and upbeat. "Let's go check it out."

He knew Carl was right. The running events were definitely his key to victory and reaffirming that would help him get his mind off the aptly-named "leech."

As they entered the portal leading out to the track, he ran through the list of his other main competitors: Russia's Yuri Stanislov who excelled in distance running, and tall, lanky Ryan Floyd from Canada, whose specialties were the dashes and hurdles. Then there was the newcomer, Cesar Enrique from Brazil. Herakles had never competed against him before, but his running stats were impressive. As for the jumping events, everyone expected South Africa's Biko Themba to continue to set the standard as he'd done now for five straight years. Recent press reports indicated that he'd improved both his running and throwing, and was in a good position to take it all. Fortunately, these competitors embodied some of Herakles' own ideals and none was a Max in any way. A few he would even consider his friends.

And so, as he entered the glorious stadium, he tried to keep these things in mind.

They emerged from the dimly lit tunnel into the full and shining brightness of morning, and it was just what Herakles needed. He took Carl's advice and loosened up with a few laps around the track, and it felt good to have some open space in front of him. With each stride, he could feel his muscles relaxing, and sense the endorphins helping to lessen his anxiety.

He heard someone gaining on him from behind, so he casually glanced over his shoulder to the outside of the track. At first he saw no one, but then suddenly, as he turned his head back around, another runner appeared on the inside, right up next to him. Kleo moved out a few steps to give him some room, but the stranger stayed close, with eyes staring straight ahead, and scarcely breathing, as if there and yet, not there.

He looked down at the stranger's feet, and out of the corner of his eye saw white running shoes with little golden wings on the heels. Left, right, left, right – the feet came down on the track just as his own, but so lightly that they seemed not to be touching the ground, and with faint footfalls, as if far off in the distance.

All of a sudden he heard a voice, ethereal, silken smooth, whispering in his mind. *Herakles of the Golden Heart, be patient. Athena has guided you to this place; she will not forsake you.* Startled, he looked at the stranger, who was still running next to him. The man glanced back, now smiling, and he again heard the voice: *We will all help you when it's time, Herakles.* Then the stranger darted out ahead, vanishing into thin air.

He stopped and looked around, shielding his eyes from the brightening Sun. *Hermes.* He laughed. *With those little wings on his shoes.* He laughed again, feeling much lighter in spirit, and releasing for the moment the weight he'd been carrying since Delphi. He started running again, with each step feeling a little better able to cope with his predicament, and taking great comfort in Hermes' words. *Athena will not forsake me.*

As he recovered his confidence somewhat, he started to notice his surroundings. Rows of clean, orderly bleachers lined the sides of the stadium, gleaming in anticipation of the 100,000 spectators who were expected to attend the track and field events. On his second pass, it finally dawned on him that the enormous red shroud along the north wall was concealing the Grand Propylaia – the colossal piece of sculpture commissioned especially for the Games. Though there had been ample speculation about it, they'd somehow managed to keep the details a secret, planning to unveil it for the world at the Opening Ceremony. He felt a twinge of anxiety as he passed the cloaked monument, but picking up his pace, was able to put it aside.

A few more people were out now, running the track and starting to use the equipment. He ran by the discus area...long jump...pole vault...scanning the crowd for a glimpse of Alanta, but alas, to no avail. As he came up on the high jump, he saw his pal, Yuri, going smoothly over the bar and then rolling off the thick blue landing mat. He ran over to him, and the two embraced like old friends, even though they'd only known each other for three years.

Yuri slapped him on the back good-naturedly, and they spent some time catching up. Kleo told him about his training in Olympia, and Yuri spoke excitedly about his own plans to travel there. After their conversation, Kleo felt a renewed faith in the spirit of honest competition, reminded that thankfully, the Maxes of the world were becoming increasingly rare.

He was able to stay focused for most of the morning, with respectable times in the sprints and hurdles, and solid, consistent long jumps – nothing spectacular but nothing embarrassing either. However, while practicing the javelin, he saw his nemesis emerge onto the field, looking more like an unruly marauder sizing up a village he's about to sack. Just the sight of him triggered profound revulsion in Herakles, reminding him just how tenuous his concentration really was. To make matters worse, he knew that because he'd shown his sensitivity in the weight room, Max would take every opportunity to add insult to injury and there would be little escape.

As Max approached, he tried to appear indifferent, as though he were just leaving anyway and couldn't possibly have cared whether Max was there or not. He unscrewed the sections of the long, pointed spear, feeling grateful that civilized men no longer settled their disputes through violence, mindful that in times past, he would have been obligated by considerations of manliness and good taste to impale the vulgar being with the full sharpness of it. He exhaled loudly, and put it safely away in its case.

"Go ahead and run away, pussy," Max barked, coming still closer.

Herakles walked away, shaking his head at the pathetic creature. "Later, Max."

"Sure would like to get some of that dark meat for myself. What do you say, Speros, share and share alike?"

"Kleo," Carl said, catching up, obviously trying to distract him as they walked away. "I think we should go over to the pole vault. What do you say? You can practice the shot put later."

Then, at that moment, as though compelled by some powerful, mysterious impulse, Herakles looked up — and there she was, watching him from across the field. She waved, and his heart lifted like a song rising upward on a zephyr at dawn. He waved back, resisting with every ounce of strength the urge to run to her, and hold her and kiss her...and tell her he loved her. But he couldn't do that. He promised he wouldn't and she had agreed. It was best not to mingle during training; no need to call more attention to themselves, they'd said. He'd have to tuck away his desire and try to savor the anticipation. Besides, just knowing she was there was enough, for now.

Had she not been there, he might have come unglued and let Max have it. The brute must have planned his attacks, because whenever the other athletes were out of ear shot, he showed up with increasingly reprehensible remarks, most of them involving Alanta. Only when Carl threatened him with disciplinary action, did he make himself scarce — until around 4:30, when Kleo was back at the shot put area, and Carl was a few minutes behind.

"Hey, rookie," Max taunted, appearing out of nowhere and catching him by surprise. "Have you done her up yet, you dirty Greek?"

Herakles suddenly felt flush, becoming acutely aware of the

16-pound cast-iron ball he was holding in his hand, wanting now more than anything to shove it down Max's throat. However, conscious of the ever-present roving television cameras, he managed to keep it together as he calmly walked over and addressed him.

"What is the matter with you? You call yourself an athlete, but in reality, you're a disgrace to everything these Olympics stand for. And if you think your infantile comments are going to help you win, let me assure you, they'll only make me that much more determined you don't."

Max thrust his pug nose down and smirked. "The gold is mine, Speros. Do you hear me? The gold is *mine.*"

"Knock it off, you two," Carl shouted, hurrying over to them. "Kleo, please take a few more laps and then cool down. I'll meet you back in the locker room."

Herakles dropped the shot put close enough to make Max jump, then took off in a run. *Get a grip*, his inner voice said as he leapt onto the track. *Get a grip!*

As he ran, he tried to evaluate his first day's performance. At best, it was fair. His focus was off and he knew it. With his soul hovering over perdition, and his resulting inability to concentrate, he was just another adequate competitor. The realization bothered him profoundly, but it was nothing compared to the helplessness he felt about the impending catastrophe. Atlas had dropped the weight of the world on top of his mortal shoulders, and at the moment, he wasn't sure he had the strength to hold it up.

He spent the next three days on a roller coaster of wildly fluctuating emotions. One moment he felt like he had it all together, and the next, he thought he would scream from the sheer frustration of it all. He was nauseous, irritable, and at times unable to keep up the calm facade he knew he had to maintain. He was not meeting anyone's expectations, least of all his own, and there was no escape from the torment.

He couldn't very well just stay out of sight, hide away until his appointment with destiny. No, he was under the world's microscope, trapped inside a petri dish where he was the grand experiment. Would he meet his greatest challenge and save Athens from horrific destruction, or would he fail, allowing ruination to engulf the land?

Of course, neither the media nor the other athletes had any idea what he was going through; they were thinking about "failure" in terms of this race and that medal, whereas for him, failure could mean the end of everything. It could mean armageddon, and they didn't have a clue.

And so, the gossiping began. People were polite enough, and except for Max, he really didn't sense any gloating or nastiness on the part of his competitors; it was more as though they all felt sorry for him, the pitiful thing. The Olympic hero wannabe who was falling apart under the pressure.

"If they only knew," Carl had said to him.

*If they only knew*, he would try to remind himself.

Fortunately, by the grace of the Immortals, he did have his occasional high point as well – his 26' long jump, and the 10.84 sprint – but they were few and far between. One step forward, two back. Like the beleaguered Odysseus, doomed to endure many tribulations before his difficult task could be accomplished, enjoying moments of hope, then plunging into hours of despair, surviving Poseidon the mighty Earthshaker only to fall into the clutches of the dreaded Cyclopes, where he remained trapped with all the world, about to be devoured whole, down to his marrowy bones.

Thank Heavens for the loyal Alanta – his Kalypso, loving Goddess on her splendid island, amidst this rough and turbulent Sea. However, unlike wretched Odysseus, who wept great tears of lamentation as he felt marooned and desolate, Herakles wept with great relief to have found safe harbor in the storm. Without her to hold him in her embrace, he would surely perish into the gloomy depths.

And dear Maria was always there, with her unwavering support. He knew he was fortunate to have these two exceptional people in his life; he also knew his best hope was to trust their belief in him, even if he couldn't yet muster it himself.

He lay back on his bed with his hands behind his head, thinking about their evening together, feeling grateful the two of them had gotten along so well. He'd always known they would, but there was still the lingering worry that somehow the chemistry wouldn't mix, and he couldn't have borne it, not at this point. As he replayed the events, he felt a warm glow within his heart....

"He's my angel," Maria proclaimed.

"I can believe *that*," Alanta affirmed, smiling at him.

"We better order," Herakles said, picking up the menu, trying desperately to change the subject.

"You're so cute when you're blushing," Alanta added, clearly delighted with the situation.

"Oh, you should have seen him as a baby," Maria said, reaching over and ruffling his hair. "This mop was even curlier when he was a toddler, and he had the roundest, cutest little face with the rosiest little cheeks...."

He smiled at the thought of them fawning over him like that. Of course he was mortified at the time, but now it felt reassuring, comforting. Their faith in him was all he had, and as he went to sleep that night, he clung to it with desperation.

# 13

# THE CHAIRMAN'S DESCENT

High atop the TExxonMobico Tower in the Kingdom of Qatar, the Chairman of the Chairmen sat alone in his darkened penthouse suite, smoking another hand-rolled Havana, idly shuffling a deck of playing cards. He leaned back in his overstuffed leather chair, kicked off his wingtips and put his feet up on the mahogany table. From across the room, on the cherry wood pedestal in the corner, a statue of Zeus stood, staring back at him, with thunderbolt ready to fly. He'd acquired the piece from an underground antiquities dealer, as a way to commemorate his latest missile factory acquisition, and was very pleased with himself for finding such a deal. That little statue had been his inspiration for the course he'd recently decided to take, and seeing it there reassured him.

He turned his attention back to the cards and started randomly cutting the deck to see if he could better his last draw. He paused to set the cigar down in the marble ashtray mounted in the chair's left arm, then retrieved his crystal tumbler from its holder on the right, and took another hefty swig of Chivas. It was late and his eyes grew heavy as he resumed his game of one-upsmanship. Ten of spades, shuffle shuffle, five of clubs, eight of clubs, shuffle, nine of clubs...all the faceless cards...shuffle shuffle, nine of spades, six of clubs, seven of spades. Dark ones, hundreds of them, marching past him…marching around him…lifting him up and carrying him into sleep. His massive head rolled down onto his shoulder, his arms went limp, and the cards fell to the floor in disarray.

He found himself atop a skyscraper made of playing cards, wearing a robe of royal red and sitting upon his gilded throne, donning a crown festooned with sparkling diamonds. All of the Cosmos arched overhead in its interminable luminescence, and his vast kingdom spread out in every direction below. King of the Universe, smug and ungracious, reveling in the power he wielded over others, marveling at the order he brought forth from Chaos.

But woe be upon him, he was so enamored with himself and his possessions that he failed to notice old silver-haired Zeus, who was seated upon another gilded throne nearby. When he finally saw him, the Chairman's tranquility drained away. "Who the hell are you?"

"You were just looking at a representation of me, you pitiful thing. I am Zeus, Fallen King of the Immortals, and I have come to show you your fate."

"Horse shit, I don't believe in you."

"You idiotic and puny-minded mortal. Must we always spell it out for you? Don't you see, I am you, and you're me: the once mighty, now fallen…"

"What are you talking about? I'm at the height of my glory. You're the one who's dead and turned to ashes. Listen, whoever you *really* are, you can just get the hell out of here. This is *my* territory."

"And if I refuse to leave, just what do you propose to do?"

"I'll have you forcibly removed."

"Consummate fool. You're blessed with the presence of an Immortal and instead of showing him civility and respect, what do you do? Utter a pathetic and hollow threat, oblivious to your inability to carry it out. For crying out loud, you liken yourself to a God and yet you perceive none of the magic within you. In days of old, I would have struck you dead the first time I laid my eyes upon you. However, I have since learned to contain my wrath, and have now forsworn the killing of others. You would do well, way-ward mortal, to heed my daughter, Athena; replace your banner of conquest with her mightier scales of justice."

"Are you threatening me, old man?"

"Still, you fail to comprehend. What is a God to do? Perhaps the only way I can reach you is to rely one last time on my previous devices." Zeus contemplated what he was about to do as he looked at the wretched little despot. "Perhaps in this act of violence I can undo some of the harm I've caused."

The King of the Gods then stood and, mustering all of his former Eminence, addressed the Chairman, his deep voice thundering from all around. "Behold yourself, mortal! Your kingdom is an illusion, built upon the pain and suffering of others while you remove yourself to a palace of luxury, insulated, protected from the devastation you would cause. You are the foolish king, for you believe your station will preserve you and your self-indulgent way of life. However, the power you seek to unleash will most certainly overcome you. Behold the future you wish to incite." Formidable Zeus, who once ruled the domain of wide Heaven, then raised his mighty arm and a blazing thunderbolt did appear, pulsating in his tightly clenched fist.

The Chairman cowered, shielding his eyes from the fearsome glow.

"I have here my last thunderbolt, and with this final act of violence, I seek only to prevent that which I helped inspire, for I am becoming a God transformed. And so, I make a solemn promise to my Immortal Kin. I, Zeus, once King of the Gods, who sought to destroy all who dared challenge me, will henceforth lay down my weapons forever more." With that, he let his final bolt of lightning fly.

Beneath the Chairman's throne, the bolt exploded with a dreadful flash, and in the blinding furor of its superheated wind, his house of cards disintegrated beneath his feet. In an instant, the penthouse diamonds were incinerated, and as the Queen cried in horror, bits of her burning card swirled about him. Then he himself became a card – the King of Diamonds – flat and stiff, unable to move. At the mercy of the hideous gale, he began his slow, protracted free-fall into purgatory.

Diamonds and hearts all around him, burning, screaming as they blew, like a cyclone, past his eyes. Unholy inferno, melting his fine wax coating, searing his paper skin. Burning...burning!

Ruther, Jack of Diamonds, suddenly emerged from the spinning chaos. "I warned you, you idiot," he screamed, with little hands waving madly from the edges of his cardboard rectangle. "You should have listened to Arthur. Now it's too late. Everything is gone!"

"Ruther," the Chairman replied, trying to look composed, "don't be such a God damn pessimist. We'll rebuild!"

"You moron! Look around you, our world is on fire. There's nothing *left* to rebuild." He cried in desperation as his defenseless, combustible form suddenly went up in flames.

"Ruther! Ruther!" the Chairman bawled, as death and mayhem and playing cards churned with him in the fierce and burning wind. He tried to see through the mêlée, perceive something of what was yet to come, but the one-eyed king could not. This malevolence had completely vanquished his two-dimensional form, and now he could only suffer through it. Falling...falling.... He called to his other diamond friends, "Morris! DP!" But the Chairman's steadfast cronies could not hear his wailing.

However, the spades and clubs did hear him. In an instant, they surrounded him, filling his perception with their blackness, conjuring visions of their suffering, and the suffering of all the subjugated life on Earth. The once-silenced people were now shouting, shouting at him with the force of all the warring ages, pleading, demanding he see his way past the evil he had purveyed. Battlefields and missile launchings came into his vision, and all the victims of his age of modern warfare, bombed-out cities and ragged children, bleeding and crying, dying in the streets.

"No more!" he finally pleaded, and the black cards receded, leaving him still falling.

The burning sky turned to smoky haze and large, gray flakes of ash began to coalesce. There the smoldering king wafted, back and forth, back and forth...for countless eons, staring up at nothingness. Helpless. Knowing not what lay in store, or when. Sometime later, the ash began to thicken, becoming dense. Choking him. Choking. Eyes stinging. Getting colder now, and darker. On and on. On and on. Isolation, desolation....

Then stillness grew from the eternal rocking and he came to rest, singed and still smoldering, flat upon the ground.

The Queen and King of Hearts appeared, hovering above him. "It's never too late to open to love," they said, as they ascended upward through the dismal sky, voices echoing ever fainter until they eventually disappeared.

Suddenly, without warning or fanfare, Zeus himself materialized in the empty space they left behind. "Well," he said impatiently, "get up!"

The Chairman looked up at the imposing figure, looming over him with menacing intent. He mustered what was left of his strength, first wiggling his stubby fingers until they loosened from the card, and then thrusting his arm into the air. With sheer determination of will, and a great stretching of skin, he peeled himself up from his sidelong prison and back into his three dimensional form, now stripped of his royal red robe.

He looked himself over, and whattaya know? Good as new, not even a scratch. "Hah," he laughed, brushing some dust from his trouser leg. "I am invincible, Zeus, do you hear me? Invincible."

"Impudent mortal! Have you not observed the destruction which surrounds you?"

The Chairman shaded his eyes from the glare and looked around. They were standing on a hill, overlooking the ruins of a decimated city. Fine gray ash continued to fall, creating a pallid haze over the barren, colorless landscape, and a terrible smell of burnt flesh permeated the air. He surveyed the charred, smoldering wreckage extending out in every direction, as far as he could see. Human and animal skeletons littered the ground and not a sign of life remained. A few yards away, a strange row of marble pillars lay flattened, melted, almost fused to the ground.

"What's this?" The Chairman asked, trying to disguise his shock. "Where am I?"

"You do not recognize your handiwork?"

"What are you talking about?"

"This is Athens, you simpleton, shortly after your bomb exploded. We are on the Acropolis, where the glorious Parthenon once stood." Zeus raised his arms to the sky and again his voice thundered. "I could cry great tears of lamentation, and for endless moontimes sing songs of mourning – for close to three millennia, this impressive work of mortal hand endured, and now it is no more. Goddess Athena's once great and shining city, reduced to hideous waste."

"It's only one city," the Chairman retorted.

For a moment, Zeus looked as though he'd at that instant strike the Chairman dead, but then he calmed himself. "Look closer, foolish king, and you will see the extent of your responsibility." He pursed his lips and with a great exhale, blew the chalky dust into a swirling tornado, sweeping them back in time to just moments before the blast. From their vantage point they could see the Olympic Stadium and the thousands of cheering, happy people watching the athletes compete in their track and field events. Surrounding it lay the bustling metropolis of Athens, crowded with summer tourists.

Then abruptly, the deafening roar of the bomb's detonation ripped through the air, and the gruesome mushroom ballooned up from the city center, instantly vaporizing it. The cloud reached ever higher and the death wave expanded outward, leveling the landscape which had been so vibrant, so alive only a moment ago. The Chairman felt the rush of the blinding, hot wind as it incinerated the people around him. One second they were there, the next, they were gone.

"Your plan will work all too well," Zeus proclaimed. "Humanity will have lost its last best hope to save itself and you will be the one most responsible. Your pitiful little life will end along with the rest of your fragile species. Take a good look, fool. The path you are on is the path of total destruction. Surely it will lead you precisely where you're going, and in your arrogance, you'll bring all of humankind down with you."

"You are not my God," the Chairman replied defiantly. "My

God believes that might makes right and I will answer only to Him."

"Oh, pathetic monotheist who does not see Ares' deceiving hand!" Zeus exclaimed, pacing until he found his inspiration. "Perhaps, difficult one, there is an avenue to reach you, for yours is not the only God who can send you to the underworld you call Hell!" He raised his mighty arm and a second thunderbolt appeared, this time blazing with the heat of a hundred Suns.

Again, the Chairman cowered from the terrible light, shielding his face.

Just then, like a tender shoot, Demeter of the Goodly Crops sprung forth from the charred Earth and incarnated herself next to Zeus. The lines on her face had disappeared, and her youthful appearance had returned.

"Dear brother," she said with great concern. "You've made a solemn pledge to lay down your weapons forever more. If you were to break it here and now, I'm fearful our alliance will end, rendering us powerless to stop Ares from carrying out his hideous plan."

Zeus roared with frustration, grudgingly suppressing his desire to punish the unrepentant human. "Of course, you are correct, Demeter. I must refrain from this course of action and remain true to my oath, particularly at this crucial time."

Slowly, he brought the lethal bolt down from overhead, and gave it to his sister. As it touched her divine hands, it miraculously turned into a golden shaft of wheat.

"It has transformed!" Zeus exclaimed.

"And so can you," Demeter avowed. "If only you acknowledge it to yourself."

"I do reclaim myself," he affirmed without hesitation, "as Son and Lover of the Great Goddess of all Creation. I will no longer claim omnipotence, or reign through fear and threats of violence, but instead shall seek to coexist in harmony and peace."

As he spoke, Zeus' voice grew stronger, recovering its full and former glory; and physically, he began to transform as well, changing from the old silver-haired warrior God into a vibrant and handsome youth with golden hair, standing lean and tall.

The Earth Goddess and the Sky God then embraced, and for a moment, all seemed right. But then, Zeus remembered the Chairman, who was looking on, as smug as ever.

"So how will this mortal learn his lesson?"

"If he is to descend into Hades in search of his buried soul, then it is he who must endeavor to undertake the journey."

As she spoke, an awesome rumbling overcame the land, and the Earth began to give way beneath the Chairman's feet. Then suddenly, violently, the ground split open into a horrific chasm, and as the rift widened into a gaping maw, he was again gripped by the clutches of eternal falling…

…then thud. He landed on his ample rump, not knowing what had hit him. It was pitch black and too damn hot. Only the sound of flowing water existed, somewhere out there, in the void. On his knees he crawled toward it, over sharp, painful little rocks that jabbed and dug at his skin. "God *dammit!*" he swore, as his palms started bleeding. The water was closer now, just over there, a few more feet and, "whoa!"

Into the steaming hot river he went, and a raging current it turned out to be, carrying him swiftly, further into the depths. "Help!" he cried, bobbing under, swallowing great gulps of scalding water. "Somebody help me!"

Just then, out of nowhere, a spindly arm appeared, grabbed hold of him and pulled him up onto a rickety wooden barge. "There you go," the familiar voice said.

"Dammit!" the Chairman coughed. "I almost drowned!" When he caught his breath, he looked up. In the dim lamplight he could just barely make out his savior's face, and was mortified to see a thin, haggard version of himself. "My God! What kind of trickery is this?"

"It's no trick," his doppelganger replied. "I'm you, in the future, and this," he gestured toward his vessel, "is what you have to look forward to."

"What the hell are you talking about?"

"Hell is exactly what I'm talking about. You're destined to become the captain of this fine ship – the one who shepherds all of the poor, dead souls down the River Styx to the Gates of the Afterlife."

"That can't be..."

"Oh, but it is. You sealed our fate with that atomic bomb." The boatman returned his staff to the waters, guiding them through a dim tunnel. Suddenly, it grew much warmer in the cave and the rushing river slowed, thickening into boiling, bubbling mud. Shadows appeared along the banks, ghastly, ashen shades, desperate spirits, running, terrified. They reached out to the Chairman, clawing at him with gruesome fingers, torn and rotting flesh hanging off their bones, wailing, pleading to be delivered.

"Get away from me! Don't touch me!" he cried, trying to evade their grasp. "What do they want?!"

"To escape."

"From what?"

"From the Hell you created."

Their moaning intensified – all the tortured souls, running headlong into darkness, plunging madly into the burning river, their transparent bodies engulfed in flames as they slipped beneath the surface.

"Get me out of here!" the Chairman whimpered.

The boatman pushed them away from shore and the cavern widened, leaving the ghosts to suffer in the distance. Soon they came upon a rocky shore, and he beached his tired craft. "This is as far as I go. You'll have to walk from here."

The Chairman looked at the volcanic landscape surrounding him. Molten lava, glowing bright red-orange, flowed past him in fiery rivers, steaming geysers shot through huge cragged vents, spewing their pungent sulfuric gasses, and mud pots bubbled like cauldrons, beckoning him to fall in once again.

"Good luck!" the boatman yelled as he shoved off.

"Hey! Wait a minute. You can't leave me here. Where the hell am I 'sposed to go?"

The boatman pointed off in the distance. "That way. You can't miss the Gate." His voice trailed off as he disappeared into the sweltering haze.

The Chairman started off across the treacherous terrain that lay before him. Every few steps, another geyser erupted, or steam vent exhaled, further searing his bedraggled self. Still, he trudged on, determined to get to the bottom of this nasty situation. After what seemed like way too God damn long, he could finally make out some kind of structure up ahead. A mammoth iron gate emerged out of the gloom, guarded by some large creature stationed in front of it. As he approached, he could see the beast glowering from its post – it was Cerberus, the three-headed hound of Hell. It seemed to recognize him, and then its three heads turned into those of his cohorts: Ruther, Morris and DP. Greatly relieved, the Chairman approached them.

"Am I glad to see you boys!"

The head of Ruther was first to address him. "Well, we're *not* glad to see you."

"Why should we be?" Morris' head chimed in. "You're the one who got us into this."

"Hey," the Chairman protested. "This was not just *my* plan, you jokers endorsed it. We all share some of the blame here."

Ruther's ashen face contorted. "You're the one who gave those lunatics the device. I had nothing to do with that."

"Nothing to do with it," Morris repeated, straining at their thick, spiked collar.

"Nothing to do with it," DP lied, licking his drooling chops.

"Wait!" the Chairman said, brightening. "I have another plan. Lemme in here and I'll have a talk with the 'ole Devil Himself. See if I can't cut a deal that works out better for all of us."

"You've already sold our souls to the Devil," Ruther said, snarling as his head turned back into Cerberus. Then the other two reverted to canine form and the creature started growling, and moving menacingly toward him.

In a panic, the Chairman looked around for something he could use to defend himself. Luckily, he saw a dead tree limb caught in a lava well, and thinking fast, he grabbed it and pulled it out of the rocks. Flames leapt from the burning end as he charged the beast, thrusting it into all six of its eyes. The Great Hound cried in pain as it was temporarily blinded, and the Chairman ran past, slipping inside the impressive gate.

With all his might, he slammed it closed behind him, then collapsed up against it, clutching it with eyes closed, trying to will this all away. When nothing happened, he reluctantly peeked through squinted lids and found the iron gate had turned into a tall door of solid oak. He felt the smooth contour of the finished wood, and it was somehow comforting in the madness surrounding him. He patted his perspiring brow with what was left of his tattered hanky.

Finally working up the nerve to look behind him, he slowly turned around. He was in the foyer of a mansion, at one end of a long corridor with a high, arching glass ceiling, and above that, only darkness. A black and white parquet floor stretched out before him, disappearing into a cloudy, formless void off in the distance. Along the mirrored walls, marble busts of his favorite heroes rested on stone pedestals: Churchill, Napoleon, Caesar, Alexander – all staring at him with the weight of history's judgment etched in their glacial faces. Beyond them, there were two more tall wooden doors, one on either side of the hallway.

*This isn't so bad*, he thought, as he carefully stood up and took a few tentative steps down the long corridor. However, as he passed the bust of Churchill, all four of the bald, bleached heads came to life, their hollow eyes blinking, and their brows furrowing in garish expressions, simultaneously chattering in loud, over-exaggerated voices.

"Never, never, never give up!" Churchill pontificated, his pale lips curling back, revealing scary, bone-like teeth. "If you're going through hell, keep going!"

The other three laughed and heckled in response, and the Chairman, terrified, pleaded with them to stop.

Napoleon ignored him, offering some advice instead. "Promise everything, deliver nothing."

"Don't forget to watch your back," cackled the head of Julius Caesar, as it started spinning maniacally on its base.

The Chairman swung around, half expecting Ruther to be there, wielding a knife.

"Always, always, always know when to quit!" chortled Alexander. "You don't want to die too young!"

Their laughter became hysterical, and then suddenly stopped, their milky white faces freezing back into lifeless busts.

From the mist at the end of the vestibule, the Chairman could hear something moving toward him. They sounded like footsteps, but had an unusual clicking quality, and were growing louder and louder as they crossed the marble floor. Then, out of the darkness, a human skeleton emerged. As the terrible specter approached – click, click, click – he stood transfixed.

Nevertheless, when it said "good evening, Mr. Chairman," he recovered his flight instinct and bolted for the door. But alas, try though he did to open the mammoth postern, his effort proved futile. He turned, with his back pressed up against it, as the hideous rattling thing came at him. Again, it spoke in a masculine voice, which was somehow vaguely familiar.

"I said, good evening, Mr. Chairman."

"Who ah-are you?"

"You do not recognize me? A pity. You and I never actually met, but at one time you took a great interest in my career. Running all of those nice stories about me in your newspapers and on your network, hounding me with your reporters in the quest for tabloid fodder. Why, until recently, I was that vibrant, healthy young man you hated so. That strong, handsome youth who embodied an ideal you believed you could not attain. However, that was when I had a little more meat on my bones, wasn't it? Before my encounter with your device." It raised its arms. "Not much left to admire, I'm afraid."

"I don't know what you're talking about."

"Sure you do, Mr. Chairman. I used to be Herakles Speros, the Olympic contender."

"So, what do you want?"

"To show you the fruits of your labor." The Skeleton of Herakles gestured to the two doors in the corridor. "I'm here to take you on a little tour. Please, follow me, and we'll have a closer look at the consequences of your actions. Behind this door are the realms of the Afterlife, where first we'll visit gloomy Tártaros." One of the doors began to open slowly, and the Skeleton took the Chairman's arm and walked him through.

They stepped into the cloudy, foreboding domain and the door slammed loudly behind them, disappearing as it did so. The Chairman spun around, trying to find the way out, but there was none. Suddenly, he was floating, with the Skeleton and everything else around him, suspended in a great void. In every direction, an endless sea of phantoms – silent, amorphous murmurs of human, animal and plant forms, disjointed, yet melting together in gruesome, frightening configurations.

A recognizable image emerged from the madness, drifting slowly toward them. The Chairman gasped aloud when he realized it was his long-dead wife, holding their infant daughter in her frail arms. "Jeannette! Chloe!" he called to them, but they did not respond; they only hovered there, staring vacuously through him into the nothingness. "Why won't you talk to me?"

"They cannot," the Skeleton explained, "for they are but the shadows of the people they once were, existing now only in your memory."

"Jeannette, please. I'm sorry. I'm so sorry." The Chairman looked at the Skeleton with tears streaming down his face, as the painful memory he buried so long ago finally came forth. "I killed them," he sobbed. "I was drunk, and I got in that car, and I killed them."

The realization snuck past the many layers of armor he'd built up over the years and exploded, leaving him virtually defenseless for the first time he could remember.

"Please, Jeannette, forgive me. Forgive me," he pleaded. However, the spirits did not acknowledge him. They lingered a moment longer, then receded into the grisly mélange.

"I was supposed to protect them, and I failed," he put his massive head in his hands and wept.

Once his tears were shed, the Chairman spoke again, "is there nothing more for the dead?"

"It was once much more, before the Final Collapse. I can

show you. Come." The Skeleton pointed its bony, cragged finger at the nothingness, and as if parting a curtain on a stage, opened a rift in the gloom. They stepped through the crack in perception and emerged on the edge of a hillside, green and lush, yet still somewhat transparent. A muted Sun shone warmly against pastel blue skies, and colorful wildflower whispers swayed in the intangible breeze. Then he noticed the people and animals. Happy echoes running through the grass and climbing in trees, rowing gay wooden boats on the lake, flying lightly with birds through the clouds – all of it somehow incorporeal, dreamlike.

"This place is much more pleasant, where are we now?"

"The Elysian Fields," the Skeleton replied.

"Ah yes, where the great warriors get to spend eternity."

The Skeleton laughed. "Sure, the few who stuck to defense were welcome here; but I'm afraid most of the warrior aggressors ended up in Tártaros."

"What about the bravery, valor and courage of the conquerors? Was it all a lie?"

"The lie was putting those qualities in the service of a might-makes-right philosophy."

"All the stories? All the heroes?"

"There are many ways to be a hero." The bony finger again pointed to the surreal landscape. "These women and men were all heroic, for they lived their lives with compassion, love and forgiveness. They left their imprint on the world, on the collective human soul. Alas though, since the Final Collapse, this realm has merged with the other, where you found your wife and daughter. However, they didn't end up there because of the accident for which you blame yourself. They have been condemned to eternal suffering because of your decision to use a nuclear bomb." As the Skeleton spoke those words, the echoes vanished, the trees and grass disappeared and the lake dried up, leaking through to brown, hard cracks in the ground. The Sun went out, the beautiful blue sky turned gray and they stood silently in emptiness.

"Are you saying that I destroyed all of humanity?"

"Your actions ultimately led to it – but you're getting ahead of yourself, we have not yet concluded the tour."

"What more is left to see?"

"My dear Mr. Chairman, Hell, as it is with Heaven, really exists for those who live. Come."

Much to the Chairman's relief, the door again appeared, opening back into the foyer. He hurried through, coming face to face with the door on the other side of the hall. The Skeleton click, click, clicked across the parquet floor and approached it. "What you will witness next are not the shades and spirits of those who are dead and gone. No. This is the realm of the living, one year after you detonated your device. This is the Hell you have created on Earth."

The massive portal opened and the Chairman was thrust into the cold, unforgiving bleakness of nuclear winter. Fires raged across the devastated landscape, generating massive black clouds which continued to block out the Sun. The charred, hulking remnants of buildings and unidentifiable rubble went on for miles in every direction. He tried to imagine the city which once stood there.

"Is this Athens?"

"No. It's one of many cities nuked after your terrorist act. You see, you started a domino effect which could not be stopped. Global disarmament abruptly ceased, nation states withdrew from the UN and governments responded with paranoia and force. Old hatreds were rekindled and pre-emptive strikes taken, and this was the result."

"What? Were there no survivors?"

"See for yourself," the Skeleton gestured toward a large tent a short distance away.

The Chairman reluctantly started walking toward it, afraid of what might be inside.

It was a makeshift hospital, with hundreds of people of all ages suffering from burns and radiation poisoning, some crying and screaming with pain, others alive, but lifeless, laying there as if waiting to die. The gravity of the situation was finally weighing on the old Chairman's nearly forgotten heart. "Is there no hope for a different outcome?"

"There is always hope," the Skeleton said, unexpectedly vanishing into thin air.

"Wait! Don't leave me," the Chairman cried, running out of the hospital.

But he was alone, entirely alone, surrounded by the suffering, death and destruction he had ignited. "Noooooo!"

He sat down on the dusty ground and put his head in his hands, sobbing. For what seemed like an eternity, tears and more tears fell from the Chairman's eyes, until finally, he was all cried out.

Then and only then, did he find himself back in the foyer, sitting on the smooth, cool, black and white floor. He scrambled to get up, frantically looking for something, anything to get him out of there. The two doors towered over him, permanent reminders of the horror he'd just seen; and the stark marble heads stared straight ahead. Then, in the amorphous mist at the end of the corridor, he thought he saw something.

He timidly started toward it, looking over his shoulder every few seconds, fearful that another ghost might appear. As he neared the mysterious chamber, a female voice, rich with the power of immortality, spoke to him.

"Please, come in."

When he crossed the threshold, two large bronze torches abruptly ignited. With a great whooshing sound they came alive, blazing with fire, illuminating in radiant light the regal Queen Persephone and formidable King Hades, dressed in resplendent attire, seated beside each other on ornate thrones. The Chairman gasped, prostrating himself on the floor before them.

"So, at last you've made your way here," said the King, not too harshly. "We've been waiting for you."

"Please," the Chairman pleaded with nose pressed hard against the floor, "end this nightmare. Give me the chance to make things right and I'll promise to mend my ways. I'll end the alliance with OGOW and get the bomb back. I'll follow my nephew's advice and convert what's left of the military industrial complex into peaceful uses. I'll do anything. Please, just let me have the chance to stop this horror from happening."

"My dear sir," Persephone questioned. "What is your name?"

He looked up from the floor and into the lovely eyes of the Queen, searching the recesses of his memory. "My name? My name..."

"Poor soul," the King interjected, "he's been hiding behind his disguise for so long, he cannot even remember his own name."

For a long while, the Chairman laid there, distraught. *My name. My name. How could I forget my name? Who the hell am I?* Then suddenly, it came back to him. "Shepherd," he said in barely a whisper. "I'm Winston Shepherd."

"Please," Persephone said gently, "stand up. In reclaiming your name, you reclaim your lost humanity, and with that, you will find your hope for the future. Stand and say it with confidence."

He rose and did as he was asked. "My name is Winston Shepherd."

The Queen pointed to the space beside him and a fantastic altar appeared. "There you will find the sacred oil. Anoint yourself."

Winston approached the candle-lit shrine, which had at its center a large oblong looking glass surrounded by fragrant summer flowers. His reflection appeared in the dark mirror, but it was shifting, unsteady, coming in and out of focus. How long had it been since he'd really seen himself? Since he'd allowed himself to feel? He contemplated these things, and what he'd so recently experienced, and his image finally resolved itself into its true form. As he spoke his name again, he looked at himself squarely in the eyes, and for the first time since the death of his wife and child, he felt alive. Thoroughly, truly alive. Smiling with astonishment, he dipped his forefinger into a shallow bowl of scented oil and touched it to his round, gleaming head.

"Now," the King said, "please approach us once again."

Winston turned away from the altar and moved closer, stopping a few feet in front of them. Persephone rose and held out her graceful hands, where a red satin pillow appeared. In the tiny pucker in the center lay one small seed. "Take this seed of Love into your heart. Nurture it, and it will flower, bringing you great abundance and joy."

Winston took the seed into his palm and held it tightly, concentrating on it with every fiber of his being. Suddenly, he felt it move, and when he opened his hand, he realized it had sprouted. Roots shot forth from the little seed and hurled themselves downward, thrusting through the marble floor, anchoring into the ground below. Before his eyes, the shoot thickened into a mighty vine and, with Winston holding on for dear life, it rocketed him upward through the layers of Earth and back into the sunshine above. For the first time he could remember, love was blossoming within him, giving him a glimpse of the interconnectedness of the Universe, making him whole again.

He awoke with a start, jumping up and scattering the rest of the playing cards from his lap. "I'm alive. I'm alive!" he shouted, scrambling around the mahogany table and over to the window, where he saw the Sun coming up out of the Persian Gulf, dawning on a brand new day. He ran back to his chair and pushed the electronic keypad on the armrest. His secretary's voice came over the speaker.

"Yes, Mr. Chairman, what can I do for you?"

"The name's Winston. Call me Winston."

"Yes, Mr. Winston."

"No, just Winston. What day is it?"

"Thursday."

"And the date? What's the date?"

"It's August 5th."

"Please tell me it's still 2004."

"Yes it is, sir. Are you all right?"

"I'm fine – better than ever – and most importantly, I'm not too late! Please contact the Chairmen. Tell them we're having an emergency meeting, and I want them all here pronto!"

"Right away."

"Thank you, uh, what was your name again?"

"Patrice."

"Yes, thank you, Patrice. Go ahead and take next week off as extra paid vacation."

"Thanks!"

Within the hour, Ruther Burdock, Morris Reynolds and DP were all gathered together, and Winston was briefing them on his change of heart about the use of the nuclear weapon. "After we let OGOW know, we'll contact Arthur and tell him about our new plans. Maybe we can convince him to rejoin us. He was right – the future *is* in the peaceful use of military technology."

"Now you're talking," Ruther said, greatly relieved. "Thank God you've come to your senses."

"That must've been some dream," DP said wryly.

Winston pressed a button on his keypad. "Patrice, please connect us with our *friends.*"

"Right away, Winston."

"Winston?" Morris wheezed.

"Yes. That's my name, and I'll be using it from now on."

Patrice's voice came over the speaker, "they're coming in now."

The OGOW leader suddenly appeared on the giant screen, though only his harsh, pallid jawbone was visible under his hood. Winston informed him of the change of plans and ordered him to remove and return the nuclear bomb. As the chief terrorist received the news, he became extremely agitated. Another hooded figure leaned into the frame, whispering something into his ear. He nodded, then turned back toward the camera and replied.

"If you do not have the courage to carry out our divinely inspired plan, then we will have to take this Holy matter into our own hands. You are all cowards. I hereby end our alliance."

With that, the terrorist gave a cut-throat motion and the transmission suddenly ended.

"I knew they couldn't be trusted!" Ruther exclaimed, jumping out of his seat. "What the hell are we going to do now?"

The Chairman pressed the button on his armchair again. "Patrice, we need to talk to my nephew, Arthur Hayes. He's probably home at this hour, please call him immediately." He looked at his cohorts. "Stay calm, boys, Arthur's got some contacts at the new UN. He can help us resolve this."

"Putting him through on the speakerphone now."

"Excellent! Arthur my boy, are you there?"

"I'm here, Uncle. What do you want?"

"Arthur, Arthur. How have you been?"

"Cut the pleasantries. Just tell me what you want."

"We need your help."

"I told you I would have no part in your terrorist schemes."

"You were right. You were right. We know that now. There's nothing we can do to change the past, but we need your help to avert a disaster in the very near future."

"You expect me to believe that you've changed your ways?"

"I have, Arthur. I swear to you, I have."

"I don't believe you, Uncle."

"I can understand that, but *you've* got to understand this: we need you to arrange a meeting with Olympic Security immediately. We gave OGOW a nuclear bomb and we've lost control of them. They're going to explode it during the Games unless we prevent it. Now, are you going to help us or not?"

"A nuclear bomb! You actually gave those terrorists a nuclear bomb? You're totally insane. All of you."

"If you don't help us, we may not be able to stop them," Ruther interjected. "Please Arthur, we need you."

"All right. I'll set up a meeting, but remember this, Uncle, I still don't trust you."

"I know, but please, hurry. We don't have much time."

# 14

## COUNTDOWN TO OBLIVION

It was Friday morning, just one week before the Opening Ceremony, and Herakles was standing with Yuri and a few other people at the long jump pit. They were watching Biko Themba, the sleek, long-legged South African, as he started down the runway. With eyes focused perfectly forward, and big powerful legs carrying out his determined intent, he accelerated into the board and took off over the long sandy stretch. He seemed to defy gravity, as he cycled through the air to the far end of the pit, before landing with his usual finesse.

*Over 28 feet! There's no way I can match that,* Herakles thought. Then he realized what he was doing and felt thoroughly disgusted with himself. *You see yourself losing before you even get started. How pathetic.* He returned his attention to the next athlete in line, and tried to focus his mind.

Gradually, it occurred to him that the clear sunny day had vanished. Dark, threatening rain-clouds now covered the sky, casting a hazy shadow over the stadium. Then, Boréas, the North Wind, blew in with a brisk, damp chill, convincing him it was time to call it quits. He gave Yuri a pat on his broad, sturdy back, and jogged over to the other end of the field.

Half-way there, he encountered Carl, who was rushing toward him, talking to someone on his phone, with a grave expression on his face. "We'll be right there, good bye."

"What is it, Coach?"

"That was Ivanna Jadan," he replied, grabbing hold of Kleo's arm and hurrying them off the field. "Security wants to see us again. It seems they've corroborated your story."

"What do you *mean?*" Herakles exclaimed, with a lump the size of Kronos' stone forming in the pit of his stomach.

Just as they entered the stadium portal, the clouds burst, sending down a drenching rain. "We're about to find out. Shower and change, and hurry up, Kleo; they're waiting for us right now."

His heart started pounding and his mind went reeling as he bolted down the corridor to the locker room. He kicked off his shoes and socks and ripped off his clothes, flinging them away, not paying any attention to where they fell. He scrambled into the shower as horrifying images rushed through his frazzled imagination, washing over him with the spray of warm water, drowning him in renewed anxiety. He felt nauseous and dizzy, so he cranked the faucet to cold, trying to snap himself out of it. The coolness poured over his head and neck, taking hold of his attention, stilling his throbbing muscles, bringing him to a tenuous state of calm.

Thankfully, Coach had collected his scattered clothing and hung it up in the locker, bringing a glimmer of order to his increasingly chaotic world. As he toweled off and put on a fresh tee shirt and jeans, he tried to re-frame the situation as an opportunity to finally *do* something, and that made him feel a little better.

They took the monorail back to Olympic Village, and within 15 minutes, were once again sitting in Director Ramirez' office.

"Mr. Speros, Mr. Richter, thank you for coming so quickly," Ramirez said nervously, shaking their hands and motioning for them to take a seat. "We're sorry for the interruption, but as Ms. Jadan indicated to you on the phone, your story has been corroborated."

"Could you be more specific?" Herakles asked, trying with all his might to maintain his cool facade.

"Under one condition," Chief Harris interjected. "What you are about to be told is classified; you are *not* to reveal it to anyone."

"Of course not," Carl replied.

"Let me hear it from you too, Speros."

"Yeah, sure," Herakles responded half-heartedly, wondering how he could possibly conceal it from Alanta and his mother.

"All right then," Ramirez began with hesitation. "We have just spoken with two high ranking defense industry executives, and they've verified that a nuclear device has indeed fallen into the hands of a group of militant fundamentalists. The informants presented us with credible evidence that a suitcase-sized hydrogen bomb is hidden somewhere in the city of Athens, and the clock is ticking as we speak. They believe it's set to go off sometime during the first week of the Games."

"I knew it!" Herakles blurted out, lurching over the table. "We have to find it!"

"Please calm yourself, Mr. Speros," Ramirez went on. "An intensive search to locate and dismantle it is already underway. We have sophisticated technology designed to ferret out devices of this nature and we're confident we'll find it in time. However, as a precaution, we're also making contingency plans to cancel the Games and evacuate the entire area."

"What can I do to help?"

"First of all, we need to know if you have any further information, any new insights or intuitions?"

"No, not really. Except for a constant feeling of dread."

"Would you mind telling us your account once again, Mr. Speros, making sure to go through every detail."

Herakles launched into his tale and was pleased that, this time, they were taking notes and treating him with much more respect. He retold the story as though the events had occurred in his imagination, during his daily meditation routine, but as he spoke of Athena and Apollo, and Hermes and Zeus, in his heart he felt himself crossing back into the Mythic Realm, and experiencing once again the horror he felt the moment he learned of Ares' plan. When he got to the part about the Delphic Oracle, he had all of them spellbound, hanging on his every word.

"And finally, the Snake Goddess said that on the third day of the Games, I would be the one to prevent the evil destruction they have planned."

"Your intuition is truly remarkable, Mr. Speros," Harris commented. "The time frame you've outlined is completely consistent with our corroborating information. This has been extremely helpful, but I think we can take it from here. Thank you both for your assistance."

"Do you have anything else to add, Mr. Speros?"

"No," Herakles replied. "No, I believe I've told you everything."

"All right then," Ramirez concluded, standing. "If you have any additional insight, please contact me immediately."

"I will."

Then Carl spoke up. "I trust we'll hear from you when the bomb has been located?"

"Of course."

"And remember, Speros," Harris said as they were leaving, "not a word to anyone."

He nodded reluctantly, and following Carl, the two of them left the room.

Carl took the initiative and led them out into the Central Courtyard, but Kleo couldn't have cared less where they were going. Now there was no escaping the truth, no matter where he might try to hide, and the realization numbed him down to his very bones; as though he were nothing more than a bag of bones, exhausted, with nothing left to feel. Somehow, when the terrible knowledge spilled into the world, the living soul of Herakles went along with it.

And now Carl had that knowledge – Carl, who was walking briskly a few steps in front of him, with his hands in his pockets and head down. He hadn't said a word since they left the administration building, and Kleo could tell he was deeply troubled, which made him that much more determined to get somewhere. They cut through one of the residence buildings, and it soon became clear that he was headed for Pangaia, in search of food. He always got hungry when he was upset. Kleo was betting on the German delicatessen and sure enough, Coach went straight there.

Herakles sat down at one end of the wooden picnic table and leaned on it, staring into the opaque blur suspended before his eyes. He was just becoming vaguely aware of the Bavarian oom-pah-pah in the background, when Carl returned with two reuben plates, sliding them down on the table. Kleo analyzed the gargantuan kaiser roll in front of him, with its thin strips of pastrami escaping around the sides.

Carl pounced on his sandwich, devouring it, seemingly fixated by its shape and texture, his eyelids slightly drooping, the tension easing in his face, and before he was even half done, his familiar calm demeanor had returned. It was a miraculous transformation.

He looked back at his own plate and frowned.

"You eat that," Carl said with a mouthful, sounding like his old bossy self.

"No."

"Kleo..."

"I'm not hungry."

"You need to build your strength...fortify." He took another large bite, as if to illustrate how it was done.

Kleo looked at the sandwich but did nothing, so predictably, Carl issued several more instructions, which of course, only delayed his compliance further. Finally, he decided he didn't want to waste it, so he picked it up and took a bite. "I'm only doing this for you, Coach."

Carl nodded in satisfaction and finished off his lunch with the last chunk of a dill pickle. His German stoicism rebounded with vim and vigor, and he asserted his opinion in a direct and orderly fashion. "They will find it. I refuse to believe humankind has come this far, only to have our best hope for the future annihilated by a band of extremists. It won't happen."

"How can you be so sure? Our fate rests in the hands of a few individuals, and that makes me really nervous."

Carl shook his head, but remained quiet.

"You can't be sure, can you, now that you know it's true?

Still he didn't speak.

"You never believed me, did you Coach?"

"Well, let's say that I never appreciated the magnitude of your burden until now. I attributed your 'visions' to stress, and..."

"You thought I was losing my mind, didn't you?"

"I wouldn't put it that harshly, but yes, I had some concerns. Put yourself in my place, Kleo: the Immortals of ancient Greece and snakes breathing fire and prophesy from fissures in the Earth? You may have thought you were disguising it from me, but I could tell you believed these things actually occurred. As far as I knew, they were demons tormenting you from within.

"I can't explain what has been happening to you, and accepting that fact may be my most difficult hurdle; the fact that not everything is explainable. Not all ways of knowing are quantifiable. I have resisted this apparent reality and in the process, I have hurt you, my friend. I am very sorry for that, Kleo, but I'm afraid the only way I can trust someone else's intuition is for my logical, left-brained mind to have the verification it so desires." He smiled apologetically.

Kleo reached over and placed his hand on Carl's arm. "You've lived most of your life in a society which expected nothing less. As long as we remain open to possibilities, we will each find the right balance for ourselves. Give it the time you need."

"It's all happened so quickly...this *cultural transformation.*"

"The blink of an eye in the grand scheme of things – a bifurcation point – when anything is possible, when radical change can happen, for better, or for worse. With the Millennium four years ago, we had one for the better." He looked squarely into Carl's eyes. "Let's hope we're not now facing one for the worse."

"It won't happen," Carl replied, shaking his head and trying to sound confident. "It won't happen."

Herakles went to bed feeling sick that night, the new level of certitude churning that reuben sandwich into a nasty stomach ache. Thoughts of becoming a vegan repeatedly crossed his mind, as waves of nausea and anxiety swept through him. Tossing and turning, sitting up, laying back down, then over to the window, staring long at the steady lights of a quiet Olympic Village. On into the early hours the insomnia went, until finally he fell asleep.

The next moment, he was hurling through the wormhole of Existence itself. His emotions, tangible, in every color of the spectrum, spiraling out before him, curving and twisting, carrying him like flotsam on the endless River of Chaos. Curving fibers of thought and matter, elegantly reflecting the oneness of our Universe; graceful, ever-present self similarity, drawing him into its depths – then thud.

Dumped off in the center of the ancient coliseum, with the abominable Hercules coming at him again, big, ferocious and mean – then the brute's face became Max's and he growled, "I'm gonna kick your ass, Speros." Closer, closer, now almost on top of him, then the monster morphed into Harris, who was just about to pounce, when the ground beneath gave way, sending Herakles through another conduit. Again the whirling everything…

…and then he was sitting straight up on the red divan, next to the Aphrodite fountain in the lobby, with the sound of the water bubbling up from her marble seashell. He stared at the statue, for the first time noticing its name. *Daughter of the Sea, Child of the Beginning*, and as he said those words, the sculpture began taking on colors. The Goddess' flowing garment became a rich and vibrant blue; her hair became golden, her smooth cheeks rosy and eyes a clear aquamarine. She stepped down from the fountain, walked slowly toward him, and taking his hand, sat beside him.

"Alas, poor Herakles, you have another dilemma do you not?"

"I have made a promise, but I feel I owe a deeper obligation."

"To your loved ones, Alanta and Maria."

"Yes."

"I know well the reservoir of Love you hold within your heart. Embrace it and draw strength from its eternal source."

"Should I tell the two I love what news has come to me, or should I keep my promised word to Harris?"

"Your love for them comes with blessed trust, and as such, it is far stronger than an oath given under coercion. Therefore, be at peace with your oath and with yourself. What's more, it is vital that they know. You need them. Poor boy, you've borne a burden far greater than your years warrant, but you will endure this trial and emerge victorious. You must."

As the Goddess' voice trailed off, her fine blue shawl fell from her shoulder, revealing Ares' cursed shackle still tightly bound around her wrist. She winced as it contracted ever tighter.

Herakles touched her arm, and her skin was smooth and warm, alive, but then he felt the icy cuff. He wedged his long, slender fingers around the steely surface of Hephaistos' magic metal. Then, in his mind's eye, he bore through it, past the microscopic, on through to the subatomic, where its protons and electrons whirled about in perfect order. Deeper, he focused on the particles themselves, and like a strange attractor, coaxed them from their pre-determined paths. All at once, they flew apart and Aphrodite was free!

His eyes opened and he found himself in his bed, staring straight up at the ceiling. *Am I sleeping or awake?* For a long time he laid there, motionless, replaying the fantastic images in his mind, wondering when another miraculous encounter would occur. He heard Aphrodite's words again in the recesses of his imagination, whispering softly, *be at peace with your oath and with yourself.*

Down into the stairwell he descended, his footfalls echoing, ghostlike, off the concrete walls. The zipper on his open jacket clanked against the railing, and a harsh metallic ching-*ing-ing* reverberated through him. Round and down the passage he ran, three and four steps at a time, the seven flights feeling like 70. Finally he made it to the lobby, over the walkway and up the three floors to Alanta's room.

For an eternity of minutes he stood there, not knowing how to get her attention without waking up the whole place. *Tap tap*, his knuckle gently sounded. With an ear close to the door, he listened. Nothing. *Tap tap tap*. "Psst." He was just about to try again, when he heard her voice.

"Kleezy, is that you?"

"Yes," he whispered, looking up and down the hall.

She slipped him inside, and he spilled the news.

Listening calmly, and occasionally nodding her head, she reacted as though it was only a confirmation of what she already knew to be true.

There they were, the Keepers of the Dreaded Secret, talking together at that quiet, early hour, growing ever closer. Though he wished he could stay with her longer, forever, he knew he had to see his mother and be back in time to meet Carl. Still, before he left, he took a quiet moment to appreciate Alanta's countenance, her presence of mind and her awesome beauty – then he hugged her abruptly, again fearful it would all be lost.

She hugged him back, tightly, telling him with confidence, "don't worry, we'll get through this together."

"I believe that," he replied, trying to sound confident too.

He arrived at Thea Vasso's about 6:30, and to his relief, his mother buzzed him in. Fortunately, his great aunt slept through the whole thing, so they were able to speak freely.

If Maria had doubted him in her heart of hearts, she didn't let on. She calmly accepted the news, and urged him to have faith that the UN authorities would find and disarm the device. He drew strength from her reassurances, and though he still felt some guilt for going back on his promise not to reveal the information, he also knew that if he had a prayer of getting through this, it would be with Maria and Alanta's help.

He returned to Olympic Village feeling acutely, almost painfully aware of everything. Colors seemed unusually vibrant, and sounds amplified, some of them so loudly he felt his head would burst. The edges of everything were sharper, more clearly defined, even magnified out of proportion to reality. His lens of perception had been wiped clean, and the contrast made him realize what a fog he'd been in these last few days. Gone was the remote hope of it all being inside his head.

The epic struggle again began developing on either side of his corpus collosum: the rational, reasonable left brain needing to have a conventional explanation for what seemed to be direct communication with the Immortals, and the creative, nonlinear right brain whispering with Alanta's voice, *relax, every little ting is gonna be all right.* But how could he have known? What was the "Mythic Realm?" An actual, physical dimension, or a delusion shaped by storytelling and imagination? And what did those distinctions mean anymore?

Two days went by without a word from Ramirez. The fate of Athens and the Olympic Games were dangling with him over the very flames of perdition — a fire so hot it woke him, startled and sweating, repeatedly in the middle of the night. His fleeting hours of clarity were again replaced by an overwhelming inability to concentrate, and he became increasingly reluctant to go out onto the field, for fear he'd fall apart.

On the third day, his concentration was so bad that Carl sent him to the showers early, clearly frustrated with his performance. He ripped off his clothes and went to the back of the empty shower room. He turned on the cool water and closed his eyes, letting it pour over his head and shoulders, trying to ease the tension.

"Well, well, well," Max's voice suddenly boomed, making him jump. "If it isn't Herakles Speros. You've been avoiding me, rookie."

Now Kleo was pissed, realizing the brute had him backed into the corner. "Cut the shit, Max. I'm in no mood for it."

Max came closer, faking a punch. "What's the matter, the pressure getting to you?"

Herakles attempted to get around him, but Max cut him off. "I'm not done with you yet, Speros, and your coach is nowhere around, so listen to me and listen to me good. I'm going to haunt you like a ghost, and whether you're awake or asleep I'm going to be in your head 24 hours a day, reminding your rookie ass that the gold is mine. Do you hear me, Speros, the gold is mine, *mate.*"

There was no room to get around him, so, containing his anger and not saying another word, he waited for Max to finish.

"What's this? The smart-ass rookie doesn't have anything to say. That's better, Speros." Then he turned around, bent over and smacked his behind with the palm of his hand. "Now kiss my ass, you God damn Greek!"

Herakles stormed by, leaving Max roaring with laughter.

He got dressed and tore out of there, furious with himself for getting trapped like that. It was careless. He knew that jerk was just waiting for an opportunity, and he let it happen. Next time, he might just haul off and punch him in the face. *Listen to yourself! What are you going to do, take him on in a fight? Jesus, keep it together, Speros.*

With growing agitation, he boarded the monorail, thinking he'd better just go and hide from the world for a while. He went straight to his room, stripped down and crawled into bed. For over an hour, he laid there with his pillow over his forehead, and eyes closed, trying to shut everything out.

Then he heard a *rap rap rapping* at his door.

"Kleo?" Carl asked, a little too loudly for his frazzled nerves. "Are you in there?"

"No."

"Kleo, please let me in. We need to talk."

The sheets seemed heavy as bricks, but he found the strength to excavate himself from bed and throw on his jeans and a tee shirt.

"I'm sorry Carl," he said, letting him in. "I just can't do it. All I can think about is that bomb. I just can't concentrate."

"Listen to me, Herakles, you have nothing to apologize for. You are under extreme pressure. Most people would have buckled by now, knowing what you know."

"Why haven't we heard anything?"

"I don't know. I can only assume that they haven't located it yet."

"Do you still think they will?"

Before Carl could answer, someone else was knocking at the door.

"Herakles Speros?" came a male voice.

Kleo looked at Carl expectantly, "yes?"

He opened the door to find two security guards, who identified themselves and explained that Chief Harris had requested their presence immediately. Kleo looked to Carl who nodded in agreement, so they followed the agents down to the parking garage. They all got in a white sedan and started across town. The agents declined to answer any questions, but it soon became clear that they were being taken to the Panathenaic Stadium in the center of the city.

It had originally been built in the 2nd century c.e., and was thought to have had a capacity of 50,000 at that time. Subsequently, it was abandoned and the marble used for other construction projects. However, in anticipation of the first modern Games in 1896, it was re-built, mostly of wood; the marble was fully restored in the early 1900s. Unlike contemporary stadia, which are oval in shape, this one is long and slim, having been designed for track and field and equestrian events. During the 2004 Games, the famous 26.2-mile race from Marathon to Athens would end in this historic stadium.

Ivanna Jadan was waiting for them at the entrance.

"I'm so glad you're here," she said excitedly. "I have very good news. We've found the bomb and it's being removed as we speak. We're out of danger."

Herakles hugged her impulsively. "Are you sure, Ivanna? Absolutely sure?"

"Positive. In fact, if you'll follow me now, you can see for yourselves."

She led them past scores of security guards, down the long, narrow field, and up into the second row, where the burly red-headed Harris was standing. A four-foot section of the stone bleachers had been removed and stacked off to the side, and Herakles looked in and saw the bomb. It was sleek and metallic, about the size of a small suitcase, yet he knew it had the destructive capability of multiple Hiroshimas.

*The insanity of it all,* he thought, as he watched the bomb squad carefully remove it and place it in a large container.

"It was set to explode on day three of the Olympic Games, just as you foresaw," Harris explained. "We've successfully deactivated the timing mechanism, and are now moving the device to the weapons lab. Mr. Speros, I believe I owe you an apology. I had my doubts about you, but your intuition was dead right."

"That's okay," Herakles replied. "The main thing is that you've found it. Thank you for letting us see it for ourselves."

Harris nodded. "Now, you rest easy, the Games will go off without a hitch."

And so the Mortal Herakles fulfilled the prophecy of the Snake Goddess of Delphi. Athens had been saved and the Games could now commence.

From their Delphic Shrine, the Immortals raised their golden chalices of ambrosia to drink to Herakles of the Golden Heart and the demise of Ares' despicable plan, unaware that the Dust of Deception was clouding their view.

Yet, before their lips tasted the sweet nectar, Aphrodite called out in pain. "Wait! As we prepare to celebrate the events we have just witnessed, the wretched cuff upon my wrist tightens ever more."

"Yes!" Athena, Goddess of Wisdom, interjected with great concern. "If we were truly out of danger, would not its grip be eased?"

Zeus, now youthful and transformed, stated with confidence, "fear not, my daughters, the dreaded cuff tightens only because

Ares has finally been defeated. Now he focuses the last of his spite on you, to keep you from spreading your Love far and wide. I will find Hephaistos, Lord of the Forge, so he can remove it once and for all."

"Most generous of you," Athena continued, "but if all were good and true, would not Hermes be among us? His unexplained absence is alarming."

"Oh, typical Hermes," Dionysos remarked. "He's always slipping in and out, with nary a word of his whereabouts."

"The catastrophe has been averted," Apollo reaffirmed. "We've seen it with our own eyes." With that pronouncement, the God of Reason raised his goblet high, calling upon the Panthaeon to toast the Mortals who had foiled Ares' plan of hideous destruction.

They brought their glasses together, celebrating amongst themselves in the blissful ignorance ingeniously imposed upon them by the cunning god of war.

# 15

## OLYMPIC EVE

Gran'mama Lily was relieved to finally be off that tarmac and in the air. The hour they'd sat there, waiting for clearance, seemed more like four. Now it was time to settle in for the flight. She wrapped her scarf around her short salt-and-pepper hair and rummaged around her well-traveled bag, looking for her sarong. She found the red, black and gold fabric, festively decorated with zigzags and spirals, and placed it around her muscular brown shoulders. Leaning into the steel body of the jet, she focused her obsidian eyes out the small rectangular window. Far below, she could see the clouds' dark shadows gliding gently across the seemingly infinite Atlantic. In the east, Night was peeking up from the horizon, chasing the last rays of sunlight over the dome of the sky. *It'll be dark soon*, she thought.

She looked over at her daughter, Grace, and son-in-law, Christian, who were sitting next to her. Lily didn't often get the chance to see them side by side, at least for any length of time, as neither of them liked to sit still one bit. They were always on the move, Grace with her students and all of the field trips, performing experiments in the lab she'd built in the back room of their house, and of course, concocting herbal remedies. Christian ran their entire 10-acre farm by himself, taking care of fruit trees, vegetables of many kinds, herbs and prize-winning orchids. The two of them were also very involved in their church community, always raising money for one good cause or another.

They were both 44 and in fine shape. Grace had lost some weight this last year, and though she wasn't nearly as tall as Alanta, she could easily pass for the girl's older sister, especially since she started wearing her hair in braids. Poor Christian was already squirming in the tiny seat, trying to position his long legs comfortably. He was starting to look a little older than Grace, with his temples just getting gray, and a few lines appearing on his face. All those years working under that hot Caribbean Sun were catching up with him, though he was still as handsome as ever.

It had been a good trip so far. She'd left Dominica more than a week earlier to spend a little time with them at their home on St. Croix. She helped Christian put in a new fish pond, and took long walks on the white sand beach with Grace. Sweet Grace. She'd really settled into a beautiful life, close to the Earth and Sea, with a good husband and meaningful work, and surrounded by love.

Lily had enjoyed those walks with her daughter, talking stories about their many adventures together during the touring days and sharing their excitement over Lanna's Olympic debut. One afternoon, Grace let on that she and Christian had had some concerns about Lanna becoming involved with Herakles Speros, some reservations they couldn't really explain. Neither of them had said anything to Lanna though, as they didn't want to upset her, and so they decided just to set those thoughts aside.

"Don't push them off too far," Lily had advised her daughter, "they may be trying to tell you something you just don't want to hear."

Lily didn't allow any passing thoughts to slip by unnoticed, for each might hold some special insight into what tomorrow would bring, and though she didn't mention it to Grace just yet, she too had had similar feelings. But she didn't want to dwell on that right now. The answers would come in their own time.

Every day was a blessing, she reminded herself, and this particular day held special significance. The three of them were on their way to Greece to watch their Lanna compete in the Olympic Games. Yes indeed, this one was especially blessed.

She clicked on the overhead light and pulled her bag from beneath the seat. From it, she retrieved her reading glasses and a book about Greece, which Lanna had given her in anticipation of the trip. Lily had a funny way of reading books, not starting from the front and working through it left to right, but rather, she liked to let them speak to her at random. She stood it on its spine and pulled it open from the center, letting the pages fall where they may. Tonight, it opened to a section on the Classical Goddesses and Gods, with pictures of Zeus, Hermes and Athena. These beings were familiar to her, though she knew them by their Yoruba names, Shangó, Eshu Elegba and Nana Bukúu. Nana Athena coaxed her eye and she studied the Goddess carefully, taking note of the snake on her shield. Feared for millennia for its poisonous venom, yet symbolic of resurrection because when it sheds its skin it is born anew, the snake was a sacred creature to be given respect.

Suddenly, like a window shade snapping open, a memory appeared in her mind's eye. It was the vision she'd shared with Lanna nine years before – the flame of a roaring fire transforming into an African Goddess, holding a living snake in each hand.

"Do you see her?" Lanna had asked.

"Yes granddaughter, I see her; and she sees us," Lily whispered. "If you show no fear, we'll learn why she has revealed herself."

The Goddess smiled, and then shared with them the gift of prophecy. *Children of Africa*, the eternal voice began, *keepers of our ancient ways, embodiments of our ancient spirit, I call upon you now to prepare to fulfill your destiny. Lily, you must teach Alanta to seek, and ultimately, to trust the Wisdom she holds within. And you, Alanta, must learn well, for you will face a great challenge in the future, and it is vital to our very existence that you are ready to meet it.*

With that, the Goddess disappeared in a whirlpool of flame and the spell was broken.

Lily stared at the picture of Athena, trying to hold the vision in mind. *Great Goddess Africa*, she concentrated, *snake handler and wise woman, reveal to me the mysteries surrounding us. I sense events are transpiring in a sphere unseen, so I ask you to share your secrets with me. What role is Lanna destined to play?* She closed her eyes and awaited insight.

"Care for a beverage?" the flight attendant interrupted, startling Lily out of her trance. She peered up over her glasses, and trying to reorient herself to the present, replied, "oh, yes, an orange juice please."

*I have made my request,* she thought, sipping the juice, knowing now she would just have to be patient and wait for an answer.

Dinner followed along. It was your typical airplane fare, not worthy of excessive description, but Lily was hungry, so she took the vegan option and ate it. For dessert, she pulled out the mango she'd brought with her, grateful that security hadn't kept it for themselves. She expertly peeled the rind in one long spiral strand, sliced some of the succulent fruit for Grace and Christian, and then enjoyed the rest herself.

The attendant took the trays and Lily put her seat back. Though she usually had a hard time sleeping on planes, this flight proved to be an exception. One moment she closed her eyes, and the next, dawn was breaking outside her little window. She could just see its glowing halo, drawing the ball of fire up from Yemoja's watery home. It was a strange feeling, flying eastward, into the future so to speak, losing time and losing track of time along the way – *happens when a body is shuffled 'round the world faster than it's meant to be,* she thought, as she stretched her arms and legs, catlike, forward and then up.

The aroma of roasted coffee wafted through the cabin, a sure sign morning had come, but Lily had never acquired a taste for the bitter bean. Instead, she got some hot water for the tea she blended herself with herbs from her garden on Dominica. She packed her little mesh teabag with a good stiff dose and plunged it into the water, then held the cup between her hands, directing the fumes into her nostrils. The potent mixture awakened her senses, and soon she felt reinvigorated.

She had a nice little exchange with her kids, as they sipped their coffee and revived themselves, then she returned her attention to Lanna – Earth spirited, sweet Lanna, her only grandchild. How she'd enjoyed their recent visits. Let's see, there was her college graduation last year, when she received the scholar athlete award. That was really something, watching that beautiful child glide up to the podium, so happy, so excited to have earned such an honor. Nelson would have been proud too, that's certain. Then there were the World Championships last summer, where she set her latest records. What a thrill, what a thrill that was. And of course, there was her visit to Dominica last October, right after Hurricane Benjamin blew through, destroying everything in its nasty path. Years of the people's hard work gone in only a few hours. Lanna came down for two whole weeks to help clean up. That child truly had a special gift, an ability to turn heartache to joy. Always looking on the sunny side, always finding the reason to celebrate, to be grateful, to draw every last drop out of life.

Lily had done her best to nurture this quality, for she knew that Lanna was destined for glory – not in a personal sense, simply to feed her ego, but rather, in a way which reflected well on all of humanity. Yes, Lanna was special, what we humans could be if we put our minds to it: balanced, compassionate, and living life to one's fullest potential.

Lily also knew her granddaughter's destiny was very near at hand, and that soon her fate would reveal itself. She could feel the magnitude of it – the tug of history on one side and the pull of the future on the other. The breaking point was imminent. Every fiber of her being was telling her that the critical time was almost upon them.

They'd made a habit of talking on the phone once a week and even though Lanna didn't mention a thing about it, Lily knew something was askew. She could hear it in between the notes of that girl's melodious voice, in between the references to her new love, Herakles Speros. Lily chuckled to herself, *she calls him Kleezy….*

Then a more somber feeling returned. *He's all wrapped up in this too.*

A few hours later, they were checked into their Athens hotel. It was situated at the foot of the ancient Acropolis, tucked away in the lively market and tourist area known as the Plaka. They were on the sixth floor, and each of their rooms had a small balcony overlooking the many shops, restaurants and tavernas in the crowded streets below. After a few minutes admiring the view, they decided to take a short rest before Lanna was due to arrive.

Lily met Grace and Christian in the hotel lobby at four o'clock as planned, and before they could even sit down, that girl came bounding through the open door. Lily took one look at her and saw right through the happy exterior. Something big lurked beneath those ear-to-ear grins. She could see it, surrounding her, even emanating from her, but she decided to let it be for now – with Grace and Christian so happy to see their daughter – she'd have to wait until she could talk with Lanna alone. So, she took her hand and contented herself with the goodness she felt just to be with her family, here in Athens for the Games. What a joy, what a very special joy.

It was a little early for dinner, but Christian was hungry, so they decided to get a bite. They found a nice place right next door, and thanks to Herakles, Lanna was able to interpret some of the dishes for them. Of course, Lily and Grace had eaten Greek food along their travels, but it was Christian's first time. He decided he liked the pastítso, the velvety macaroni dish, the best.

After the meal they had a walk around, stopping in a few of the souvenir shops. Lily was looking at some Minoan reproductions and a miniature Snake Goddess figurine caught her eye. *Athena's grandmother*, she thought, holding the heavy little brass object in her hand. She admired the detailed patterns in the layered skirt, and was amused by the lion cub perched on her head. She took it up to the counter, and after politely declining the owner's offer to throw in a bust of Zeus and a Byzantine icon for a pittance, she bought it.

It started getting dark, and Lanna had to be getting back to Olympic Village. Even though Coach Jimmy had protested, she'd insisted on taking the morning off to be with her family, and so they firmed up their plans to visit the Acropolis together the next day, and said their good nights.

The hypnotic eastern sound of bouzouki music drifted upward from the tavernas below, lulling Lily into a deep and dreamless sleep. She had long ago learned to selectively tune out sounds, so she didn't even notice the boisterous merry-makers who continued well on into the early hours.

She rested peacefully until the wake up call came through, just as it was getting light outside. They'd wanted to leave in time to miss the big tourist busses, which would start arriving mid-morning, so they all met in the lobby at 7:15, and then set out for the Agora entrance a few blocks down the now quiet street.

Lily had done some reading about the ancient pilgrimages to the Parthenon. In the old days, people who wanted to pay homage to Goddess Athena would begin their journey some 14 miles away in the town of Eleusís. They followed a road called the Sacred Way, which at that time took them to Athens through olive groves and fields of wheat and barley. Sadly, most of what was once that revered path was now covered over by industrial-age urbanization and sprawl, hidden from the modern eye.

They came to a large open area, a park, with cypress trees and crumbling stone walls.

"Kleezy drew out a map for us," Alanta said, pulling some papers from her pocket, "and he told me all about this place. This whole area is called the Agora, the market, but we're actually just skirting the main part of it, which had been over there." She pointed toward the west. "Those must be some of the building reconstructions, right there through the trees. The American School of Classical Studies has been excavating the site for years, and it's a whole day trip by itself. Come on, we can pick up the Sacred Way over here." She motioned for them to follow her.

Lily stopped for a moment to notice the contrast. Behind them, modern buildings and streets, and in front, an oasis of the distant past. So, as if crossing a threshold of space-time, she stepped off the sidewalk and onto a gravel path.

She recalled what she'd learned about the Agora. Like the

modern day Plaka, where they were staying, it had been a vibrant and lively place. It was there that the people of the city congregated to sell their goods, exchange ideas, learn, debate, compete, philosophize and participate in civil society. It was also where, in a temporary resurgence of democracy, they made the decisions of state. Athenian citizens, which actually meant a few privileged males, would cast their votes by placing black and white stones into large clay pots.

However, even the powerful must have known their limitations, Lily observed, looking from the shadows skyward toward the Acropolis. She could only glimpse the temple tops behind the old stone fortress, yet she could tell that the structures were enormous. They paid their fee at the entrance booth and continued up the Sacred Way, walking past huge rectangular blocks of marble, and stone disks from once tall pillars, now spread out like fallen dominoes on the ground. Some walls had been partially reconstructed, but most of them had been left in time's grasp, and now, green grass and red poppies sprouted through their old cracks.

Lily walked the path slowly, taking note of the stones and bits of marble as they picked up the morning light. "So many people have come this way," she said out loud. "Can you hear all those footsteps?"

Her family continued on with her, silently perceiving their own whispers from the past.

They came around a curve and she looked up. High above them, and still some distance away, she could see a rectangular building, with four pillars standing firm and defiant, resting atop another huge block of stone carved right from the jagged rock face. As the Sun climbed over the mountains, it illuminated the structure, washing it down with golden light.

"Athena's Temple of Victory," Alanta whispered. "Kleezy told me the Athenians built it after they successfully defended the city against a Persian invasion, to proclaim victory to the entire Mediterranean world."

"That's certain," Lily agreed, marveling at the exquisite monument.

"That's certain," Grace echoed, smiling. "So, Alanta January, you better say a little prayer to Ms. Athena when you get up there."

"Grace," her husband admonished, a little uncomfortable with that line of talk.

"Oh, Christian," she laughed, grabbing his arm. "You lighten up."

He shrugged it off and they proceeded along the Way. Alanta stretched out her leg muscles a little more and started bouncing around, running up the hill, then sliding back down, creating small cascades of rolling gravel.

"You're kickin' up too much dust, girl," Christian said, smiling, trying playfully to pinch her belly as she darted past him.

"All *right*, you two." Grace took her turn in coming down the heavy. "Settle now."

Lily had fallen a little behind, immersed in the history surrounding her. When the people kindly regained their peace and continued on, she returned her attention to the stones. Again, she heard the footsteps...then voices, off in the distance, thousands of them – a cacophony of all the joys and sorrows of the many lives, and deaths, here over the eons.

Up. Up. Up, to where, finally, they passed beneath the Temple of Victory and approached the staircase at the grand entrance of the Acropolis. She stopped again, turning to see where they'd come from. The deep green cypress trees held their heavy morning mist, shrouding the city below. When she turned back around, she found herself alone at the bottom of the well-worn marble stairs – her family had already gone up.

She was now at the foot of the Temple of Victory, which soared above her on the right; she could barely crane her neck enough to see it. To her left, near the top of the staircase, were an array of tall pillars. Mindfully, she ascended the broad stairway into the Realm of the Immortals, respectfully passing through the majestic entrance to Athena's long revered sacred space.

At the top, she encountered a short walkway framed by more marble columns, wondering how the stone masons of antiquity were able to raise those massive rocks so high. Then, as she emerged onto the plateau, the full grandeur of the Parthenon came into her view.

The magnificent structure stood with eight colossal pillars in front and too many to count along the side. What was left of its triangular pediment thrust upward into the clear, blue sky, as if still trying to touch the Heavens. She stood motionless, taking it in.

After a few minutes, she allowed her eyes to drift to the cleft in the mountain above and beyond the Parthenon, and she noticed they were perfectly aligned. She sensed the spirit of those ancient Greeks, who had placed their holy sites in beautiful natural settings, challenging themselves to create temples complementary to the splendor of Earth Herself.

As she walked slowly toward Athena's massive temple, she started noticing some of the other buildings, and one in particular caught her eye. It had six tall pillars, carved as female figurines, all of whom supported the roof of an elaborate porch. Though Lily didn't know it by its name of the Erechthion, the place which once held the most sacred, most venerated image of Athena, she could nonetheless sense the Goddess' spirit still emanating from it.

Those statues had seen 2,500 years of history: Greeks, Persians, Romans, Byzantines, Turks, Nazis. Pilgrims, philosophers, statesmen – slaves, concubines, warriors and madmen. The whole history of the city was imprinted in the marble, and Lily allowed the images to roll across her mind.

She suddenly started to feel a little dizzy, so she looked around for a place to sit down, noticing a low marble bench under the shade of an olive tree. A minute later, Lanna came running toward her, jumping over several pillar fragments.

"Watch your ankles on this uneven ground, Lanna. You don't want to be taking any chances."

"Yes ma'am," she replied, sitting down beside her, close in. "Isn't it awesome, Gran'mama?"

"It is," Lily replied, realizing that this might be their only chance to talk for a while. "So, Lanna, is there something you want to tell me?"

She looked around nervously, and then replied, "yes, there is. I've been wanting to tell you for a long time, but I had to wait till you got here."

"I understand." Lily's heart started pounding. *How bad would it be?*

"Kleezy has the gift, Gran'mama – he went to the Oracle at Delphi and learned about a terrible plan to destroy the Games and all of Athens with an atomic bomb."

Lily closed her eyes, feeling the horror of it manifesting in her gut.

"But don't worry, Gran'mama, they've found it, so everything's okay."

"Tell me what happened."

"Right when he got here, Herakles went to UN security but nobody believed him. He didn't have any proof. I believed him though, right from the start. I haven't doubted him for a second."

"Did you leave it at that?"

"We couldn't figure out anything else to do, then about a week later, security called him into their office again. They discovered evidence that made them realize Kleezy was right. All week, we've been a mess with worries, wondering if they would find the bomb or be forced to cancel the Games. Then, two days ago we got the call. They found it in the old stadium and dismantled it, so everything's okay now!"

Lily tested her. "Are you sure?"

"Yes ma'am. Kleezy saw them remove it."

"We sometimes see what we want to see."

"Oh, Gran'mama," Lanna took her arm, "don't be worried. Everything's okay. You're just tired from your long trip, and you're picking up on all of my earlier anxiety."

Lily regarded her for some time, then finally spoke again. "Look with me, Lanna, at the fiery veins in the marble pillars of the Parthenon. See how they're absorbing the photons of sunlight, bringing life into the silent stones...remembering the way it was when the Goddess spoke?"

"Yes, I see them. They're beautiful."

"Look deeper, like I taught you. Ask these stones to release their memories to you. Be open to the vision they will give you. Now, what do you see?"

"Flames, I guess...spiraling upward."

"Go on," Lily encouraged her.

"Connecting Earth and the Heavens. Yes...I remember you talking about that before."

"What else do you remember?"

Lanna furled her brow, trying to see through to the essence of the stone. Then suddenly, her expression changed to one of comprehension. "Yeah, it's like in that vision we saw at my ceremony...when She appeared. The time when the Goddess spoke..."

As Lanna echoed those words, an opaque, ghostlike image became visible within the pillar.

"You see her, Lanna?"

"Yes, Gran'mama. Who is it?"

The ethereal figure then spoke to them in a hauntingly distant voice. "It is I, Athena Tritogenía, born from the salt marshes of Tritonis, in the land of ancient Libya. I take this form to honor my link to Mother Africa. Lily Khana and Alanta January, welcome to my beloved Sanctuary.

"I appear before you now because I fear that all is not well this Olympic Eve. Deception clouds the vision of Mortals and Immortals alike, and if it remains unperceived, it will most certainly lead to our destruction. I cannot tell you what it is that you must do, for I do not yet know myself, however, one thing is clear. Alanta, you must trust in the Wisdom within you, as your destiny is at hand."

As she finished speaking, the column returned to solid form, and Nana Athena vanished.

Lily looked intently at her granddaughter, who was now silent. "You still don't want to believe it, do you?"

"It can't be true Gran'mama. It just *can't* be."

"It must be."

Alanta lowered her head, shaking it. After a few moments, she looked at Lily. "She must be talkin' about the past. All that's already happened. The deception unperceived was about the bomb – and it's been found. Herakles saw it with his own eyes."

"I'm telling you. The threat is still here, I can feel it in my bones. If you concentrate, you will see the ruination for yourself. It's hanging heavy in the air like a thick cold fog."

"Dohn *say* that Gran'mama. It's too horrible."

"I must speak my truth, and so must you. Listen to what Nana Athena just said: trust in the Wisdom within you." She retrieved the little Snake Goddess figurine from her bag and placed it in Lanna's palm. "You must come to see the deception, Lanna. Everything depends on it."

Just then, Grace and Christian spotted them, and Lanna was all too happy to put the Goddess away in her pocket and jump back into distraction, springing off the bench and darting over to them.

And so went the morning: Alanta back to her old cheerful self, avoiding spending any time with Lily alone, not wanting to be reminded of what Lily knew to be true. Terrible destruction was near, circling like a hungry vulture overhead, and it was up to Lanna and Kleezy to prevent it.

The four of them lingered awhile at the Acropolis, but the voices of the place had become so present in Lily's consciousness they grew bothersome. She was relieved when everyone got hungry again, and they all went back down the hill to find something to eat.

This new knowledge weighed heavily on Lily throughout the rest of the day and into the evening, and as much as she wanted to explain to Lanna how things were, she knew she was going to have to leave her be, and trust that she'd come to the truth in her own time. Since they'd soon be on their way to the dinner party at "Auntie Vasso's," she resolved to set her concerns aside. The last thing she wanted to do was cast a shadow on the evening's festivities.

She tried to reassure herself there was still time. *There must be time*, she sang to herself, as if in a mantra, using all of her influence to make it so. She would just have to accept the uncertainty for now, and push that ominous storm cloud back along the horizon of her imagination. Lily was a powerful being of faith, and by the time twilight surrounded Athena's City, she was feeling much more at ease and even looking forward to dinner. Tonight, she would finally meet the other players in this epic drama.

Vasso's apartment building was close to their hotel, so they decided to walk. They followed their directions through the narrow cobblestone streets, and within about twenty minutes, came to the griffin gate. Lily admired the abundant flowers, as Lanna sped up the walkway to the directory and pressed the button. The door buzzed open and they were in.

The old elevator slowly clanked its way up to the top floor of the 12-story building, and when it opened, that girl, already starting to blush, darted over to their doorbell and rang it enthusiastically. Grace and Christian each took a nervous breath as they approached behind her. The door whooshed open and there stood the fabled Herakles Speros, bright eyed and smiling. Lily could feel the magic between and beyond the two of them, radiating outward, enveloping Grace and even touching Christian, who, though he tried, couldn't completely resist their aura.

She was introduced first, so she took Herakles' hand in hers and looked into his amber brown eyes. All at once she sensed his strength and courage, kindness and creativity, but there was also something more, she was certain – yes, below his current awareness lay denial as well. It rested quietly, deep in his psyche, nearly hidden from view, but Lily could sense it even if he couldn't. Like Lanna, on the surface he too believed everything was fine, that there was nothing left to worry about. His very desire to believe the danger had passed was keeping him from seeing the truth.

*Let it be*, she reminded herself, as she warmly shook his hand and smiled.

Lanna then introduced him to Grace, who was already noticeably under his spell. It was written all over her daughter's face. She was smiling and nodding approvingly, and even subtly batting her eyes. She always was a bit of a flirt, and Christian, well, he was still pretty stiff, but she could tell he'd come around, eventually.

Herakles escorted them into the living room, and Lily took note of the decor – various Greek frescoes and sculptures, family photos and a Byzantine icon of the Virgin Mary on the wall, and oak furniture, whispering with voices from a once sacred grove. Suddenly, the kitchen door burst open and out walked Maria and Vasso, talking rapidly to one another in Greek. Then, Vasso, noticing she'd left her apron on, abruptly spun around to the kitchen, a moment later reappearing without it. As Herakles completed the introductions, Vasso announced, now in English with a heavy Greek accent, that since it was such a pleasant evening, they should all follow her out to the terrace.

Lily crossed the dining area into the small kitchen. She smelled something roasted, with sage and oregano, but there was no sign of any food. They'd been invited for dinner, she thought, as her stomach took note, reminding her that she'd had only a light lunch many hours before.

Vasso led them through a doorway and out onto the rooftop terrace, gesturing for them to sit while she poured everyone some fresh-squeezed lemonade. They all admired the beautiful flowers, spilling out of clay pots of every size, and the green leafy grape vines growing around the walls, with their clusters of ripening fruit bursting through the white slats of an overhead trellis. A light breeze freshened the evening air as Lily sat down on the love seat next to Maria, who struck up a conversation.

The discussion quickly turned to the work they'd both done internationally, Lily with the Ogoni liberation movement and Maria with the United Nations. They expressed gratitude and appreciation for one another's efforts and for the progress which had been made over the last four years. Then Maria changed the topic to music, admitting that she'd worn out an old African Rhythms 8-track in her youth. The thought of that archaic technology sent Lily back too.

She shared stories about the early recording days and the

Rhythms' first studio. With the dilapidated equipment and constant power shortages, it was a miracle they'd recorded anything at all. She reminisced about how it had been to live a nomadic, musical life, trying to spread a message of hope, as she encountered the people, customs and cultures of the world.

They found they had a lot in common, like a commitment to helping others and working for social justice, a mutual love of travel, and an appreciation for the beauty and joy life could bring.

As they chatted, Lily also tuned in to the other conversations taking place around the patio. Auntie Vasso went on with the vigor of a seasoned storyteller, while Kleezy unobtrusively made sure everyone else got to participate in the conversation. He had a beautiful way about him that boy, with his gentle, good nature. He had Lanna and Grace completely won over, and Christian was undoubtedly beginning to thaw.

In a little bit, Vasso went inside, and much to Lily's confusion, returned with a large tray of pastries. Lanna and Kleezy were oblivious, lost in each other's company, but she exchanged a glance with Grace, who could only shrug her shoulders. She looked over at Christian and he seemed excited at the prospect of sweets, besides, he didn't care. He'd eat just about anything you put in front of him, anytime.

Lemon pie, little twisted butter biscuits, some powdered sugar cookies – her stomach growled again – a dinner of dessert. Inwardly, she laughed at herself. Even after all of her cultural experiences, there were still surprises. She selected a nice full plate and enjoyed each and every one of them, and so did the others.

The seven of them talked on, exchanging family histories, speculating about the Olympics, and reaffirming both athletes' prowess and potential of winning, then, as Lily expected, Christian finally came around. He toned down his West Indian accent, to be sure everyone would understand him, and told a story about Lanna, about the time when she was five and had been playing in the garden with him when a rain squall blew through. She splashed in the puddles and rolled in the dirt, then made a big fuss when he tried to clean her up. He told her, "Lanna, if you don't let me give you a bath this minute, you're name is gonna be Mud. Well, she put her hand on her little hip and stomped her foot, saying, 'if my name is gonna be Mud, then pack my bags, I'm moving next door to the Anthony's.' Always a mind of her own that one."

They heard that story how many times, and Lanna was still embarrassed, trying without a prayer to change the subject, as Christian in his sly way kept bringing it around again, till finally he let her be. Then, he let loose a little on Kleezy, making sure the boy was minding his competition, and gently testing him in that 'you good enough for my daughter' way fathers sometimes do.

Grace then asked Maria to share a funny story about Herakles as a boy, and she was obviously delighted to tell a tale which Lily suspected had also been recounted on many occasions. Kleo was three and his curly hair was so darling, so adorable, she just couldn't bear to cut it. It grew and grew, and soon he started looking like a 'kukla,' a cute little doll. Maria, who didn't have a daughter, couldn't resist, just that one time, putting him in a frilly pink dress — just to see how cute he could be. It was so confining, and the lace so picky, he yanked it over his head, literally ripping it apart at the seams. Everyone laughed and Kleezy took it all in stride, blushing a little and changing the subject as quickly as possible.

Just about when Lily thought they'd be calling it a night, Vasso went back into the kitchen. Kleezy sprung into action to retrieve place settings from a credenza, and Maria started taking drink orders. A moment later, Vasso returned, bearing a large bowl of cucumber-tomato salad and a basket of bread. Then it just kept coming: roasted lemon chicken, rosemary sage potatoes, a creamy pasta casserole sprinkled with nutmeg, delicate spinach and cheese stuffed triangles, and it was already close to 11:00. *Oooh, on top of all those sweets?!* She looked at Grace, who widened her eyes and blew out her cheeks. Predictably, Christian was beaming with anticipation. Just where the piping hot food was coming from was a total mystery to all of them.

When the commotion settled down and the people were again seated, she took a small serving of everything and ate till she could fit no more. Then, as she was finally setting her fork down, to her utter astonishment a fresh tray of pastries appeared, along with a bowl of cantaloupe and honeydew slices. She exhaled fully, sat up a little straighter and politely accepted some fruit.

In front of each person, Maria then placed a small porcelain demitasse cup, and Vasso filled them with Turkish coffee.

"Drink with me," Maria said, looking at each of the guests, "from the well of the future."

Kleezy smiled at his mother's dramatic style and looked around the room to see the reactions of the others. When his eyes met Lily's, she detected a little pang of fear and a subtle change of demeanor. *Good. It's on its way up to the surface.*

He abruptly looked away, and started explaining his mother's remark. "When we're finished enjoying the coffee, the wise and lovely Maria will read everyone's cup."

"Like tea leaves?" Grace wondered, reaching for hers.

"Exactly," he replied, taking his own.

"Where does the tradition come from?" Lily asked, sipping on hers at first to be polite, but then another surprise, it was oddly attractive, bittersweet.

"The Greeks learned it from the Ottomans, during the occupation," she replied. "As I understand it, the custom goes back to China, where they originally read the dents in their temple bells. I guess, as the practice became more widespread, they must have run out of bells!"

Everyone laughed, and they shared a few more stories. Then, as each of them finished the coffee, Maria demonstrated how to turn the cup over onto its saucer. "You have to do it quickly, like this, so the grounds are properly distributed," she said, encouraging the others to follow her example. After allowing a few moments for the cups to drain, she announced she would begin with her son's. She looked at him and smiled, sliding his saucer toward her and grasping the cup with her right hand. She turned it over and held it in her palms, rolling it gently in one direction then the other, as she looked inside, into the secrets of the cup.

"I see a man on the slope of a mountain, and like poor Sisyphos, he's pushing a formidable boulder upward, toward a high plateau."

Herakles' brow furled slightly, almost imperceptibly. "It must be Max," he laughed, trying to deflect the omen. Then he and Lanna exchanged glances, and Lily could tell that a slight pall had been cast on their enthusiasm.

Maria took Lanna's cup next. "Well, Alanta," she began, "I see a ring, no, a hoop, like a hula hoop," she kidded. "It's hovering above the ground...and on the other side of it stands a pedestal. Here, have a look."

"What does it mean?" Lanna wanted to know, looking inside.

"That's for you to determine. I can only tell you what I see."

"Yes, I see it too," Lanna replied, a little troubled by the image.

Lily could tell that her granddaughter was going to look her way any moment, and when she did, Lily gave her a clear affirmation. *You've got to go through that hoop before you get to the prize.*

But Lanna shook it off.

"Your cup is next," Maria said to Christian, smiling, as she slid his saucer over.

To Lily's eyes, Christian looked skeptical. He didn't go too much for the old ways, but as he was a guest and wanted to be congenial, he went along with it. *Poor thing*, Lily thought, *he's had too much dogma in that church of his. It scares people for no reason.*

"Beautiful," Maria exclaimed. "This one's easy. A dove carrying an olive branch, it's right there. It's all in the cup." She handed it back to him.

The gesture was not lost on son-in-law Christian, who by now seemed much more comfortable as he replied. "Thank you, Ms. Maria."

Grace's cup was next. "I clearly see a palm tree," Maria said, "and these figures here look like a group of people sitting together."

She handed the cup to Grace. "It's our family! We're out front at the house. There's the beach, and the Sun rising on the horizon."

Maria went to lift Vasso's cup, but Vasso scooped the whole saucer up herself and held it close to her chest. "No," she said dramatically, "I do not wish to have my cup read."

"Very well," Maria said, reaching instead for Lily's, "that leaves mine and Ms. Lily's. May I?"

"By all means."

Maria studied Lily's cup much longer than the others, and so the prolonged sound of silence took on a mystical air. "Lily," Maria finally said, looking for a moment into her eyes, "I see someone sitting high up on a ledge, overlooking a little town down in the valley...and the Sun is low in the sky."

Lily took the cup and peered inside, studying the dark brown pattern left behind by the coffee grinds. Suddenly she saw what Maria described and her heart fluttered – *am I to sit there, a passive observer with a bird's eye view, yet powerless to influence events? And is that Sun rising, or setting?*

She returned her attention to Maria, "what a wonderful custom, Ms. Maria. Thank you so much for sharing it with us."

"It's my pleasure," Maria replied, seeming to note her reaction. "Uh, perhaps you'll do me the honor of reading my cup? It's bad luck to read my own."

Lily shook off the feeling and nodded politely, taking Maria's saucer. She turned the cup over and looked in, allowing an image to emerge. The corners of her lips curled up ever so slightly, and she pronounced her reading. "Well Maria, it appears that there's a man with a mustache in your future."

Lily watched with interest as Maria's eyes darted over to her son's, whose eyes likewise moved to meet hers. Immediately, she sensed the pain someone had caused deep within both of them. *What part would he play in the drama unfolding?*

"I hope I didn't say something wrong," she said with concern.

"No," Maria replied, trying to mask her feelings, "you read the cup exactly as you should have. Thank you for sharing in our custom."

They continued talking until just after midnight, and although Vasso looked as though she could carry on for hours, everyone agreed that they should call it an evening. Lily gauged the mood as she said her goodnights. The excitement everyone felt at the beginning of the evening was still there, but Maria's poignant readings had also stirred up some anxiety. Boulders and hoops, palm trees and doves, mountains and Suns – and the mystery man in the cup. It would all be coming together soon.

And so, on this Olympic Eve, the two families affirmed the goodness of their meeting and took leave from one another, each embarking on the journeying ways.

# 16

# LET THE GAMES BEGIN!

Magenta mountains and swirls of lavender and pink adorned the twilight sky over Athena's city. The 28th Olympiad was about to commence with the start of the Opening Ceremony, and 100,000 people were in attendance, filling Olympic Stadium to capacity. Over three billion more viewers watched over the e-waves, getting a bird's-eye view from the ENN dirigible circling silently overhead. Each spectator had been given a miniature laser, and from above, as darkness fell, they morphed into an enormous phosphorescent horseshoe.

Then, on cue, everyone turned off their lights and the stadium went dark. Anticipation permeated the air, as a low, electronic note slowly, sneakily crept into the audience's consciousness, then began to crescendo, building, building, adding violins, woodwinds and horns, intensifying expectation. Spotlights suddenly thrust upward into the Heavens, illuminating the nation-state flags waving in the gentle summer breeze from atop the stadium rim. The timpani sounded and another set of floodlights ignited, casting their powerful beams on the Grand Propylaia, the massive sculpture still draped in its red shroud, waiting to be revealed. Above it, ascending even taller poles, were two more flags, one with the familiar interlocking rings, and the other with the bright blue and white Earth against a Cosmos of deep indigo. The Olympic Anthem rang out, and the crowd erupted in applause, cheering and whistling and clapping.

When they finally calmed down, the performance began. From seven different directions around the field, hundreds of African drummers emerged, each dressed in the colorful clothing of their native country. With diverse and elaborate drums, they created a heavy, methodical pulse – lub*dub* lub*dub* lub*dub* lub*dub* – and as they drummed, they formed a ring encircling the whole field, their intense, primordial rhythm enveloping the stadium, connecting one and all to the ancient heartbeat.

Then, as they transitioned to a more energetic, melodic beat, long streamers of fabric began to unfurl from the south end of the field, swiftly carried by runners hidden underneath. Some had banners of the land and some had banners of the sea, and together they formed a colossal map of Greece: the Mainland, the Pelopónnisos and islands of the Sporádes, Dodekánisos, Kikládes and Kríti all spanning the field. Those familiar with the country would have noticed an island missing; but not for long.

The drumming intensified and, as if by magic, what looked to be red-hot lava shot up from the "sea" north of Kríti. A three-dimensional form began to rise from the stadium floor, becoming a purplish blue cone which grew larger and wider, and as the image of the map receded off the field, the island of Thíra was born.

The volcano grew and grew, towering up into the air, and when it attained full height, the drumming stopped. The drummers receded and all was momentarily silent...then birdsong could be heard. A forest of tree puppets rose around the base of the cone, and then sparrow, finch and hummingbird puppets appeared. More runners carried ribbons of iridescent blue fabric, becoming the Mediterranean and Aegean Seas, where whales, dolphins and octopi swam amidst the silken waves.

Then from across the ocean, in glorious sailing ship floats, the Minoans came to make the island their home. Musicians with harps and lutes and castanets struck up their lively music, while from the wings, dancers appeared with large three-dimensional banners much like Chinese kites. One after another they came out – bull vaulters, cup bearers and priestesses, followed by lilies, blue monkeys and griffins, all gliding majestically around the field. One of them, massive in scale, was a splendid recreation of the great Temple at Knossós, restored as it might have looked 3,600 ago, with its multiple tiers of red pillars and distinctive bulls' horn frieze. The last to appear was an enormous replica of the circular Linear A tablet, which would carry the Minoan Message into the future.

They sang and danced their harmonious life – until horsemen started appearing at the water's edge. Around and around the field the riders went, brandishing their spears and yelling in a threatening manner. The island people took note of their arrival, but for the moment they were still protected by the sea, so they went on with their lives as best they could, albeit with growing concern.

Then suddenly, a sound much like thunder could be heard and the mighty volcano shook, silencing the celebrants. Abruptly, the music ceased, the banners fell still, and all of the horses came to a halt. Again it thundered, gripping everyone in its presence with fear. The Minoans then knew that the end of their way of life was at hand. They boarded their ships and set out across the ocean.

The volcano roared, erupting with furious laser flames and shaking the whole of the stadium, then, in a single moment of great misfortune, it suddenly collapsed into the sea. As the Minoans reached the distant shores, they fell into the waiting arms of the warriors, who picked them up and carried them off the field. The lights went out and the audience sat in darkness, quiet.

Again, a long, low note claimed their attention, then it grew into a cadence, aggressive, staccato. Images began to appear on the large video screens mounted around the perimeter of the stadium: the gold Mask of Agamemnon, the Trojan Horse, then geometric amphorae and large stone kouroi followed. Periklean Athens with its classical statues, temples and theaters; the conquests of Alexander and the emperors of Rome. On they flowed, from the Byzantine patriarchs and the sultans of the Ottoman Empire, through to 1846 when Greek revolutionaries gained independence. Images of patriarchal culture interspersed with those of warfare, slavery and human suffering – our glorified, yet ultimately dishonorable, heritage of domination.

The final montage showed the rebirth of the Games in Athens in 1896, starting with an old black and white photo of the lighting of the torch. Then, one by one, the Olympic Flames of each of the modern Games came across the screen, from Paris to Moscow to Sydney, bringing hope to the world throughout the tumultuous 20th century. The Olympic rings then appeared with "ATHENS 2004," the lights of the stadium came on, and with the audience roaring their approval, the Parade of Athletes began.

As is now customary, the athletes of Greece were the first to enter, and when they came onto the field, the crowd again went wild. Hope and anticipation graced their young faces, each filled with the excitement of living out their dream. State by nation-state, the competitors poured onto the field, Albania, Algeria, Andorra, Angola, and on through the alphabet to Zaire, Zambia and Zimbabwe – the alpha and omega of the world, all beaming with good will. Humanity in all our glory and splendor.

Alanta watched the spectacle from one of the athlete waiting areas, where large monitors had been set up. Excited, nervous energy enveloped her, and as she thought about entering the stadium, past and present memories raced through her mind – running the high roads of her own Caribbean island home, the vision with Gran'mama Lily so many years ago, her World Championship races, Olympic Village, the bomb and terror now relieved, Athena at the Acropolis, the horses circling the periphery – and with Herakles standing beside her, she could feel the glorious thread connecting all the events of her life, all the different experiences which had brought her to this moment.

The roll call approached the United States and they moved closer to the door, their anticipation continuing to build. They waited a few minutes more, and then, as the first few notes of the anthem began, they burst out onto the track, suddenly surrounded by a universe of flickering lights and loud applause.

What energy! Raw, creative, ever-expanding energy, and she and Herakles were sharing it together. The music, the colors, the people, the cameras, the sense of history and above all, the good vibe. It was exhilara*ting*.

She looked up into the stands, and even though she couldn't possibly pick them out, she clearly felt her family's presence there amongst the multitudes. She thought about Momma and Daddy, which made her feel safe and good, but when Gran'mama Lily popped into her head, she cringed. Brushing it aside, she waved to the cheering crowd, trying to concentrate on their excitement. Then, she just happened to put her left hand into her jacket pocket, and there was the Snake Goddess figurine Gran'mama had given her. A cool, solid reminder of everything she didn't want to be thinking about right now.

Once all of the athletes entered the stadium, and all of the anthems were played, a mighty drum roll sounded and all else trickled into silence. The eyes of the world moved to the unveiling of the Grand Propylaia, the symbolic entrance through which one reaches into the past, and at the same time, steps into the future. Suddenly, as if pulled by an unseen magician, its silken shroud was whisked aside and the magnificent work of art revealed for the first time.

Before the spectators and the wider world, the Classical Greek Panthaeon appeared, gathered together under the Tree of Life. Carved out of a huge triangular slab of marble, each figure and tree-limb was perfectly formed in three dimensions. But this was not the smooth, white marble of museum pieces, with every fleck of paint, bit by bit worn away by the eons. No, these figures had been fully infused with natural, lifelike features, vibrant colors and spectacular adornments.

Hera with jet black hair against fair skin, standing tall beside a strong and youthful Zeus – the Partners – together with their family, the Goddesses and Gods, laughing and lounging beneath the branches down either side of the pediment. Artemis was seated before them, attended by a deer and hare, and to her left, radiant Apollo stood, reaching for a piece of fruit from the abundant Tree. By his side, Demeter sat, holding shafts of grain in the cradle of her arm. Reclining at her feet lay the sumptuous Dionysos, with head thrown back in laughter and golden chalice raised. Past his legs, from the east, rose the Sun with the horses of Helios.

Next to Zeus, the august Athena stood, accompanied by an owl and a pair of snakes. Beside her, enchanting Aphrodite danced, her delicate garment seeming to ripple in the wind. Below them, winged-footed Hermes reclined with his legs outstretched, and the horses of Moon Goddess Selene charged off toward the west into Night. Beneath them all, a gentle stream flowed, connecting each with the other and the natural world.

This whole magnificent pediment rested on two colossal columns, one on either side of the tall bronze chalice which would hold the Olympic Flame.

Then, a girl in a red cloak, wearing a crown of laurel, ran onto the field and approached the steps leading to the base of the shining chalice. With her, she carried the sacred flame, which had begun its journey in the Grove of Altis at Olympia, and then circumnavigated the globe, touching thousands of people in many countries. Complete and utter silence now filled the air as she started up the stairs, and then slowed to more respectfully ascend the steep bronze steps, all the way up to the massive lip. She bowed gracefully, raised the torch and, invoking Hestia of the Ancient Flame, lit the bronze cauldron. With a *whoosh*, it burst forth with fire and the stadium again erupted in applause.

Lively Greek music filled the air and the athletes of the world rejoiced. Herakles lifted his arms Zorba-style and started dancing, encouraging Alanta to join. She linked her right arm with his left and tried following his steps: one two three, kick, kick, one two three, kick, kick...a few more of their teammates joined in, and soon they had a serpentine line of exuberant dancers.

When the music stopped, Global Council President, CeCe Kim, began her welcoming remarks and they turned their attention toward the podium.

"This is an historic moment," President Kim declared. "Not only have the Olympic Games returned home to Greece..."

The audience applauded and didn't stop for a long time. When they finally settled down a bit, the President continued, "...but I'm also *very* pleased to announce that the ancient custom of ceasing all hostilities during the Games, the Sacred Truce, has been achieved!"

The applause intensified, with people now jumping to their feet and clapping with unprecedented jubilation.

"Late last night, the remaining two nations signed on to the Resolution and for the first time in recent history, all of the countries of the world have laid down their weapons." Again, more ecstatic applause. "It is a beginning, an important step toward finally ending warfare once and for all. Amidst this celebration, let us now take a moment to envision the future. With our continued efforts, what we have accomplished today will become the norm for all of humanity. Governments will no longer condone or participate in the intentional killing of other human beings for *any* reason, and the barbarous practice will have been banished to the distant past. Let us continue to foster..."

As Alanta looked into the blazing Olympic flame, trying to take the President's words to heart, she thought she saw the fire leap upward. Yes, she could see it now, above the Propylaia. She blinked and rubbed her eyes, but it remained burning, emanating from one of the figures in the pediment in an intense circular glow. She reached for Herakles' arm, suddenly overwhelmed with a gut-wrenching feeling.

"Kleezy?"

He turned toward her, his expression abruptly changing to concern. "What is it?"

With terror consuming her face, and barely able to speak, she pointed toward the pediment. "Look! Do you see that?"

"See what?"

"Up there on the right side of the pediment, the third figure from the end. A ring of fire is circling his head. And I can feel it...nasty and destructive...full of hate." She felt weak in the knees, gripping his arm tighter as she stared up at the figure, wide-eyed.

"That's the statue of Apollo," he explained, tentatively.

"Oh, *no* Kleezy," she said, remembering the Oracle. "'Herakles of the Golden Heart, you must find the weapon which *springs forth from the head of Apollo.'"* She turned and faced him. "The bomb is up *there.*"

Herakles looked up at the statue, repeating the prophecy, "...springs forth from the head of Apollo..."

"Exactly."

"I don't see anything. Are you sure?"

"Absolutely," she replied, retrieving the figurine from her pocket and laying it out in the palm of her hand, getting his attention. "I know it with every fiber of my being. Gran'mama Lily knows it too. She's been tryin' to get me to see. Athena herself tryin' to get me to see. And now I see. I just didn't want to admit it before."

"How can that be? The bomb was found at the other stadium. I saw it with my own eyes, Alanta."

"I don't know. But ahm tellin' you, it's up there."

Herakles looked at the statue again. "I still don't see anything."

"Concentrate Kleezy. See through to what lies beneath the surface."

"I don't see it," he repeated, shaking his head.

As Alanta came to the horrifying realization that the terrible threat still loomed, Herakles stared at the statue, slackjawed, and the President completed her speech.

"Let the Games begin!" her voice rang out as the laser fireworks went off, filling the nighttime sky with festive colors and starburst patterns. The music resumed, the people cheered and the athletes danced with joy, for they knew not the danger confronting them. But Alanta knew. All too well she knew.

She would have a hard time convincing Kleezy of it, though, she could tell by his reaction. He was in denial, just like she'd been. He saw that bomb being pulled from the bleachers, and so it was over, disaster averted and that was that. She could see it on his face. And at the moment, with all the noise and commotion, they couldn't possibly carry on a conversation, let alone one of such magnitude. It would just have to wait. She reached deep down into her reservoir of strength and pulled herself together.

During the hour it took them to get back to Pangaia, Kleezy kept trying to reassure her, without drawing too much attention to it. However, his concern was far more focused on her well-being rather than the impending disaster, and by the time the monorail left them off, she could tell he was ready to move on to the festivities.

There was no shortage of distractions – the beaming athletes pumped up on adrenaline, the upbeat world music playing all over the place, conversations in every conceivable language and Kleezy engaging everyone else but her. *Poor thing*, she thought. He's been through so much, and just when he thought it was over, he's about to realize it's just begun.

She tried to tell herself that he'd come around in his own time, but she also felt a pressing urgency to address it. Finally, when she was just about to lose it with all the people and noise and revelry, she grabbed his arm and stopped him. "Kleezy, listen to me. We have to face this, now. We may not have much time left!"

"Alanta, relax. There's nothing to worry about. You must be picking up on some residual energy or something."

"You're in denial," she said flatly, starting to walk away.

He laughed, nervously. "What are you talking about?"

"You don't want to face the possibility that the bomb is still out there. You want to rely on the "evidence" of what you saw the other day. Well, I don't have to tell you Hera*kles* Speros that things are not always what dey seem. You think about what I saw: a ring of fire around Apollo's head. That can only mean one thing. And so I ask you, can you really say that the Oracle has been fulfilled? You think about that tonight, okay?"

"Okay."

"*Oh*-kay. All right." She leaned over and kissed him on the cheek. "Get some sleep. We gotta be makin' a new plan tomorrow. Good night, Kleezy."

"Wait. I'll walk you to your room."

"No. You have to get the celebration out of your system and I need some time alone. I'll be seeing you soon."

Without any hesitation, Alanta turned and made a bee-line

to the Village, her mind reeling with the images of the fire surrounding Apollo's head, the milieu of the Opening Ceremony, the prophetic hoop in the demitasse cup, and Athena addressing them at the Parthenon. When she got to her room, she threw herself onto the bed, and with her pillow over her face so as not to be heard, she cried and cried and cried, not realizing just how much she'd been holding in. This was her nightmare scenario, and it was now more real than ever: the mushroom cloud over Athens, the death of hundreds of thousands of people and the devastation of an entire city.

Then it hit. The scratchy throat, the tightening in her back and chest, and all of a sudden she could barely breathe. She took a few puffs of her inhaler, but the wheezing persisted, and it was all she could do to get the front desk on the phone. They rushed her an order of two black coffees, and fortunately, she could tell they would eventually work. The attack finally subsided enough so as not to be life-threatening, but it was still almost four hours before she could fall asleep, and by that time, she was completely and utterly exhausted.

# 17

# WITHIN THE GRAND PROPYLAIA

The Olympic Stadium had been darkened for the night, and was now quietly resting in the warm glow of the Sacred Flame. The security guards were making their rounds, and the cleaning crew was sweeping up the confetti from the Opening Ceremony. Above them, on the resplendent pediment of the Grand Propylaia, the immense marble statues stood, towering in a formless, dense mass of shadows.

Nevertheless, a wonderous potential lay within that stone, a place where thought, imagination, and the hopes and dreams of all humanity could coalesce. And so it was here that the Immortals came, united once more to witness the splendor of the Games and the triumph of the heroic Mortals.

They'd departed Delphi unaware of the effects of Ares' Dust of Deception, secure in the false knowledge that the weapon had been found. Each went on their own journey to Athens, exploring the land from which they'd arisen so many centuries before. They all had their favorite bubbling spring or rushing river, hidden cave or mountain meadow, and they visited these places, happily reminiscing about times past. Alas, but Apollo, forlorn, did not venture far, choosing instead to remain at Delphi, to soothe his damaged ego in the rejuvenating mineral waters of the Kastalía Spring.

After Zeus' experience with Winston Shepherd, and his subsequent trip into the depths of his own being and soul, he was again youthful and strong, yet tempered. He went to Límnos to find Hephaistos and fulfill his promise to Aphrodite, though much to his great sorrow, the once-mighty God was nowhere to be found. Only an echo of his hammer and anvil has remained, occasionally heard in the town of Hephaistia after dark. Demeter journeyed back to Eleusís to celebrate her Mysteries, feeling renewed and healthy once again after so many years of decline. Hera traveled to her beloved homeland of Argos, returning to the Heraion, the 3,000-year-old temple which had always borne her name. She'd looked out over the vast plain and recalled the past, contemplating all that had changed. Artemis, as Protectress of Animals, climbed Mount Taíyetos to be with her kindred creatures. And of course, Dionysos was guest of honor at the wine festival in Thebes, where the villagers had been preparing for his celebration all year.

Though still ensnared in the spell of Ares' deception, Athena and Aphrodite knew all could not be right. The two of them had felt compelled to go directly to Athens, to Athena's temple at the Acropolis. From there, they could see all of the events unfolding around them, and be alert for opportunities to free Aphrodite from her wicked bond. It was then that they had found Lily and Alanta, when Athena had addressed them in her Tritogenía incarnation, a form she could just barely recall from her own very distant past. It was a strange and troubling encounter, for what had been intended as a greeting had somehow been transformed into a warning, validating both Goddesses' perception that something was indeed amiss.

Fortunately, the Fates had not completely abandoned the Immortals. In the split-second after the blanket of Dust was laid, and unbeknownst to Ares, swift-footed Hermes scooped up the potent substance intended for him and slipped away from Delphi. He traveled back to the great desert wilderness in search of more information, and using Ares' own deception against him, cloaked himself in anonymity. Upon uncovering the plot against the Panthaeon, he transported himself to Athens, and as the first to reach the Grand Propylaia, it was he who discovered the nuclear device deviously planted within the marble head of Apollo.

When the other Immortals arrived, Hermes, Bestower of Blessings, stepped forward with his proof. In his hand he held a vial of the Dust, and as the Immortals perceived it, the veil of deception was lifted. Together and all at once, they saw the bomb. The tool of their destruction was right there in their midst, and they could no longer deny the horrific truth. As they made the terrible realization, their confidence and vigor drained away.

The weight of the burden immobilized poor Apollo, who was overcome by guilt and remorse. He sat upon the pediment, staring out into the night sky, looking old and tired.

Finally, Athena fully understood her encounter with Lily and Alanta. So, with Aphrodite, she devised a new plan to again reach out to the young Olympian, and this time to Herakles as well, seizing the moment at the Ceremony's end to reveal the truth. They concentrated on the evil device, and with all their magic, manifested its fire, radiating forth from Apollo's head.

Now, high atop the Olympic Stadium in the seemingly doomed city of Athens, as the oblivious Mortals tidied up, the Goddesses and Gods talked amongst themselves.

"Woe be upon us," Dionysos exclaimed. "Behold our glorious forms, carved by the Mortals in this magnificent stone as a testament to our eminence, but within us sits a device designed to perpetrate utter destruction. Another Trojan Horse, but with a capability the clever Epeios could not have hoped to dream of. And here we are, proud, ever-changing Goddesses and Gods from an ancient era, powerless to stop the devastation. What should we do now, Phoebos Apollo?"

"I do not pretend to know anymore." Apollo replied, dejected.

"Our powers may have receded with the years," Hera reluctantly conceded, "but there are still realms where we have some influence. In the Dreamworld, and the Realm of Visions, as Athena and Aphrodite so cleverly demonstrated earlier this evening."

"Yes," Zeus affirmed, "though they were unable to get through to young Herakles."

"And though Alanta has become pivotal to our success," Athena reminded them, "the prophecy requires Herakles to find the weapon and prevent the destruction."

"Perhaps you should go to him once again," Artemis suggested.

"Yes," Athena agreed, "I will beckon him to the Labyrinth."

"Splendid idea," Zeus concurred. "We may not have our former powers but we are far from powerless. Hear my words Apollo, we cannot allow you to indulge yourself in your shame, we need your keen mind now more than ever if we are to prevail, and we *will* prevail. Personally, I feel stronger and better than I have in years."

"It must be the Deception Dust again, Great Zeus," Dionysos chided. "Don't you see? We're *not* the ones in control here. Without the Mortals, we do not exist. They created us, and if they choose to do so, they can also destroy us."

"Dionysos," Athena interjected. "Perhaps what you say is true, but I will not give up on our sister, Hope. Remember, she is again free in the world, touching nearly every Mortal soul. We must have faith in humanity, and in those young athletes we saw before us today. Herakles and Alanta are the future. They can, and will, prevent the destruction, and restore us all to glory."

"So it is spoken," Zeus proclaimed.

"So it shall be done," they all affirmed.

"Well, Zeus," Hera gently teased. "I suppose if *you* can transform, anything is possible."

"It is," Zeus agreed, stepping closer to his partner and offering his arm. She hesitated, but then she smiled, a little, and took it.

"Very well," Athena agreed, seeing no dissent. "I will go to Herakles tonight, and release to him a buried memory. He will overcome his denial and finally see the danger."

"Make haste," cried Aphrodite in agony, "Hephaistos cannot be found and the wretched cuff of Ares still persists!"

"Fear not, dear sister," Athena replied. "I shall go to Cape Sounion and find Poseidon's swiftest stallion, to be certain to reach Herakles in time."

# 18

## HERAKLES REMEMBERS

As Alanta disappeared into the crowd, Herakles was abruptly wrenched into the realization that he had really let her down. The steadfast Alanta, who had completely supported his visions and intuitions, yet when given the chance to reciprocate, how did he respond? Selfishly – not wanting to spoil the joy he was feeling in his heart, the excitement of the Opening Ceremony, the relief that the threat was over – all about himself. He wanted to go to her that instant, apologize for the way he had acted and reaffirm his support, but something was holding him back.

Suddenly, the surrounding noise came crushing down and a wave of claustrophobia overcame him. The dreaded Cloud of Doom took its place in the forefront of his mind and he saw the flash he'd seen a thousand times in his imagination: the bright light and violent storm surge inflicting instantaneous annihilation – all the athletes, the fans, the Olympic venues, all the ancient sites and people of Athens – gone. He leaned up against a tall Minoan pillar to steady himself. *That's what will happen if Alanta is right.*

*I have to get out of here.*

He wormed his way out of the crowd, through the columns and down the steps of Pangaia, trying to remain as inconspicuous as possible. When he was relatively clear, he bolted onto the lamp-lit walkway, and with easy strides, made it the kilometer back to

Olympic Village in no time. He was about to reach for the door to the complex when it dawned on him. *I can't go in that cramped little box. I need to be outside.*

He went around to the front of his building, Santoríni, and realized there was a walkway under the ramp where he and Carl had stopped to look out at the Central Courtyard. He ducked under the stone arch and was suddenly in the midst of the large circular park. Off in the distance, he could still hear the celebration at Pangaia, though it seemed to be fading, becoming more remote, when the hoot of an owl stopped him in his tracks. He searched the treetops, and then spotted her nearby, sitting on a thick branch of one of the old oaks. She glared at him, then flapped her wings and flew into the center of the grove. He followed.

The foliage grew dense, but the light of the full Moon still crept through the canopy overhead, illuminating the pathway in silver light. Just as he came into the clearing, he again saw the owl, perched on a bough with wings spread wide, at the entrance to the Labyrinth. Her large golden eyes were fixed on him, as if urging him to walk the sacred path.

"Athena, Goddess of Wisdom," he addressed the awesome creature. "I need your guidance now more than ever. Please, be with me as I journey to the center."

With a slow, measured step he began.

Straight ahead he ventured, directly toward the heart of the Labyrinth, then suddenly, a curve to his right, sending him out and away from center, far around the outside of the ring...then back to the left, again approaching center, but only for a moment, before swinging again to the outer reaches. On and on he traversed the winding, curving path, with each step trying to focus his fractured mind on the beauty of the mosaic, to see each of the inlaid stones carefully set in the ancient serpentine pattern.

When finally he reached the center, he stopped, taking care to be aware of his approach to the threshold. The walking had helped to calm him, and when he felt ready, he stepped into the grassy center and sat down, crossing his legs and closing his eyes.

A moment later, the sky of his mind clouded over with angry

blue-gray storm clouds, and as a sinister rumbling sound took dominion over him, he fell into the grip of the thunder. He wanted to scream, he was screaming, but his voice could not be heard above the roar. His very soul was being consumed by the emptiness of a malevolent eternity he could not see. He was at the mercy of its hatred, the focal point of its revenge.

He struggled against it, fighting as he had with Hercules in the coliseum, with all his might wrestling with its shifting form, at once glacial, smooth, then fierce and terrible. Relentless, it drew him in, closer, closer to its depths, and then he rebounded, calling forth all of his will to resist, pulling himself free from its grasp.

For a moment, the Snake Goddess appeared in his mind's eye, as she had at Delphi, a vision of strength and empowerment.

In response, the threatening force thundered back, clutching him by the throat and seizing his attention, whirling him up in its vitriolic cyclone of violence and hatred. He fought for his very life, trying to reclaim his thoughts, trying to grab hold of something stationary, permanent, to keep from being sucked into this evil snare of death and destruction. Random thoughts, fragmented and ethereal, grazed his ruptured consciousness. Everything was chaotic, distorted, overwhelming, becoming louder and louder until the sound itself completely engulfed him. It was the sound of pounding hooves, pulverizing the ground beneath them, coming toward him from either side.

On the left, Athena in her classic garb, with bronze helmet and mighty aegis, astride a fine black stallion, hugging its bare back with her long, slender legs, swiftly closing the gap between them.

From the right, a robust white stallion appeared close at hand, carrying the dreaded Ares, his face guarded with a titanium mask and his arm wielding a razor-sharp sword high over his head.

On the one side, his protector, and on the other, his executioner. He was trapped, unable to move, and they drew closer still. Back and forth he looked, not knowing who would reach him first, then when it seemed as though they would surely collide, Athena burst ahead and swept him up behind her on her horse. He held on tightly and she reined hard around, just as Ares' sword came slicing by his head. They galloped away to safety, and Herakles looked back to see the white stallion coming to a sudden stop and rearing up on both hind legs, with Ares still brandishing his blade, furious and defiant.

For a moment more they rode together, free from harm or danger – then the buried memory was released, and suddenly the venue changed.

Now he was at the first meeting with Olympic Security, but this time as an observer, seeing the whole scene from a third perspective, watching himself interacting with them. Ivanna and Ramirez, politely hearing him out, and Harris, agitated, visibly upset that he was being allowed to go on. When they got to the part about the Oracle, and Herakles being the one to find the weapon which springs forth from the head of Apollo – just then, Harris jumped to his feet, sending his chair sailing across the tiled floor and into the wall.

The sound of the impact jolted his eyes open and brought him back to the center of the Labyrinth. He laid down on the grass and stretched out his legs, looking up through the branches at the bright Moon. *It's Harris! It's got to be Harris*, the words repeated in his mind. Over and over he relived his encounter with the Security Chief and soon he was certain. Then another memory came forth: their conversation at the old stadium where 'the bomb' had been discovered. Harris made sure that he saw it being removed, all the while invoking the prophecy and telling him that he'd fulfilled his destiny. *The bomb was set to detonate on the third day*, Harris had said, but that wasn't the prophecy. The Oracle had clearly stated that he was to *prevent* it on that day. Harris needed a way to convince him the plot had been foiled, and so the duplicitous Chief orchestrated the whole charade. It was all a ploy, a deception to put his mind at ease, along with everyone else's. Was Ramirez involved too? And what about Ivanna Jadan, could she be trusted? Could anyone? The implications became alarmingly clear.

If the Chief of Security was involved, then Herakles' every move and every communication was probably being monitored. Paranoia instantly overtook him. He easily convinced himself that his room had been bugged the whole time and that he was under round-the-clock surveillance. Encounters with seemingly friendly security personnel now became suspect, as did those with Olympic competitors and acquaintances.

As he started spiraling into a chasm of mistrust, surely it must have been Apollo himself who thrust forth an image into his present awareness. It was the Grand Propylaia, with the marble Panthaeon, but this time, Herakles saw the halo of fire around the head of the mighty God. That's when he came full circle back to Alanta. The threat *was* still imminent. The bomb was undoubtedly inside the marble figure, and on the third day of the Games, he somehow had to fulfill the prophecy and prevent it from going off. The owl flapped her wings and hooted, then flew into Night.

He suddenly felt an overwhelming urge to go to his love of life, to be with her, to acknowledge the truth she had somehow glimpsed at the Opening Ceremony. He scrambled to his feet and ran across the mosaic, then over the moonlit path and out of the woods, right up to her building. As he went in, he noticed a clock, and it was already 4:30 in the morning! He must have once again been in the Mythic Realm, where time follows its own course.

The halls were empty, but he still moved through them as though he were being followed. When he got to her door, he looked both ways, and seeing no one, lightly knocked. There was a brief silence, then the rustling of bed sheets.

"Is that you, Kleezy?" Alanta answered groggily.

"Yes," he whispered back.

She opened the door.

"I'm sorry to come so early but we have to talk."

"That's all right."

He brought his index finger to his lips, signaling her to remain silent, then whispered as softly as possible into her ear. "Please, come with me."

She nodded, put on her sweats and sneakers, and followed him out into the hallway. Neither said a word as they made their way outside to the Central Courtyard, to the bench near the little pond.

In the bright moonlight, he could see how tired she was. "Alanta, are you okay?"

"Had a little asthma," she said, coughing, "but I'm all right."

"It's my fault. I'm so sorry I didn't take your vision seriously. I know now that you were right. Please forgive me for doubting you."

"It's okay," she replied. "And it's not your fault I had a stupid attack."

"Are you sure you're okay?"

"I'm sure, and I'm sure glad you're back with me, 'cause that thing is tickin' away."

Herakles gently grasped her hands. "I think I know who deceived us."

"Who?"

"Harris, the Chief of Security."

"How do you know?"

"It came to me in the Labyrinth, but it was right in front of me the whole time. Do you remember me telling you how he reacted when I recited the Oracle to them? How he jumped up, sending his chair crashing across the room?

"Yes, I remember you saying that."

"What I didn't remember until this morning was the timing of his reaction. It was precisely as I said 'the weapon which springs forth from the head of Apollo.'"

"As soon as you got too close for comfort, he put on a big show to try to divert attention away from what you were saying."

"Exactly, and it worked. Ramirez ended the meeting right after that."

"So you think Ramirez and Jadan are involved?"

"I don't know. They did claim they'd received other credible information, but that may have all been part of the ultimate ruse, to make me believe I'd fulfilled my prophecy when I saw them find the bomb."

"Which was really a decoy," Alanta concluded.

"It must have been. Now the question is, where do we go from here?"

"And who can we trust?"

"Indeed, who can we trust? If Harris is corrupt, any or all of the officials could be too. I can only trust you, my mom and Carl. What about you?"

"I always go to Gran'mama Lily when I'm in trouble. Besides, she pretty much knows what's going on anyhow. That reminds me, there's something I didn't get a chance to tell you about yet."

Herakles listened as she recalled her experience with Lily at the Acropolis. Her story reaffirmed everything, and helped him to clarify the path they must now take. "I think we should bring everyone together to help us figure out what to do."

"Sounds good," she agreed. "Where and when?"

"My mother can find us a safe place, I'm sure of it. As to when, as soon as possible."

"We gotta be careful, make it look like we've left our worries far behind. Otherwise, Harris and his gang might notice."

"You're right. Even this is risky."

"Then it has to be at the mid-day break, that's our only free time. I'll tell Jimmy we're going to lunch."

"Agreed. I'll sneak out right now and arrange it with my mother. Hopefully, she can bring Lily with her."

"Okay, why don't you, me and Carl rendezvous outside the locker room at the stadium, after morning workouts, say 11:45."

"Perfect," Herakles agreed, taking her hands and giving them a squeeze. "We can do this."

She squeezed back. "We will."

And so, determined and reconnected, Herakles and Alanta parted ways this uncertain Olympic morning.

He tightened his shoelaces and headed for the street exit. No one seemed to be overly preoccupied by his presence, and the guard waved him on. Once outside the Village complex, he eased into a spirited pace, which swiftly carried him along the paved streets of the far-famed city, all the way to Thea Vasso's.

He got a pen and paper from his pocket, and scribbled a note for Maria. *Mother, the threat is not over. Security cannot be trusted. We need a safe place to meet at noon today. Bring Lily.*

Now he had to get it to Maria without alerting his aunt. He loved her, but she couldn't be trusted to keep a secret, and with one or two strategic calls, she could fire up the Athens grapevine in less than a heartbeat.

He went through the gate and rang the buzzer.

"Who is it?" Vasso's groggy voice eventually came crackling over the speaker.

"It's me, Thea Vasso, Herakles, here for breakfast."

"What breakfast? Do you know the time? It's barely 6:00. We're not even out of bed."

"Mitéramou invited me. I'm sure she told you."

An irritated grumble crackled back at him and the front door buzzed open.

The elevator seemed to take a lifetime, but it finally opened and there was Vasso, at her doorway at the end of the hall, arms crossed, indomitable. He'd better make it good. He gave her a kiss on both cheeks, trying his best to warm her up.

Maria appeared from the guest bedroom, and he walked passed Vasso and over to her, surreptitiously giving her an expectant look. "Mother, you *did* invite me for breakfast today, didn't you?"

"Yes, of course," she replied, looking at Vasso. "I'm sorry, I completely forgot about it."

"Breakfast at this hour?" Vasso retorted. "I don't believe you, but I don't care, I'm going back to bed. I'm getting old and I need my sleep. Try not to make too much noise, eh?"

"We'll keep it down," Herakles promised, watching Vasso disappear into her bedroom. Once the door was shut, he brought his index finger to his lips and handed Maria the note. She read it, then looked deeply into his eyes.

"I'm sorry, Kleomou, I guess my memory is slipping." She took his pen and paper, wrote something and handed it back to him.

"That's all right, mother, I'll just have one of these bananas, and we can do it another day."

He read the note. *We'll meet at noon at the old string factory in the warehouse district, the one I used to take you to when you were a boy.*

*I'll bring Lily.* He nodded his head in agreement and hugged her tightly, then left.

He set off on the streets again, surveying the urban landscape for anything unusual, and as he ran by the Bank of Greece, its flashing time display read 6:26. *Good.* He could still make it back for breakfast with Carl at 7:00, their regular time, so nobody should be suspicious.

However, as he entered the Olympic Village, he felt the gaze of the security guards, this time seeming to notice his return, especially the one with the headset. He diverted to the restroom, where he could write another note. It was similar to the one he'd written to Maria, but it also mentioned his suspicion of Harris and informed Carl of their meeting after the morning workout. He ended it with, *I'm not imagining this! Please, you have to trust me.*

Herakles folded the note in half and headed to the cafeteria in their building. Once again he slipped into a feigned role of nonchalance, while discreetly passing the note which told the awful truth.

Carl read it slowly, as though he were weighing out all the possible repercussions, then nodded his assurance that he would do what Kleo had asked.

They continued on as normally as possible, making it to the monorail and the Olympic Stadium without incident. He had to convince anyone who might be watching that he was completely focused on his upcoming competition, even if he had to fake it once again.

But it turned out that he didn't have to fake it at all. He started off in the weight room with a light workout, and while he expected the inability to focus and heightened anxiety to return, much to his surprise, that did not occur. Instead, he found himself accepting this new reality and his role in it. He realized that Harris and the other henchmen of Ares were his competitors just as surely as was Maximilian Leach, and that he would have to be in perfect balance – physically, mentally and spiritually – in order to be able to surpass them. As his resolve to succeed solidified, his performance improved dramatically. Instinctively, he knew he was entering his peak zone.

Even though security personnel made the rounds wherever he went, and were no doubt reporting to Harris his every breath, nothing was able to distract him from his newly found determination. Carl immediately noticed his improvement and channeled it where Herakles needed the work most. They went out to the field and practiced the shot put, javelin and discus under the watchful eyes of the Panthaeon. Although he couldn't see the ring of fire, he could undoubtedly feel the presence of the Immortals, watching over him and offering their support.

Time ticked away and the lunch hour was soon upon them. Alanta was waiting outside the locker room, and the three of them boarded the monorail, being sure to let as many people on before them as they could. Herakles paid special attention to see whether a security guard would also get on, and sure enough, one did. He was a slim, older man and he entered the same car through the other door. Herakles turned his back to the agent and whispered to his cohorts, "we have to get off at the last possible moment. I'll hold the doors."

The train moved ahead, smoothly traversing the distance in about a minute and a half. "Next Stop: the Olympic Pool," the electronic voice said in multiple languages.

The doors opened and they stood motionless, pretending to be remaining on board, but then, as the doors were about to close, Herakles stepped in front of them, blocking them just long enough for everyone to slip out, leaving the agent behind.

They cut through a group of swimmers, and slipped past the security checkpoint before word of their presence had been received. From there, it was easy to get down to the street, and then hail a cab to take them to the old abandoned string factory.

The cabbie kept pretty much to his own business, save for his repeated glances in the rear view mirror. Herakles thought he must have recognized them, but thankfully, he didn't engage them in conversation.

They got out in the middle of the warehouse district of Athens, where there were still a few small-scale shops and artists' lofts amidst mostly abandoned buildings. Herakles led Alanta and Carl down a back alleyway, taking a few extra minutes to circle around to the factory. If memory served, it should be right around the corner, and *yes!* There it was: a tall, narrow door with its red paint chipped and worn, and the same old sign hanging over the sidewalk, which said, "Klostí," Greek for "string."

He looked around, then knocked on the door. After what seemed like an eternity, he was greatly relieved to see Maria, who opened it and hurried them inside.

It had been 15 years since he'd been there, and back then it was still in operation. His mother's side of the family had owned it for generations, but sadly, three of the brothers had had a falling out, the business dissolved and a cousin of theirs got stuck with the warehouse.

Sunlight crept through its dust-covered windows, casting a muted light on the abandoned old place. It looked pretty much the way he'd remembered, with large wooden spools at the end of long poles, some of them laid out on tables in rows, and others suspended from the rafters overhead. Though now, with the passing of the years, cobwebs interlinked them all.

They joined Lily in the center of the room, where a few crates had been arranged as chairs.

"I'm glad we all made it safely," Lily said, acknowledging each of them.

As Maria sat down, she reassured everyone. "Don't worry, my cousin Petro has the only other key, and he has no reason to come here."

Herakles then introduced Carl to Lily, and asked Alanta to start.

"You were right, Gran'mama," she said, taking Lily's arm in hers. "We aren't clear of danger. During the Opening Ceremony, I saw a ring of fire around the head of the Apollo sculpture, and that's when I finally realized it."

Lily nodded knowingly.

"I didn't believe her at first," Herakles interjected, "then I remembered something last night." He told them his tale of Harris' deception and concluded that they urgently needed to act.

"Let me get this straight," Carl interrupted. "You believe the bomb is actually *inside* the Apollo statue in Olympic Stadium?"

"Yes," Herakles and Alanta replied simultaneously.

"Then we need someone with 007 kind of stuff, radiation detectors and the like, who can *confirm* it."

"There may not be enough *time*," Alanta rebuffed. "According to the prophecy, we only have till day after tomorrow to get Kleezy goin' on whatever it is he has to do. I agree with him, we have to act now."

"How can we possibly act right now?" Maria asked pragmatically. "Carl's right, we need someone who's an expert at this kind of thing."

The room fell silent as they each searched for an answer, and after a long moment, Maria spoke. "I can only think of one person," she said, looking at Herakles, "who would have contacts like that."

"The man with the mustache in your cup," Lily said matter-of-factly, as if she knew exactly who Alexander was.

Herakles looked at this impressive woman...*how* does *she know these things?*

"Yes," Maria responded, "my estranged husband, Alexander." She turned to her son. "Kleo, I didn't want you to have another Alex-induced upheaval to contend with at this critical time, so I didn't tell you earlier."

He shifted uncomfortably, tipping the wooden crate on end. "Tell me what?"

"Your father contacted me yesterday morning; he's in Athens."

Kleo's heart fluttered. "What did he want?"

"To see if we were okay."

His stomach dropped. "Do you think he knows what's going on?"

"I can't be absolutely sure. I didn't divulge anything, but during the whole conversation, I got the feeling he was trying to press me for information. He was attempting to disguise it, but I know him too well. It's very possible that he could know all about it."

"But which side is he on?" Carl interjected, with great alarm.

"That's a good question," Herakles affirmed, suddenly realizing that the time of their encounter might be just a stone's throw away. In a split second, images came rushing back to him – forgiving Alexander at Delphi, then Olympia and the unexpected visit, the wipe-outs on the hurdles and pole vault, and then Athena's proclamation, *you must come to terms with your father before you can be victorious.*

"Mom, do you trust him?"

"Under some circumstances, I would trust him completely. If, for example, someone appeared at the door with a gun, I really believe he'd die trying to protect us."

"Isn't that what we're dealing with here?" Kleo exclaimed, wanting desperately to believe in him. "A group of fanatics holding a nuclear gun to our heads?"

"We must remain cautious," Carl reminded them skeptically.

"He wouldn't have been in the cup if he wasn't to be in the play," Lily chimed in.

"I can't believe he'd *knowingly* let such a catastrophe happen," Maria said confidently.

"I think we should trust him," Herakles blurted out, looking to Alanta.

She looked a little scared, but nodded her head in agreement.

Maria looked around the room. "Then I'll call him. We'll meet here again at six this evening. "

"No," Lily asserted. "It's too risky trying to get everyone together. I suggest you and Kleezy meet with Alexander alone."

They all agreed, and with brief and frightened good-byes, they concluded their meeting.

Herakles, Alanta and Carl made it safely back to Olympic Stadium, seemingly unnoticed, which in and of itself made Herakles suspicious in his heightened state of mind. However, nothing appeared to be amiss, so with confidence and determination, he focused himself forward. They were really getting down to the nitty gritty now.

# 19

## REUNITED AT LAST

Throughout the rest of the afternoon, Herakles practiced his sprints and hurdles, with an intensity his competitors had not seen in him before. He didn't think about his mother's meeting with his father, or whether Alexander would be willing or able to help them. Nor did he worry about the bomb overhead and how they would be able to stop it. No, he set all of that aside and instead concentrated on perfecting his start, his stride and his finish. He now knew that it would be his ability to perform at his absolute peak, without distraction, under extremely stressful and risky circumstances that would not only enable him to win the gold, but would also ensure that he could play his part in preventing the catastrophe.

In this state of mind, time flew and before he knew it, he was once again leaving Olympic Village. He threw security off by telling the guard that he was going to take a run downtown to meet his aunt, when in reality, he cut over on a side street and hailed a cab to take him to the string factory. Maria was there, and while they waited for his father, she related to him what had previously transpired.

She had reached Alex shortly after she left the warehouse, and they arranged to meet in the lounge at the Grande Bretagne. She'd immediately gotten to the point, testing his willingness to go out on a limb for his family. He responded with convincing sincerity, so she divulged all that had taken place and asked for his assistance. He quickly made two phone calls and arranged a meeting with a trusted friend, who, throughout the years, had been able to supply him with just about anything he'd ever needed. Apparently, today was no exception. This friend promised to arrange for a specially equipped "television news" helicopter to fly by the Grand Propylaia later that afternoon.

Suddenly, there was a loud knock on the red string factory door.

Herakles walked over to it, listening. "Who is it?"

"It's me, Alexander."

It was definitely his voice, so Herakles opened the door and let him in, quickly closing it again behind him. "Thank you for coming. After our last meeting, I wasn't sure if you'd want to help us."

"I assure you, son, there is nothing I would like more than to be able to help you. Thank you for allowing me the opportunity. I know it isn't easy for you to trust me."

"Did you *find* it, Alex?" Maria interjected impatiently.

"Yes," Alexander replied. "You and Alanta are right, Kleo, there is a nuclear device in the head of the Apollo statue."

"How much time do we have left?" Maria asked.

"We cannot determine that with certainty unless we get inside. However, if the prophecy is correct, we know we have at least until the third day of the Games. Beyond that, only Ares and his henchmen know. The track and field events begin that morning, so the stadium will be filled to capacity. We should do it then, when security will be sufficiently distracted."

"Then, it can be deactivated?" Herakles wanted to know.

"Yes. However, it will be a very dangerous operation, and you, Herakles, will be the one who carries it out."

"At last, the prophecy is coming full circle," Herakles responded, feeling a strange sense of relief. "How am I to accomplish it?"

"I have a plan, but I need 24 hours to work out the details and get the supplies. I suggest we meet here again, the same time tomorrow night, and we'll thoroughly go over it then."

"Okay," Herakles agreed, affirming his allegiance to his father. "Good luck."

"We will need it. Harris cannot be underestimated."

"You know him?"

"Yes. He is a former CIA operative who, like many of my old colleagues and myself, couldn't cope with the new era of peace. Most of us drifted about, barely connected to the fringes of society, but a few went much further – too far. They joined an alliance which has come to be known as One God One Way, a loosely connected group of fundamentalist terrorists and Harris is among them.

"He is unusually cunning, as he has obviously been able to maintain impeccable credentials. However, under that facade lies a fanatic, who wouldn't hesitate to kill himself in what he would consider a supremely holy act. When I heard he'd been appointed Olympic Security Chief, I knew the Games, and the two of you, could be in grave danger."

"Is that why you contacted me the other day," Maria asked, "out of concern for our safety?"

"Yes, and that is why I went to Olympia, Herakles. You are the most intuitive individuals I know. All I had were my suspicions about Harris, but I knew if danger were in the air, you two would sense it."

As Herakles listened to his father's words, trying to gauge his sincerity, the first strands of trust caught hold, and like the string which used to wind around the old wooden spools overhead, a memory buried long ago came reeling in.

In an instant, his mind's eye perceived it. He and Iphe were seven, and they were sitting under a trellis on an old man's patio, in Alexander's home village. Their parents were taking a walk, and the old man used the occasion to tell the boys about the terrible things that had happened in this now peaceful little town.

"Your father is a remarkable man, to have overcome the atrocities he witnessed as a child. When he was only a boy, no older than the two of you, he saw his parents shot dead by the soldiers, right there in front of the bell tower. Days later, he was found in a crawl-space, and then taken away to a hospital and isolated because of his bone disease. Eventually, he ended up in an Athens orphanage. It was a horrific time, and I tell you this against his wishes, because it is something none of us should ever forget."

The two boys were terrified by the old man's story, and they imagined the same events being played out around them at that moment. When Maria and Alexander returned, they found their children wailing, distraught with the fear that they'd been left alone. Alexander knelt down and took them both in his arms, assuring them that the old man had only imagined those stories and that there was nothing to worry about. Nothing bad was going to happen to anyone. He affirmed the version that his parents died a natural death, and told them to forget everything the villager had told them.

Herakles realized then and there that he'd always known about his father's true childhood, but had learned to dismiss it as the ravings of that "crazy old man." In reality, Alexander had been trying to protect them from the horrible truth. All of a sudden, he saw his Delphi experience in a new light as well, feeling an urge to apologize for the way he'd treated his father at Olympia. And so, speaking with winged words, he did.

"Father, since last we met at Olympia, where my anger toward you went unchecked, I have undertaken the searching of my soul. In doing so, I have remembered the truth about what happened to you and my grandparents when you were a child – their murder, your illness and isolation and your eventual relocation to Athens, all of which must have profoundly affected you in ways I can only try to imagine. Remembering your experiences has helped me to find compassion for you, and in the process, forgive you. I no longer hold that anger in my heart. So, now I say to you, I am willing to try to reconcile our differences once we have put this threat to rest."

His father responded with a heavy sigh. "The Fates have truly blessed me to be given this chance to redeem myself, so please allow me to take this moment to speak from my heart. The tragedy which befell me as a child most certainly affected my ability to love and trust, but yet, as a young man I thought I had overcome it. When I met and fell in love with you, Maria, my soul was at peace. I was happy for the first time I could remember, and I vowed not to let anything come between us. I never questioned that vow until the boys were born.

"I could not accept that one of my sons had been afflicted with the dreaded disease, and therefore, could not face the fact that he was imperfect. Consequently, I could not find a place for him in my heart. I could not love Iphikles and I did not – my own flesh and blood! My own son, and I could not show him love." Tears welled up and out of the corners of his eyes as he continued his confession.

"I have searched my own soul these last years, and have come to believe that my inability to love Iphe was the root of my other transgressions, and I'm sorry. I'm so sorry." He broke down with heavy sobbing.

Maria stepped forward, tears of grief and compassion mingling on her cheeks. Taking Alexander into her arms for the first time in years, she whispered, "oh, Alex." After a moment of silence, she added, "I'm glad to see you're finally realizing that we had *two* wonderful sons."

As he pulled away, he regained his composure and strength. "Thank you again for trusting in me. I know I can never make it up to Iphe, but I promise, I *will* make it up to both of you. I will not let you down again."

And with that, Alexander headed toward the door, giving one final caution as he left. "Kleo, you know Harris will be watching you closely. He cannot see us together, as it would surely arouse his suspicion. I'm quite certain he would remember me. And Kleo, you must continue to prepare yourself for competition. We *must* retain the element of surprise."

Herakles nodded his agreement and, with a handshake, said goodbye to his father.

Before he could say another word, his mother hugged him and apologized for helping to hide the truth of Alexander's past.

"Oh, Honeymou, forgive me. I'm so sorry to have kept it from the two of you, but he asked me to promise when we married. It was so important to him that his children grow up free from the horrors he'd experienced, and I too felt it was for the best. Now that you're an adult, and can put it in perspective, I'm glad that you've recalled the truth."

"Of course I forgive you. I probably would have done the same thing in your place. Honestly, I think it was better that I didn't know until I could truly appreciate the magnitude of it, so please don't give it another thought. In all my life I have never mistrusted your intentions, and I'm certainly not going to start now."

And so, further unified, they ventured forth once more upon the journeying ways.

# 20

## ALANTA'S DESTINY REVEALED

Alanta paced back and forth in front of the hotel elevator door, waiting for Gran'mama Lily to emerge. It had already been two days since she'd seen the ominous ring of fire, and to say her concentration was off was a serious understatement.

At first, she'd been overwhelmed with the sheer impact of the realization, then, when Herakles told her of the plan, she felt useless. Coach Jimmy kept giving her that look, like he knew something was up but he couldn't quite put his finger on it. She desperately wanted to tell him of the mythic struggle engaging her, but it was way too late for that. Had he been in on it from the start, things would be different, but at this point, it was just too much. Besides, she wasn't even supposed to be paying attention to *politics*, let alone getting involved in something like this. In any event, if she had a prayer of keepin' it together, she needed him to be staying completely focused.

She'd wanted to do more to help with the plan, but Kleezy's daddy had insisted that the deactivation attempt take place tomorrow morning, as she was getting ready to run her first race. So she was supposed to carry on as if nothing were out of the ordinary.

Kleezy seemed obsessed with the idea that he would only be successful if she ran the best race she could. She'd reassured him, *yeah Kleezy, I'm gonna be rippin' it up...you go climb Apollo and stop the nuke and I'll run like the wind.* However, if the truth be told, she wasn't feeling so sure. She'd barely made it through the qualifying heats that afternoon, squeaking by with some of her worst times that year. With Herakles risking his life and so much on the line, she just wasn't able to give it her all. She needed Gran'mama Lily to set her straight. So, even though it was risky, she snuck out to the hotel.

Finally, the elevator opened and there was Gran'mama, flanked on either side by Momma and Daddy. She tried to appear un-phased, but the presence of her parents completely threw her off. She had expected to speak with her grandmother alone, and had specifically requested that, so she couldn't understand why Lily had brought them. As she was about to say something, Gran'mama attempted to put her mind at ease.

"I hope you don't mind, Lanna, but I thought it would be best if we had a *family* conversation. Let's all go out to the terrace, where no one will interrupt us."

Alanta hesitated, until she looked into her parents' eyes, full of love and longing to help, then her agreement just slipped out. "All right Gran'mama, *oh*-kay. If you think it's for the best."

"I do," Lily replied with certainty.

And so they sat in close together around a small table, and with Lily's encouragement, Alanta spilled the beans. She'd kept a lot of emotional stuff from her mother and father over the years, not because she didn't trust them or didn't think they cared, but because she had Gran'mama. Now she realized she needed them like never before, and the words poured out about the strange and frightening events which had entangled her.

She told them about the Delphic Oracle and the meetings with Olympic Security, the ups and downs of the past few weeks, and her experience at the Parthenon with Lily. Grace and Chris-tian listened quietly to the whole re-telling, and despite the shock and fear she saw on their faces, they seemed determined to stay strong and believe in her.

She told them about the ring of fire at the Opening Ceremony, Kleezy's realization that the Chief of Security was involved, and the plan they were devising to dismantle the nuclear bomb. And that somehow, with all that going on, she now had to mentally prepare for her most competitive event, the 100-meter sprint. Being able to finally speak of it was cathartic for her, and as she gave her mom a hug she felt a great release.

"It's all right, Lanna," Grace said, patting her back. "It's gonna be all right."

Christian placed his hand on his daughter's shoulder and offered his support. "Kleezy's gonna do it, and so are you, Alanta January. We haven't come all this way just to get blown to smithereens."

Alanta lifted her head from her mother's shoulder and looked up at her daddy, a few stray tears still rolling over her cheeks. She laughed a little bit. "That's *exactly* what I told Kleezy when I first found out."

"Then it must be true," Grace affirmed.

Lanna looked to her Gran'mama, who had quietly been taking in the whole scene. She was magnificent. Calm, even serene, and wise beyond Alanta's comprehension.

"You know what you have to do," Lily pronounced. "Run that race with a good, strong wind at your back."

Alanta sat up straight and wiped away the last few tears, remembering her encounter at Congo Square, with the Spirit of her nameless ancestress who had been sold into slavery.

Then, Christian, who never cared to get too emotional, got up. "Now Lanna, you need to get your rest." She stood and he gently took hold of her shoulders. "Next time we see you, you'll be wearin' a gold medal 'round your neck!"

She smiled and hugged her father tightly, and then her mom, and her grandmother, until he finally shooed her off.

She took the monorail back to Olympic Village, on the surface feeling a little better, but still fundamentally unsettled underneath. She wandered around for awhile, dodging people she knew and avoiding conversation, until finally she returned to her room. Then she stared at the ceiling for what seemed like hours, until finally, sleep emerged from the weariness.

She found herself in a small boat on a river, drifting along its meandering course, through a green cathedral of trees arching from shore to shore. After what seemed like a long while, she came out onto a tranquil bay illuminated by the full Moon overhead, when all at once, the boat disappeared and she was under water amidst the sparkling phosphorescents. At first she was afraid, but then, when she realized she could breathe, she relaxed, feeling the mystic coolness of the liquid surrounding her, incubating her, leading her to center, where she would make her request. And so, in the quiet solitude, she asked the Universe for guidance.

Gradually, she felt herself expanding, radiating outward, slowly merging with the consciousness of the primordial Sea, becoming one with Yemoja, Goddess of the Watery Realm – there she saw the race she was destined to run.

She was in the starting blocks at the Olympic Stadium, surrounded by tens of thousands of cheering fans. The gun sounded and she sprung forth, like the cheetah bursting with Ashé. Her stride and alignment were perfect, and her competitors never had a chance. As she swept past the finish line, the crowd roared, jumping to their feet. The electronic timer, in fluorescent neon and much larger than life, read 9.276: A NEW WORLD RECORD, then kept flashing, 9.276! 9.276!

She suddenly awoke in her bed, knowing exactly what she was going to do – run the 100-meter faster than any human being ever had.

That morning, she went to the track with her newly found purpose, not at all understanding how her performance would help stop the unthinkable from occurring, but trusting in herself that somehow, it would.

# 21

# THE PILLARS OF HERAKLES

It was the morning of day three of the Games, and the aquatic competitions were largely over. The Australian swimmers had triumphed with eleven golds, though the diving medals had completely eluded them, being swept up by the Japanese. In an unexpected victory, an Icelandic contender won the 200-meter butterfly in record time.

And now, the world's attention was shifting from the Olympic Pool to the Olympic Stadium, where 100,000 fans eagerly waited for the main event to begin. Their focus was on the track and field competitions, especially the women's 100-meter, the race in which Alanta January would seek her first Olympic medal.

Herakles Speros was there as well, but not as a competitor and not as a spectator. He was there instead to complete the Thirteenth Labor. Just as the mythical Hercules had relied on physical strength to perform many of the first Twelve, so too would our hero have to rely on his own athletic abilities to accomplish his feat. However, instead of killing man and beast to serve King Eurystheus, Herales would have to scale the 60-foot statue of Apollo and deactivate a thermonuclear device, thereby saving all of Athens from utter ruination.

His father had used his most reliable contacts to formulate what turned out to be a simple plan. Once Herakles climbed the monument, he would find the hidden panel, expose the bomb and introduce a computer virus into its operating system.

Alex was convinced they'd be dealing with old technology, surmising that the fundamentalists had probably acquired surplus materials. He obtained a sophisticated computer program which would over-write the bomb's existing software, disengaging its detonator and deactivating its timing device in the process; he gave Kleo a copy on disk, and just in case they were a little more up to date, a CD version as well. As a last resort, if the computer plan failed, Herakles would attempt to physically detach the timing mechanism from the bomb itself, but that could take upwards of twenty minutes, leaving him further exposed.

In order to access the marble pediment, he would have to traverse the colossal, steel-grid support structure concealed behind the rows of bleacher seats. He and Alexander had studied the blueprints of the Grand Propylaia and the interior of the stadium surrounding it, planning every step of Herakles' route, trying to foresee all the obstacles and hazards lying ahead. Fortunately, Alex made sure they had the equipment they needed, including a special rappelling suit and shoes, and a miniature communication device so they could talk to each other as Kleo carried out the plan.

During the night he rested, though his mind remained alert, actively playing out the events to come. Over and over again he visualized himself, catlike, carefully negotiating the stadium's interior grid, scaling the massive marble sculpture, finding the bomb and then successfully planting the virus.

Now, as Helios gathered his horses and set forth across the morning sky in his golden chariot, Herakles readied himself to go. He dressed inconspicuously, in a tank top and shorts, combed his hair neatly back into a ponytail and brushed his teeth. As he took one last look in the bathroom mirror, his brother's face for a moment appeared in his own, making him smile. "Well, Iphe, here we go."

With that, he grabbed his pack and set out from Olympic Village for his rendezvous with Destiny.

"Pssst," he whispered into the invisible mic, "father, can you hear me?"

"Yes, Kleo," came Alexander's response. "I hear you perfectly. I trust you're going to the stadium now?"

"I'll be taking the next train out."

"Right on schedule, excellent. I'll be with you every step of the way, Kleo – and good luck. I know you can do this."

Herakles felt confident in his father's assurances, for he was convinced that Alexander would not desert him now.

The train ride was uneventful, and he was soon at the Olympic Stadium locker room. Many of the competitions began today, so the atmosphere was tensely charged. His adversary, Maximilian Leach, was there, calling out to him sarcastically, attempting to get his goat, but Herakles remained single-focused, impervious. He breezed through the room, through another set of doors, and around a corner to a utility closet.

He stepped inside and quickly closed the door, changing right away into the special suit. It was black, skin tight, with short sleeves and short pants, and had a built-in harness with caribiners for fastening the ropes. He put on the rubber-tipped shoes and shoved his stuff in the pack, then turned his attention to the closet wall. Behind a row of buckets and mops, he found the grate, which he pried loose and set aside. He climbed through, into the dark, inner guts of the stadium, then replaced the grate behind him.

The sound of stomping feet and cheering fans reverberated around him, echoing throughout the cavernous interior. He got out his flashlight and shined it on the vast network of steel girders which would take him, unseen, beneath those unknowing spectators all the way up to the base of the pediment. He gripped the metal firmly and proceeded carefully, section by section, gate by gate, around the curvature of the stadium's midsection, until he reached the area directly behind the Grand Propylaia. Then he began the arduous climb, one foothold at a time.

He moved with precision and confidence, his muscular legs

and arms rippling with power and strength, taking him steadily, methodically up into the web of steel, until at last, he reached the very top. He scanned the area for the access door, and when he spotted it, he let Alexander know.

"Remember," Alexander replied, "once you go through that door, you'll be in the open air, so you must be especially careful. If security sees you, I have no doubt they will try to kill you."

"I understand. How many are there?"

"Six around the staircase to the Olympic Flame, at least another dozen on the field and five on either side of the Grand Propylaia. Harris is up in the security loge, and I'm keeping an eye on him."

"Okay."

And with that, Herakles took a deep breath and pushed through the small door, emerging onto the eastern edge of the triangular pediment platform, which supported the glorious statues of the Olympic Panthaeon. He positioned himself behind the four-foot marble horse heads at the base, and looked up at the magnificent work of art, astonished at its titanic size.

Next to him was the huge foot of a sensual, reclining Dionysos, who held an overflowing stone chalice high in the air, in a toast. Toward the top of the pediment, he could see Demeter holding her bundles of grain, and above her, Apollo, reaching into the tree branches to pluck a piece of fruit. Beyond that, he could only glimpse the profiles of the other impressive Immortals.

He peeked his head out over the neck of one of the horses, and could easily see the spectators sitting closest to the Grand Propylaia. Mostly, they seemed to be focused on the activity down on the field, though some did appear to be watching the large video screens mounted near the top of the stadium wall.

He located as many of the guards as he could, counting eight on the field, and four of the six he knew to be stationed below him at the base of the Flame. None of them seemed to be alarmed, so he continued on. As long as the Fates remained with him, and he was careful and quick, he could proceed without being detected.

A gun sounded, startling him for a moment, until he realized it was only a starting signal for another contest. In the back of his mind, he'd heard the announcer calling the race and naming the athletes, but he hadn't really paid attention.

Alanta's event would be taking place soon, and she was down there somewhere, getting ready. He tried to spot her amidst the athletes warming up in the inner circle, and sure enough, there she was! Though he couldn't make out her features, he knew those moves. Just seeing her gave him a powerful rush, renewing his determination to push forth and carry out his task.

He took a few deep breaths, centering himself...settling his mind...and when he felt ready, he scurried up Dionysos' long, reclining leg and torso, up to his shoulder, then carefully, on the fold of marble fabric at the neck of his robe, walked around the back of his ten-foot, laurel-crowned head and crouched down low. He looked down at the guards, who were all still in their places. *Good*.

With a running leap, he landed on the most lateral folds of Demeter's two-story marble robe, then shimmied up into her lap and hid behind the shafts of wheat. Still, no one seemed to notice him.

As he pulled the rope from his pack, he again considered the bizarre scale of the images around him, feeling a lot like Cary Grant climbing the heads of Mt. Rushmore.

"Kleo?"

"Yes?"

"Are you okay?"

"I'm fine – exhilarated even."

"Excellent. You're doing well. You're right where you need to be, but you must keep moving. Harris appears preoccupied, agitated, and he keeps looking at his watch. We don't have a moment to spare."

"Understood."

Wasting no time, he leaped onto Demeter's shoulder, and staying as low as he could, inched his way over to the curving edge. He looked up at Apollo's massive head, looming above, and visualized the throw as he'd already done a thousand times. When he had his footing, he checked the position of the rope in his hand, then cast it upwards. The loop sailed past the impressive ear to the top of the head, falling neatly around one of Apollo's knobby stone curls.

Herakles knelt down, trying to remain inconspicuous while he calculated his trajectory. To get to the back side of the statue, he'd have to jump out in a wide arc, bounce off of Apollo's arm and swing around and onto the shoulder blade.

He stood, pulled the rope until it was taut, and then hooked himself up. One last look, then he jumped into the air, bouncing gently off the arm and landing on the back, just about where he'd planned. His rubber-toed shoes gripped the stone, and once he regained his balance, he began the last stretch of his ascent.

Calling on all the mind-body energy he could invoke, he projected his being skyward, allowing the steady pull of Gravity's invisible hand to pass right through him. He glided up, step after buoyant step, imagining himself being lifted by a delicate thread of chi energy emanating from the crown of his own head. His biceps and quads glistened under the sizzling Sun, building, pumping, bursting at the seams of his sleek suit, until at last, he reached the broad, flat shoulder of Divine Reason, where he laid down and caught his breath.

A few seconds later, he rolled over onto his stomach, and bellied up just far enough to check the guards. No unusual activity. *Okay.* He wriggled back over and behind Apollo's neck, and then, with the rope, nimbly pulled himself up the remaining distance, to the row of carved curls on the head. He gripped the stone, and carefully, hoisted himself on top of the magnificent shelf of hair.

"Alex, are you with me?"

"Right here, Kleo, but where are *you?*"

"Sitting comfortably in Apollo's immortal hair."

Alex laughed, "good boy."

"Father, the view is stunning; I can see all of our beloved Athens below."

"And you're going to save it right now, Kleo. Do you see the panel?"

Herakles turned his attention to the ribbed stone and tried to find some evidence of it.

"I don't see anything, Alex."

"Keep looking, and don't panic, it's got to be there somewhere."

Herakles tried to follow his father's advice as he desperately searched the surface of the stone with his fingers, trying to sense something, anything unusual. Then he saw it – a thin horizontal line about two feet long, and another one parallel to it. "I found it!" he said excitedly.

"Try to activate the retraction device."

"Right." Herakles pressed the lower corners simultaneously and the panel released. "It worked!" He pulled it slightly toward him and it lifted up, revealing the dreaded device – a hydrogen bomb encased in a steel box about the size of a carry-on bag. On its face was a small computer screen with a keypad and digital readout: 5:25 – and counting!

"Holy shit! The clock is ticking, Alex, and we only have five minutes and 22 seconds left!"

"What else is on the screen?"

"Their *logo*," Kleo replied in disgust. "One God One Way."

"How is its operating system accessed?"

"It's their Achilles' Heel," he answered, retrieving the virus-laced disk from his pack, "a floppy drive. You were right."

"Go ahead then, you know what to do. Good luck."

Herakles loaded it, and a message appeared on the screen:

- - - a: drive is replacing c: drive – time to completion 4:41 - - -

He looked up at the timer, which now read 4:52. "Okay, it's working," he whispered, "and just in the nick of time."

"Watch it carefully," Alexander reminded, "and make certain it continues to load...and be careful not to be seen, and..."

"Okay, okay," Herakles cut him off, feeling glad for a moment to hear his father's concern, even under these circumstances. That wore off quickly, however, as anxiety started creeping in.

*Everything is going exactly as planned*, he tried to reassure himself. *No one sees me and the virus is still transferring* – but it all seemed a little too easy.

Nervously, he inched up the side of the hair to check on the guards and the action on the field below, and still, no one appeared to notice him. He surveyed the dramatic scenery. Towering above him were the mighty stone heads of Zeus and Hera, and directly across, his beloved protectress Athena, looking out at the cheering fans, as if watching the competitions with anticipation. He checked the screen again - - - processing - - - *three minutes left.*

Down on the field, Alanta was pacing around, trying to stay loose while she waited to be called. *Good luck Alanta.*

The seconds now seemed to stretch into hours.

*Two minutes.*

His patience was thinning but there was no way to speed things up. All he could do was wait and watch.

*One minute left - - - processing - - -*

The announcer introduced all seven competitors, though he only heard her name. "...in lane three, representing the United States of America, Alanta January. In lane four...."

His heart fluttered as he watched her walk confidently over to the starting line. The rest of the names were called and the runners settled into the blocks. *I love you Alanta, I know you're going to do it.*

The starting gun sounded.

He watched her slingshot out of the blocks into an instant lead, which widened and widened and widened, the entire length of the track. She broke the tape at the finish line and sent her arms skyward in ecstasy. The stadium erupted in applause, and he wanted to cheer at the top of his lungs, but he kept himself in check. A moment later, as her time flashed on the giant stadium screen, the audience went wild.

9.276 – A NEW WORLD RECORD!

He looked back to the timing device. *Twenty seconds left. Nineteen, eighteen, seventeen,* then suddenly, unbelievably, it stopped and a new message appeared - - - security code required - - -

"Father! A firewall has gone up. It's asking me for a password and the bomb is still ticking – what do I do?!"

"Enter whatever numbers come to your mind, Herakles, and do it now! I love you, Kleo!"

Just then, a bullet clipped the lobe of Apollo's ear – he'd been discovered! As he dodged a second one, he again saw Alanta's world record flashing on the giant stadium screen. 9.276 A NEW WORLD RECORD 9.276!

Without hesitation, he turned back to the computer and tapped "9276 enter." The screen went blank and the words that Herakles prayed to see, appeared - - - download resuming - - -

Another bullet whizzed by his head. He ducked, but he remained where he was, needing to make sure he did everything he could. The timer ticked down, :05, :04, :03 and then it stopped, and a final message appeared - - - download complete - unable to execute - error9276exe - - -

The shots had alerted the fans and television cameras to the drama occurring overhead and a hush had fallen over the crowd. Herakles secured the rope to his harness again, and swung out from behind the marble head, down around the massive shoulder and over the folds of Apollo's robe, evading the last, futile bullets of Ares' henchmen. He stood atop Apollo's giant foot on the pediment base, and before him, the Olympic Flame burned, its tendrils of fire slithering forth from the huge bronze chalice, hissing with intensity. From the audience's perspective, he seemed to jump down into the Flame and a great collective gasp arose.

Spider-like, he dropped the last 50 feet behind the flaming cauldron to its marble platform, then disconnected the rope and darted around to the front, where a pack of security guards stood between the two pillars, blocking the steps to the field. Three of them lurched toward him and Herakles delivered a series of well-placed kicks which brought each of them to the ground. Three more guards tried to block him, and they too easily fell. He took off down the steps and yet four more were scrambling up toward him. With a mighty leap, he dove over them all and onto the field, rolling right through his landing to an upright position, and then with full momentum, ran toward the gaggle of press.

Suddenly, Alanta broke through the line of reporters and came speeding toward him. The press ran after her, and when she and Herakles embraced, completely surrounded them. Then they kissed for real, not caring that the whole world was watching. When Herakles finally pulled away, he looked into her expectant eyes. "We did it!"

"Yes!" came her response.

"Did what? Did what?" the reporters pressed, encroaching ever closer.

The two Olympians turned to address the crowd.

"Everything is all right," Alanta exclaimed, beaming.

A radiant Herakles then called for the arrest of Harris, and revealed the terrorists' plan to a stunned and grateful public. "I was able to access the nuclear device and successfully plant the computer virus, but then, when the timer was ticking with only 11 seconds to go, the firewall went up demanding a password I didn't have. Luckily, I saw Alanta's record time on the screen. I put in the numbers, held my breath, and lo and behold, it worked!"

"So," the ENN reporter interjected, "the two of you have saved all of Athens!"

"Alanta and I have played a role in the events which have unfolded, but it is humanity's collective benevolence that will carry us all into the future."

Alanta gripped his arm, and with a smile, added, "Love is all we need."

And so it was, Herakles of the Golden Heart and Wing-Footed Alanta saved humanity from Ares, the god of war, thereby fulfilling the Prophecy of the Oracle at Delphi.

Our two Olympians now had a momentum so incredible, so unstoppable, it carried them both to victories only dreamed of. Alanta set world records in every race she ran, finding herself with five gold medals at the close of the Games. Herakles earned the gold as well, by winning each of his ten events. He also set world records for earning the highest point total ever scored in the decathlon, and achieving the widest margin of victory.

Of course, it simply would not be a tale worthy of the Homeric tradition without Herakles matching Alanta's new record for the 100-meter sprint. Indeed, he too ran a 9.276, tying him with his beloved in the record books forever.

Herakles' rival, Maximilian Leach, ended his career in disgrace. Not only had Herakles defeated him in every event of the decathlon, but he was stripped of his previous Olympic medals when his former trainer came forward with evidence that he'd been using illegal steroids for years, and had paid off the screeners to accept his phony urinalysis samples.

When it became obvious that the plan had failed, mastermind Harris attempted to escape from the security loge. However, as he came out, he was stopped cold by a tranquilizer dart from the hand of Alexander Speros. It rendered him unconscious until the Athens police arrived and took him into custody, where he would wait until his trial before the International Criminal Court for attempted crimes against humanity.

Ivanna Jadan and Marco Ramirez were cleared of all wrongdoing. However, Winston Shepherd and his three cohorts were arrested and charged with conspiracy to commit crimes against humanity. They quickly agreed to cooperate with the prosecution in the Harris case, and to assist in the ongoing OGOW investigations. Nevertheless, they were still looking at serving time in prison, paying enormous fines and having their corporate charters and CHAOS ONE broadcasting license revoked.

At the Closing Ceremony, Alanta and Herakles were honored with a special commendation for their extraordinary acts of bravery and heroism. As the Olympic anthem played, and the Earth banner rose to the Heavens, President Kim of the UN Global Council presented them with two-of-a-kind medals made of shining platinum. They accepted the keys to the city from the Mayor of Athens, and spent the next day trying to satisfy the insatiable appetite of the press.

For the rest of the world, the end of the Games closed another chapter of Olympic history. For Herakles and Alanta, it signaled the beginning of the Mythical Journey of Love they were destined to take.

# 22

## RETURN TO MOUNT OLYMPOS

For the first time in almost 2500 years, the Goddesses and Gods of the Hellenic world gathered atop Mount Olympos to celebrate their glorious triumph. They raised their chalices of ambrosia and toasted all of the Mortals who so brilliantly played their parts in the epic saga. As they did so, off in the distance, they spotted Ares on his white stallion, traversing the plains below. Aphrodite, free at last from the dreadful bond, called to him with open arms, inviting him to put down his weapons and join them.

The god of war hesitated, for just a moment, and then he turned away and rode off, back toward the wilderness.

Meanwhile, Alanta and Herakles had finally escaped the cameras and the crowds of Athens, and were now themselves on their way up Mount Olympos, on the first leg of their extended journey. By the time the golden Sun was setting over a distant ridge, they reached the cave where they'd be spending the night. Arm and arm they sat together, on a ledge overlooking all of Greece.

A slim waxing crescent Moon hung in the western sky, cloaked in a shroud of orange – just as they had seen it so many months before. And as the crescent symbolizes Rebirth, the beginning of the cycle, so did the Partners feel born anew as they began their lives together.

Night came upon them and Hera's milk sprayed against the darkening sky, creating the expansive arc of our Milky Way. Flying amidst the white clouds of stars, Cygnus the Swan soared with Aquila the Eagle high up toward the Heavens, and there was nothing to be said with words.

They gently removed each other's clothing and embraced in mutual tenderness. As ecstasy overtook them, their minds, bodies and souls merged with the consciousness of the Earth Herself and, finally, the veil lifted.

The Greek Panthaeon appeared, and with them, all the deities of every culture ever existing on Planet Earth – from throughout Asia and the Far East, from Europe, the Americas and Australia, Oceania and the continent of Africa – all the Immortals who were ever imagined by the human mind, spreading out in every direction, animating every molecule of space.

Then, out of those divine personas, the original form coalesced, becoming Mother Africa, the Great Goddess Herself: the Oldest One, all-encompassing primeval Creatrix, ancestress of all others. She surrounded Herakles and Alanta with Her eternal Love and sent their spirits soaring into the vast Cosmos beyond.

# 2004: AN OLYMPIC ODYSSEY
Interpretive Guide

For those of you who are familiar with Greek mythology, you'll notice as you read *2004* that we've taken certain liberties with the stories. Therefore, in order to provide a basis of comparison, and more fully explain our point of view, we've written this *Guide*. It includes many of the figures and places occurring in the novel, and one or more versions of what is commonly accepted as the "Classical" interpretation. (*See* Hesiod, Homer)

However, we believe the origin of many of these myths dates back to a much earlier era, to a time well before Zeus ruled the wide Heavens. Though a fortress of obfuscation was constructed in the path long ago, with a simple change of perspective, we saw the terrifying hell-like dungeon of the Minotaur's maze transform back into the dancing floor it once was. By following Ariadne's Thread, which has been woven through many of the tales, we were able to navigate the dim, frightening corridors of warrior hero cosmology back through time – all the way to the Golden Age. (*See* Ariadne, Labyrinth)

The stories about humanity once living in peace and prosperity can now be shown to have their roots in the actual lives of our Neolithic ancestors. Through the remarkable scholarship of two individuals in particular, Drs. Marija Gimbutas and Riane Eisler, abundant physical, cultural, historical and literary evidence has been put forth to support the proposition that humans did in fact once live in the "Garden of Eden."

Gimbutas, a renowned linguist and archeologist who analyzed data from countless excavations throughout Europe, and conducted five major digs of her own, documented the existence and ultimate downfall of what she called the Civilization of Old Europe. Eisler, a cultural historian and evolutionary theorist, expanded on Gimbutas' theories, persuasively demonstrating how a cultural transformation occurred in so-called prehistory, when the peaceful, creative agriculturalists were overrun by nomadic herders who idealized the warrior hero above all else. (*See also* Civilization of Old Europe, Neolithic, Partnership)

What has emerged is a fundamentally different view of the historical events which occurred between approximately 7000-1628 b.c.e., and it is with this conceptual framework that we've reinterpreted the Classical stories. Throughout the process, we not only found many links to the symbolism of the older Civilization, but also, when seen in totality, the myths themselves document the societal transformation from a peace-loving, egalitarian way of life, to one where dominance and violence reigned supreme. (*See* Indo-European) Mythologically, the central deity of prehistory, whom Gimbutas characterized as the "Great Goddess," was conquered by the all-powerful sky Gods, and her sphere of influence divided, compartmentalized, and carefully assigned to a multitude of lesser Goddesses, whose names have nevertheless survived into the present.

In this *Guide*, we first present a synopsis of the Classical version of a given tale, and then, looking through what Eisler would call a "Partnership" lens, find the links to the older culture and follow them through to a new interpretation.

In addition to the mythological information, we've also included phonetic pronunciations. Where applicable, the first is an approximation of how the word would be said in Greek, and the second, as we have come to know it in English. If a mythological character or place has its own entry, the pronunciation will be found there. If a word occurs within the body of an entry, only the Greek pronunciation is given. The occasional Roman era equivalent has also been included.

To honor the Greek language and the enduring Hellenic spirit (and where we thought it wouldn't cause too much confusion), we used a spelling which most closely approximates the Greek. For example, the letter "c," as used in the Latin version of a given word, has been changed back to "k," and in some cases (not involving the letter upsilon), we've replaced "u" with "o." We've left most occurrences of "ch" as is, because it usually represents the Greek letter "xi," a sound which has no equivalent in English. The Letter "e" at the end of a word often represents the letter "ita," which is pronounced as a long "e." Accents are widely used in Greek, so we've left a few of them in, mostly with place names.

At times, we've also tampered with capitalization conventions to emphasize words which, in our opinion, have not been given proper respect (such as "Goddess" or non Judeo-Christian "Gods"). Conversely, we've also withheld capital letters from those words we believe should be de-emphasized, such as the names of particular wars. Capitalizing this or that battle, particularly when so many have occurred during the last 5,000 years, only serves to perpetuate the glorification of warfare and dominance.

With respect to the Yoruba culture of West Africa, their traditions are extensive and complex, and in no way are we presuming to sum them up. We're only introducing a few of their deities to illustrate some of the interesting links and parallels between Greek and African mythology.

**Achilles (ah-khee-leh-EECE or a-KILL-eez):** Considered to be the greatest of the Greek warriors from Homer's Trojan war epic, the *Iliad*. He was the son of a Sea Goddess, Thetis (THEH-teece), who, in one version, tried to make him immortal by holding him by his heel and dipping him into the waters of the River Styx. All but his heel were then impervious to death, and tragically, that's where the arrow of his Trojan enemy mortally wounded him.

Dominator cultures value the warrior hero over all other figures, because they obtain and maintain an authoritarian ordering of relations through violence or the threat thereof. Without warriors who are willing to kill to enforce the dominator way of life, it cannot be sustained. Consequently, those who die in the process are glorified as "heroes." (*See* Dominator)

In Partnership cultures, the ability to kill other beings would not be glorified. Heroes in such a culture would overcome adversity through their wits and intelligence, as well as through their physical strength, and would kill others only in self-defense. They would also show compassion and mercy to those intent on disrupting or destroying their way of life through violence. (*See* Partnership)

**Acropolis (ah-KHRO-poh-leece or a-KROP-oh-liss):** The fortified citadel of an ancient Greek city, which usually contained multiple structures. In our story, we're referring to the temple complex in Athens, which is situated on a plateau at the top of a steep hill. (*See also* Erechthion, Parthenon)

**Aegis (eh-GHEECE or EE-jiss):** A goat-skin shield or breastplate imbued with magical powers, and usually associated with Zeus or Athena. The skin of this shield is said to be that of Amalthea, the goat whose milk sustained the infant Zeus while he was hidden from his father in a cave on Mount Díkti. Athena's aegis was often depicted with the head of Medusa, the Gorgon. (*See* Medusa)

**Agamemnon, Mask of (ah-ghah-MEHM-nohn):** A gold death mask found in one of the circular graves at Mikínai, and attributed to Agamemnon, King of Argos. In Homer's *Iliad*, he was the commander of the Greek army. (*See also* Dominator)

**Ages of Civilization:** In his *Works and Days*, Hesiod told of five distinct ages of human culture. The first, and most desireable, was the *Golden Age*, existing long before his own time of the 8th century b.c.e. During this Age, people lived joyfully with carefree hearts, free from toil or misery. In one translation, "all good things were theirs, and the grain-giving soil bore fruits of its own accord in unstinted plenty, while they at their leisure harvested their fields in contentment amid abundance." (West) Hesiod went on to describe this race as being covered by the Earth, and indeed, it is these people who have now come to light through the work of Dr. Marija Gimbutas and other archeologists. The Minoans were probably the last, and certainly one of the most gifted cultures of this civilization. Next came the *Age of Silver*, and it is a time when humans lost many of their positive attributes. As Hesiod put it, they were mentally and physically inferior to the people of the previous Age, and "could not restrain themselves from crimes against each other." (West) Zeus hid them out of sight, and they too were covered over by the Earth. This Age likely recalls the early warrior invasions, when dominator influence began to take hold. The *Bronze Age* brought multiple Indo-European incursions, which intensified the disruption to the societies of Old Europe. The barbarians now had weapons of bronze, which further facilitated their conquest of the peaceful peoples, and as Hesiod put it, they "were a terrible and fierce race, occupied with the woeful works of Ares and with acts of violence." (West) In the end, they destroyed themselves and went to Hades without leaving their name. The fourth is the *Heroic Age*, and as the Trojan war is invoked, probably refers in part to Mycenean times, when the Indo-Europeans were becoming more "just." Nonetheless, Hesiod recounts that after "ugly war and fearful fighting destroyed them," the fortunate were sent to eternal paradise on the Isles of the Blessed. (West) Finally, the poet laments his own time, the **Age of Iron**, and his account is chilling in its applicability to our contemporary political situation. He says that the Iron Age will end when, among other conditions, men "will sack another's town, and there will be no thanks for the man who abides by his oath or for the righteous or worthy man, but instead they will honour the miscreant and the criminal. Law and decency will be in fists. The villain will do his better down by telling crooked tales, and will swear his oath upon it." (West) (*See also* Bronze Age, Dominator, Neolithic)

**Akrotíri (ahk-roh-TEEHR-ee):** The site of an archeological excavation on the volcanic island of Thíra, Greece. In about 1628 b.c.e., what was once a massive volcano exploded in one of the most tremendous eruptions in human history. Ironically, while that catastrophe contributed to the destruction of the Minoans, the last of the Partnership cultures, it at the same time preserved in volcanic ash remarkable evidence of their civilization.

The buried villiage now known as Akrotíri has only been partially excavated, but what's been found to date suggests an egalitarian society, which held women and men in equal esteem, and valued music, the arts and the celebration of life. Everyday rooms were painted with colorful, floor-to-ceiling frescoes depicting whimsical and highly creative connections with nature. Interestingly, at Akrotíri, Kríti and other Minoan sites, no military fortifications have been found, suggesting a culture which was not driven by warfare. This 3600-year-old city offers us a rare glimpse into the world of these ancient people, and consequently, into a way of life which had flourished for thousands of years before the ideology of the warrior was imposed. (*See also* Atlantis, Civilization of Old Europe, Neolithic)

**Alanta (ah-LAHN-ta):** We chose this name for one of our main characters to remember Atalante, the fastest woman in the world of Greek mythology. She refused to marry any man who could not beat her in a foot race, and those who tried and failed were executed by her father. The suitor who was ultimately successful had to cheat in order to "win" her hand. (*See* Atalante)

**Alexander:** King of Macedonia (mah-kheh-doh-NEE-ah), who conquered the Greek city-states, Persia, Egypt and much of Asia, thereby spreading Greek culture far and wide. He is usually referred to as "Alexander the Great," a title which reflects our culture's dominator bias of glorifying the warrior hero, or in this case, the warrior king. (*See also* Dominator)

**Alkmene (alhk-MEE-nee or alk-MEE-na):** Mother of the half-twins, Herakles (by Zeus) and Iphikles (by Amphitryon [ahm-fee-TRHEE-ohn]). Zeus, with his infamous treachery, disguised himself as Alkmene's husband, Amphitryon, thereby tricking her into having sex with him and stealing her virginity. Her real husband returned and was informed of "his" misfortune by the Theban prophet, Tiresias (teehr-eh-SEE-ahs). Amphitryon tried to punish her by burning her on a pyre, but Zeus doused the flames, so she was forgiven and they consummated their marriage.

Her story is a poignant example of how women are considered to be little more than chattel in dominator cultures. (*See* Dominator)

**Alphiós (ahl-fee-OHS):** A river originating in the Arkadian Mountains in the Pelopónnisos; it flows past Olympia on its way to the Ionian Sea.

**Altis (AHL-teece):** The Sacred Grove at Olympia, where the temples to Hera and Zeus, and the public hearth or prytaneion (pree-tahn-eh-EE-ohn) were located. The Olympic Flame is still lit in this grove at the beginning of each Olympiad. (*See also* Hestia, Olympia)

**Amalthea (ah-MAHL-thee-ah or am-al-THEE-a):** The goat whose milk sustained the infant Zeus while he was hidden from his father in a cave on the island of Kríti. Her skin was used to make Zeus and Athena's aegis. In some stories, she is a Nymph.

**Amphora(e) (ahm-FOR-ah; ahm-FOR-ee [plural]):** A large, egg-shaped vase, often beautifully decorated, with a narrow neck and two curved handles, used for the storage of wine, olive oil and other liquids.

**Anastasía (ah-nah-stah-SEE-ah):** The surname of Herakles Speros' mother in our story.

**Aphrodite (ah-froh-DEE-tee or af-ro-DIE-tee):** Daughter of Ouranos alone (Celestial Aphrodite), or of Dione (dee-OHN-eh) and Zeus (Aphrodite Pandemos [pahn-DEH-mos] meaning "of all of the people"). In her Pandemos form, Aphrodite was the Goddess of love, laughter, beauty and all things which delight the senses. She was married to Hephaistos, the Lord of the Forge, but also had liaisons with Hermes, Apollo and Ares as well as many others. She was said to have loved Ares, the God of war, a linking of sex and violence which began with the earliest Indo-European invasions. She was also depicted as being prone to outbursts of anger and revenge, inflicting a variety of punishments on those who failed to offer proper veneration.

Celestial Aphrodite was herself a child of sexual violence. In the well-established cycle of power usurpation, Ouranos was castrated by his son, Kronos, who threw the immortal genitals into the sea, thereby creating the Goddess. From this perspective, and Plato's, the "highest" love arises from the male principle alone, completely negating the need for any feminine aspect of divinity.

Consequently, the power of creation was shifted from the Great Goddess of prehistory (from whom everything once originated) to the Sky God who procreates through violence. Further turning the original story on its head is Plato's interpretation of Aphrodite Pandemos, which characterized the Sacred Marriage, as represented by physical love, as more "base." What was once considered to be holy had been twisted into something profane.

Aphrodite was associated with the island of Kíthera, where one of her ancient temples still stands today, and also Cypress, a place with its own Partnership past and links to Minoan Kríti. Her symbols were the dolphin, bee, swan and dove, which were all sacred creatures with long Partnership lineages. The Latin version of her name has been given to Earth's closest planetary neighbor, Venus.

**Apollo (ah-POH-lohn [ancient], ah-POH-lohn-ahs [modern] or a-PAHL-o):** Lord of Light and Reason. He was one of the twin children of Leto and Zeus, who, with the help of his sister, Artemis, was born on the rocky island of Delos (DEH-lohs) (the brilliant). He grew to be one of the most esteemed of the Immortals. The title "Phoebos," which means "bright," was often associated with him in his capacity as Sun God, though it was also used long before he was directly linked with the Sun. He was best known for his supremely rational mind and clarity of vision, but was also associated with the practice of medicine and the oracular arts of prophecy and healing, as well as with the realms of poetry, song, music and archery. His temple at Delphi was at the very center of Classical Greek spiritual life, and as such, pilgrims from throughout the Mediterranean went there, with the hope of receiving a favorable prophecy. Homer depicted Apollo as someone who would ultimately possess uncontrollable power, and as the God has often been associated with the realm of science, particularly as it has been employed in the pursuit of furthering institutionalized warfare, time has proven Homer's prophecy to be accurate on many occasions.

The stories of Apollo give us further insight into the cultural transformation which occurred in prehistory. The Oracle at Delphi had been a sacred place of Goddess worship for many centuries before the Indo-Europeans installed Apollo. In order to establish his pre-eminence, it was necessary for him to slay Python (PEE-thohn), the serpent who attended the Oracle for the Goddess, Gaia. There are also several links to the earlier Minoan culture, and one is particularly poignant. It is the story about Apollo's recruitment of the devotees of the Temple at Knossós on Kríti. In that myth, Apollo transformed himself into a dolphin, jumped up on their ship and then guided them swiftly to his newly-built temple at Delphi, before revealing himself and commanding them to serve him. (*See also* Python)

The transfer of power at Delphi reveals yet another example of co-optation through conquest. The conquerors, with Apollo as their God, reordered the mythical realm and reassigned to him the powers of the older deities. However, the links to the previous Goddess tradition remained abundantly clear. For example, the God's prophecy continued to be pronounced by a temple priestess, known as the Pythia. Also, an egg-shaped stone, known as the Omphalos, continued to be kept there. That word means "navel," and signified the physical and spiritual center of the Earth, connecting all of humanity to its Mother. (*See also* Pythia)

**Apples of the Hesperides (ess-pehr-EE-dess or hes-PEAR-i-deez):** The three daughters of Nyx (neeks) (Night) lived in a land beyond the sunset, and there they kept a beautiful garden, where the Tree of Life, with its Golden Apples of Immortality, grew. The Tree was carefully guarded by Ladon (LAH-dohn), a hundred-headed serpent who was sent by Hera to protect it. For Herakles' eleventh labor he had to steal the Apples, which he did with the help of Atlas. Herakles held up the sky while Atlas snuck into the garden and retrieved them, then clever Herakles tricked Atlas into resuming his heavy burden. Herakles delivered the Apples to king Eurystheus, but they proved too dangerous to keep, so with the help of Athena, he returned them to the garden. In Euripides' version, Herakles killed the serpent and absconded with the Apples.

The Tree of Life, the paradisiacal "Garden of Eden," the presence of the Triple Goddess and the snake all recall the earlier Partnership culture where this imagery was central. Through this story, Herakles usurped all of the older, sacred symbols and incorporated them, as though they were trophies, into his warrior hero persona.

**Arachne (ah-RAHK-nee):** A peasant renowned for her skill at weaving, which was an art attributed to Athena. Arachne was unwilling to properly credit her skill to the Goddess, and so an outraged Athena disguised herself as an old woman and paid her a visit. The unsuspecting Arachne made blasphemous comments and challenged the Goddess to a weaving contest. Athena revealed herself and accepted the challenge, weaving a tapestry depicting her contest with Poseidon for the rule of Athens, as well as several scenes of mortals who were foolish enough to challenge the Immortals, and as a result, were changed into various creatures. Arachne, however, was undaunted. She wove a vivid scene showing Zeus, Poseidon, Apollo, Dionysos and Ouranos conquering Goddesses and mortal women through deceit and violence. Athena inspected Arachne's creation and had to admit defeat. In retaliation, she bludgeoned the poor girl with her own loom shuttle, before pouring a wicked herb over her, which like acid, burned her hair, shriveled her limbs and left her in spider form.

This story reaffirms a number of dominator themes, including caste, and the imposition of violence to establish superiority. However, Arachne remains in the depths of our subconscious, spinning her own thread of truth throughout the vast web of time. The imposition of a social order which relies on domination and violence cannot be morally justified. (*See also* Dominator)

**Ares (AHR-eece or AIR-eez):** The God of war, born in Thrace to Hera and Zeus. In Homer's *Iliad*, his own father called him "most hateful," for Ares, and what he represents, derives from what some have called the "reptilian brain" – that part of the human brain where, among other characteristics, ruthlessness, viciousness and cunning developed long ago on the evolutionary continuum. Ares was a personification of those undesirable traits, which have been cultivated, and even sacralized by dominator ideology, making him the ultimate warrior. (*See also* Dominator, Indo-European)

In the stories, he was not married, though he did have numerous lovers, the most famous of whom was Aphrodite, in what at first appears to be an incongruous matching. Yet, a closer look at dominator cultures reveals a long-standing pattern of the linking of sex and violence. This tragic phenomenon most likely started when the Indo-European invasions began, and has continued right up to the present day. The Latin version of Ares' name has been given to the red planet, and our next door neighbor, Mars.

**Argo (AHR-goh):** Swift (ancient Greek). Jason and the Argonauts' famous ship, which had as its crew a virtual who's who of Greek warrior heroes, including Atalante and Herakles. This roving band traveled the sea's wide ridges and overcame many challenges on their quest to find the Golden Fleece of Immortality.

**Argos (AHR-ghos); also, Argolís (ahr-gho-LEECE):** The region in the northeastern Pelopónnisos which was a primary focal point for the worship of Hera. The Heraion is one of the many temples to this Goddess, and though now a ruin, it has been there for almost 3,000 years. Argos is also where the ancient city of Mikínai once stood (*circa* 1600-1100 b.c.e.). In Homer's famous tale, the *Iliad*, it was the place where Agamemnon rallied his troops before setting sail for Troy, at the start of what would become a long, bloody conflict.

**Ariadne (ahr-ee-AHD-nee):** The daughter of Queen Pasiphae (pahss-ee-FAH-ee) and King Minos of Kríti. In one of her most well known stories, Ariadne fell in love with the Athenian hero, Theseus, and helped him to defeat the Minotaur by giving him a ball of thread so he could find his way back out of the Knossós Labyrinth (which in this story was really a maze). To avoid her father's wrath, she fled with Theseus on his sailing ship, but unfortunately, was then deserted on the island of Náxos. Dionysos discovered her as she slept on the beach, fell in love with her and, ultimately, married her.

Some scholars believe the labyrinth itself originated as a dance, possibly involving an initiation rite, which symbolized the process of death and regeneration. In this context, the "Thread of Ariadne" becomes symbolic of the path itself, the negative space created by the contours of the labyrinth shape. Metaphorically then, because Theseus needed the thread to find his way out, he had to rely on the Goddess' help to be reborn. Ariadne's original spirit is also remembered through Dionysos and the Partnership resurgence his popularity sparked. (*See also* Labryrinth, Minotaur)

**Arkadía (ahr-kah-DEE-ah):** A region of Greece in the central Pelopónnisos.

**Armageddon (arm-ah-GHED'n):** A story from the Book of Revelations in the New Testament of the Bible. It's the place where the ultimate, and horrific, final battle will take place between "good" and "evil." It has also come to mean the occurrence of that battle and the resulting annihilation of humanity.

**Artemis (AHR-teh-meece or ART-a-miss):** Goddess of the Wild Animals. She was one of the twin children of Leto and Zeus, and was associated with remote places, especially the wildflower meadows and solitary forests of snow-capped Mount Taíyetos in the Pelepónnisos. Shortly after her birth, she helped her mother bring forth Apollo, so she was also known as a Goddess of childbirth, though she herself remained a virgin. Her brother ultimately usurped her once-significant oracular and healing powers, as well as her sources of inspiration, the Muses, which he subsequently claimed as his own. Like him, she was an accomplished archer, and so when the crescent moon is waxing or waning, it is her bow we see hovering in the heavens. Independent, confident and strong, she undertook many adventures, sometimes inflicting great cruelty and pain (*See* Niobe).

She was worshipped throughout the Mediterranean region, and a particularly interesting representation, the "many-breasted" Artemis, is a statue from Ephesus, in Asia Minor. Artemis embodied the forces of nature and our primal need to connect with them. She was one of the oldest Goddesses of the Greek Panthaeon, with lineage dating back to the Paleolithic Goddess of the Wild Animals, and later, the Neolithic bear, bird and weaving Goddesses.

**Ashé (ah-SHAY):** In the Yoruba culture of Western Africa, Ashé is the divine force incarnate, the morally neutral power to "make things happen." It is the vital energy of the Universe, embodied in the main Yoruba God, Olorun (oh-lo-RHOON). This energy came to Earth manifested in different animals, representing various aspects of "life power." It is represented by the color red, the color of the blood of life. (*See also* Itútu, Yoruba)

**Asia Minor:** That part of Turkey which borders the Aegean, Mediterranean and Black Seas. Also known as Anatolia (ah-nah-TOH-lee-ah).

**Atalante (ah-tah-LAHN-dee or ah-tah-LAHN-tah):** A virgin huntress, who as an infant was abandoned by her father and left to die in the wilderness. However, she was found and nursed by a mother bear, and later discovered by hunters who raised her. She grew up to become part of the crew of the sailing ship, *Argo*, who embarked on the journey to find the Golden Fleece.

Atalante was the fastest woman in the mythological realm, and refused to marry any man who could not beat her in a footrace. Those who tried and lost were executed by her father, who was now back in the picture. Finally, a suitor named Milanion (mi-LAHN-ee-ohn) devised a plan to trick her into losing. He obtained three of the Golden Apples of the Hesperides and planted them strategically along the route. Of course, the Apples of Immortality were irresistible to her, and so she stopped during the race to pick them up, allowing Milanion to cross the finish line first. After they consummated their marriage in a sacred grove, an angry Zeus turned them into a lioness and lion. (*See also* Apples of the Hesperides)

Atalante's refusal to go by the patriarchal norms of Greek society, where women were tantamount to chattel, reveals her more ancient roots. She was likely connected to an earlier Partnership tradition, where relations between men and women were more egalitarian. The presence of the Apples and the animal references in this story also clearly link her with Neolithic cultures and their symbols, including the Tree of Life, the bear and the lioness.

**Athena (ah-thee-NAH or a-THEE-na):** Protector of the City. Daughter of Metis (one of the Oceanids [oh-keh-ah-NEECE]), and Thunder God, Zeus, this Goddess was not born in the usual manner. Metis was destined to give birth first to a daughter, and then to a son who would one day rule the wide heavens, so when she became pregnant by Zeus he swallowed her whole, to ensure the prophesy would not ultimately be fulfilled. Shortly thereafter, he complained of a headache and, depending upon the version, either Prometheus or Hephaistos hit him in the head with an axe, and Athena sprung forth, fully grown, fully armored and screeching a battle cry. She was first and foremost a warrior Goddess, and as such was the guardian of Athens, from which she may have derived her name. She was bright-eyed (sometimes known as grey- or pale-eyed) and brilliant, and was considered to be ethical, at least according to the dominator code of relations. (*See* Arachne) She was a supreme strategist in military matters, though she was also an accomplished mediator and judge, using her wisdom to interpret and uphold the law. Athena was especially close to her father, Zeus, and took particular interest in various warrior heroes, including Odysseus, Herakles, Perseus and Achilles, acting as their protector, mentor and guide. She was also credited with more domestic qualities, and was honored as the creator of cooking, spinning and weaving. In addition, the gifts of the olive tree and the flute were attributed to her benevolence.

Athena was often depicted with snakes, which reveals her link to the older Minoan Snake Goddess, and by extension, pre-patriarchal culture. Her "birth" from the head of Zeus was a blatant co-optation of her powers by the Indo-European invaders. While she was allowed to retain significant influence, she could do so as long as it remained clear that her authority came from, and was subordinate to, her father. (*See also* Metis)

As an aside, when the Greek people say "ah-THEE-nah," they are referring to the city of Athens; "ah-thee-NAH" refers to the Goddess.

**Athloi (AHTH-lee or ATH-loy):** Contests undertaken for a prize (ancient Greek). It also referred to the "Labors of Herakles." As Herakles was credited with the founding of the Olympic Games, the word eventually evolved into the contemporary English word, "athlete."

**Atlantis (aht-lahn-DEECE or at-LAN-tiss):** The highly sophisticated and technologically advanced island civilization that, according to Plato, "in a single day and night of misfortune...disappeared in the depths of the sea." (Demos) The story of Atlantis comes to us through Plato's *Dialogues*, specifically the discussion between Critias (khree-TEE-ahs) and Timaeus (tee-meh-EECE), which relies on the authority of Egyptian priests. Many scholars believe that the myth refers back to the ancient Minoan civilization, and though not all of the descriptions match, in part because Plato was reaching so far into his own distant past, there are many similarities. Among other characteristics, he described them as a refined, elegant people, who had a very high standard of living, and who were talented artists and proficient sailors.

From as early as 3100 b.c.e., the pre-Greek Minoan culture thrived in the Mediterranean region, most notably on the islands of Kríti and Thíra. At that time, Thíra was a massive volcanic cone, rising above the ocean perhaps as high as a mile. However, in about 1628 b.c.e., in one of the most horrific eruptions in human history, the island blew its top off, and as the walls of the mountain came crashing down, forming a caldera in the sea, tidal waves reaching 800 feet in height swept across the region. Of all of the possible explanations for the origin of the Atlantis myth, the Minoan culture seems the most likely candidate. Not only are many of the descriptions similar, but a volcanic eruption is one of the few geological events which could sink an island overnight. (*See also* Akrotíri, Knossós, Minoans)

**Atlas (AHT-lahs or AT-lis):** Son of Clymene (klee-MEH-nee) and Iapetos (ee-ah-peh-TOHS) or Ouranos, and one of the Giants (GHEE-ghan-dess), an earlier generation of Earth-born divinities who arose to challenge Zeus' overthrow of the Titans. He was punished with the task of holding up the sky.

**b.c.e.:** Before the Common Era. A secularized version of b.c. (before Christ).

**Boréas (vor-EH-ahs or bor-AY-ahs):** The North Wind.

**Bronze Age:** The historic period between the Neolithic and Iron Ages, approximately 3500–1250 b.c.e. It is during this time that warrior cultures used the innovation of bronze to devise more deadly weapons, with which they completed the conquest of the Civilization of Old Europe.

Interestingly, the pre–Greek Minoans were able to thrive during the first half of this period, choosing instead to utilize the new technology for ritual and agricultural purposes. From what is suggested by the archeological evidence, they apparently shared the abundant fruits of their labor fairly and equally amongst their populations. (*See also* Ages of Civilization, Civilization of Old Europe, Minoan, Neolithic)

**Byzantine (vee–zahn–tee–NOHS or BIZ–ahn–teen):** Referring to the Byzantine Empire (*circa* 395 c.e. to 1453 c.e.)

**Calibishie (kal–i–BEE–shee):** A fishing village on the northeastern shore of the Caribbean island of Dominica.

**c.e.:** Of the Common Era. A secularized version of a.d. (anno Domini), which means "in the year of the Lord."

**Centaurs (KEHN–dahv–rhee or SEN–tawrs):** A mythical race of fierce warriors, who had the head and torso of a human, and the body and legs of a horse. They were defeated in battle by the Lapiths, a scene which was carved in stone on the west pediment of the Temple of Zeus at Olympia.

**Cerberus (KEHR–vehr–ohs or SIR–bir–us):** The three-headed hound of Hades who guarded the entrance to the Underworld. For Herakles' twelfth labor, he ventured into the realm of the dead, subdued the dangerous dog and delivered it to King Eurystheus. Then he returned the creature back to its home, thereby symbolically conquering death itself.

**Chaos (KHAH-ohss or KHAY-oss):** The Chasm (ancient Greek). According to Hesiod, the original void or "yawning" from which the primordial deities emerged: Gaia (Earth), Tártaros (a place deep within the Earth), Eros (representing "Celestial Love"), Erebos (the gloominess of Tártaros) and Nyx (neeks) (Night).

**Charybdis (KHA-rheev-deece or ka-RIB-diss):** Daughter of Gaia and Poseidon, she was cast into the sea by a thunderbolt of Zeus. She, as the whirlpool or water spout, presents a dangerous obstacle for ships sailing through the Strait of Messina, which separates Italy and Sicily.

**Civilization of Old Europe:** A phrase coined by archeologist Dr. Marija Gimbutas, to denote the European civilization which existed for thousands of years prior to the Indo-European invasions (*circa* 6th - 4th millennia b.c.e.). The people of Old Europe had a matrilineal, egalitarian social structure, an agricultural economy, and they lived in unfortified villages and townships. Gimbutas presents a compelling case that they were also peaceful and artistic, and that they conceptualized divinity as the "Great Goddess." (*See also* Great Goddess, Neolithic, Partnership)

**Cycladic or Cyclades:** *See* Kikládes.

**Cyclopes (KEE-kloh-pess or sie-KLOH-peez):** Round-eyed (ancient Greek). The three one-eyed sons of the Sacred Marriage of Earth and Sky (Gaia and Ouranos). Each had an orb-like eye in the middle of his forehead, perhaps signifying oracular wisdom. They were gifted metallurgists who created lightning and thunder, and they resided in remote mountain caves. One of them captured and held Odysseus and his comrades, but the clever hero escaped by tricking the Cyclops into getting drunk, and then blinding him with a burning olive wood stake.

This story is another example of mythological co-optation.

The warrior hero used his cleverness and brutality to overcome the more ancient diety, who had been turned into a dumb, but threatening, monster. The earlier origin of these creatures is suggested by several of their attributes: their lineage as children of the Sacred Marriage; their dwellings were in caves, which had long been sacred places of earlier religions; and their wisdom, as symbolized by the exaggerated eye, was destroyed through violence.

**Daidalos (DEH-dah-los or DEE-da-lus):** Famed artisan and engineer who was credited with being the architect of the Labyrinth at Knossós, and the creator of many inventions, including wings affixed with wax. Tragically, while trying to escape from King Minos, his son, Ikaros (EE-kahr-ohs), disregarded his warnings and flew too close to the Sun. The wax melted, the wings fell off and the boy plunged into the sea and perished.

**Delphi (DEL-fee or DEL-fie):** The sanctuary of Apollo, located high on the slopes of Mount Parnassós in central Greece, and the site of the famous Oracle. Delphi was at the very center of Greek spiritual life, so pilgrims from all over the Mediterranean journeyed there, bringing important questions, both personal and political, with the hope of glimpsing their future. In order to claim Delphi as his own, Apollo had to slay the serpent, Python (PEE-thohn). From that word, the title "Pythia," or Priestess of Apollo, was derived, as was "Pythian" (pee-thee-OHS), an epithet for the God himself. Athletic contests known as the Pythian Games also took place here every four years. (*See also* Apollo, Pythia)

The snake was a sacred creature to our pre-Indo-European ancestors, because it not only had the power of life and death, but each time it shed its skin, it was reborn. Therefore, as a potent symbol of the earlier belief system, it had to be conquered, and its powers controlled, as part of establishing the new order.

Prior to its usurpation, Delphi was the Oracle of Gaia, and

habitation of the site likely stretched back into the Neolithic. The name was derived from "delphini" (del-FEE-nee), the Greek word for dolphin. (*See also* Delphinios)

**Delphinios (del-FEE-nee-ohs or del-FIN-ee-us):** One of Apollo's titles, derived from the Greek word "delphini" (del-FEE-nee), which means dolphin. It originated from the story of how Apollo transformed himself into a dolphin in order to enlist the devotees of the Temple at Knossós to be his sanctuary attendants at Delphi. (*See also* Apollo)

**Demeter (dee-MEE-teehr or deh-MEE-ter):** Goddess of the Fruitful Soil. She was a daughter of the Titans, Rhea and Kronos, and mother of Persephone, who is the subject of one of her most well-known stories. Persephone was a budding Earth Goddess, who drew the amorous attention of Hades, God of the Underworld. He conspired with Zeus (Persephone's father) to lure her with the intoxicating scent of a narcissus flower, then abducted her and took her to his realm, far from the fields of her mother. Demeter searched in vain, grief-stricken, causing the once abundant fields to become barren and a cold winter to envelop all of the Earth. Things got so bad that Zeus finally had to intervene, demanding his brother release her. Hades did as he was told, but only after he forced Persephone to eat the seeds of a pomegranate (a fruit connected with death and regeneration). She was then required to return to his realm for one third of every year, and so the cycle of the seasons was born. Each winter, when her daughter must descend into the Underworld, Demeter causes the fields to go barren in her grief. And each spring, when mother and daughter are reunited, the Earth rejoices and the crops again grow and flowers bloom. To celebrate their initial reunion, Demeter established the Mysteries at Eleusís. (*See* Eleusís)

Demeter is another ancient Earth Goddess, who, in her form as Grain Goddess, dates back to the seventh millennium b.c.e.

Later portrayed with a sickle and shaft, she represented the cyclical nature of the seasons and the art of agriculture she taught to humanity. She was the Goddess of the Ancient Harvest, and as such, also represented abundance. She was linked to the island of Kríti, most notably through Persephone, who was born there; Homer suggested that it may also have been her place of origin. The poppy was sacred to her, as it was to the Minoan Snake Goddess.

This story is one in a long line of vegetation myths invoking the cycle of life, death and regeneration, which is a recurring theme throughout the mythologies of the world. The Romans knew her as Ceres (SEER-eez) (root of the word "cereal").

**Díkti (DEEK-tee):** A mountain on the island of Kríti, where, in a cave, the infant Zeus was hidden to protect him from his father, Kronos. Some stories also place his birth there. Caves were sacred to Partnership cultures and symbolic of the womb of the Earth Goddess, so it is not surprising that the Indo-European invaders chose to hide (or incubate) their king of kings in a cave, thereby co-opting the religious significance of the site, and by extension, the body of myth originating on Kríti.

**Dionysos (dee-OH-nee-sohss or die-oh-NICE-us):** Vegetation God of the Grape and Vine. Originally the son of Persephone and Zeus (called Zagreus [zah-greh-EECE] in that incarnation) he was dismembered by the Titans, but then reconstituted as the child of Semele (seh-MEH-lee) and Zeus. However, like Athena, he was not born in the usual manner. Semele was killed through the trickery of Hera, which caused her to be incinerated by Zeus' lightning. At the moment of her death, the premature infant God was snatched up and placed in the thigh of Zeus, to await "birth."

Dionysos brought prosperity and happiness to those who offered appropriate worship, but to those who did not, he would bring only madness and death. Also known as the bull-horned God, he carried an ivory covered staff called the thyrsos (THEEHR-sohss), and on occasion, wore a crown of serpents. He was attended by Maenads and Satyrs, a passionate and lively bunch, who relished in carnal delight. As the God of the Grapevine, and of Ecstasy, his festivals were renowned for the pleasure they brought to the celebrants. He also represented rebirth and resurrection, as evidenced by numerous vegetation-related stories, and the tale about his trip to the Underworld to bring his mother back to life.

His links to the earlier culture of Minoan Kríti are also substantial. He's associated with the symbols of the bull and snake, and he married the Minoan Goddess, Ariadne, after Theseus deserted her on the island of Náxos. Importantly, his celebratory nature emphasizes the joy of life, rather than the glorification of death. His popularity during Classical times (*circa* 480-323 b.c.e.), particularly with the revival of the older ritual celebrations, suggests a Partnership resurgence. (*See also* Partnership)

The story of Dionysos' ultimate "birth" nicely illustrates the co-optation of the earlier cosmology, accomplished by the overt usurpation of the maternal role, and by extension, the mysteries he represented. The Romans knew him as Bacchus (BAHK-us).

**Dodekánisos (doh-deh-KAH-nee-sohss):** A group of twelve islands in the southeastern Aegean Sea, near the coast of Turkey.

**Doha (DOE-heh):** Capital city of the independent emirate of Qatar.

**Dominator:** A term used by Dr. Riane Eisler as part of her Partnership/Dominator Continuum. What follows is a description of an extreme dominator culture, which is reflective of the warrior tribes that invaded and destroyed the Civilization of Old Europe beginning as early as 6000 years ago. Most contemporary cultures still exhibit these tendencies to one degree or another.

Dominator ideologies tend to be hierarchical and authoritarian in nature, conceptualizing "power" as something to be used to dominate and subjugate other members of society. They are by and large patrilineal and patrifocal, and masculinity is often equated with violence. This model of social organization typically relies on strong-man rule to reinforce the so-called social "norms" of institutionalized warfare, second class status of women as a group, economic injustice and environmental destruction. Technology and resources are strictly controlled to ensure the political status quo. Dominator cultures can be either patriarchal or matriarchal.

In these societies, warrior heroes are valued over all other figures, because they obtain and maintain an authoritarian ordering of relations through violence or the threat thereof. Without warriors who are willing to kill to enforce the dominator way of life, it cannot be sustained. Consequently, those who die in the process are glorified.

In Partnership cultures, the ability to kill other beings would not be glorified. Heroes in such a culture would overcome adversity through their wits and intelligence, as well as through their physical strength, and would kill others only in self-defense. They would also show compassion and mercy to those intent on disrupting or destroying their way of life through violence. (*See* Partnership)

**Doomsday Clock:** Created in 1947 to measure the liklihood of nuclear weapons being used. The closer the clock ticks toward midnight, the greater the danger. It was at its closest, 11:58 pm, in 1953, and at its furthest, 11:42 pm, in 1991. It's maintained by the Bulletin of the Atomic Scientists. www.thebulletin.org/clock.html

**Echo (ee-KHO or EH-koh):** Mountain Nymph who could only repeat the last word someone else said to her. She fled from Pan's advances, and in retaliation, he whipped his shepherd devotees into a frenzy, spreading "panic" and "pandemonium." In their collective madness, they tore her to pieces, leaving only her voice.

Another version credits Hera with limiting her speech, because when Zeus was out carousing with the other Nymphs, Echo would prevent Hera from catching them by delaying the Goddess with her repetitive words.

The two variations of this myth illustrate that both Gods and Goddesses used the tactic of maiming to reinforce their authority in dominator culture.

**Ekecheiría (eh–keh–kheer–EE–ah):** The Holding of Hands (ancient Greek); also, the Sacred Truce (ancient and modern Greek). When the city-states sent athletes to Olympia to compete in the Games (beginning in 776 b.c.e.), they had to agree to honor the Ekecheiría, and observe the cessation of all hostilities, so it would be safe to travel. Even in that barbarous age, the warrior heroes were able to lay down their weapons, something we, in our modern era, have not been able to accomplish on a large scale.

However, in very recent times, there has been significant progress toward reviving this remarkable tradition. In 1992, the Olympic Committee finally called upon the international community to observe the Truce. They didn't. In 1994, the Truce was partially achieved, as the factions in war-torn Sarajevo ceased hostilities during the Winter Games in Lillehammer, Norway. The Resolution of the 50th Session of the UN General Assembly (1995) reaffirmed the Olympic ideal as a key to global peace. In 1996, the Athens 2004 Committee pledged to revive the Truce and promote it through the Olympic Flame Relay. Another UN Resolution was passed for the 1998 Winter Games in Nagano, and it was partially achieved in the Persian Gulf region. In 1999, a record 180 UN Member States co-sponsored a resolution to observe the Truce during the 2000 Summer Games in Sydney. The International Olympic Truce Foundation and the International Olympic Truce Centre were founded in 2000, and also in that year, at the UN Millennium Summit, 150 heads of state adopted a Declaration which included an affirmation of the observance of the Olympic Truce. On September 26, 2003, Greece introduced to the UN General Assembly a new resolution entitled "Building a Peaceful and Better World through Sport and the Olympic Ideal," with the hope that all 191 Member States will endorse it prior to the 2004 Games in Athens. www.olympictruce.org

**Eleme (eh–LEM-eh):** One of the six kingdoms of Ogoniland within the country of Nigeria, Africa. Also the name of one of the four main Ogoni languages.

**Eleusís (eh–lehf-SEECE or eh–LOO-sis):** The place of happy arrival (ancient Greek). A town about 14 miles from Athens, and the Goddess Demeter's sacred site where, in antiquity, her Mysteries had been celebrated. They honored the agricultural cycle of life, death and regeneration, and were performed for at least two thousand years, evidencing the significant influence that the older religion continued to have on the Greek imagination. During the time the Mysteries were held, the city-states declared a truce, and people came from all over the Mediterranean. (*See also* Demeter)

The rites were an outgrowth of an even earlier festival known as the Thesmophoria (thess-moh-FOHR-ee-ah).

**Elysian Fields (eh–LEEZ-ee-en):** Paradise, or Heaven. The ancient poets situated this realm of the afterlife in essentially three different locations: at the western edge of the Earth; on the Isles of the Blessed far in the western ocean; and later, in the lower domain of Hades. Though they were worlds apart, they all had something in common: a philosophy that the ideal life could only be found upon death.

Contrasting this view with Hesiod's Golden Age and Christianity's Garden of Eden, where life itself was paradisiacal, an explanation becomes apparant. Once the Indo-European warriors had conquered all of the peaceful agriculturalists (the Civilization of

Old Europe), they justified their actions with the promise of an eternal paradise after death, which ironically, attempted to embody the very way of life they'd destroyed.

**Ennead (eh-NEH-ahs or eh-NAY-ad):** The Nine (modern Greek), as in the nine Muses. (*See* Muses)

**Eos (ee-OHS or EE-os):** The saffron-robed Goddess of Dawn, whose rosy fingers painted the sky each morning as she traveled in her two-horsed chariot. She was the youngest daughter of the Titans, Theia and Hyperion, and known to the Romans as Aurora.

**Epeios (eh-pee-OHS):** In Homer's *Odyssey*, he was given credit for building the Trojan Horse, though he did have a little help from Athena. (*See also* Trojan Horse)

**Erebos (EHR-eh-vos or EHR-i-bus):** Another of the realms of Hades, this one being the gloomy darkness of Tártaros, or Tártaros itself.

**Erechthion (eh-rhek-THEE-ohn):** An elegant temple next to the Parthenon, on the Acropolis in Athens. Its famous porch has six larger-than-life female statues, known as the Karyatides (kehr-ee-AH-tee-dess), supporting the roof. It was named after Erechtheus (eh-rhek-theh-EECE), an early king of Athens, but it had formerly been known as the temple which housed "the ancient statue." (The latter refers to a wooden statue of Athena from distant antiquity called the Athena Polias (POH-lee-ahss)). It's also the place where Athena and Poseidon had their contest for control of the city.

**Eros (EHR-ohs):** This Immortal had several different traditions associated with his birth. In Hesiod's stories, he was an early cosmic deity born directly from Chaos, and was the embodiment of Classical Greek beauty. Another story places him as the son of Aphrodite and Ares, thereby solidifying the connection between sex and violence. The cherub version of Eros (Cupid) arose during later Roman times (*circa* 200 c.e.). For the purposes of our story, we've combined the various attributes to come up with the Cherub of Love. In modern Greek, the word "erotas" (EHR-oh-tahs) is a root for many words relating to romantic love.

**Eshu-Elegba (EH-shoo eh-LEG-ba):** The Messenger of the Gods and Goddesses in the Yoruba (West African) Panthaeon. He represents the crossroads, the place of sacred intersection between the mortal and immortal realms, and he also has a reputation for mischievousness. Eshu-Elegba shares these characteristics with the Greek God, Hermes.

**Eurystheus (ev-rhis-theh-EECE or yoo-RISS-thee-us):** A king of Mikínai whose birth was hastened by Hera to ensure that he, and not Herakles, would fulfill the prophecy of becoming ruler of the race of Perseus (pehr-seh-EECE). Consequently, Herakles was destined to complete his twelve labors in service to the king. Monarchies, with their hierarchical structure and chain of command, by necessity tend toward a dominator configuration. (*See* Dominator, Partnership)

Ευχαριστώ **(ehf-kahr-ee-STOH)**: Thank you (modern Greek).

**Fates:** In Greek they are known as "Moira" (MEEHR-ah), and there are three of them: Klotho (KLO-tho), Lakesis (LAH-khee-seece) and Atropos (AH-troh-pohs). Klotho spins the thread of each life, Lakesis measures it and Atropos cuts it.

**Gaia (GHEH-ah or GIE-a):** Earth. Also known as Ge (ghee), which in ancient and modern Greek means "Earth." Primordial Cosmic Mother Goddess who emerged from genderless Chaos, and then, alone, gave birth to Ouranos (the Heavens), the Mountains, and Pontos (POHN-tohs) (the Sea). Gaia united with Ouranos, and then gave birth to the Titans. (*See also* Son-Lover)

In Greek mythology, she was the original parthenogenic Goddess – from her, and without the male principle, the Creation came forth. The figure of Gaia recalls a time when humanity was one with nature, and divinity resided in the body of the Great Goddess. (*See also* Great Goddess, Pangaia, Parthená, Parthenos, Sacred Marriage)

Today, scientists such as James Lovelock and Lynn Margulis invoke Gaia when they're describing the self regulating and self-perpetuating nature of our Earth system. Others have put forth the idea of Gaia Consciousness to describe the notion that at some level, not fully understood, the Earth itself is conscious. Perhaps, as Anne Baring and Jules Cashford have said, by naming her again, we can restore her sacred identity "so that a new relationship might become possible between humans and the natural world we take for granted." (*See also* the Global Consciousness Project at http://noosphere.princeton.edu)

**Geo:** A fictional currency which is based on a just, sustainable economic system.

**Golden Age:** *See* Ages of Civilization.

**Golden Fleece:** *See* Argo.

**Goondiwindi (goon-di-WIN-dee):** A town on the border of Queensland and New South Wales in Australia.

**Great Goddess of Prehistory:** The Giver of All. When our Paleolithic ancestors first anthropomorphized a creator deity, they drew from their experience. Because they witnessed life coming forth from the body of woman, they quite naturally tended to see all of Creation coming forth in this way. And so, the Great Mother came into being. The archeological record is replete with figurines and images evidencing this development.

She was likely seen as an all-encompassing entity with many aspects, a few of which are listed here. As the Goddess of Life, Death and Regeneration, our ancestors recognized her presence in the lunar cycles of the Moon: the waxing crescent emerges from the womb of the Great Mother, grows brighter each night until it reaches full, and then wanes into the total darkness of the new Moon, where it incubates for three days before its rebirth as a crescent once again. As the Bird Goddess, she laid the Cosmic Egg from which the Universe was born; upon death, our spirits take flight to the Heavens. As the Snake Goddess, she was symbolic of the primordial rivers, had the power of life and death, and was reborn each time she shed her skin. During the Neolithic, she was the Goddess of Vegetation and Grain, when the cycle of life, death and regeneration became increasingly significant, as the agriculturalists learned the cycle of planting, growing and harvesting. As the Bear Goddess she was the nurturing mother of all wild creatures. As the Bee Goddess, she reminded us of the interconnectedness of our existence, a grand honeycomb with sweet nectar in abundance. And as the Butterfly Goddess, she taught us about spiritual transformation. (*See also* Old Europe)

**Griffin:** A mythological winged creature which is half lion or dog, and half bird. They were prominent figures in Minoan art, recalling the lioness and bird aspects of the Great Goddess of prehistory. They provide an important contrast to the Harpies and Sirens who were demonized in later myth. (*See* Harpies, Sirens)

**Hades (EH-deece or HAY-deez):** The Invisible (ancient Greek). God of the Underworld, son of the Titans, Rhea and Kronos. His realm included the Elysian Fields (Heaven), Tártaros (Hell) and Erebos (the gloomy darkness of Tártaros). In one of his most notorious acts, he abducted Persephone and forced her to marry him. (*See also* Demeter)

**Harpies (AHRP-neh or HARP-eez):** The Snatchers (Greek). Dangerous birdlike creatures with female faces, who often appeared as strong, violent winds and were capable of causing great harm. Archeologists have found countless Paleolithic and Neolithic artifacts depicting the Bird Goddess, a figure who, in earlier belief systems, laid the Cosmic Egg from which the Universe came forth. She also symbolized the flight of the soul upon death. The Harpies are an obvious demonization of an important pre-patriarchal figure.

**Helikon (ee-ehl-ee-KOHN or hel-i-kon):** A mountain in Boetia (vee-oh-TEE-ah) and one of the traditional homes of the Muses. It reaches a height of 5,738 feet. (*See also* Muses)

**Helios (EE-lee-ohs or HEE-lee-us):** A Sun God, he was the son of the Titans, Theia and Hyperion. Each day, he rose in the east and traveled across the dome of the sky on his golden chariot, until he reached Mighty Oceanos in the west. As Oceanos completely encircled the Earth, Helios was then able to sail, horses, chariot and all, back along the horizon to his dwelling in the east.

**Hephaistia (ee-FEH-stee-ah):** The site of an ancient town on the volcanic island of Límnos, first established about 1000 b.c.e. (*See also* Hephaistos)

**Hephaistos (EE-fess-tohs or heh-FESS-tus):** God of Creative Fire and Lord of the Forge, he was the son of Hera and Zeus, and spouse of Aphrodite. He was a gifted artisan who created countless items of utility and beauty. He was usually described as "deformed" and "lame," and as such, Aphrodite and he were an early representation of the beauty and the beast tale. He was linked to the volcanic island of Límnos, and his metallurgical tutelage was attributed to Thetis (THEH-teece) and her sister Sea Nymphs, the Nereids, who rescued him from the Aegean (after Hera or Zeus threw him off Mount Olympos). He spent nine years with the Nymphs, dwelling in their cave, and it was during that time he learned his trade. Metallurgy is a gift from the Earth and Hephaistos' tale honors that link.

**Hera (EEHR-ah or HEHR-ah):** Goddess of the Sacred Marriage. She was a daughter of the Titans, Rhea and Kronos, and spouse of Zeus. She and Zeus had four children of their own, Eileithyia (ee-lee-THEE-ah), Goddess of Childbirth, Hebe (EE-vee), Goddess of the Youthful Bloom, Hephaistos, God of the Forge, and Ares, God of war. The two often argued about Zeus' sexual conquests and she would seek her revenge by tormenting his victims and "illegitimate" offspring.

Prior to Classical times (*circa* 480–323 b.c.e.) she was a Great Goddess figure, the Creator, Sustainer and Destroyer of all things. Homer called her the Queen of Heaven and Hera of the Golden Throne. As the white-armed Goddess, she was associated with the role of Moon Goddess, casting her beams far and wide. She was thereby connected to the cycle of life, death and regeneration, which the Moon plays out every 29.5 days. Hera was often depicted with snakes, thereby closely associating her with her predecessor, the Minoan Snake Goddess.

Her name is not of Indo-European origin, which suggests she was a powerful Goddess prior to the invasions. As such, she had to be co-opted and subjugated to reflect the new world order, so she was married off to Zeus, stripped of her powers and relegated to the role of nagging wife. She was known to the Romans as Juno. (*See also* Heraion)

**Heraion (eehr-ah-EE-ohn or hehr-EH-ohn):** Temple to the Goddess, Hera. There were many of them throughout the Greek mainland, the Pelepónnisos and the islands of the Aegean; the most famous was located in Argos, near Mikínai.

**Herakles (eehr-ah-KLEECE or HEHR-a-kleez):** Hera's Glory (ancient Greek). Son of Alkmene and Zeus. He was a legendary warrior hero, more familiarly called Hercules, and best known for his Twelve Labors, which he undertook upon the order of King Eurystheus.

1. Slaying the Lion of Nemea (neh-MEH-ah)
2. Slaying the Hydra of Lerne (LEHR-neh)
3. Capturing the Keryneian Stag (keh-rhee-nee-OHS)
4. Capturing the Boar of Mount Erymanthos (eh-RHEE-mahn-thohs)
5. Cleaning the Stables of Augeias (ahv-GHEE-ahs)
6. Killing the Stymphalosian Birds (steem-FAH-lee-dess)
7. Capturing the Bull of Kríti
8. Taming the Mares of Diomedes (dee-oh-MEE-deece)
9. Killing the Amazon, Hippolyte (ee-poh-LEE-tee) and Capturing her Magic Girdle
10. Capturing the Cattle of Geryon (GHEHR-ee-ohn)
11. Stealing the Golden Apples of the Hesperides
12. Capturing Cerberus (Kerberos) the Three-headed Hound of Hades

The Labors give us further insight into the conquest of the Civilization of Old Europe. Nearly all of the killed or captured figures were once central to the symbology of earlier Partnership cultures. The lion, snake, stag, boar, bird and bull were all linked to the Great Goddess of prehistory, and therefore had to be demonized and conquered so their powers could be usurped. The Tree of Life, the Magic Girdle and the Golden Apples all have their roots in the mythology/religion of those cultures as well.

Of all of Zeus' children born outside of his marriage to Hera, Herakles was the focal point of much of her rage. The two of them were usually depicted as having an antagonistic relationship, though the young hero's name suggests that at one time, they may have felt much more fondly toward one another. Interestingly, after he became immortal, he married Hera's daughter, Hebe (EE-vee), Goddess of the Youthful Bloom. One wonders if the Eve of Christian myth has her roots in Hebe. (*See also* Hera, Milky Way, Son-Lover)

As the supreme hero, Herakles played a critical role in early Greek society, because dominator cultures value the warrior hero over all other figures. Their philosophy is to obtain and maintain an authoritarian ordering of relations through the threat or use of violence, and the hero's willingness to kill enables the dominator way of life to persist. It's not surprising then, that Herakles was ultimately rewarded with immortality. (*See* Dominator)

In Partnership cultures, the ability to kill other beings would not be glorified. Heroes in such a culture would overcome adversity through their wits and intelligence, as well as through their physical strength, and would kill others only in self-defense. They would also show compassion and mercy to those intent on disrupting or destroying their way of life through violence. (*See* Partnership)

Herakles was often credited as being the founder of the Olympic Games. (*See also* Athloi)

**Hermes (ehr-MEECE or HER-meez):** Messenger of the Gods. He was the son of Maia (MEH-ah) and Zeus, born in the Arkadian mountains in the Pelopónnisos. He was a God of shepherds, a bringer of luck and ultimately, the herald who conveyed the dictates of Zeus. He was associated with flocks and music, and within hours of his birth, made a reputation for himself by using a tortoise shell to invent the lyre, and by stealing Apollo's cattle. He was often depicted with winged sandals, and carrying his caduceus (ka-DOO-see-us), his snake bearing wand, which links him to the Earth-based cultures preceding him. As Psychopompus (pseekoh-pohm-POS), he was the God of the Crossroads, or Gateway, who guided souls into the Underworld. He was thereby connected with the mysteries of life, death and regeneration, a realm associated with his feminine contemporaries, all of whom have their origin in the Great Goddess of prehistory. The Latin version of his name has been given to the planet Mercury, because, as the closest to the Sun, it has the quickest orbit.

**Hesiod (EE-see-ohd or HE-see-id):** A Greek poet from the late 8th century b.c.e. whose compendium, the *Theogony*, is one of the primary sources of Greek mythology, especially concerning the relationship between Zeus' generation and their predecessors, the Titans. His *Works and Days* is also an important source. He was from Boetia (vee-oh-TEE-ah) in central Greece.

**Hesperides (ess-pehr-EE-dess or hess-SPARE-i-deez):** Nymphs of the Setting Sun. The three daughters of Nyx (neeks) (Night), who, with Ladon (LAH-dohn) the serpent, guarded the Tree of Life which bore the Golden Apples of Immortality. (*See also* Apples of the Hesperides)

**Hestia (ess-tee-AH or HESS-tee-a):** Protectress of the Home. The oldest daughter of the Titans, Rhea and Kronos. She is the Virgin Goddess of the Fire, the "essence of things" which burns within the hearth. Because hearths were critical to day-to-day living in ancient times, they were constructed in the very center of Greek houses, and shrines to Hestia were often kept there. Additionally, each city center had a public hearth known as a prytaneion (pree-tah-neh-EE-ohn). Both the domestic and communal hearths were considered holy.

Only a few of Hestia's stories have survived the millennia, but they clearly point to a very ancient deity who was once highly revered. She still remains with us today, embodied within the flame of the Olympic Torch as a symbol of hope and peace, recalling the memory of our Partnership heritage – a flame which cannot be extinguished. In modern Greek, the word can mean a number of things: hearth, fireplace, home, origin and even cradle.

**Himalaya (hi–MAHL–ya or him–ah–LAY–a):** The mountain system in southern Asia, which consists of numerous peaks over 20,000 feet in height, including 29,028-foot Mount Everest, the tallest on Earth.

**Hippodemeia (ee–poh–DAH–mee–ah or hip–poh–da–MEE–a):** Daughter of Oenomaos (ee–NOH–mah–ohs), King of Pisa, an area which included Olympia. Her father refused to allow anyone to marry her unless they could fend him off in a chariot race to the death. Thirteen suitors were each given a head start, but none could beat back the king, all being killed by his royal hand. However, with a wink and a nod from Zeus, Pelops (PEH–lops) outwitted the king by sabatoging the wheels of his chariot. Hippodemia was consequently forced to marry Pelops.

Her story is a poignant example of how women are considered to be little more than chattel in dominator cultures. (*See* Dominator)

**Hiroshima (heer–oh–SHEE–mah or heer–OH–sheh–mah):** A Japanese city at the western end of the Inland Sea in Honshu (HOHN–shoo) province. On August 6, 1945, the United States dropped an atomic bomb here, completely destroying the city and instantly killing over 80,000 civilians. Thousands more died of radiation exposure in the aftermath. Three days later, the United States dropped another atomic bomb on Japan, this time destroying the city of Nagasaki (nah–gah–SAH–kee), killing another 40,000 people on the spot and countless others over time.

To date, these two attacks are the only instances that a nuclear device has been used in warfare. Of course, over 30,000 of these weapons of mass destruction remain, while ever more destructive ones continue to be created. The United States is currently a leading proponent of increased research, development and production of a whole new generation of these deadly weapons. (*See also* Doomsday Clock)

**Homer:** A Greek poet from the 8th century b.c.e. (or thereabouts) who is thought to have come from Asia Minor. He is the one to whom the *Iliad* and the *Odyssey* are ascribed, though the authorship of these works is a source of great debate. It's likely that the poems had been developed through oral tradition over a period of centuries, until they eventually stabilized in the form we know them today. They were first written down sometime between the 8th and 6th centuries b.c.e. The *Homeric Hymns,* a set of thirty-three poems honoring the Olympic dieties, were written over a period of four hundred years (also beginning in the 8th century b.c.e.); they provide an important source of information about the attributes of particular Immortals, as well as the cosmology of the ancient Greeks.

**Hope:** The Goddess who remained trapped in Pandora's jar (or box) while all of the "evils" escaped into the mortal realm. In our first novel, *The Coming of a New Millennium*, Hope escapes from her prison and is now free to spread her good will around the world. (*See also* Pandora)

**Hydra (EE-drah or HIE-dra):** A child of the sea deities Typhon (tee-FOHN) and Echidna (EKH-eed-nah), this creature was actually a nine-headed water serpent with poisonous blood (though the number of heads varies considerably in the stories). It lived in the swamps of Lerne (LEHR-neh) near Argos. For his second labor, Herakles had to slay Hydra, but every time he chopped off one if its heads, another grew in its place. He overcame that obstacle with the help of his nephew, Iolaos (ee-OH-lah-ohs), who cauterized the neck-stumps, thereby preventing the heads from growing back. However, according to some authors, the central head was immortal, so Herakles had to settle for burying it under a huge rock.

The serpent was a central symbol in the belief system of our Neolithic ancestors. It was an aspect of the Great Goddess of prehistory and her mysterious cycle of life, death and regeneration, because not only did it have the power of life and death, but through the shedding of its skin it was reborn, thereby transcending death itself. As this story so clearly demonstrates, the earlier divinity can be conquered, but her spirit is indominable.

**Hyperboreans (ee-pehr-VOR-ee-ee or hie-per-BOR-ee-enz):** Mythical people who lived on an island paradise at the back of the North Wind, possibly referring to the British Isles.

**Hyperion (ee-pehr-EE-ohn or hie-PEER-ee-en):** As one of the Titans, he was a child of the Sacred Marriage of Earth and Sky (Gaia and Ouranos). He united with his sister, Theia, and together they had three children, Eos (Dawn), Helios (Sun) and Selene (Moon).

**Indo-European:** A designation used to refer to a number of different tribes of steppe pastoralists (herders) who invaded the lands of the peaceful agriculturalists, and over a period of several millennia, approximately 4300-1628 b.c.e., destroyed the Civilization of Old Europe. According to Dr. Marija Gimbutas' synthesis of the archeological record, their arrival completely disrupted Old European culture, radically changing habitation patterns, social structure, the economy and religion. These peoples shared common traditions and cultural norms, most notably a social structure with a rigid dominator configuration. (*See* Dominator)

Neolithic peoples buried their dead collectively, along matrilineal lines. In contrast, early Indo-Eurpoean (Kurgan) graves were found to have had one important male with many possessions, including war implements, wives, dogs and gold buried alongside him. These people were the nomadic hunters and herders of the cold northern steppe lands and inhospitable eastern deserts, whose survival relied on the killing of animals and an unsustainable pattern of consumption. Once they used up the resources in any given area, they had to go in search of more, taking whatever they could find, and in the worst cases, killing or enslaving everyone in their path. Over the course of a few thousand years, they substantially decimated the peaceful and prosperous Civilization of Old Europe, establishing the model for the never-ending series of violent conquests which have plagued our planet right up to the present day. Their language is the parent tongue of many modern languages, including Greek, English, French, Spanish, Italian, German and Russian. (*See also* Civilization of Old Europe, Neolithic, Partnership)

Throughout this *Guide*, we use the word "Indo-European" broadly, to encompass a long span of time and all of the various invaders, including the Aryans, Semites and those from other parts of the Asiatic and European North.

**Ionian (ee-OHN-ee-ahn):** Descendents of early Greek invaders who preserved some of the pre-Hellenic traditions. They inhabited the islands of the Kikládes and parts of Asia Minor.

**Iphe (EE-fee):** Nickname of Herakles' brother in our story; short for Iphikles.

**Iphikles (ee-fee-KLEECE or IF-a-kleez):** Son of Alkmene and Amphitryon (ahm-fee-TREE-ohn) and twin half-brother of Herakles. (*See also* Alkmene)

**Isles of the Blessed:** *See* Elysian Fields.

**Itháki (ee-THA-kee or ITH-i-ka):** The rocky island home of the warrior hero, Odysseus. It lies in the Ionian Sea, off the north-western coast of the Pelepónnisos.

**Itútu (ee-TOO-too):** Mystic Coolness. In Yoruba (West African) culture, Itútu is the balancing principle to Ashé (the power to make things happen). It also conveys gentleness of character, serenity, devotion and generosity, and is considered to embody the greatest degree of morality. (*See also* Ashé, Yoruba)

**Jupiter:** *See* Zeus.

**Kafenéo (kah-feh-NEE-oh):** Coffee shop (modern Greek).

**Kalí epitehía (kah-LEE ep-i-teh-HEE-a):** Good luck (modern Greek).

**Kalimeára sas (kah-lee-MEHR-ah sass):** Good morning to you (modern Greek).

**Kallisto (kah-leece-TOW or ka-LEECE-tow):** A young girl who was another of Zeus' unfortunate victims. The God became enamored with her, disguised himself as Artemis or Apollo, and then raped her. When Hera learned of it she became furious, then with all of her wrath, further victimized the poor girl by turning her into a bear. (Some stories attribute the transformation to Artemis or Zeus.) Years later, Arcas (ahr-KAHSS), Kallisto's son from the rape, was out hunting when he encountered his mother. Just as he was about to kill her, Zeus intervened, whisking the two of them into the heavens. They became the constellations Ursa Major, the Great Bear, and Arcturas or Boötes, the Bear Warden.

The Bear Goddess was an important figure to our Paleolithic and Neolithic ancestors, as she symbolized the nurturing mother aspect of the Great Goddess of prehistory. Kallisto's placement in the sky acknowledges her previous significance.

**Kalypso (kah-leep-SO or ka-LIP-so):** Daughter of Pleione (plee-OH-nee) and Atlas, and in some stories, one of the seven sisters of the Pleiades (plee-AH-dess). After she rescued shipwrecked Odysseus, she detained him on her island, Ogygia (oh-GHEE-ghee-ah) for seven years. Though she loved him, provided for his every need and even offered to make him immortal, he could not forget his beloved Penelope, and so he spent his days in mourning. Zeus finally sent Hermes with a mandate to release the beleagured hero, and Kalypso complied, helping him build a raft so he could continue on his journey home to Itháki.

**Kastalía Spring (kah–stah–LEE–ah):** A natural fresh water spring at Delphi on Mount Parnassós, where the Pythia bathed herself in preparation for the act of prophecy. In one version, the spring was named after a girl, or Nymph, from Delphi who, while fleeing from Apollo's pursuit, threw herself into it. (*See also* Apollo, Pythia)

**Katse (KAHT-seh):** Sit down (modern Greek).

**Khana:** The name of one of the four main Ogoni languages (Niger Delta, Africa).

**Kikládes (kee-KLAH-dess or SIK-la-deez):** A group of about 220 islands in the Aegean Sea, so named because they encircle the island of Delos, Apollo's birthplace. Partnership cultures thrived here during the Neolithic and early Bronze Age, as evidenced by the exquisite, and numerous, female folded-arm figurines found throughout the archipelago.

 **Kíthera (KEE-thehr-ah or SITH-er-a):** A rocky island off the southern tip of the Pelopónnisos, which in some stories is associated with the birth of Aphrodite.

**Kladeos (KLAH-dee-ohs):** A river near Olympia.

**Knossós (k'noh-SOHSS or NO-suss):** Located on the island of Kríti, this was the site of the most extensive of the Minoan temple complexes, dating back to about 2000 b.c.e. In 1903, English archeologist Sir Arthur Evans began excavating and reconstructing this remarkable site.

Though it has been referred to as a "palace," with the "oldest throne in Europe" there is no persuasive evidence a monarchy existed in the Minoan culture prior to the Mycenean conquest (*circa* 1600 b.c.e.). (*See also* Mikínai, Minos) Further, there's no indication that their social structure revolved around a male-dominated hierarchy. Most of the frescoes found there depict women, and the men who are represented are portrayed neither as warriors nor as servants. The evidence discovered to date suggests a society where both halves of humanity were valued. (*See also* Partnership) One particularly interesting and beautiful fresco, *The Bull Vaulters*, shows both women and men participating in an event where they performed acrobatics over the back of a bull, perhaps in a ritual dance. (Contrast this practice with bull "fighting," where the animal is killed in a cruel and painful manner.)

At its peak, as many as 100,000 people lived in and around the temple complex at Knossós, and the temple itself must have at one time been an amazing structure. It consisted of approximately 1,500 roofed areas, all arranged in an intricate series of squares and rectangles, and it may have reached five stories in height. It was constructed with porticoes, corridors, grand staircases, and light wells, which also provided fresh air. It was hydraulically engineered, with fountains and lustral basins (bathing areas) which had running water and flush toilets. Importantly, there were no military fortifications, a feature the Minoan cities shared with the Civilization of Old Europe. While they did have weapons, elaborate daggers for example, there is no indication they idealized or sanctified warfare or violence. (*See* Minoans)

The Minoans carved a bow-tie shaped image, called the labrys, on walls throughout the stone corridors of Knossós, and as a result, the structure became known as the Labyrinth — the dwelling of the labrys. We don't know if Knossós was an actual labryrinth, or if it was just remembered that way, being confused over the centuries because of the architectural layout of the temple complex. (*See also* Ariadne, Labrys, Labyrinth)

Knossós is also the place where, in our first novel, *The Coming of a New Millennium*, time traveling archeologist Dr. Zoee Nikitas discovers a Linear A tablet, and then miraculously experiences that moment in prehistory when the Minoans sent their message of Partnership and peace to the future.

**Koh Phangnga (ko-pahn-GAH):** An island in the southwestern part of the Gulf of Thailand.

**Komboloi (khom-boh-LOH-yee):** Greek worry beads.

**Kórinthos (KOHR-in-thohs):** Corinth. One of the original city-states. Today, it is a city and region in the northeastern part of the Pelopónnisos, across the Corinth Canal from mainland Greece. In order to link the Gulf of Kórinthos with the eastern Mediterranean Sea, a long narrow canal was cut through almost four miles of solid rock. It has tall, sheer sides and is deep enough for the largest ships to navigate.

**Kouretes (KOOH-rhee-tess):** The young men, or spirits, who protected the entrance to the cave where infant Zeus was hidden from his father, Kronos. They masked Zeus' crying by beating their spears against their shields and loudly dancing about, thereby ensuring that the older Thunder God could not find his young rival. Their noisemaking recalls the ritualistic fertility celebrations associated with the ecstatic worship of the Great Mother Goddess, Cybele (kee-VEH-lee), of Asia Minor.

**Kouriambiethes (koo-rhee-ahm-BHED-ess):** Almond butter cookies encased in powdered sugar.

**Kouroi (KOOH-rhee); Korai (KOHR-eh) (feminine):** Plural of "Kouros" (KOUR-ohs) and "Kore" (KOHR-ee). Very tall, upright stone statues, nude and rigid, with one leg extended and a gaze fixed straight ahead (*circa* 600 b.c.e.). The style is reminiscent of ancient Egyptian sculpture, though it's somewhat more realistic.

**Kríti (KHREE-tee):** Crete. The largest and most southern island of Greece, with a high central mountain range, plentiful streams and groves of olives and citrus fruit. Situated equidistant to the continents of Europe, Asia and Africa, it is a crossroads, where many cultures have mingled throughout the millennia. Kríti was also the center of the Minoan civilization. (*See also* Knossós, Minoans)

**Kronos (KHRO-nohs):** Time (ancient and modern Greek). The youngest of the Titans, born of the Sacred Marriage of Earth and Sky (Gaia and Ouranos); also spouse of Rhea. It was Kronos who castrated his father and assumed dominion over the immortal realm, until his own son, Zeus, in turn defeated him. In the Classical tale, Rhea gave birth to Hestia, Demeter, Hera, Hades and Poseidon, but Kronos devoured each of them to ensure that none would threaten his rule. However, he was deceived by Rhea, who conspired with Gaia and Ouranos to hide the last of her children, Zeus, in a cave on Mount Díkti in Kríti. Kronos was then tricked into swallowing a stone wrapped in swaddling clothes. Further woe was to be upon Kronos, as he was ultimately manipulated into regurgitating all of Zeus' siblings, who then conspired to overthrow him.

At the time these stories were coming into existence, the Indo-European invasions had already been occurring for well over

100 generations. Kronos' tale foreshadowed Zeus' ultimate rise to power as "King of the Gods," and continued the custom of power usurpation established by the earliest invaders. The Latin version of his name has been given to distant, ringed Saturn, the sixth planet from the Sun.

**Kyría (keehr–EE–ah):** Feminine courtesy title.

**Labrys (LAHV–rheece or LAH–breece):** The symbol of the labrys appears in many cultures throughout prehistory, but is most often associated with the great Temple at Knossós on the island of Kríti. The ancient Minoans carved the symbol on walls throughout the stone corridors of Knossós, and as a result, this remarkable structure became known as the Labyrinth – the dwelling of the labrys. Since the word "labrys" is of pre Indo-European origin, we can only speculate what it might have meant to the Minoans, but there is little doubt that it was of great importance to them. Archeologists have recovered hundreds of small bronze labryses, as well as numerous artifacts which bear the image, including exquisite gold jewelry and tiny sealstones.

In Neolithic art, the Great Goddess of prehistory was sometimes represented as a double triangle, in an hourglass configuration, which when tipped on its side bears a close resemblance to a labrys. The symbol itself could therefore recall the time when the Civilization of Old Europe thrived.

The labrys has often been referred to as a "double axe." However, during Minoan times, there is no evidence that it was used as a weapon, or to perform ritual sacrifices. On the contrary, nearly all of the labryses found at Minoan sites are decorative in nature, and many were discovered in rooms where sacred rituals are believed to have taken place. Perhaps the symbol was a reminder of the double-edged nature of technology. In their time, bronze was the technology of the day, and most warrior cultures were using it to make stronger and more deadly weapons with which they could carry out their conquests. The Minoans, however, chose to use the metal to make ritual objects and more durable tools, in order to further the common goals of the entire community. Did they understand that technology in and of itself was neither good nor bad, but rather, could be used to create *or* destroy? By making the labrys a central part of their rituals, it's possible they were reaffirming their conscious choice to use the new technology for altruistic purposes.

The symmetry of the labrys also suggests the idea of yin-yang, the balance between the feminine and masculine energies, which together, make up the whole within each of us.

**Labyrinth (lah–VEEHR–in–thohss or LAB–i–rinth):** The underground "maze" at Knossós where the dreaded Minotaur lived. Theseus made his way through the cold stone corridors of this terrifying dungeon, slew the Minotaur, and with Ariadne's Thread, successfully navigated his way back into the light of day.

The words "labyrinth" and "maze" are almost always used interchangeably, however, they are very different. A labyrinth does not contain false choices and dead ends designed to trick and confound, but rather, it consists of one long, circuitous path to the center, and when it's used as a walking meditation, becomes a metaphor for the journey to the center of one's spiritual and emotional self. The idea is to release the burdens of life with each step along the path, so that by the time you reach the center, you are less encumbered and more able to connect with your inner self.

The shape of the labyrinth was known in Minoan Kríti in the second, and possibly the third, millennium b.c.e. It most likely had its roots even further back in the Neolithic. Many scholars believe that the labyrinth was originally a dance pattern, and there are a number of references suggesting this interpretation. For example, "Ariadne's dancing floor" is mentioned in Homer's *Iliad*, and it refers to one of Daidalos' creations at Knossós. The first writing which mentions the word "labyrinth" is from about 1400 b.c.e., on a Linear B (an early form of Greek) inscription. According to one interpretation, it says, "[o]ne jar of honey to all of the Immortals and one to the Mistress of the Labyrinth." (Kern) Because of its womb-like shape, the labyrinth could have been connected with a mystery rite or initiation ritual, such as those relating to the cycles of life, death and regeneration. (*See* Eleusís)

During the "holy" wars of the Middle Ages, Christians would walk the mosaic labyrinths on the floors of the great cathedrals to the Virgin Mary (for example, Chartres [shart] Cathedral in France), as a surrogate for making the dangerous pilgrimage to Jerusalem, the center of Christianity.

Labyrinths can be found in every age since then, in art, literature and architecture, as well as in three-dimensional form, such as hedge and turf labyrinths. During the last few decades, there has been a tremendous resurgence in their popularity, as hundreds have been installed in churches and public spaces around the world. Indeed, the path of the labyrinth, which has come to be known as the "Thread of Ariadne," continues to be used in many contexts, as has likely been the case throughout the ages. (*See also* Knossós, Labrys)

**Lapiths (lah-PEE-theh or LAH-peeths):** A tribe of warriors from Thessaly, in northern Greece, who are credited with defeating the Centaurs. The battle scene was carved in marble on the west pediment of the Temple of Zeus at Olympia.

**Leto (lee-TOW or LEE-tow):** Daughter of the Titans, Phoebe (FEE-vee) and Koios (KEE-ohs), and mother, with Zeus, of the twin deities, Artemis and Apollo. She had a terrible time finding a place to give birth because Hera pursued and intimidated her, and threatened those who dared to offer her refuge. Depending on the version, her roots were in Asia Minor, Kríti or the land of the Hyperboreans. The Romans called her Latona. (*See also* Niobe)

**Límnos (LEEM-nohs or LEM-nohs):** A volcanic island in the Aegean Sea often associated with Hephaistos, the God of Creative Fire.

**Linear A:** The undeciphered language of the Minoan civilization (*circa* 3100–1628 b.c.e.). Clay fragments containing this script have been found in Greece and Turkey, and on numerous islands, including Kríti, Thíra, and Samothráki (sahm-oh-THRAH-kee).

**Mae Hong Son (mah-hawn-sawn):** A town and province in northwestern Thailand, in the foothills of the Himalaya.

**Maenads (meh-NAH-dess or MEE-nadz):** Female Nature Spirits who dwelt in the forest and were devoted to Dionysos. (*See also* Nymphs)

**Mars:** *See* Ares.

**Medusa (MEH-dee-sah or meh-DOO-sa):** The most famous of the three Gorgons (gohr-GOHN-ess), who were the children of sea deities Keto (kee-TOW) and Phorkys (FOHR-keece). Their hair was a writhing tangle of snakes, their necks were protected by dragon scales and they had boar tusks, golden wings and hands of bronze. Mortals who dared to look at them were instantly turned to stone by their penetrating, and ultimately deadly stares. Perseus (pehr-seh-EECE) slayed Medusa with the help of some Nymphs, who gave him a helmet, rendering him invisible, and winged sandals with which he could fly. Athena also helped him by holding a polished bronze mirror over Medusa, so that Perseus could avoid her lethal stare when he cut off her head.

This myth is one of the best examples of the demonization of the Minoan culture through the symbol of the snake. Numerous Snake Goddess figurines found at Knossós and other archeological sites evidence the importance of the snake to that earlier culture. It was a symbol of life, death and regeneration, because not only did it have the power of life and death, but each time it shed its skin it was reborn, thereby ultimately transcending death itself. One is also reminded of the frescoes depicting Minoan women and men with their long curly black locks, transformed through the Medusa story into threatening, hissing serpents. (*See also* Aegis)

**Mentes (MAHN-theece or MEN-tess):** In Homer's *Odyssey*, this character was actually the Goddess Athena disguised as the old man, Mentor. She guided Odysseus' son, Telemachos, in the fulfillment of his destiny.

**Mesolóngion (mess-oh-LOHN-ghee-ohn):** A port city on the southwestern shore of the Greek mainland, at the entrance to the Gulf of Kórinthos.

**Metis (MEE-teece or MEE-tiss):** Wisdom (ancient Greek). Daughter of the Titans, Tethys (tee-THEECE) and Oceanos, and mother of Athena. Metis was destined to give birth first to a daughter, and then to a son who would one day rule the wide heavens, so when she became pregnant by Zeus he swallowed her whole, to ensure the prophesy would not ultimately be fulfilled. Consequently, the Goddess of Wisdom and her offspring were brought under his control. (Recall that Athena "sprung forth," fully armored, from his head.) (*See* Athena)

This story reflects the conquest of the peaceful, Goddess-based Partnership cultures, and their subordination to Indo-European dominator ideology. There is no attempt in the myth to explain the logic of such an unnatural event as a male giving birth from his head. Rather, the mythmakers defy the human experience, and in the process create a new ordering of relations, which is expected to be followed without question. Yet, in between the lines of the story, "Wisdom" remains, revealing herself as a direct link to our Partnership past, to a time when divinity was conceptualized as female. In further support of this proposition, a review of contemporary Greek words shows that the root of the name "Metis" occurs in the words for "mother" and "womb." (*See* Mitéramou)

**Mikínai (mee-KEE-neh):** Mycenae. A city in the northeastern Pelopónnisos near the archeological site by the same name. (*See also* Mycenaean)

**Milky Way:** Our Galaxy. In Greek myth, Zeus lulled Hera to sleep while Hermes put the infant Herakles to her breast, and there are at least two versions of what ensued. In one, the young hero allegedly bit her, and when Hera awoke, she thrust him off, thereby sending her milk across the heavens. Another account says she suckled him until she realized who he was, then she shook him off and the excess milk spurted out, forming our Galaxy. (The Greek word for "milk" is "gala" [GHAH-lah]).

The image of the Son-Lover sitting in the lap of a Mother Goddess is an old one, linking back to the Egyptian Goddess, Isis (EYE-siss) and her Son-Lover, Osiris (oh-SIE-riss). It is also prominent in Christian symbology, as exemplified by the many similar images of Mary and Jesus. By drinking Hera's milk, Herakles is imbued with her ancient powers (and some stories even attribute his immortality to it). However, his biting of her breast is indicative of a Son-Lover turned warrior hero, whose relationship with the once-revered Mother Goddess has been altered.

**Minoan (mi-noh-ee-KHOS or mi-NOH-an):** The highly creative and technologically advanced civilization which thrived on Kríti and the surrounding islands from approximately 3100 to 1628 b.c.e. They were named after King Minos, though he is a figure who arose after the Mycenaean conquest of the pre-Greek society, whose actual name is not known. The pre-Greeks are the people to whom we are referring. (*See also* Knossós, Partnership)

The Minoans were accomplished sailors and architects, and gifted in the arts of painting, pottery, weaving and jewelry making. Their architecture, frescoes and statuary reflect a sophisticated culture with an egalitarian social structure. Ruins have been found on the islands of Kríti and Thíra, as well as several others in the region. On Kríti alone, five main temple complexes have been discovered, along with numerous smaller settlements and abundant ritual sites on mountains and in caves. They constructed large-scale public works projects, including aquaducts and irrigation systems, as well as roads extending from one end of the island to the other. However, in contrast to most of the other cities of the same period, there were no military fortifications. The evidence suggests they had a lifestyle very different from that of their contemporaries, as well as the Mycenaeans (*circa* 1600-1100 b.c.e.) and the Classical Greeks (*circa* 480-323 b.c.e.) who succeeded them.

According to Drs. Gimbutas and Eisler, the Minoans were the last of the Partnership cultures, which in so-called prehistory had thrived in many of the rich, fertile valleys of Europe, the Mediterranean and Mesopotamia (the area in southwestern Asia between the Tigres [TIE-gress] and Euphrates [yoo-FRAY-teez] Rivers). The Minoans were able to hold onto this ancient way of life well into the Bronze Age because, as an island people, they were protected from the Indo-European invasions by the barrier of the sea. The actual events and timing of their demise are uncertain. However, it's likely that the explosion of the Thíra volcano (*circa* 1628 b.c.e.) made it possible for the Minoan civilization to be fully absorbed by the Indo-European Mycenaeans. (*See also* Knossós, Mikínai, Old Europe, Partnership)

**Minoan Message:** The fictional message sent to the future by the doomed Minoan civilization on the eve of their destruction. The Message tells the story of the cultural transformation which took place in our prehistory, and calls for a return to Partnership values as the remedy for many of our societal ills. It is conveyed by a Linear A tablet, which is discovered and deciphered by the time-traveling archeologist, Dr. Zoee Nikitas, in our first novel, *The Coming of a New Millennium*.

**Minos (MEE-nos):** A legendary king of Kríti during Mycenaean times (*circa* 1600-1100 b.c.e.). It is to him that the Athenians paid tribute every eight years, by sending seven young men and seven young women to be sacrificed to the Minotaur in the underground Labyrinth at Knossós (which in this story was really a maze). (*See* Labyrinth)

In dominator cultures, such as that of the Mycenaeans, strict hierarchies are reinforced through the threat or use of violence. Since they had conquered the Athenians, the requirement of human sacrifice to maintain dominance is not wholly unexpected. However, the eight-year time interval takes on special significance, because that's when the full Moon coincides with the Solstice (shortest and longest day). Robert Graves maintained that in early monarchies, this was the time when the king's power had to be renewed, and originally required the actual sacrifice of the king himself. Over time, others were substituted so that the king could continue to rule, and eventually, animal sacrifice became the norm.

In pre-Greek Minoan times, it is unlikely that a king, or even a queen for that matter, "ruled" in the sense of a top-down, authoritarian hierarchy. We can only speculate about how they may have governed themselves or celebrated their cosmic rituals, but there's no evidence they practiced human sacrifice. (*See also* Knossós, Minotaur, Partnership)

**Minotaur (mee-NOH-tahv-rhoss or MIN-oh-tawr):** The half human, half bull creature who lived in the underground "Labyrinth" at Knossós. He was ultimately killed by the Athenian warrior hero, Theseus, who, with the help of Ariadne's Thread, was able to escape from what was really a maze in this particular story. (*See also* Labyrinth)

The myth very likely refers back to Mycenaean times (*circa* 1600-1100 b.c.e.), after a monarchy had been imposed on Kríti. The story demonizes the bull, a creature sacred to the Mycenaeans, by placing it in a hell-like dungeon and construing it as a monster who consumes children. The mythmakers thereby successfully co-opted the symbols of the Mycenaeans, and in the process, obscured the rich legacy of the pre-Mycenaean Minoans. (*See also* Ariadne, Knossós, Labyrinth, Minoan, Minos, Mycenaean, Theseus).

As an aside, considering the half-human nature of the horned Minotaur, one is enticed into speculating whether this character is the pre-curser to the Devil of Christian myth.

**Mitéramou (mee-TEHR-ah-moo):** My mother (modern Greek). Used as an endearment. (*See also* Metis)

**Monemvasía (moh-nem-vah-SEE-ah):** City on the far south-eastern coast of the Pelopónnisos.

**Muses (MOO-seh or MEWZ-ez):** The Reminders (ancient Greek). The inspiration of all artists, especially poets and musicians. In some stories, they are the nine children of Zeus' conquest of the Titan, Mnemosyne (m'nee-moh-SEE-nee) or Memory. Some of the Muses are associated with additional gifts, though only their primary area of influence has been included here: Klio (KLEE-oh) (history), Euterpe (ehf-TEHR-pee) (lyric poetry), Thalia (tha-LEE-ah) (comedy), Melpomene (mel-poh-MEH-nee) (tragedy), Erato (ehr-ah-TOW) (love poetry), Terpsichore (tehr-psee-KHOR-ee) (light verse and dance), Polyhymnia (poh-LEEM-nee-ah) (sacred music), Ourania (oo-RHAN-yah) (astronomy), and Kalliope (kah-lee-OH-pee) (epic poetry). They all eventually came under Apollo's control, and were known as the Ennead (from "ennea" [eh-NEH-ah] which means "nine").

Before they were divided into nine separate deities (*circa* 8th century b.c.e.), there had been three Muses (the Triple Muse) who resided on Mount Helikon; they were then known as Memory, Meditation and Song. Mount Pieria had been their earliest home, during the time when the Muse was seen as a single deity, the Moon Goddess, or perhaps even the Great Goddess of prehistory.

**Myanmar (my-an-MAR):** Country in Southeast Asia, formerly known as Burma.

**Mycenaeans (mee-ken-ee-a-KOHS or my-CEEN-ee-anz):** The Indo-European Achaeans (ah-KHEE-anz) who conquered large areas of late Bronze Age Greece. Their preeminence lasted 500 years, from approximately 1600-1100 b.c.e. One of their most significant palaces was located in the northeastern part of the Pelepónnisos, near the city still known as Mikínai (mee-KEE-neh), or Mycenae (my-CEE-nee). In the late 1800s, it was discovered and excavated by German archeologist Heinrich Schliemann, who wanted to prove that the stories of Homer's *Iliad* and *Odyssey* were grounded in historical fact. (Schliemann also discovered and excavated Troy, in Asia Minor.) The entrance to the complex at Mikínai had an elaborate stone gate, with a pair of lionesses carved on top of a massive stone archway; it's considered to be an excellent example of megalithic architecture because of the large boulders or "cyclopean" stones used in its construction. In the circular tombs of the palace, Schliemann uncovered the gold "Mask of Agamemnon," and many other well preserved items, including a trove of gold jewelry, statuary, pottery and a variety of weapons.

These artifacts reveal a people who, though they appear to have co-existed for several centuries, ultimately absorbed the older Minoan civilization. The Mycenaeans adopted many of the Minoans' artistic conventions, though they were more restrictive, and reflective of their warlike nature. They still decorated their walls with elaborate frescoes, and painted their pottery with sophisticated designs, but the subject matter had radically changed. Instead of the priestesses, lilies, sparrows and blue monkeys favored by their predecessors, they increasingly chose the symbols they cherished: warrior heroes ("action figures" in modern parlance), horses, chariots and battle scenes. The takeover likely occurred after the explosion of the Thíra Volcano in about 1628 b.c.e., which substantially destroyed the Minoan civilization, and brought to an end the last of the Partnership cultures. Mycenaean rule continued until approximately 1100 b.c.e., when they fell to another band of Indo-Europeans known as the Dorians (DOOR-ee-anz). Interestingly, the names of some of the prominent Olympian deities, including Hera, Athena, Artemis, Zeus and Hermes were mentioned in tablets dating back to the latter part of the Mycenaean era.

**Nana Bukúu (NAH-na boo-KOO-oo):** Fearless Yoruba warrior Goddess who either destroyed whole cities or brought them to victory, depending on which king won her favor. She is an African counterpart to the Goddess, Athena.

**Náxos (NAX-ohss):** One of the islands of the Kikládes, in the southern Aegean Sea. (*See also* Ariadne)

**Neolithic (nee-oh-LITH-ik):** New Stone Age, when the Partnership cultures of Old European Civilization rose and fell (*circa* 7000-3500 b.c.e.). According to Dr. Marija Gimbutas' chronology of the archeological record, during the first 500 years of this period, food production and village settlement were just beginning in the Aegean Basin and on Kríti. Between 6500-5500 b.c.e., the cultivation of grains and the domestication of all animals (except the horse) became established. From 5500-5000 b.c.e., the food producing economy spread through east-central to central Europe. Copper metallurgy began, and sacred script started appearing on ceremonial items. For 700 years, between 5000-4300 b.c.e., Old European culture climaxed. Ceramic art, copper and gold metallurgy, and architecture (including two-story temples) flourished. Megalithic tombs were built in western Europe.

Between 4300–3500, the first Indo-European invasion wave occurred, affecting primarily the Danube Basin. Their arrival completely disrupted Old European culture, radically changing habitation patterns, social structure, the economy and religion. There was also a significant decline of art. During this period, figurines, polychrome ceramics and temple buildings were nowhere to be found in the archeological record in that area. The invasions accelerated between 3500–3000 b.c.e., yet Old European culture was still able to continue in the Mediterranean region, and in northern and western Europe, where there was continued construction of megalithic temples, for example, in Malta and Ireland. During the period between 3000–2500, another invasion wave, this one from Russia, further eroded Old European culture in eastern and central Europe, Greece, and as far west as the Iberian Peninsula and the British Isles. In the aftermath of the volcanic eruption of Thíra (*circa* 1628 b.c.e.), and the subsequent downfall of the Minoan civilization, Partnership culture, as it had been known for many thousands of years, ceased to exist.

Excavations at Neolithic sites reveal a preponderance of artifacts depicting the female body, suggesting a civilization centered around a female deity. Gimbutas spent her life excavating and analyzing the artifacts of both the Neolithic and the Bronze Age, and in the process, substantiated the premise that during so-called prehistory, a "Civilization of the Goddess" had in fact thrived throughout Old Europe, Asia Minor, Africa and the islands of the Mediterranean. (*See also*, Partnership)

**Nereids (neehr-EE-dess or NEAR-ee-idz):** Sea Nymphs. The 52 daughters of Nereus (neehr-eh-EECE) and Doris (dhor-EECE) who lived in the watery realm. Their father was an "old man of the sea" figure, and their mother was one of the thousands of Oceanids (oh-kheh-ah-NEECE) who were children of the Titans, Tethys (tee-THEECE) and Oceanos. In modern Greek, "neráida" (nehr-AH-ee-dah) means "fairy" or "beautiful woman."

**Nike (NEE-kee or NIE-kee):** A winged creature known as the Goddess of Victory. Also a title of the Goddess, Athena. The Temple to Athena Nike still stands today at the entrance to the Acropolis in Athens. In 420 b.c.e., after the Athenians repelled a Persian invasion, it was built as a public declaration of victory.

**Niobe (nee-OH-vee or NIE-oh-bee):** Queen of Thebes. Traditionally, the women of her city bestowed gifts and offerings to Leto, mother of the immortal twins, Artemis and Apollo. Niobe had the temerity to claim herself more deserving of the honor because she had given birth to 14 children, when Leto had only borne two, albeit with all-mighty Zeus. Leto complained to the twins, who rushed to the palace at Thebes to avenge her honor. One by one, with their golden arrows, Apollo killed the boys and Artemis the girls, with the exception of the youngest. As Niobe pleaded for her daughter's life, Artemis turned the Queen to stone and then, in a fearsome whirlwind, sent her to a mountain in her homeland of Phrygia (FREE-ghee-ah), in Asia Minor, where tears continue to flow down her marble face.

This is another case of twisted dominator logic – the killing of innocents to avenge the name of another is a perverse order of justice indeed. However, it does serve its purpose of reinforcing the established hierarchy through fear, intimidation and brutal force.

**Nótos (NOH-tohs):** The South Wind.

**Nymphs (nimfs):** Female Nature Spirits. The Naiads (nee-AH-dess) were nymphs of the watery realm, as were the Nereids, though the latter lived primarily in the sea. On land, the Maenads dwelt in the forest, while the Dryads (dree-AH-dess) were usually found in trees. Often associated with fertility rights, Nymphs give us a glimpse into the ritualistic gatherings which took place before the Indo-European conquests. Their spirits live on in all wild places.

**Oceanos (oh-keh-ah-NOHS or oh-SEE-an-us):** God of the Ocean. He was the oldest of the Titans, conceptualized as a stream of water encircling the Earth. He united with his sister Tethys (tee-THEECE) and she gave birth to the Oceanids (oh-kheh-ah-NEECE), including Metis, who was the Goddess of Wisdom and mother of Athena.

**Odysseus (oh-dee-seh-EECE or oh-DISS-ee-us):** In Homer's epic tale, the *Odyssey*, Odysseus was the clever warrior hero who, with the help of Athena, overcame many hardships and challenges in his quest to return home to the island of Itháki. (*See also* Dominator)

**Ogoni (oh-GOH-nee):** A West African people who inhabit the Niger Delta region. (*See also* OPM)

**Old Europe:** *See* Civilization of Old Europe.

**Olympia (oh-lim-PEE-ah or oh-LIM-pee-a):** Located in a grove called Altis in the western Pelopónnisos, near the confluence of the Alphiós and Kladeos Rivers. This is the site of the original Olympic Games, dating back to at least 776 b.c.e. Every four years, the men of the various Greek city-states laid down their weapons and gathered at Olympia to compete in sport (*See* Ekecheiría). During Classical times (*circa* 480-323 b.c.e.), the site was dedicated to Zeus, but prior to that, and for an unknown span of time, it was dedicated to the Goddess, Hera.

As groves have often been linked to Goddess worship, the conquest of the sacred grove at Altis marked another clear shift to patriarchal culture. (*See* Altis) Apparantly, no expense was spared in the creation of the majestic Temple of Zeus which, towering over Hera's more reserved temple, housed a 36-foot gold and ivory figure of the King of the Gods. The message was unequivocal: there was a new world order, maintained by strong-man rule, where might makes right. If one dared step out of line, Zeus would not hesitate to hurl his mighty thunderbolts of destruction.

 **Olympos (OH-leem-bohs or oh-LIM-pus):** A snow-capped mountain, over 9,500 feet in height, in northeastern Greece. Also, the famed mythical home of the Classical Greek Panthaeon. (*See also* Panthaeon)

**Omphalos (ohm-fah-LOHS or OHM-fah-lohs):** Navel (ancient and modern Greek). The egg-shaped stone at the sanctuary of Delphi, signifying the place on Earth which connects all of humanity to its Mother. (*See also* Apollo)

**OPM:** The Ogoni People's Movement. A fictional organization based on the work of the Movement for the Survival of Ogoni People (MOSOP). MOSOP is a nonviolent political organization, which is trying to bring economic, social and environmental justice to the Ogoni people of the Niger Delta. The oil-rich ancestral lands of the Ogoni were for all intents and purposes stolen by various corporate oil interests beginning in 1958, and over the last four and a half decades, their way of life has been destroyed. They organized in 1990 and were quickly and violently repressed by the military dictatorship. The former President of MOSOP, well-known Nigerian poet and writer Ken Saro-Wiwa, along with eight other Ogoni leaders, were convicted of bogus charges and sentenced to death by a military tribunal on October 31, 1995. They were executed by hanging ten days later. Tragically, the Ogoni's struggle continues to this day. www.dawodu.net/mosop.htm

**Ottomans (OTT-oh-menz):** Referring to the Ottoman or Turkish Empire (*circa* 1453-1922).

**Ouranos (OOHR-ah-nohss or YUR-a-nuss):** In Greek mythology, the original Sky God who embodied all of the Starry

Heavens. Brought forth by the Earth Goddess, Gaia, he was first her son, and then lover. Their sacred union brought forth the Titans, and ultimately, everyone and everything else. In the Indo-European tradition of usurpation through violence, Ouranos was castrated by his youngest son, Kronos, who was the father of Zeus. The Latin version of his name has been given to the gas giant planet known as Uranus, seventh from the Sun. (*See also* Kronos, Sacred Marriage, Son-Lover)

**Paleolithic (pay-lee-oh-LITH-ic):** The Old Stone Age (*circa* 750,000-13,000 b.c.e.), characterized by human's use of chipped stone tools, and a gatherer-hunter way of life. Somewhere in this hazy period of our evolution, and likely by 50,000 b.c.e., "humanity" was coming into existence on the continent of Africa. We began to conceptualize the creator of the Universe as a Great Mother, projecting onto the world around us the first anthropormorphic notion of divinity. She is known to us now as the Great Goddess of prehistory, and some scholars believe the early humans took that cosmology with them as they migrated around the world, populating the Earth. (*See* Great Goddess)

Beginning in the upper Paleolithic (*circa* 50,000-30,000 b.c.e.), the glaciers, which had come and gone in four great Ice Ages, started melting. They finally disappeared in about 10,000 b.c.e. Between 20,000 and 15,000 b.c.e., the grasslands started giving way to vast forests, and the bison, horse and cattle herds were forced to move east. The people who would become the Indo-Europeans moved with them. The people who would become the Partnership Cultures of the Civilization of Old Europe remained, moving into caves in fertile river valleys. This is the period when the cave paintings such as those at Lascaux (LAH-skoe) in France, and the numerous Goddess figurines were created. For example, the Goddess of Willendorf (WILL-en-dorf) (Austria), dates back to about 20,000 b.c.e., as does the Goddess of Lespugue (leh-SPUHG) (France). The Mesolithic (*circa* 13,000-7000 b.c.e.) was a transitional period during which the roots of agriculture took hold. (*See also* Neolithic, Partnership)

**Pallas (PAHL-ahs):** An epithet for the Goddess Athena, meaning "maiden." After Athena's emergence from the head of Zeus, she was raised by the God, Triton, who was likely from the region in Libya where there had been a river or lake by that name. Triton had a daughter named Pallas, who loved to play war games with Athena. One day, during an argument, Pallas was about to strike the Goddess, when Zeus intervened by placing his aegis (shield) in front of his daughter to protect her. Pallas was startled, and Athena reacted, accidentally killing her friend. She was overcome with remorse, and so to atone, she created a statue of Pallas, adorned it with her aegis and named it the Palladion (pah-LAH-dee-ohn). The statue was said to protect the city which possessed and worshipped it.

**Panayía Arkoudiótissa (pahn-ah-YEE-ah ahr-kou-dee-OH-teece-ah):** Mother of God of the Bear (modern Greek). This is an excellent example of how the bear aspect of the Great Goddess of prehistory continued on, first through Greek mythology in the form of the Goddess Artemis, and then through Christianity in the figure of the Virgin Mary.

**Pandora (pahn-DOHR-ah):** A woman created by Hephaistos and Athena per Zeus' order, in retaliation for Prometheus' theft of fire from the immortal realm. Pandora, like Eve in later Christian mythology, is responsible for letting unspeakable evils loose upon the world, in her case when she opens her infamous jar (or box). This myth is a poignant demonstration of the status of women in dominator ideologies – a tragic contrast to the esteem in which women were once held. (*See also* Hope, Minoans)

Despite being scapegoated for all of the woes of humanity, her name means, "all-gifted," which refers to the gift (or charm) each

Immortal gave Pandora. The word can also be interpreted as "all-giver." In that sense, her name becomes a reference back to the Great Goddess of prehistory, who once bestowed blessings as well as misfortune (though there is no indication the earlier cultures deified the concept of punishment). (*See* Great Goddess)

**Pangaia (pahn-GHEH-ah or pan-GIE-a):** In a geological context, "pangaea" (pan-JEE-a) means "all Earth," and it refers to the single, enormous continent which formed approximately 270 million years ago. Then, about 255 million years ago, it's believed that a "superplume" of molten lava came rocketing through the Earth's mantle, shattering the giant land mass into pieces, creating what would become the continents.

In modern Greek, "Panayía" (pahn-ah-YEE-ah) is used to refer to the Virgin Mary, who is currently one of the best known incarnations of the Great Goddess of prehistory.

**Panthaeon (pahn-THAY-ohn):** This word is derived from "pantheon" (PAHN-theh-ohn), which in Greek mythology, has traditionally meant "all the Gods." We inserted the "a" to recognize the feminine aspect of divinity. "Pantheon" has been used to refer to the fourteen most prominent Olympian deities: Hestia, Hera, Demeter, Zeus, Apollo, Athena, Artemis, Aphrodite, Hermes, Hephaistos, Hades, Poseidon and Ares. Hades was later omitted, as his realm was under the Earth. Dionysos, as a relative late-comer to Classical myth, replaced Hestia, and the traditional number was reduced to twelve.

**Parakaló (pah-rha-kah-LOH):** Don't mention it (modern Greek).

**Parnassós (pahr-nah-SOHS or par-NASS-us):** The sacred mountain overlooking the Gulf of Kórinthos, where the sanctuary of Delphi is located. It reaches a height of 8,061 feet.

**Parthená (pahr-theh-NAH):** We're using the feminine form of this word as a title, to recognize the parthenogenic nature of the Great Goddess of prehistory, from whom Athena is ultimately derived. "Parthenos," the title used in the stories, is masculine in gender, as if the mythmakers were trying to imbue her powers with a male principle simply through the speaking of her name. In modern Greek, the word means "virginity," "maiden" or "first." (*See also* Parthenon, Parthenós)

**Parthenon (pahr-theh-NOHN):** The Temple to Athena Parthenos on the Acropolis in Athens. It was built between 447 and 438 b.c.e., and housed a 36-foot ivory and gold statue of the Goddess. This incarnation of Athena recognized and paid tribute to the Great Goddess of prehistory, the original mythological figure, from whom, without a male principle, all life came. (*See also* Parthená, Parthenos)

**Parthenos (pahr-THEH-nohs or PAR-theh-nohs):** A title of Athena, usually translated as "virgin," though it actually refers to the idea of parthenogenesis, or reproduction through the development of an unfertilized egg. In Greek mythology, the Earth Mother, Gaia, is said to have brought forth Ouranos (the Heavens), without partnering with a male deity. The Parthenogenic, or Virgin, Goddess therefore has all the elements necessary within Herself to create life. (*See also* Great Goddess, Parthená, Parthenon)

Today, evolutionary biologists point to the parthenogenic nature of many microorganisms as being essential to the very creation of life on Earth.

**Partnership:** On Dr. Riane Eisler's Partnership/Dominator Continuum, Partnership-oriented cultures are exemplified by a lack of fortifications and warfare, an egalitarian social structure in which men and women share equally in all aspects of life, and the absence of a strict, violently reinforced hierarchy. Technology and resources are shared by all for the good of all. Creativity and the celebration of life are highly valued, and "power" is viewed as something to be shared with, as opposed to exercised over, the other members of society. These cultures tend to be more democratic, and focus on the principle of linking, rather than ranking, in terms of how societal relations are ordered. A key indicator of the degree to which a culture is Partnership-oriented is the status of women, and the extent to which altruism is reflected in public policy.

In Partnership cultures, the ability to kill other beings would not be glorified. Heroes in such a culture would overcome adversity through their wits and intelligence, as well as through their physical strength, and would kill others only in self-defense. They would also show compassion and mercy to those intent on disrupting or destroying their way of life through violence.

Eisler refers to the Minoan civilization as the last of the Partnership cultures of prehistory, but she also notes that there have been numerous Partnership resurgences since then. The flowering of Classical Greece, the emergence of Christianity, the creation of the grand cathedrals during the 12th and 13th centuries, and the Renaissance and Enlightenment can all be viewed from this perspective. At present, the countries of Scandinavia provide some of the best examples of Partnership culture, whereas those in the Middle East, such as Saudi Arabia and Afghanistan serve as excellent examples of ones tending toward a Dominator configuration. (*See also* Dominator, Minoans, Neolithic) www.partnershipway.org

**Pediment (PED-i-ment):** A large triangular ornament crowning the front of a Classical Greek temple.

**Pelopónnisos (pel-leh-POHN-ee-sohs or pel-leh-pohn-EE-sus):** Pelops' (PEH-lops) Island, named for the mythical King of Elis (EE-leece). Geographically, it is the southern peninsula of Greece, which is separated from the mainland by the Corinth Canal.

**Periklean (pehr-ih-KLEE-ahn):** Referring to the time of the Athenian leader, Perikles (pehr-ee-KLEECE) (*circa* 463-429 b.c.e.) when a quasi-democratic form of government was in place, and the arts and sciences flourished.

**Persephone (per-seh-FOHN-eh or per-SEFF-oh-nee):** Budding Earth Goddess and Queen of the Underworld. Daughter of Zeus and Demeter. Also known as Kore (KHOR-ee) or Kora (KHOR-ah). She was abducted and raped by Hades, and then forced to spend one-third of each year with him in the Underworld. (*See also* Demeter)

**Phaedriádes (feh-dree-AH-dess):** A mountain range in central Greece. The Horns of the Phaedriádes are the two mountain peaks which rise close together over the sanctuary at Delphi.

**Phoebos (FEE-vohs or FEE-bus):** Bright (ancient Greek). A title often associated with Apollo. Although he was not originally a Sun God, he eventually assumed those duties and powers. The word was also used in its feminine form, Phoebe (FEE-vee), to describe Apollo's twin sister, Artemis, who had assimilated the powers of earlier Moon Goddesses.

**Pieria (pee-EHR-ee-ah):** A mountain in Thessaly (theh-sah-LEE-ah) in the far northeastern part of Greece; it's thought to be one of the earliest homes of the Muse. (*See also* Muses)

**Pillars of Herakles:** The two promontories at the eastern end of the Strait of Gibraltar (the waterway connecting the Atlantic Ocean and the Mediterranean Sea). For his tenth labor, Herakles had to journey to the western edge of the world to capture the cattle of Geryon (GHEHR-ee-ohn). As a monument to his success, he created the Pillars, also known as the Rocks of Calpe (KAHL-pee) (Gibraltar) and Ceuta (THAY-oo-tah).

**Pleistos (PLEE-stohs):** A river near Delphi.

**Pompeii (pahm-PAY):** An ancient city at the foot of Mount Vesuvius (veh-SOO-vee-us) in Italy, near what is now Naples. It was completely buried in volcanic ash and debris when Vesuvius erupted in 79 c.e.

**Pontchartrain (PAHN-shehr-train):** The large salt water lake near New Orleans, Louisiana. It connects to the Gulf of Mexico via Lake Borgne (born), and to the Mississippi River via canal.

**Poseidon (poh-see-DOHN or po-SIE-den):** The Earthshaker. Son of the Titans, Rhea and Kronos, he is known as the supreme God of the Sea. Like most authoritarian rulers, he protected his realm with the threat and/or use of violent force.

**Prometheus (pro-mee-theh-EECE or pro-MEE-thee-us):** Forethinker (ancient Greek). Son of the Titan, Iapetos (ee-ah-peh-TOHS) and Clymene (klee-MEH-nee), though some sources name Themis (THEH-meece), also a Titan, as his mother. He is often portrayed as the maker of humans and/or their primary benefactor, especially against Zeus. Though he and Themis sided with Zeus in the war against the Titans, afterward, he turned on Zeus, elaborately deceiving him into choosing a pile of bones as an offering rather than the meat of a butchered ox. In retaliation, Zeus took fire from humanity. Prometheus then further tricked the old Thunder God by retrieving the fire in a fennel stalk and returning it to the mortal realm.

As punishment, Zeus had Prometheus bound to a mountain rock, where an eagle would tear at his immortal liver for eternity (though he was eventually rescued by Herakles).

Zeus also decided that humanity deserved to be punished for the brazenness of Prometheus, so he ordered the creation of Pandora, who let loose the "evils" from her jar. (*See* Pandora)

**Propylaia (proh-pee-LEH-ah):** At the Acropolis in Athens, this structure was the grand entranceway into the temple complex, where the Parthenon, Erechthion and other buildings stood.

**Pseira (PSEEHR-ah):** A small island off the shore of northeastern Kríti. It was inhabited by Minoans during the Bronze Age. (*circa* 3100-1628 b.c.e.)

**Psyche (psee-HEE or SIE-kee):** The Greek word "psyche" can mean many things: soul, heart, energy, courage and even butterfly, a symbol of transformation. We use the term to mean the "soul" or "mind" in an expansive sense. In Roman mythology, Psyche is married to Cupid (Eros).

**Pythia (pee-THEE-ah):** The High Priestess at Delphi, who would cleanse herself in the Kastalía Spring, and then receive the Earth's utterings (the Oracle) as they emanated from the sacred place beneath Apollo's temple. Her title derived from the snake, Python (PEE-thohn), whose name came from the Greek verb "pytho," which means "I rot." Apollo slayed it in order to usurp the sanctuary of Delphi.

So powerful was the previous oracular tradition (as represented by the snake), that it wasn't enough simply to kill the creature, but rather, it was made to *rot*, thereby sending a strong and unambiguous message that the older order was not only dead, but decayed. (*See also* Apollo, Delphi)

**Qatar (k'TAHRH or KOT-er):** An independent Arab emirate located on the Arabian Peninsula. It's actually a small peninsula itself, jutting into the waters of the Persian Gulf.

**Rhea (RHEE-ah):** A Titan, born of the Sacred Marriage of Earth and Sky (Gaia and Ouranos). She united with Kronos, then gave birth to Hestia, Demeter, Hera, Hades, Poseidon and Zeus.

Kronos devoured them all, except for the last-born, Zeus, whom Rhea protected in a cave on Mount Díkti. Rhea is closely linked with the Great Mother Goddess, Cybele (kee-VEH-lee), another, older Goddess from Asia Minor. (*See also* Zeus)

**Sacred Marriage:** Also known as Hieros Gamos (ee-ehr-OHS GHAH-mohs) (modern Greek). The union between an Earth Goddess and a Sky God. In Greek mythology, examples include Gaia and Ouranos, and Rhea and Kronos. The concept originated during the late Neolithic, well after the Indo-European invasions had begun, perhaps in an attempt to restore the balance lost as a result of the conquest. The male principle, which until then had been represented by animals such as the bull, boar and stag, was now deified through the Son of the Great Goddess. He eventually grew into manhood and became the Goddess' lover, and then their union evolved into the Sacred Marriage. Unfortunately, the Son-Lover turned Sacred Partner eventually became the "Almighty," once again disrupting the balance. (*See also* Great Goddess, Neolithic, Partnership)

**Sacred Way:** The contemplative path pilgrims took to visit a sacred site, for example, the approach to the Parthenon in Athens, or the steep climb to Apollo's temple at Delphi.

**Santoríni (sahn-tohr-EE-nee):** *See* Thíra.

**Satyr (SAHT-eehr-ee or SAY-ter):** Male Nature Spirits who were part goat or horse and part human; they were ardent followers of Dionysos.

**Selene (seh-LEE-nee):** Moon Goddess, and daughter of the Titans, Theia and Hyperion. She traversed the heavens in a silver chariot drawn by two white horses, carrying on the timeless tradition of linking the Goddess to the cycles of the Moon. Like the three aspects of the Triple Goddess, Maiden, Mother and Crone, the Moon Goddess is reborn each month as a waxing crescent, grows until she's full, and then wanes again into the total darkness, or death, of the new Moon. After three days, she will be resurrected once again, and the lunar cycle continues.

**Shangó (shahn-GO):** The mythical Third King of the Yoruba people. He is the Thunder God whose power is embodied in meteorites and lightning bolts. He is considered to be a moral God who focuses his wrath on those who would commit immoral deeds. He shares many traits with the Greek God, Zeus.

**Siam (sie-AM):** The Kingdom of Thailand in Southeast Asia.

**Sirens (see-RHEEN-ess or SIE-renz):** Birdlike creatures with women's heads, who, with their enchanting songs and music, lured sailors onto the rocky shores of their island. Once the unfortunate passers by became shipwrecked, the Sirens devoured them. Archeologists have found countless Paleolithic and Neolithic artifacts depicting the Bird Goddess, a figure who, in earlier belief systems, laid the Cosmic Egg from which the Universe came forth. She also symbolized the flight of the soul upon death. The Sirens are an obvious demonization of an important pre-patriarchal figure.

**Sisyphos (SEECE-ee-phohss or SISS-i-fiss):** The King of Kórinthos who, in one version, identified Zeus as the abductor of Aegina (EH-ghee-nah). In retaliation, Zeus struck him with a thunder bolt and cast him into the Underworld, where he was condemned for eternity to push a boulder up a hill. Dominator cultures always reinforce their hierarchies through the threat of pain and punishment, and in this case, eternal pain and punishment.

**Son-Lover:** Our Paleolithic and Neolithic ancestors conceived the idea of a Great Goddess or Great Mother who gave birth to all of Creation. Male "Gods" as such were unknown to those early people. However, the male principle was still integral to their cosmology, as reflected by a wealth of important symbols, including the bull, boar and stag.

By the late Neolithic, domination and conquest were firmly established by the Indo-European invaders, and in most of those cultures, the Sky Gods ruled supreme. (*See* Dominator, Neolithic) Even though the conquerors imposed their ideology on those whom they vanquished, the figure of the Great Goddess persisted. And so, the concept of the Son-Lover subsequently arose, perhaps as an attempt to restore the balance which had been lost as as result of the conquest. The male principle was then deified through the Son of the Great Goddess. He eventually grew into manhood and became the Goddess' lover, and their union evolved into the Sacred Marriage. Unfortunately, the Son-Lover turned Sacred Partner eventually became the "Almighty," once again disrupting the balance. (*See also* Great Goddess, Partnership)

**Sounion (SOU-nee-ohn):** The rugged headland on the tip of the Attica peninsula, where the Mediterranean and Aegean Seas meet. In 5th century b.c.e., temples to both Poseidon and Athena were built there, and his is still partially intact. Legend has it that this was the place King Aegeus (eh-gheh-EECE) threw himself into the sea which now bears his name, when he thought his son, Theseus, was dead.

**Sphinx (sfeenks):** An enigmatic winged lion with the face of a woman. Child of Echidna (EH-kheed-nah) and Orthros (OHR-throhs) or Typhon (tee-FOHN). It terrorized the people of Thebes by devouring them if they failed to solve certain riddles. Finally, Oedipus (ee-DHEE-pooce) correctly answered the questions, and thereby destroyed the Sphinx's power.

The Sphinx is likely a demonization of the Great Goddess of prehistory, who was first associated with lions during the Neolithic. The symbol of the wings can be traced back much further in time to the Bird Goddess figurines of the Paleolithic.

**Sporádes (spohr–AH–dess):** A group of islands in the northwestern part of the Aegean Sea, off the coast of mainland Greece.

**Styx (steeks or sticks):** The River of Hate in Hades' Underworld.

**Syntagma Square (seen–TAHG–mah):** Constitution Square. This is the central area of Athens, where the Parliament Building and the National Gardens are located.

**Syphnian Treasury (SEEF–nee–ahn):** Síphnos (SEEF–nos) is one of the islands of the Kikládes, in the southern Aegean Sea. At Delphi, their treasury, or place of offering, was among the finest and best preserved of all the treasuries along the Sacred Way. During Classical times (*circa* 480-323 b.c.e.), in order to win the favor of the Immortals, each of the city-states and islands would try to out do the others with their splendid offerings.

The pediment of this elegant structure depicted the struggle between Herakles and Apollo for the Delphic Tripod, the seat upon which the Pythia or Priestess of Delphi would sit to receive the Oracle from Gaia. Mythologically speaking, the contest was for control of the prophetic tradition. The tripod also symbolically represented the Triple Goddess (Maiden, Mother and Crone) and her various lunar aspects of the waxing crescent, and the full and new Moons.

**Taíyetos (teh–EEGH–ah–tohss):** A mountain near Sparta in the southern Pelopónnisos. In some accounts, it is the mythical home of the Goddess, Artemis.

**Tártaros (TAHR-tahr-ohs):** The realm of Hades' Underworld where punishment was inflicted. In modern Greek, "tártara" (TAHR-tahr-ah) means "bowels of the Earth."

**Telemachos (tee-LEHM-ah-kohs):** In Homer's *Odyssey*, he was the son of Penelope and Odysseus, the latter of whom was the well-known warrior hero who was trying to find his way home after the long Trojan war. When his father failed to return to Itháki, Athena, disguised as Mentes, urged the young Telemachos to go in search of him.

**Thalassemia (thal-a-SEEM-ee-a):** Also known as Cooley's Anemia. A genetic blood disease afflicting people of Mediterranean, Middle Eastern and Asian descent. It prevents the body from producing sufficient hemoglobin, and consequently, the bone marrow cannot produce enough red blood cells to carry an adequate supply of oxygen to the rest of the body. For more information, contact the AHEPA Cooley's Anemia Foundation, 1909 Q Street NW, Suite 500, Washington, DC 20009 202.232.6300 ahepa@ahepa.org or www.cooleysanemia.org

**Thebes or Thebe (THEE-veh):** A town in the east central region of mainland Greece, and a city-state during Classical times.

**Theia (THEE-ah):** A Titan, and daughter of the Sacred Marriage of Earth and Sky (Gaia and Ouranos). She united with her brother, Hyperion, and they had three children, Eos (Dawn), Helios (Sun), and Selene (Moon).

**Theseus (thee-seh-EECE or THEE-see-us):** The Athenian warrior hero who slayed the Minotaur, and with the help of Ariadne's Thread, escaped from the underground Labyrinth at Knossós (which in this tale was really a maze). Here, we again see the co-optation of once-sacred symbols (bull, labyrinth) to fit the new Indo-European myths, thus reinforcing domination as the key principle of social organization. (*See also* Ariadne, Dominator, Knossós, Labyrinth, Minotaur)

**Thíra (THEER-a):** A volcanic island in the Kikládes, a group of islands located to the north of Kríti. In about 1628 b.c.e., a massive eruption blew the top off of this once-immense volcanic cone, creating a sea-filled caldera and dividing the remaining land mass into three main islands. This eruption hastened the end of the Minoan civilization, and a way of life which had flourished for many thousands of years. An entire Minoan village, now known as Akrotíri, was perfectly preserved in volcanic ash. It was discovered in 1967 by Greek archeologist, Spyridon Marinatos. (*See also* Atlantis, Akrotíri, Minoan)

**Tholos (THOL-ohs):** The mysterious circular temple at the sanctuary of Delphi, and part of a larger complex dedicated to Athena.

**Típota (TEE-poh-tah):** Don't mention it (modern Greek).

**Titans (tee-TAHN-ess; tee-tahn-EE-dess [feminine] or TITE-anz):** The twelve children of the original Sacred Marriage in Greek mythology. Earth Goddess, Gaia, united with Sky God, Ouranos, and brought forth Oceanos, Koios (KEE-ohs), Krios (KHREE-ohs), Hyperion, Iapetos (ee-ah-peh-TOHS), Theia, Rhea, Themis (THEH-meece), Mnemosyne (m'nee-moh-SEE-nee), Phoebe (FEE-vee), Tethys (tee-THEECE) and the last to be born, Kronos. They were the earliest generation of Immortals, who were subsequently overthrown by the Olympian deities. (*See also* Zeus)

**Tree of Life:** The mythical tree which bore the Golden Apples of the Hesperides; it was guarded by the serpent, Ladon (LAH-dohn).

The Tree of Life later made its way into Christian myth, becoming the familiar scene of the serpent's seduction of Eve, but by then, the Apples had come to signify Knowledge, and the Judeo-Christian God had forbidden mortals from tasting that fruit. (*See also* Apples of the Hesperides)

In the Eve story, "knowledge" could very well have meant the understanding of earlier cultural norms, and so, as an extremely threatening influence, it had to be prohibited. (*See also* Neolithic, Partnership)

**Tritogenía (tree-toh-ghen-EE-a):** A title of Athena, referring to her birthplace near a river or lake called Triton, in what is now Libya. It seems clear that humans first evolved in Africa, so it is not surprising that Athena, and probably the earlier Minoan Snake Goddess, both had their early origins there.

**Trojan Horse:** After an arduous conflict, the ruse of the Trojan Horse finally led to the fall of Troy. With Athena's help, the Greek hero, Epeios (eh-pee-OHS), built a giant wooden horse, in which the most important warriors were concealed. The Trojans were tricked into bringing the horse inside their walls, and when night fell, the warriors escaped and took the city, leaving great destruction in their wake.

**Typhon (tee-FOHN):** Also known as Typheus (tee-feh-EECE), and meteorologically speaking, typhoon. A monstrous dragon, with 100 snake heads, who came from the sea, and whose mighty winds were the scourge of sailors and coastal peoples. Zeus is said to have killed him after a fierce battle.

In order to justify the conquest of the earlier belief system (as represented by the snakes), the mythmakers had to exaggerate that once-sacred creature into a terrifying, even supernatural, monster, which then had to be destroyed for the good of all. Variations of this myth occur in many cultures around the world, suggesting that perhaps the phenomenon of cultural transformation was global in scope. (*See also* Medusa, Neolithic)

**Underworld:** The realm of Hades, which lies beneath the Earth. It consists of the Elysian Fields (Heaven), Erebos (EHR-eh-vohs) (the gloomy darkness of Tártaros), and Tártaros (Hell) itself. As a whole, the realm is referred to as Tártaros or Erebos. In some of the stories, "Paradise" was located in a far-off place of the upper world, called the Isles of the Blessed. (*See also* Elysian Fields, Hades)

**Yai ya (yah-YAH):** Grandmother (modern Greek).

**Yeia sas (YHAH-sahss):** A greeting, meaning "to your health," or more generally, a polite form of "hello" (modern Greek).

**Yemoja (yeh-MO-ja):** One of the river rain Goddesses of the Yoruba tradition in Nigeria, who is also associated with the sea. She is known as Yemayá (yem-eye-YAH) in the western hemisphere, where she became linked with the Virgin Mary in some traditions, notably in Brazil. Both are thought to share qualities of sacred love, faith and purity. (*See also* Yoruba)

**Yoruba (YOHR-uh-ba):** A culture in West Africa, especially Nigeria, once comprised of kingdoms. They believe they're descended from Goddesses and Gods who live in an ancient spiritual capital known as Ile-Ile (EE-lay EE-lay). One of the most urban of the traditionally African civilizations, it dates back to the Middle Ages, a time when it was comprised of self-sufficient city-states similar to those in Classical Greece.

They are highly creative artisans and poets, with a vibrant and complex cosmology. Their culture has spread around the world, with major populations in North America, Brazil, Haiti, Cuba, and other parts of the Caribbean. (*See also* Ashé, Itútu, Yemoja)

**Zephyros (ZEH-feehr-ohs):** The West Wind.

**Zeus (zeh-EECE or zooce):** King of the Gods. He was the youngest son of the Titans, Rhea and Kronos, and was thereby destined to usurp his father's throne. In an attempt to prevent this fate from occurring, Kronos intended to devour all six of his children upon their birth. However, unbeknownst to him, Rhea had conspired with Gaia and Ouranos to save the last-born, Zeus. Rhea fled to Kríti, gave birth, and then Gaia hid him in a cave on Mount Díkti. Rhea then returned to Kronos, and presented him with a rock in swaddling clothes, which, apparently without paying much attention, he swallowed. Meanwhile, Zeus was safe in the cave, being nursed with milk from the goat, Amalthea, and honey from the Bee Goddess, Melissa (meh-leece-eh-EECE). The Kouretes, the young men (or spirits in some accounts), prevented Kronos from hearing the infant's crying by clashing their spears against their shields, and noisily dancing about. Zeus survived into adulthood and eventually, with the help of the Cyclopes (including Thunder, Lightning and Thunderbolt) and the three Hecatonchires (ehk-ah-TOH-gheer-ess) (the hundred-handed creatures) engaged in an epic war with the older generation of Immortals, the Titans. After a ten-year struggle, the Titans were defeated when the dextrous threesome buried them with 300 rocks, painfully binding them in gloomy Tártaros for all eternity (though some stories say that Zeus eventually let them out). Then, also with remarkable violence, Zeus battled and defeated the Giants, including Gaia's youngest, Typhon, the dragon with 100 serpent heads. Finally, as mightiest, Zeus achieved supremacy over Mount Olympos.

    Zeus had a dramatic and highly mercurial personality, expressing many human emotions. Far from perfect, he angered easily, occasionally slipping into violent rage, and lusted after Goddesses and mortal women alike. With his sister/spouse, Hera, he sired four children, and through the rape and deception of countless others, fathered many more. The Latin version of his name has been given to the largest planet in our Solar System, gas giant Jupiter.

Viewed from a Partnership perspective, it is important to acknowledge that he was born on the island of Kríti, a place which had long been sacred to the ancient Minoan civilization. By placing his birth there, the Indo-European mythmakers effectively co-opted the religious significance of the site, and the whole body of myth originating on Kríti.

His defeat of the Titans and the Giants, who were from a previous generation of deities (for the most part personifying different aspects of nature) in effect, chronicled the Indo-European conquest of the earlier cultures that once thrived on Greek soil, and by extension, in all of Old Europe. His marriage to Hera, a much older deity who once held the power of creation and destruction, enabled him to annex her powers. Similarly, his many conquests, which led to the births of Goddesses like Athena, Artemis and Persephone to name a few, enabled him to control their powers as well, for each of them also predate Zeus' Indo-European origins. However, it is interesting to note that the conquerors chose not to extinguish the powers of these Goddesses, but rather to subordinate them to Zeus. Perhaps this led to a swifter acceptance of the new world order, because the vanquished could still worship their deities even though the context had been radically altered. It was the continuation of a process which had been occurring since the earliest Indo-European invasions. The deity who had once been the Great Goddess of prehistory was now fragmented and compartmentalized, allowed only to govern certain spheres, while Zeus, the Father, reigned supreme.

Nevertheless, the enduring presence of such strong and powerful Goddesses in the Classical myths, along with the abundant symbols and imagery those tales contain, provide remarkable clues about our ancestors' world view prior to the downfall of the Civilization of Old Europe.

# BIBLIOGRAPHY

Our source information comes from a variety of writings and reference materials, the most important of which are listed below. We encourage you to embark on your own odyssey – delve into the stories and draw your own conclusions. Who knows what might come of it?

*Atlas of the World,* 7th ed. New York: Oxford University Press, 1999.

Baring, Anne, and Jules Cashford. *The Myth of the Goddess: Evolution of an Image.* New York: Arkana Penguin Books, 1991.

Biers, William R. *The Archeology of Greece.* Ithaca NY: Cornell University Press, 1987.

Campbell, Joseph. *The Hero with a Thousand Faces,* 2nd ed. Princeton, NJ: Princeton University Press, 1972.

Eisler, Riane. *The Chalice and the Blade: Our History, Our Future.* San Francisco: HarperSanFrancisco, 1987.
———. *Sacred Pleasure: Sex, Myth and the Politics of the Body; New Paths to Power and Love.* San Francisco: HarperSanFrancisco, 1995.

Gimbutas, Marija. *The Civilization of the Goddess: The World of Old Europe.* San Francisco: HarperSanFrancisco, 1991.

———. *The Language of the Goddess.* San Francisco: HarperSan-Francisco, 1989.

Graves, Robert. *The Greek Myths,* vol. 2. New York: Penguin Books, 1955.

———. *The White Goddess: A Historical Grammar of Poetic Myth.* New York: Farrar, Straus & Giroux, 1966.

Grimal, Pierre. *The Penguin Dictionary of Classical Mythology.* New York: Penguin Books, 1991.

Homer. *Iliad.* Translated with an Introduction by Richmond Lattimore. Chicago: The University of Chicago Press, 1951.

———. *Odyssey.* Translated with an Introduction by Richmond Lattimore. New York: Harper & Row, 1965.

Hornblower, Simon, and Antony Spawforth, eds. *The Oxford Classical Dictionary,* 3rd ed. New York: Oxford University Press, 2003.

Kern, Hermann. *Through the Labyrinth.* New York: Prestel, 2000.

Kofou, Anna. *Crete: All the Museums and Archeological Sites,* 2nd ed. Athens: Ekdotike Athenon S. A., 1990.

Levy, Peter. *Atlas of the Greek World.* New York: Facts on File, 1980.

Lovelock, James. *Gaia: A New Look at Life on Earth.* London: Oxford University Press, 1979.

Margulis, Lynn, and Dorion Sagan. *Microcosmos: Four Billion Years of Microbial Evolution.* Berkeley: University of California Press, 1997.

*Merriam Webster's Geographical Dictionary,* 3rd ed. Springfield, MA: Merraim-Webster, 1998.

Morford, Mark P.O., and Robert J. Lenardon. *Classical Mythology,* 5th ed. White Plains, NY: Longman Publishers, 1995.

Plato. *Plato Selections.* Edited by Raphael Demos. New York: Charles Scribner's Sons, 1927.

Powell, Barry B. *Classical Myth.* Englewood Cliffs, NJ: Prentice Hall, 1995.

Pring, J.T. comp. *The Pocket Oxford Greek Dictionary.* New York: Oxford University Press, 1982.

Sagan, Carl, and Ann Druyan. *Shadows of Forgotten Ancestors: A Search for Who We Are.* New York: Random House, 1992.

Scully, Vincent. *Architecture: The Natural and the Manmade.* New York: St. Martin's Press, 1991.

Sjoo, Monica, and Barbara Mor. *The Great Cosmic Mother: Rediscovering the Religion of the Earth.* San Francisco: HarperSanFrancisco, 1987.

Thompson, Robert Farris. *Flash of the Spirit: African and Afro-American Art and Philosophy.* New York: Random House, 1983.

*Webster's New International Dictionary of the English Language,* 2nd ed. Springfield, MA: G&C Merriam, 1957.

*Webster's Universal Dictionary and Thesaurus.* Montreal: Tormont, 1993.

# ABOUT THE AUTHORS

Nicholas George Manolukas was born on December 9, 1961 in Youngstown, Ohio to first generation Greek-Americans. His grandparents emigrated from Greece at the turn of the century, leaving their village life in pursuit of the American dream. Nick graduated from Yale with the class of 1984, and received his JD from John Marshall Law School in 1988.

Heidi Joanna Neale was born on August 26, 1961 in Dearborn, Michigan. Seven years later, her family left suburban Detroit and moved north to Cheboygan, near the beautiful Straits of Mackinac. Her ancestors emigrated from England and Germany in the mid 1800s, but after 17 years with Nick, she's become Greek by osmosis. Heidi graduated from Michigan State University in 1983, and earned her JD from DePaul College of Law in 1991.

Their partnership began on the Summer Solstice of 1986, when they met at the Printer's Row Book Fair in Chicago. In 1991, they left the Windy City to embark on a year-long trip around the world, and it was near the end of this journey, while visiting the Greek islands of Kríti and Santoríni, that they learned about the ancient Minoan Civilization – a discovery which inspired them to write their first novel, *The Coming of a New Millennium*, and the screenplay adaptation, *Knossos! Return to the Labyrinth*.

When they returned to the US, they moved to Corvallis, Oregon, to live near the volcanoes and rainforests of the Pacific Northwest. Since 1997, they've lived in Berkeley, California, the US Virgin Islands, and Sarasota, Florida.

Nick and Heidi have also worked extensively as activists, lawyers, mediators and consultants, promoting the ideals of social justice, sustainability and progressive political change.

*2004* is their second novel.

# 2004: AN OLYMPIC ODYSSEY
## ORDER FORM

www.olympicodyssey.com online

888.362.3133 telephone

**LABRYS** mail
PO BOX 18341 ( check or money order )
Sarasota, FL 34276-1341

| NAME | | | PRICE | $14.95 |
|---|---|---|---|---|
| ADDRESS | | | QUANTITY | |
| | | | TAX (FL)* | |
| CITY | STATE | ZIP | SHIPPING & HANDLING* | |
| TELEPHONE | | | AMOUNT ENCLOSED | |
| EMAIL | | | | |

* *Shipping and Handling*: Please include $4.00 for the first book and $2.00 for each additional book. Books will be sent by Priority Mail. *Sales Tax*: Florida residents, please add $1.05 per book. **CALL FOR BOOK CLUB DISCOUNT.**

For more information, call or email:
**olympicodyssey@earthlink.net**

## THANK YOU FOR YOUR ORDER!
Or order it through your favorite neighborhood or on-line bookstore. **ISBN** 0.9659778.1.1